A REAL MAN TELLS THE TRUTH

"I was wrong before," he said between breaths.

"About what?" She'd already figured what he meant, but wanted to hear him say it.

"That you and I shouldn't be together. That's bullshit. I want you." One of his hands left her waist to splay over her backside. "All of you."

Time would tell if he truly wanted all of her—including her heart—but for tonight the confession was enough. She slipped a finger behind the knot of his tie and tugged. "I'm yours for the taking."

His body tensed, radiating torrid, male need. He drew her lower lip into his mouth and ran his tongue across it. "Right now."

The terse demand sent a shot of arousal through her. Right now sounded just exactly perfect.

She looked around the lobby. Mr. and Mrs. Parrish were watching them with wrinkled noses, judging. Others darted glances, smiling knowingly, and no doubt filing away the juicy news of Matt and Jenna's heated embrace for later.

Matt seized hold of her chin and forced her attention back to him, his eyes relentless in their hunger. "Right now, Jenna."

She licked over her lower lip, tracing the path his tongue had taken. Sweet sundae, she loved the way he tasted. "Guess we'd better find ourselves an empty room."

MAY 2014

Books by Melissa Cutler

The Trouble With Cowboys

Cowboy Justice

How to Rope a Real Man

Published by Kensington Publishing Corporation

How To ROPE A REAL MAN

MELISSA CUTLER

ZEBRA BOOKS
KENSINGTON PUBLISHING CORP.
http://www.kensingtonbooks.com

ZEBRA BOOKS are published by

Kensington Publishing Corp.
119 West 40th Street
New York, NY 10018

First Mass-Market Paperback Printing: May 2014
ISBN-13: 978-1-4201-3008-9
ISBN-10: 1-4201-3008-0

First Electronic Edition: May 2014
eISBN-13: 978-1-4201-3009-6
eISBN-10: 1-4201-3009-9

10 9 8 7 6 5 4 3 2 1

Printed in the United States of America

To Rachael, Janet, Georgie, Tami,
Cori, Lisa, Marie, and Shoshana—
my honorary sisters

Chapter One

Jenna Sorentino was nothing if not self-sufficient. That trait had served her well for twenty-four years, but it was a bitch of a problem tonight. Because Matt Roenick—hard-bodied, bright-smiling Matt—was only interested in people he could save. Try as she might, she couldn't figure out a palatable way to land herself in that position.

Seated two seats down from the head of the table at the rehearsal dinner for her older sister Amy's wedding, she watched Matt cut up Tommy's chicken strips like he was the daddy she wanted him to be, all the while trying to dream up a problem Matt could solve for her that wouldn't make her feel helpless.

It wasn't that Jenna didn't have problems. Besides the problem of Matt never giving her more than the time of day in the eight months she'd known him, she had a category-five hurricane brewing with her two sisters. But there wasn't another person on earth who could save her from that storm except herself, not even the noble and dashing Matt Roenick.

That particular problem would have to wait until after Amy's wedding, though, because she hadn't damn near killed herself to put on the best wedding in Catcher Creek history only to ruin it with the truth.

A loud, banjo-heavy song exploded from the speakers. Jenna sipped her diet cola and tried not to wince outwardly. "It's too early for banjo," she called to Matt over Tommy's head.

He smiled, revealing the very same dimple that had made her go weak in the knees the first time she'd seen it so many months ago. "Is it ever the right time for banjo?"

She swirled the ice in her glass and gave him her most scholarly expression. "There's a banjo window, but it's very narrow. Only nine to eleven at night."

His brows pushed together. "Not eight or seven, but nine?"

"Eight's too early. You have to get nice and relaxed before banjo sounds good."

He rewarded her joke with a laugh. "That makes perfect sense, even though I'd never heard the banjo rule before tonight."

She shook her hair away from her cheek and smiled, trying to tell him without words how much she loved their easy camaraderie. "Yes, well, some things are so obvious, they don't need to be said."

His eyes glimmered, like he loved their conversations as much as she did. "I'll bear that in mind if I ever get the chance to take you to a bluegrass concert."

Her smile fell. To distract herself from the urge to point out that he had the chance any old time he wanted because Smithy's Bar had a standing event with a bluegrass band every Saturday night and all he had to do was ask, she picked a couple pieces of sawdust out of Tommy's hair that she'd apparently missed on his first brushing-off, then ruffled his dark blond locks.

Leave it to a five-year-old to get himself coated with

sawdust in the scant amount of time since they'd entered the Sarsaparilla Saloon and been seated on the far side of the dance floor.

"Uh-oh, buddy," Matt said, nudging Tommy with his elbow. "I hate to break it to you, but it looks like your head's sprouting sawdust."

Tommy giggled. "If our floor ever got this dirty, Mama would pitch a tent."

Matt quirked an eyebrow at Jenna. "Translation?"

Love for her earnest little boy roused a smile from her lips once more. "I think you meant pitch a fit, and you're exactly right. You know Mama loves clean floors, but this is a saloon, so it's supposed to be messy. It's part of the ambiance."

"Am-bee-ance," Tommy repeated, as though committing it to memory. Ever since it had dawned on him that he'd be starting kindergarten in the fall, he'd been obsessed with rattling off big words, so Jenna made sure their conversations were dense with them.

It'd been her idea to hold the rehearsal dinner here. Kellan, her soon-to-be brother-in-law, had requested someplace casual, with dancing and beer. As small a town as Catcher Creek was, nothing in its blink-and-you'll-miss-it downtown district fit the bill. Good thing Jenna was intimately familiar with just about every bar with a dance floor in New Mexico between Albuquerque and the Texas state line.

A glance at Amy made her stomach drop. Amy's eye twitched and she was using the steak knife that'd come with her top sirloin to dice the side of steamed vegetables into tiny cubes—a sure sign her wedding nerves were getting intense.

Kellan was the only person in the world who could talk Amy off the ledge when anxiety got the best of her, but he was deep in conversation about steer prices with Vaughn, Jenna's other soon-to-be brother-in-law. As much as Jenna wasn't going to let her own problems get in the way of Amy's perfect wedding, she wasn't about to stand by while Amy ruined it either.

"How's your meal, Ames?"

"Fine." Her voice was strained, and she'd answered without meeting Jenna's eyes, focusing instead on slicing a baby carrot.

Oh, crap.

Jenna pushed up from the table, smoothing the skirt of her swishy cotton dress as she stood. She met Matt's startled look. "Will you keep an eye on Tommy for a bit?"

"Of course."

"Amy, I need to talk to you outside. Could you spare a minute?"

Amy's knife and fork froze. She blinked at her plate for a couple beats before standing. "Okay, yes. Outside would be good."

Their movement must've caught Rachel's eye because she broke from her conversation with Kellan and Vaughn and stood. "Where're you going?"

As the oldest sister, Rachel had always been the mother figure and rock of the family that Jenna had needed growing up, supporting her through the toughest of times. As close as two sisters could be, they had an understanding of each other that ran deep and didn't need words. However, from Jenna's first recollection of her sisters, Amy and Rachel had gotten on like two tomcats locked in a barn. There wasn't a situation the good Lord could throw at one that the other couldn't make worse without even trying.

With Amy looking like she was going to blow a gasket at any moment, the last thing she needed was Rachel getting involved before Jenna had a chance to run damage control.

Without relinquishing her hold on Amy's shoulders, she

pressed close to Rachel. In as low a tone as she could muster, she hissed, "Bring us three shots of tequila, STAT."

"What? You don't drink."

But Jenna was already hustling Amy from the table. She drilled Rachel with a *Don't mess with me* glare behind Amy's back. "Tequila. Now!"

The fenced-in patio out back of the saloon was bathed in a soft yellow glow from the strings of twinkle lights crisscrossing the tin roof. As they stepped out, a weathered, older man was snuffing a cigarette in an ashtray. He tipped the brim of his hat to them, then made his way inside. The door bounced a few times before sealing shut, dulling the music to a muffled rhythm of vibrations.

Jenna spun Amy to face her. "Okay, what's wrong?"

Amy wrapped her arms around her middle. "Nothing. What makes you think something's wrong?"

Jenna pinched the bridge of her nose and silently recited the alphabet backward, a mom trick she'd learned to maintain patience when under duress. And it worked near about all the time. Well, sort of. If she didn't count the fact she'd never once made it past N.

"Spill it, Amy."

Amy's tongue poked against the inside of her cheek, and Jenna could tell she was fighting hard to keep her composure. "Jake texted Kellan on our way here. *Work emergency.* That's it. Two words. And Kellan can't get him on the phone."

From everything Amy had told her, Kellan had made his only brother, Jake, his best man as an olive-branch gesture, trying to mend their decades-old rift. And it seemed to have had the desired effect, if they all ignored that Jake hadn't attended Kellan's bachelor party or shown up for the rehearsal that afternoon. She'd figured intimate gatherings like this made him uncomfortable given the fragility of his and

Kellan's reconciliation, but it'd never occurred to her he might blow off the actual wedding.

"Jake's a cop, and not a rural cop like we're used to dealing with. LAPD is a different beast," Jenna said. "I bet work emergencies are par for the course. There's nothing he can do about that. Besides, he still has time. The wedding's not until three."

"That's what Kellan said, but I looked up flights from L.A. to Albuquerque on my cell and the next one's not until tomorrow at nine thirty, L.A. time. It's a two-hour flight, then a three-hour drive here, if everything goes perfectly. And that's not counting time spent in the airport or at a car rental place. With the time difference, it's impossible. But Kellan's acting like nothing's wrong. He still believes Jake'll make it work. I don't know what to do."

It wasn't like they could delay the ceremony, because every detail of the wedding and reception, from the caterer and DJ to the photographer, was hinging on a three o'clock start time, including the minister, who had a second wedding to perform later that evening. Still, a little fake optimism never hurt anything. "I bet everything will work out and he'll make it on time." *If he hooks up with Superman or bribes his way onto a private jet.*

Wide-eyed, Amy shook her hands, palms out, fingers stretched. "Don't patronize me. I'm freaking out here!" The shrillness of her voice made Jenna's teeth ache.

She grabbed hold of Amy's shoulders and rubbed, praying that Rachel materialized with their shots in the next thirty seconds.

"Even if Jake doesn't make it, everything will be fine. Vaughn is Kellan's best friend. He'll stand in as best man at the wedding and he's really good in front of crowds so he'll be able to pull off a last-minute toast at the reception, no sweat. I'll make sure he has a speech planned, okay? I'm not going to let anything spoil your special day, so calm down."

The doors burst open. "Don't tell her to calm down. She hates it." It was Rachel, balancing three shots in her hands. "Here, take a glass before I drop one."

Jenna passed a shot to Amy, then took one for herself.

Amy frowned down at hers. "What are we doing with this stuff?"

Jenna clinked the lips of their glasses together. "What do you think? Shooting it."

"I get really silly when I drink, Jen. You know that," Amy said.

"That's what I'm counting on." And if one shot didn't turn her from stressed to silly, Jenna wasn't above buying round after round until Amy's buzz set in.

Rachel nudged Jenna. "How long's it been since you had a drink?"

"Well, Tommy's five, so . . . six years. Wow. But I need it tonight. We all do."

"Isn't this what AA calls enabling?" Rachel asked. "Am I causing you to fall off a wagon or something?"

"I'm not an alcoholic and you know it. It's just that I lost my appetite for the stuff when I got pregnant."

Rachel sniffed her shot, then screwed up her face. "This tequila is making me lose my appetite. Why can't we shoot whiskey instead?"

"Because whiskey's not ladylike. Now hush up. You're not weaseling out of this shot by whining. Do it for Amy."

"You don't have to do it, Rachel," Amy said.

Jenna pinned Rachel with her best scolding expression. "Don't listen to her. She's the bride; she doesn't know what she's talking about. As the wedding planner, my word trumps all."

Amy shook her head. "I don't think that's—"

"Fine. For Amy." Rachel raised her glass in a toast, then tossed the tequila back.

Jenna and Amy followed suit. The liquor flooded Jenna's throat with the warmth of an old friend—or maybe her worst enemy.

The taste and burn reminded her of high school, which was pretty pathetic, but there it was. It sent her right back to long nights of partying in the vacant desert with Carson Parrish and all the other misfits she'd wasted her teenage years with. She might've been angrier at the memories or at herself except that she was damn proud of how she'd turned her life around.

Back in the day, her tolerance had been such that it had taken her at least three shots to work up a buzz. Tonight, the drink settled in her muscles and brain almost instantly.

Amy shuddered and handed her empty glass to Jenna.

"All right, why did we do that?" Rachel said, stacking her glass on Amy's.

Jenna draped a fortifying arm across Amy's shoulders. "We're not sure Kellan's brother is going to make it to the wedding."

Rachel didn't flinch. "That's because he's an asshole."

"Rachel, he's family now!" Amy scolded.

Jenna rolled her eyes. *Here they go . . .*

"Yeah, I get that," Rachel pressed, "but there's no rule that says family members can't be assholes. In fact, I'd wager there's no more focused collections of assholes in the world than people have in their own families."

Amy made a sound like a snort that got Jenna's attention fast. The second she looked her way, Amy burst out in giggles.

God bless tequila.

A squeak warned of the patio door opening again. Kellan stepped out, ducking under a strand of low-hanging twinkle lights. Amy smushed her lips together and tried to stop laughing.

"Okay, womenfolk, what's this powwow all about?"

Jenna rattled the stack of empty glasses. "We were getting some fresh air and enjoying a splash of New Mexico's finest tequila."

"Not really," Rachel said. "I only sprang for the cheap stuff."

Jenna patted her arm. "That was called sarcasm, sweetie."

Kellan's eyes twinkled as he gave Amy a once-over. "Are you getting my bride drunk on our wedding eve?"

Amy snorted through her nose, clearly fighting another bout of giggles. Kellan's smile broadened, and he pulled Amy from Jenna's arms into his own.

This was a good man Amy was marrying. The kind of man who took care of things and people. Like Rachel's fiancé, Vaughn, did. That her sisters had found such fine matches eased some of Jenna's guilt about her plan to leave town.

Amy threaded her arms around Kellan's ribs. "Just a little bit drunk."

"Good. That makes it easier for me to take advantage of you."

"I'm always easy for you to take advantage of like that."

"True enough."

Rachel groaned and started for the door. "I don't care that you're getting hitched tomorrow. I'm not going to stand around listening to you two talk dirty to each other. I'm going back in."

Jenna poked her arm as she passed. "Like you and Vaughn are any different."

Rachel kept moving, but flashed Jenna a coy smile that hinted at the love and happiness Vaughn had brought into her life. The kind of love Jenna wanted for herself. She stared blankly at the swinging door as it closed behind Rachel, almost afraid to look back at Kellan and Amy in the throes of their own love story for fear that jealousy would turn her insides ugly.

A fast song came on in the bar, along with the DJ calling out a line dance.

No more pity party. Not with a song beckoning for her to whisk Tommy to the dance floor and boogie down.

She wound through the crowd pouring off the bar stools, then zigzagged through tables en route to the dance floor, searching out Tommy and Matt as she moved. Lo and behold, they were already dancing, along with Kellan's six-year-old goddaughter, Daisy. Matt didn't see her, busy as he was modeling the steps to the Watermelon Crawl for the kids.

In Jenna's experience, kids made lots of men nervous, especially those of the unattached variety, but not Matt. From the day he'd come into her family's life to negotiate an oil rights contract, he'd gotten down to the kids' level and played or talked with them as if it was the most natural thing in the world.

Blame it on her hormones or Darwin's theory of evolution, but seeing a man interacting with kids got her blood stirring and her imagination looking into the future. To top it off, clearly Matt could hold his own on the dance floor. He handled the kids and the steps like he did everything else in his life—with smooth, easygoing confidence and genuine enjoyment. It was this uncommon quality that had caught her attention all those months ago and dropped her deeper and deeper into longing every time they were together.

And, sweet sundae, did she long for him tonight.

She hung back, watching. Daisy didn't give two wits

whether she did the steps right, but Tommy's tongue was poking out the side of his mouth in concentration as he watched Matt's boots.

During the butt shimmy part of the choreography, Tommy hammed it up, and Jenna couldn't stifle a laugh, he was so cute.

The laugh caught Tommy's attention. "Mommy, I'm dancing! Just like we practice at home."

She met Matt's amused expression with a wink, then smiled at her son. "I can see that. Great job." She scooted close to the kids and grabbed Tommy and Daisy's hands to help them into a turn.

Matt leaned her way during a kick and weight change. "He told me you two do a lot of line dancing and two-stepping in the living room before bedtime."

True enough. She could dance until her boots wore out and the band went home or the radio broke. It was her favorite way of letting off steam since she'd stopped raising hell in order to raise her son right.

"I can't think of a better way to end the day." Well, she could, but it'd been a while—too damn long, in fact—since she'd had the pleasure of indulging in that particular pastime.

They turned again. She helped Tommy line up in front of her, then got busy staring at Matt's behind as he kicked and moved with the music. It was such a fine view, she nearly hummed her appreciation out loud.

Maybe it was the tequila, or maybe the prolonged view of Matt's posterior, but she wasn't as worried about tomorrow as she had been for months. She'd run herself into the ground organizing every detail of the wedding and reception, and she felt great about what she'd accomplished.

She deserved a little R & R tonight before the wedding-day craziness was upon them.

On the far side of the bar, she caught a glimpse of Kellan, Amy, and Rachel laughing while Vaughn told them an animated story with lots of gesturing. Her sisters and Tommy, and now Kellan and Vaughn, were her only living family, and she'd do anything to make sure they were happy.

A stab of conscience cut through her gut. That wasn't entirely true.

She'd do anything for her sisters and brothers-in-law . . . except stay in Catcher Creek one day longer than was absolutely necessary. She shoved the unpleasant awareness from her mind. Tonight wasn't the time to worry about that. Neither was tomorrow. After the wedding would be soon enough to deal with the coming storm.

The ending notes of "The Watermelon Crawl" blended with the beginning of a waltz. Jenna's favorite dance.

Even so, she refused to ask Matt to dance with her or even look his way with hopeful anticipation. She was far too proud to beg for his interest if he wouldn't give it freely. Not that he'd notice her looking. His brown leather boots seemed glued to the ground and he cracked his knuckles, his dark eyes haunted as they followed Tommy and Daisy off the floor with Daisy's mom, Lisa.

She'd seen that shadow of a look flash over his features before in moments of unguardedness that hinted at a private fight being waged in his mind. She'd become aware of its presence two months ago, the day he'd joined their family to celebrate Tommy's birthday with cake and ice cream at the Catcher Creek Café. And now that she was aware of it, not a night with him went by that she didn't notice that haunted look cross his face at least once. As soon as it revealed itself, it was gone and he was back to being easygoing, happy Matt.

Talk to me, she wanted to press. *What is it, and does it have to do with why you won't let me into your life?*

But she never did ask because she couldn't get him alone no matter what she tried. She couldn't even get him to dance with her tonight. Irritation flared, but she tamped it down. There she went, making everything complicated. Maybe interest had nothing to do with it. Maybe he didn't know how to waltz. He'd nailed the Watermelon Crawl, but partner dancing was a whole different bale of hay.

She swished her skirt with her hands as she debated the merits of a trip to the ladies' room to save her from standing there awkwardly for much longer. This was one of her least favorite parts of being single—never knowing if she'd have a partner for the next dance. Nothing brought her aloneness into starker focus than when she was prevented from doing the thing she loved most because she didn't have a man in her life.

Salvation came fast on the heels of those dark thoughts in the form of a cute, young cowboy flaunting a starched red western shirt and shiny belt buckle. He was too good-ol'-boy for her taste, complete with a wad of chew puffing his cheek, but she smiled invitingly anyway. Dancing a waltz didn't bind her to the guy for life.

"Care to dance, miss?"

Her answer was on the tip of her tongue when Matt appeared at her side, a proprietary hand sliding around her waist. Well, well, well . . . perhaps all he'd needed was a rival to remind him she wasn't going to wait forever while he made up his mind.

"Sorry, man. She's spoken for on this dance."

Jenna bit back a swoon. Lord have mercy. She'd never thought she had much use for testosterone-fueled machismo, but the aggressive edge in his tone called to the feminine part of her psyche in a way she hadn't expected.

Doing her best to turn her smile apologetic, she mouthed a *sorry* to the young cowboy, but he was already wandering off, scanning the crowd for another potential partner, leaving her free to concentrate on the big, solid man at her side. She ran her gaze along her shoulder, then up Matt's body until it landed on his face. "I don't remember you asking me to dance."

He turned her in his arms and took her right hand in his, his eyes flashing down the length of her. "Some things don't need to be said."

It was the first time their hands had touched outside of a handshake. His hand was strong, with calluses she hadn't expected to feel on a lawyer. With a motion so slow it seemed to stretch time, he dragged his thumb over the back of her fingers as though cradling her hand in his wasn't nearly enough friction to satisfy him.

She responded with a slow crawl of her other hand up the muscles of his arm to settle into closed hold position. His body was unyielding beneath her touch—deliciously hard and male. A fantasy flashed in her mind of the two of them in her bedroom, standing together like this but without a stitch of clothing. Without any of the barriers that presently stood between them.

A corner of his mouth kicked up into a wolfish grin. "I guess we'd better get to waltzing before the song ends."

Before she could answer, he stepped her back into the swirl of dancers and let the lilting rhythm of the music carry them away.

The lights had been dimmed to blues and purples, hushing the party crowd, while a disco ball gave life to the dreamy lyrics about summer love under a blanket of stars in the big old Western sky.

When they reached the far end of the dance floor, the

arm at her waist pulled her nearer. His mouth dipped close to her ear. "Are you ready for Amy's big day, Miss Wedding Planner?"

His breath lighted across her neck, igniting a tremor of sensation through her body. "I'm ready, all right, but by the skin of my teeth. I thought six months was plenty of time to plan a wedding reception. What a joke. Now I understand why people plan these things a year or more out. There was no convincing Amy and Kellan to take their time, though."

"I've known Kellan going on ten years, since I was a T.A. in an oil law course he was taking, and he's always been the jump-in-with-both-feet type."

No wonder he and Amy were perfect for each other. Amy gave new meaning to the term *full steam ahead*. Jenna turned her face to meet his eyes. "But you're not like that. You're more of a wade-in-slowly kind of guy." If their relationship moved much slower, they'd be going backward.

He tipped his head, considering. "I guess I am. Wasn't always that way, but I suppose I've gotten more cautious with age."

"That makes you sound old, but you're only, what, thirty-one? Thirty-two?"

He guided them around a couple who looked brand-new to the world of country-western dance, staring at their legs and counting the steps aloud. "I'm thirty-three."

"Still too young to be cautious."

His expression turned teasing. "I know it's taboo to mention a lady's age, but pardon me if I have trouble taking aging advice from someone who hasn't even hit thirty yet."

"Then maybe I shouldn't let on that I only just turned twenty-four in June." He got quiet, probably doing what everybody else did when they realized how young she was. She beat him to the punch. "I had Tommy when I was nineteen."

He was gentlemanly enough to mask his shock, but not before his eyebrows flickered up.

"I know, so young." With a flippant wave of her hand, she smiled warmly to let him know it was okay for him to be shocked. She'd been pretty darn shocked when she'd first found out too. "I guess I'm way too fertile for my own good."

Matt's shoulders stiffened. "Most people are."

What an odd comeback. In all the times she'd made that same joke about her pregnancy, she'd never heard a response quite like that. She was in the process of formulating a question, when, without breaking his impeccable rhythm, Matt added pressure to the hand at her waist, her cue that they were about to get fancy with their dancing.

Bring it, she thought as he lifted the hand she held, then expertly partnered her through a triple spin into a reverse that erased the questions from her mind. She nearly laughed with the giddiness at performing the complicated steps and the deftness of his execution. Now *this* was how dancing was supposed to be.

Breathless, she met him in closed hold once more. His hand slipped to her back with the control of a man who'd spun a lot of women around the dance floor in his day.

She shoved the petty thought aside. After all, she'd been spun around the dance floor plenty of times by plenty of men. And she refused to hold anyone else to their pasts when she hated that she couldn't escape her own.

"I didn't know you could dance like this," she said.

His cocky, lopsided smile sent a flash of heat through her. "One of my many secrets."

Before she could respond to such a baiting remark, he

spun her in a double turn that twisted into a side-by-side shadow hold. Swinging her chin over her shoulder, she met his warm, confident smile. Hot damn, this man lit her fire.

With a wink that told her he knew exactly how good a dancer he was, he launched them into windmills and reverses. A bit flashy given the prying eyes surrounding them, but it satisfied her womanly sensibilities that he was showing off for her. It would be nice for a change to have the good folks of Catcher Creek spreading rumors about her for something other than her days as a wild youth or the identity of Tommy's missing father.

When they'd returned to closed hold, Jenna shook her hair back and pinned Matt with her most flirtatious look. "You can't lay down a challenge like that and expect me not to take it up."

"What challenge? Are you saying you think you could best me in a dance-off?" He scoffed. "I'd like to see the day."

The dare had her *tsk*ing good-naturedly. "That's not what I meant, though I have no doubt that in a dance-off, I'd shine the floor with your ass."

Continuing with a basic one-two-three around the floor, he laughed through his nose, his eyes twinkling. "You talk a big game, darlin'. Makes me concerned about what other challenge you think I've laid down for you."

The song ended and they slowed to a stop on the outer edge of the floor. People moved around them as a new song, a faster song, picked up pace. She traced the edge of his chiseled shoulder muscle below his chambray shirt. This is how it would be between them if they were a couple—smooth and romantic, like the waltz.

She moved her fingertips from his shoulder to his jaw. "Matt Roenick, one of these days you're going to tell me all your secrets."

He swallowed and his focus dipped to her lips, so she angled them up, parting them, closing her eyes. All he had to do was lower a few inches and she'd finally—*finally*—know what his mouth felt like on hers. Didn't matter that they were surrounded by people. She'd waited eight long months for this. *Come on, Matt. Kiss me already.*

Chapter Two

Any guy who'd ever thought dancing was unmanly had obviously never danced a waltz with Jenna Sorentino.

All his childhood years of being forced by his parents to attend cotillion classes, the innumerable dance partners throughout his life who'd stepped on his toes, and too many late nights in loud, smoky country-western bars were all made worth it with the look Jenna gave him when she realized he knew what he was doing.

It was a breathless look of arousal that sent a surge of lust and machismo pumping thick and fast through his veins. Those same men who thought dancing was for sissies were probably the same ones who thought anything more than a hard, fast fuck was a waste of time. Their loss, his gain, because dancing with Jenna was one of the most erotic forms of foreplay he'd ever experienced.

Dangerously so. Every swish of her hips and arch of her back led him deeper into wanting. In his hand he held her delicate fingers, which ended in white-tipped nails. He could imagine those nails, those fingers, grazing him all over, wicked and hot. Her skin and hair smelled of honey and almonds, and damn, he wanted to feast on her something fierce.

He'd never danced a waltz with a hard-on before. Any dance, for that matter. Probably should've expected as much tonight; after all, a man didn't want a woman for as long as he had Jenna without experiencing some sort of visceral reaction the first time he touched her body. And Jenna was, quite simply, the sexiest, most luscious creature he'd ever laid his hands on.

He should've never dared to dance with her.

But the alternative would've been that slick rodeo cowboy taking her for a spin around the floor, and there was no way in hell he was going to watch another man leading her in Matt's favorite dance while he stood on the sidelines.

What a crazy, messed-up way of thinking. It didn't matter how much hot-blooded testosterone pounded through his body when he was dancing with Jenna or how many nights he'd dreamed of holding her, because none of it meant shit when all the chips were down and she was standing there, pressed into him, offering her lips. He may have wanted her worse than he'd ever wanted a woman, but he still wasn't going to kiss her.

He didn't date single moms.

Not anymore. Not even those who were beautiful and smart and got his engine revving like Jenna did.

The policy sounded arrogant and callous. Even knowing the reasons behind it, he disgusted himself. Looking down at Jenna's sweet, rosy lips, he knew he was the most pathetic man in history. But precedence and fear had a way of settling priorities. After everything he'd been through the past eleven years, there were only a handful of things in the world he feared more than single moms.

Tonight, fear won out over longing.

He smoothed a fingertip along her jaw, wishing he could be what she needed, knowing it was hopeless. But how could he turn her away? This soft, clever woman who'd done nothing wrong except try to get closer to him. He rested his cheek against hers and tried to find the words.

They were standing close enough together that he felt her phone vibrate in a pocket hidden in her dress. It was the out he needed.

"Your phone," he said lamely, cringing at the rawness of his voice.

She opened her eyes and backed her face up to regard him with disbelief. "What?"

"Your phone's vibrating. I think you should answer it."

Her jaw tightened and in her eyes he read pain. *Hell.*

"You do?"

"What if it's important?"

She pulled her lower lip into her mouth and bit down, nodding. A ripple went through her body like she was resetting herself. "Silly me. I thought something important was going on right here."

Giving him a look that told him exactly how much he'd hurt her, she turned on her heel and stalked across the middle of the dance floor, fishing her phone out as she went.

He stepped back, out of the way of the dancers, and inhaled sharply.

Stupid, stupid jackass.

His first instinct was to leave. He could settle the bill, say good-bye to Kellan and Amy, and get in his car. But all that was waiting for him at the end of the drive was a lonely hotel room, and besides that, he wasn't the walk-away kind.

True, he was the leading-a-good-woman-on-and-causing-her-undue-pain kind, but running and hiding was a shade more cowardly than he was willing to stoop.

What he really needed to do was cowboy up and talk to Jenna tonight so things weren't weird between them at the wedding. To make that happen, he needed to figure out a way to explain why they couldn't get involved without telling her the whole, hideous truth.

A little liquid courage first wouldn't hurt either.

He started for the bar. Halfway there, a man clapped him on the back. "Where I come from, we call dance moves like yours skirt flippers."

He turned to face Kellan, all six-foot-something of bulky rancher build, grinning from ear to ear as any dopey-in-love man should be.

Kellan's smile was infectious. Matt found himself following suit despite his lingering frustration from disappointing Jenna. "Something tells me you've never made a girl want to flip up her skirt because of your killer dance moves."

Kellan swigged on his beer, then hid a belch behind his hand. "The only way my dance moves would be killer is if a girl could die from squashed toes. Lucky for me, my intended bride forgives me of my shortcomings."

"Does that mean for your first dance as husband and wife you'll be doing the prom hang?" Out of the corner of his eye, he saw Jenna slip in from the patio. If he and Kellan didn't move fast, she was going to walk right into them and he was nowhere near ready to face her yet. "I was headed to the bar. Join me?"

"Sounds good. I missed my prom, but if you're implying that Amy and I are going to rock back and forth while bear hugging, that's exactly what I had in mind."

The casual acquaintance he and Kellan had struck up a decade earlier had strengthened into a solid friendship over time, thanks in large part to the massive oil deposit sitting under Catcher Creek and Kellan's family ties to big oil. Over the years, Kellan had called on Matt a lot to help home owners negotiate fair contracts with his uncle's less-than-altruistic oil corporation.

Matt loved practicing the kind of law that helped ordinary,

hardworking people. The royalties he negotiated on behalf of the people with the oil sitting beneath their properties paid mortgages, sent kids to college, and kept struggling farms in the black.

It had been Kellan who'd hooked him up with Jenna's family last December. The contract he'd negotiated for the sisters had saved the farm that'd been in their family for generations. Victories like that were the reason he'd become a lawyer and were the legacy he wanted to leave. Even if he wasn't destined to start his own family, he could help other families stay intact.

"Getting any closer to biting the bullet and opening up your clinic?" Kellan asked as they sidled up to the bar.

Matt had dreamed about opening the low-cost legal clinic since law school, a business that would get him out of his corporate job at the law firm and into helping down-on-their-luck families full-time. He'd been socking away money and building industry connections for years, and a month ago, he'd finally gotten serious about going after his dream and hired a Realtor to help him find the perfect storefront.

They'd narrowed the choices to two locations—one in downtown Santa Fe, near his family, and the other in Catcher Creek, the heart of oil country. The trouble was, some gut-level instinct was holding him back from making a choice and he couldn't for the life of him figure out why he was dragging his feet.

Matt signaled for two beers from the bartender. "I've got the paperwork and loans figured out, but it's a scary prospect, giving up my salary and security at the firm." That had nothing to do with it, but it was an excuse people readily accepted. Matt was in a unique position not to care about such things. Not only did he live a modest lifestyle, but he didn't have a family to worry about providing for and he lived on his family's property, which meant he had no mortgage or major expenses.

"Will the senior partners at your firm support you striking out on your own?"

"Yes. Absolutely. I've talked extensively with them about my plans and they're being great about it. They don't do much pro bono work, so I won't be any sort of real competition."

"Glad to hear it. I've said it before and I'll say it again, Catcher Creek would be lucky to have you. Vaughn's old house is on the market, now that he's living out with Rachel on the farm. I'm sure he'd be thrilled to sell it to a friend."

The beers arrived, their sides dripping with icy water. Matt snagged one and relished the bite of cold, bubbly brew sliding down his throat. "That's definitely something to consider. The storefront I'm looking at in Catcher Creek is more affordable than the one in Santa Fe and it'd make my clinic easy to find for Quay County folks who need help." But Jenna was here and he wasn't sure he could stand seeing her on a regular basis, knowing she could never be his.

"How do you think your folks would handle their baby boy moving off the homestead?"

"Aw, do you have to put it like that? It's not like I live under their roof like some overgrown slacker. Our houses aren't even in shouting distance of each other. And that's by design."

Kellan pounded the last of his old beer and picked up the next. "Just bustin' your balls. Santa Fe's only three hours away from Catcher Creek, so it wouldn't be like you're moving to Mars."

"Too true. How are you faring with the wedding? Nervous about tomorrow?"

After another swig of beer, Kellan shrugged. "Nah.

Ready to get the show over with so I can whisk Amy away on our honeymoon."

"The Caribbean, right?"

Kellan chortled. "I don't see why we have to spend a whole day traveling to get to a private room with a comfortable bed, but apparently it'll make Amy happy to know the ocean's right outside our door, even if we never get around to seeing it."

He dug for his wallet, but Matt waved him away and threw a twenty on the counter. "What time is your brother getting in for the wedding?"

Kellan's face turned stony, and Matt knew he'd stepped in it. Jake wasn't coming. Shit.

"I'm sorry," Matt said.

"Me too." He squinted at a blank space on the far wall.

The awkward silence that ensued had Matt debating his next move. Change the subject or say something sappy? It was a tricky situation because he and Kellan didn't have that kind of relationship. They'd been buddies for a long time, but more like beer-drinking, hunting pals than the *let's talk about our feelings* kind.

What the hell, he decided. There were worse things in life than letting your friends know you cared about them. Didn't make him any less of a man.

"That really sucks. He's your family and he should be here for you on the most important day of your life. You deserve better than that."

Kellan's eyes shifted to Matt, the stoniness replaced by regret. "I really don't. That's the thing. I'm not sure what I was thinking, asking him to be my best man. That was jumping the gun on my part. We only just started talking again this December. It should've been enough for me to invite him instead of putting him front and center like I tried to."

Matt would probably be kicking himself too, if he were

in Kellan's situation. The thing of it was, with five siblings and an extended family that would fill the Superdome, nothing like that would ever happen to him. Still, he knew what it meant to blame yourself for things out of your control.

"Listen, that's bullshit, man. If Jake wasn't comfortable being in the wedding party, then he should've never agreed. You can't control what other people say or do any more than a farmer can make it rain when he wants to."

Which was exactly the mantra he'd been telling himself since the accident that had changed everything. If only the words were as easy to believe as they were to say.

Kellan pressed a finger to the spot between his eyebrows and squeezed his eyes closed. "My mom's still holding out hope that Jake will make it to the wedding. I think I'll wait until I drive her home to break it to her that he won't be there. No sense in ruining her night sooner than necessary. Mostly, I don't want Amy worrying about this. I can tell she already is, even though she's doing a decent job of hiding it."

Good plan. "Neither you or Amy has anything to worry about. It'll be smooth sailing from here on out. Jenna's done a great job planning this shindig, and tomorrow, Vaughn, Chris, and I will be standing up there with you, and you know we've got your back. It's going to be a great day, okay?"

Kellan mustered a grin and socked Matt on the shoulder. "Damn right it will."

A clatter of boot heels had both men turning to find the source of the noise. Jenna shouldered her way between them and waved her phone, her eyes wide. "We've got a problem. A big one."

Chapter Three

The pain that had been in Jenna's eyes when she'd looked at Matt only a few minutes earlier had vanished, replaced with cool indifference, as if he were any other man she barely knew. That was what he wanted, wasn't it? For her to stop pursuing him? So then why did his chest ache with the loss?

"You were right to have me take that call," she said, pointing her phone in his direction. "It was Philomena, the florist." Her eyes shifted to Kellan. "You know, the one I told you about who Marti at the salon recommended because she did her sister's wedding?"

Kellan fiddled with his beer, wide-eyed and clueless, as if to say, *I'm just a guy. Don't expect miracles.* "Was that the night the Cardinals beat the Dodgers?"

Jenna gave a little head shake. "Anyhow, the van bringing the flowers in from Texas broke down outside of Amarillo this morning. Complete engine failure in the middle of nowhere. With this summer heat, by the time the tow truck got there, every flower in the back had languished."

"Languished?" Matt and Kellan echoed at the same time.

Jenna held up her palms. "Philomena's word, not mine. And when I asked her to clarify, she said she'd mail back the deposit, along with a bouquet of stargazers as an expression of her apology."

Kellan lifted his hat and ran a hand over his hair, his vibe turning desperate. "She can't pull out now. The wedding's tomorrow."

"I know that, sweetie."

"She should have called you hours ago."

"I know that too." Her smile was serpentine, her voice low and tight. "And I fully plan on shoving those stargazers up Philomena's you-know-what where they won't ever see the stars again, but that's going to have to wait until after I've thrown my sister the most beautiful, most perfect wedding Catcher Creek has ever seen."

Kellan cursed and turned away to stare at the wall like he was thinking about kicking a hole in it.

Matt tried a smile on for size and attempted to lend some perspective to the crisis. "It's not like the reception hall burned down or something catastrophic. They're just flowers, right?"

Until that moment, standing before Jenna, Matt wasn't sure he'd ever seen the full capacity of a woman's wrath. It made him take a few cautionary steps back in case she burst into flames right there in the middle of the Sarsaparilla Saloon.

Her eyes got small. Beneath her dusting of freckles, her skin turned pink. She rose up to her full height, then higher still, as if anger were a substance lighter than air, making her body levitate.

"For your information, all Amy wanted—her only request—was a wedding filled to bursting with flowers. We planned for flowers lining the pews and altar at the ceremony, bouquets, boutonnieres, and corsages for the bridal party"—with each word, her body levitated higher—"flower centerpieces for the tables at the reception, topping the limousine, topping the cake, and fashionably nestled in her updo. Think of her updo, Matt!"

Matt didn't know what an updo was, but he sure as hell wasn't about to ask. He looked to Kellan for rescue, but he was still drilling a hole in the wall with his eyes. Turning his focus back to Jenna, Matt held up a finger like a timid kid hoping the teacher would call on him to speak.

She didn't.

"It's nine o'clock on a Friday night, the wedding is eighteen hours away, and Catcher Creek is smack in the middle of Bumfuck, Egypt!"

Those were all valid points, but Matt knew something she didn't. Something that had a high certainty of fixing the problem. "Take a breath, Jenna. I have a solution."

Kellan's head whipped their way, his eyes pleading, but Jenna was unconvinced. She wagged a finger in warning. "This better not be more of your glass-half-full optimistic bull—"

He wrapped one hand around her finger and the other over her lips. "My sister Tara is a florist."

Could've been another optical illusion, but she seemed to drop her boots back to solid ground. Even her expression relaxed a shade. He shoved his hands in his pockets lest he was tempted to pull her closer and help her relax even more.

"Where?" Kellan asked.

"Santa Fe. If we left right now and called her from the road, we'd get there in under three hours."

Jenna flattened her hand against Matt's chest, breathing and blinking. "Three hours is midnight. She'd have to work through the night to make enough flower arrangements, and that's if she has the flowers to spare. That's a lot to ask of anyone. I mean, she doesn't even know Amy."

His heart rate sped up at her touch and he wondered if she could feel it pounding. He took a breath, pushing his ribs into her palm. "When I tell her how important this is, I guarantee she won't even blink. She's family. Besides that, Tara owes me. Big-time."

Finally, Jenna met his eyes. Her lips twitched and then spread into a smile, her expression no longer panicked, but amused and maybe a little awed. "You're going to save me, aren't you?"

He wrapped a strand of her wavy blond hair around his finger, then let it spring away. "I'm going to try."

Shaking her head, she fiddled with his shirt collar. "This is unbelievable. What're the odds you have a florist in your family?"

Matt rocked on his heels. "Pretty good, actually. Five siblings, plus four spouses and an ex-spouse makes ten different careers. Add to that eight aunts and uncles and eighteen cousins, all in the general Santa Fe area. Yeah, I'd say my family's got you covered no matter what kind of help you need. Well, except dentistry."

"No dentists?" She faked some shock and lightly scraped his forearm with those white-tipped nails. He fought to ignore his body's response.

"You'd have to look all the way to my third cousins on my mom's side to find one, and even then, I wouldn't trust him with my teeth. He's a shifty sort."

Kellan clapped his hands together, reclaiming their attention. "Let's do this thing. You and me, Matt, let's go. Right now."

"Not you," Jenna said. "You've got enough on your plate keeping your mom and Amy from worrying. Don't tell them about this yet. Let them get a good night's sleep and you can break the news in the morning."

Kellan glanced across the room to where Amy and Rachel were fumbling through a two-step together. "You're right. That'd be the best plan."

"Matt and I are going to fix this, Kellan. We're going to save the wedding."

Vaughn chose that moment to enter their circle, chuckling. He hooked his arm around Kellan's neck. "K, I think our women are tipsy. I like it. How much tequila did you make them drink, Jenna?"

"Just the right amount." She snagged Vaughn's other arm. "Hey, listen, would you and Rachel take Tommy home with you tonight? There's something I've got to do." She waved dismissively. "Last-minute wedding prep."

"No problem."

She fished a set of car keys from her pocket and set them in Vaughn's hand. "For Tommy's booster seat."

Matt handed him the key card to his hotel room. "Room one-twelve, in case you need to grab my tux and meet us at the civic center."

Though Amy and Kellan had originally planned to marry at the farm, the ballroom at the Tucumcari Civic Center, thirty miles east of Catcher Creek, had proved to be the only air-conditioned reception hall in the whole of Quay County that could fit the lengthy guest list they'd drummed up. The ceremony would take place in the center's sprawling atrium.

"What? Why would you be late?"

"No time to explain." Matt tucked Jenna's hand around his elbow, exhilarated by the idea of spending the night with her—even if it was nowhere near the kind of night he'd fantasized about. "See y'all tomorrow. Wish us luck."

Kellan stuck his hand out. "Thank you, man. When you get hitched, you'll understand how grateful I am for your help."

Matt shook his hand and smiled, but his heart sank. There probably wasn't a man in the free world who wanted to get married as badly as he did, but every year the prospect seemed less and less likely. He simply couldn't figure out what kind of woman would have a man who wasn't whole. Certainly none of the women he'd met.

Except maybe single moms, but that was a beehive he was through kicking.

He angled Jenna toward Tommy, who was back on the dance floor, this time with his grandma. "You say good night to your son and I'll bring my car around. Time for you and me to make some wedding magic."

It took Jenna a few minutes to wrangle a kiss from her busy son and explain that he'd be going home with Aunt Rachel and Uncle Vaughn. His eyes lit at the prospect. Sleeping in the big house on the farm with two of his favorite grown-ups—and Mom nowhere in sight—was a rare pleasure indeed for an independent little guy like he was.

She couldn't find Amy to say good-bye, but that was probably for the best. Ever since their sister huddle and tequila shots, Amy had looked so happy and distracted from her wedding nerves that Jenna didn't want to put herself in the position of trying to explain why she was ducking out early.

On the flip side of the heavy wooden saloon door, she stepped into the sultry summer air. Matt had brought his red SUV near the entrance and stood leaning against the passenger door, his arms in the pockets of his jeans and the slight breeze ruffling the tips of his dark hair. She loved how he wore his hair, styled with product to give it a youthful, mussed-up look. The carefully constructed illusion made her want to muss it up for real.

He offered her a lopsided smile. The appearance of her favorite dimple almost made up for him begging off from kissing her earlier with one of the lamest excuses she'd ever heard.

"You ready to ride with me, young lady?"

"You know it, cowboy. I've been trying to get you alone in a car for a long time." Damn it, she'd vowed not to flirt with him anymore and there she went, already back at it. The kicker was, she knew he had to be aware of their compatibility. The attraction that sizzled between them was too palpable for him not to feel it like she did, all the way deep down to her heart and soul.

Maybe she shouldn't let her pride talk her into giving up on him quite yet. Maybe this night together would prove the tipping point in their relationship.

He pushed off the door and opened it. "Are you confessing that you sabotaged the flowers on purpose to set up this all-night road trip?"

She sent him a sidelong look filled with intrigue. "My lips are sealed."

"Oh, no. Don't you dare try to distract me from your mischief by talking about your lips. That's double dirty dealin'."

She slid onto the seat, catching the way his eyes followed the swing of her bare legs into the car. She was busy congratulating herself on choosing to wear a sundress instead of jeans when her boot touched down on something hard. A crunch like an aluminum can buckling filled the space. She moved her foot off the can, inadvertently kicking a second.

"Oh geez, sorry," he muttered, diving down around her legs in search of them.

As he groped along the floor, his cheek brushed her leg. Her breath caught.

He jerked his head away, face averted, one hand holding an empty energy drink and the other covering his cheek. "I didn't mean to . . ."

He tossed the can into the backseat and stared into the darkness beyond the parking lot.

God, Matt, what's it going to take for you to overcome whatever's haunting you?

Determined to reclaim his attention, she ground the heel of her boot into the other can.

Their eyes locked. The band of tension that had been pulling between them all night stretched tighter.

A twist of her ankle crinkled the aluminum again. She cocked an eyebrow in challenge. *Get the can, Matt. Reach on down there, big guy.*

He crossed his arms over his chest and narrowed his eyes. "Miss Sorentino, are you trying to seduce me?"

"I'm just trying to clear some room for my legs." She smoothed her hand over her thigh.

Those must've been the magic words because with a jolt his expression thawed. His focus shifted to her lower body. Unfolding his arms, he stepped into the doorway, looming over her.

And then his fingertips were on her bare knee. She sucked in a deep breath and held it, letting her lungs burn.

With a feather touch and a gaze as dark and hot as the air outside, he dragged his fingers higher, to the edge of her skirt.

She slid her eyes to his hand and watched as he ever so slowly pushed the hem higher.

Her whole body flushed with awareness and an ache flared to life between her thighs. She arched into his touch, relishing the sound of his quickened breath that told her he was as turned on as she was.

"You make me forget myself, Jenna," he whispered, throaty. His hand left her skirt and dipped to the inside of her thigh.

"That's a shame because I was looking forward to getting to know you better tonight." Before she had time to second-guess the move, her hand shot to the back of his head. Fingers delved into his thick hair, pulling his head to her. His hand grabbed a firm hold of her thigh as the distance between their lips closed.

The door of the saloon opened with a bang so forceful both Jenna and Matt turned to look. Kellan stood in the doorway, his expression homicidal. "What are you two still doing here?"

Matt rose to his full height, his hand falling away from Jenna's leg, and pivoted to face Kellan. "What's wrong?"

Kellan angled his focus around Matt and stabbed a finger at Jenna. "No more tequila for Amy—ever again. She's in the bathroom, sick."

Jenna sat back against the seat, her mouth falling open. "What? She only had one shot." Sure, Amy was a lightweight, but not *that* big of one. "Has to be wedding nerves."

"This wedding is turning into a circus, for shit's sake. I'm this close to grabbing Amy and finding a judge to get this thing over and done with so we can get on with the rest of our lives." He knocked the toe of his boot hard against a brick planter box. Jenna had never seen him this upset before. He looked like a big, angry bear.

Matt moseyed his way, casual and slow, counterbalancing Kellan's agitation.

"No, you won't," he told Kellan in a smooth, confident tone, "because Amy wants a big wedding, and I've seen you with her enough that I know you'd do anything for her. We're going to celebrate you and Amy coming together to start a family, and it's going to be a beautiful time, even if it's not exactly like you planned. But that's life, right? Messy as hell. Weddings are no different. Wouldn't it set a terrible tone for your marriage to kick things off by quitting?"

Despite her concern for Amy, Jenna got a fluttery feeling listening to Matt's eloquent words. She'd never been around a man who had such a graceful talent with language, and it turned her on as much as the way he filled out a pair of jeans or that boyish dimple, which was saying something.

Kellan's anger deflated. His shoulders dropped. He went from kicking the planter box with force to bouncing the toe of his boot off it with light taps. "Don't you ever annoy yourself, what with being right all the time?" He looked sideways at Matt, a conciliatory smile on his face.

"It's a burden I have to carry. Listen, I'm serious—all weddings are circuses. Every single one of my brothers' and sisters' weddings had about a million last-minute problems. But everybody pitches in and gets it back on track. Take Amy home and get some water and aspirin in her. Jenna and I will take care of everything else."

Kellan scrubbed his hands over his face. "Okay, okay. I came out here in the first place to pull my truck around, so I'd better get to it. Rachel's going to bring her out when she's done in the bathroom."

Matt pulled keys from his pocket. "That's our cue to get out of here. See you in the morning. And try not to worry."

Jenna tugged her door closed, astounded that Amy's nerves had made her physically ill. As far as she knew, that had never happened to Amy before—and she, Jenna, and Rachel had been in some seriously stressful situations.

Matt climbed in the driver's seat and maneuvered the car onto the highway, heading west into the night. Jenna settled back in her seat and got comfortable.

She loved long drives. Loved singing along to the radio and cracking the windows to breathe in the dried-sage smell of the desert. She loved the exhilarating rush of anonymity and freedom when no other cars were in sight. The times Tommy was with her, long trips through the empty desert were when they had their best talks. It was when she and her sisters had their best talks too. There was something about the vast sky and the wide, flat land that opened people up.

Tonight, the moon was bright and nearly full, casting gray shadows over distant buttes and rolling hills. And she was alone with Matt. Maybe he'd finally open up to her too.

After adjusting the temperature and turning down the classic country song on the radio, he fiddled with the earpiece for his cell phone, then dialed a number.

"Hey, Len. It's Uncle Matt. Shouldn't you be in bed already?" Whatever Len said made Matt chuckle. "I like it when books make me stay up past my bedtime too. Is your mom around?"

In the pause that followed, Jenna's heart took a dive. She pressed a hand to her chest and fixed her attention on the white line that edged the road. What if this didn't work? She'd have to ambush florists in the morning, begging for help. She'd have to throw money she didn't have at the problem. Amy was already nauseous with nerves; how would this latest disaster affect her?

Matt rapped her thigh with the back of his hand. When she turned his way, he offered a reassuring smile before his attention was recaptured by the phone.

"Hiya. Sorry to—" His face crinkled into a grimace. "No, I don't need a reminder about your no-calling-after-nine rule." The grimace intensified. "Stop it. Ugh. I don't want to hear the gory details of your bubble bath and hair-removal regimen. I need to bleach my brain now. Thanks for that." He sighed, shaking his head. "I know, I know, *then don't call after nine*. I get it. But I need a favor."

Defeat tightened Jenna's throat. Interrupting a lady's personal beauty routine to beg a huge favor didn't exactly get the conversation off to the best start. If Tara didn't appreciate the phone interrupting her personal time, then she certainly wasn't going to want to cut her evening short to pull an all-nighter at her flower shop for a complete stranger's wedding.

In response to something Tara said, Matt rolled his eyes. "Give me a break. Do you remember last December at Disneyland?" After a pause, he grinned, triumphant. "Yes, I'm bringing it up. Get over it. Because guess who volunteered to stay in the hotel with Brittany when she had the stomach flu so the rest of you could enjoy your day at the happiest place on earth? That's right. Her favorite uncle did."

Jenna's anxiety gave way to affection. She should've guessed Matt was the same way with his family as he was with others. Always the one saving the day.

"And who babysits your kids every other Friday so you can date?" he continued into the phone. "I know I told you I'd never hold that against you, but all bets are off. I've never needed a favor this big."

Matt's smile got so wide, his teeth practically glowed. Jenna wanted to press a finger, or maybe her tongue, into his dimple. "Oh please, I'd never ask you to take the bubbies to synagogue for Torah study again. What did you say after last time? That you'd reached your annual quota of guilt trips about being a better Jew?"

Tara must've said something funny because Matt chuckled, then flashed Jenna a thumbs-up. "All right, here it is: I'm a groomsman in Kellan Reed's wedding tomorrow afternoon. You remember him, right? He's bought a few horses from Mom and Dad over the years. Well, we have a flower emergency, along with a very nervous bride who needs your expertise."

Despite Matt's obvious confidence that Tara would help, Jenna held her breath.

"Excellent. Thank you. Okay, details. Uhh . . . I have no clue. But I've got the bride's sister Jenna with me, who also happens to be the wedding planner. Let me pass the phone to her."

After more fiddling with the earpiece to turn it off, he handed the phone across the seat. Jenna wasn't easily intimidated, but her pulse pounded in her ears as she took it from him. After the back-and-forth between Matt and his sister, she half expected to be greeted on the phone by a royal bitch.

"Hi, Tara. My name's Jenna. Thank you so much for this. I'm sorry we're interrupting your night."

"That's okay. I like to give Matt a hard time, but I'm happy to help." Her voice was relaxed and warm, jokey even. Definitely not a bitch. "It's my weekend with the kids, but I'll call their father and see if he can come stay on the sofa tonight to watch them."

"Yay, Daddy!" a girl's voice hollered in the distance.

"You're supposed to be asleep, Brit!" A little-girl giggle sounded in the background. Tara let loose with an incredulous snort. "I swear, getting these two to settle down and go to bed is like trying to stop a Slinky on an escalator. And now that they know Ira's coming, forget about getting them to sleep. That man is a rock star around here. He'll probably let them have pie for breakfast."

"I'm sorry to put so many people out. Are you sure he won't mind?"

"Not at all. He and I weren't meant to be married, but he's a great dad. He won't mind in the least. Tell me, what kind of flower emergency are we talking about here?"

Jenna took a deep breath. "The florist called less than an hour ago and pulled out of my sister's wedding tomorrow afternoon." *And the best man is a no-show, and the bride is puking her guts out at the moment in the nasty-ass bathroom of a saloon, and this is turning into the wedding from hell.*

"That's a hundred shades of horrible," Tara said with genuine outrage. "I don't have a huge overstock in my refrigerator at the shop, but we'll work something out, then hit the wholesale warehouse when it opens in the morning. Every bride deserves beautiful flowers at her wedding. Heck, my motto is that every woman deserves to be surrounded by flowers all her life."

Relief washed through her. Maybe everything would turn out okay after all. "I like that motto, even though the only time I've ever been surrounded by flowers is when I pass through them in a store or attend a memorial service."

Tara scoffed. "You and just about every other woman in the world, which is a crime, if you ask me."

"Agreed. Listen, thank you for this."

"You bet. Fill me in on the wedding colors and flowers you had planned."

Tara listened intently, asking questions and pausing to take down notes. She promised to make haste to the shop and get busy, and Jenna agreed to show up with plenty of coffee and sweets to get them through the night.

When they ended the call, Jenna held the phone to her chest and released her exhale in a slow, peace-inducing stream.

"You okay?" Matt asked.

"Better than I've been the past hour. We might actually pull this off, thanks to you and Tara."

He waved off the praise. "Do you think Amy's going to be all right?"

Nodding, she watched the dark terrain out the window, gathering her scattered thoughts. "I know Amy freaks out easily, but she's tougher than she looks. We had it rough growing up and all three of us sisters ended up damaged in one way or another. But in a twisted way, I'm grateful for what we went through because I think it turned us sisters into fighters. In this crazy world, being a fighter is a good thing. Amy's going to be fine tomorrow. It's just a wedding."

Matt snorted. "And here I was under the impression that

throwing Amy the ultimate wedding was of the utmost importance to you."

She turned his way, faking wide-eyed innocence. "Whatever gave you that idea?"

He shot her a sidelong glance. "Do the words 'best, most perfect wedding in Catcher Creek history' ring a bell?"

"I did say that, didn't I?"

"I've never taken you as a control freak or the kind of person obsessed with appearances, so what gives? Why are you putting so much pressure on yourself to make this wedding perfect?"

He had the most uncanny way of getting to the heart of the issue. It would be unnerving if his concern was less than sincere, but she'd had her eye on Matt for a long time and he was the genuine article.

She knew exactly why she cared so much, but it was complicated. Still, she supposed he deserved to understand why he was working through the night to save the wedding— or at least as much of the truth as she could share.

"Our parents mismanaged our alfalfa farm, and about the same time as the economy took a dive, our business started going under. Rachel and I couldn't pay the bills. I'd never felt so helpless and I hated it. The only job I could get within driving distance was as a waitress, and juggling that, and a precocious preschooler, and—" She choked back the words that had been on the tip of her tongue.

Weird. She'd never come close to telling anyone that particular nugget of information before. She'd never wanted to. She liked the secret. It felt safer to keep it inside—a part of her nobody else could get to.

Shaking off the close call, she cleared her throat and forged ahead with her story. "That's about when you came into the picture last December, right after Amy swooped in to save the farm. She was the only one of us sisters who had any money or assets. She quit her job in L.A., sold her condo, moved home, and put up the collateral to start Heritage Farm Inn and the restaurant.

"Between her and Kellan, and your efforts negotiating those oil rights contracts, we were saved. Rachel's livelihood as a farmer was spared, as was the legacy we wanted to pass to Tommy. You asked why this wedding is so important to me, and the answer is that I owe Amy more than I could ever repay her. The wedding of her dreams is the least I can do."

His eyes on the road ahead, he gave a thoughtful nod. "Fair enough. That's my favorite part of being a lawyer, by the way. When I get to help families stay in their houses."

"I already knew that about you. You like to save people." Affection, warm and heady, almost had her reaching out to stroke his arm. She rubbed her own arms instead, knowing that if he flinched from her touch, the spell of the moment would be broken.

"I'd like to believe I'm more humble than to think about it in those terms, but I am proud that I have a skill that helps people."

"That's really noble."

He balked. "I wouldn't go that far. It was kinda inevitable, given the way I grew up. My family's huge on public service, like, big-time. *Tikkun olam* is what it's called in the Jewish community. Any time one of us kids would talk about what we wanted to be when we grew up, our parents, aunts and uncles, and grandparents made us explain how it fit in with tikkun olam."

Jenna chuckled. "No wonder you turned out to have such a way with words, needing to explain yourself all the time like that. Are your brothers and sisters passing on the tradition to their kids?"

"To varying degrees."

"I bet you will too when you have a family. The more I think about it, tikkun olam would be a good philosophy for Tommy and me to practice, too."

His expression hardened, smile gone.

A flash of regret pulsed through her. Had she said something wrong? Was she not allowed to practice tikkun olam because she was Christian? Would something like that matter to Matt? He'd never seemed conservative in his beliefs, but there was so much about him she didn't know.

You make me forget myself, he'd said.

Could their differing religions be the reason for the dark flash of inner turmoil she sometimes saw cross his face? Maybe that was the reason he wouldn't ask her out or kiss her. It was so tempting to scold herself for making things unnecessarily complicated again, but what if religion was a deal breaker for him?

She was still mulling over the possibility when he cracked the knuckle of his middle finger and said, "I have a question I've been wanting to ask you. And I bet you've been asked it a hundred times."

Boy howdy, had she ever. She'd been asked it enough that she could hear the question coming by the timbre of a person's voice. People all sounded the same when they broached the topic—tentative, with each word a slow labor of speech. Men sometimes smiled nervously. Women leaned in, their expressions solemn, as if they were Jenna's confidantes.

As far as transitions went, this one was about as smooth as a dirt road after a rainstorm, but rather than press him about their religious differences, she decided to follow his train of thought around the mental U-turn. "You want to ask me about Tommy's father."

"That obvious, huh?"

She grinned and offered a shrug to show him she didn't

mind. "He's not in the picture at all. Never has been, never will be."

Matt's breath gushed out in a *whoosh* and his torso folded in as though he would've doubled over if not for the support of the steering wheel. "What an idiot. I can't understand men like that."

One of Jenna's greatest sins was letting people believe Tommy's father wasn't around because he was a deadbeat. The truth was, the reason Tommy's father wasn't fulfilling his fatherly duties was because she'd never told him she was pregnant with his child. And unless she were to divulge the whole story of why she'd made that choice—which she'd never do because lives and livelihoods were at stake—then she came across as a borderline criminal, keeping a little boy and his daddy apart for no good reason.

"How's Tommy coping with that?"

She loved that Matt thought about her son's happiness. Most men she dated were only concerned with whether or not they'd have to fight off a jealous ex-boyfriend. "Tommy doesn't know any better. When he asks about his daddy, I tell him he's one of a kind because he doesn't have one, but that he's a lucky boy because he's got a mommy, two devoted aunties, and two soon-to-be uncles who love him dearly and look out for him."

"What about you? How are you coping with it? It's none of my business, but does the creep at least pay child support?"

Child support would've been nice. The money might have helped her cut down on her waitressing hours and given her more time with Tommy when he was little. "Tommy and I have managed all right. Rachel's helped a lot and now we've got the oil money coming in regularly." She touched his arm because gratitude was a good excuse to get her hand on him. "Thank you for being concerned about us."

He eased his arm away from her. "You almost told me

something earlier but stopped yourself. You said you were juggling being a waitress and mom and something else."

It took her a lot of blinks to catch up with his second directional shift in as many minutes. And this time, she didn't like where they were headed. Not at all. "I was hoping you missed that."

He pointed at himself. "Hello, lawyer here. I was trained to deal in details."

Her first instinct was to follow his lead by changing the subject. Then she thought about what a ridiculous conversational dance they were doing, twisting around every sensitive topic. How did she ever expect him to open up to her if she refused to do the same?

Besides, everyone was going to find out sooner or later. Confessing to him would be great practice for telling her sisters, and she had a feeling Matt would keep her confidences.

She scooted sideways in her seat, her heart pounding with a sudden burst of adrenaline. "I'll tell you something about me I've never told anyone, but it can't get around. Not even to my family."

Chapter Four

Déjà vu smacked Jenna hard.

She ground her teeth together, fighting panic. Holy shit. Whatever made her phrase it like that, it must've come from deep down in her psyche.

I'll tell you something about me I've never told anyone, but it can't get out. Not even to my family. Those had been Carson Parrish's exact words. Followed by the secret that had changed everything for both of them. Not that the secret itself was to blame, but it had been the tipping of the first domino.

Matt set a hand on her knee. "My lips are sealed."

It wasn't like this secret was dangerous—not like Carson's had been. But still, what Jenna had been hiding from her sisters for four years would complicate everyone's lives all over again. It would be as if someone had reengineered the dominos she and Carson had tipped that fateful night and she was going to start a whole new chain reaction.

"For the past four years, I've been going to college and I'm graduating next month," she blurted before she could overthink it to death. She sucked in a breath and studied his reaction.

His brows squeezed together and he hit the brakes, maneuvering his truck onto a turnout on the shoulder of the road. Jenna tensed, feeling confused and defensive.

He unbuckled his seat belt and twisted, hitching a knee on the seat. Then he looked her square in the face with a huge smile. In the glow of the car's instrument panel, she could just make out her favorite dimple. "I was trying to guess what you were going to say, but it sure wasn't anything that cool. Where? When? Let's hear some details."

His enthusiasm was irresistible. Her body instantly relaxed with relief. "The University of New Mexico has a correspondence program. For the most part, my classes have been online except for midterms and finals. Once a week, I have a computer lab on the UNM campus in Albuquerque."

"You're getting a degree in something computer-related? That's perfect for you. Let me think . . . graphic design?"

Graphic design was a great guess. After she, Amy, and Rachel had transformed their farm into an inn and restaurant, Matt had asked for a referral to their website designer to help him create one for the legal clinic he was thinking of opening. Jenna would never forget the bold admiration on Matt's face when he'd discovered it to be her. That had been a moment of clarity for Jenna, outside proof that she had marketable skills to go along with her passion for computer programming.

"Close. Computer engineering."

He whistled, clearly impressed.

"Why did you stop the car?"

He gave her hand a squeeze. "News this extraordinary deserved my full attention."

Well, that was something. She'd been bending over backward for eight months trying to get his full attention. If she'd had any idea that her secret life as a college student would do the trick, she might've taken him into her confidences months ago.

He rubbed his chin. "Let me get this straight. When you were twenty, you had a one-year-old son, a job as a waitress, a sick mom, and a farm to take care of—and you signed up for college on top of all that? And you're graduating after only four years, even though you chose not to seek any support from your family or friends?"

"Yes," she answered breathlessly. What was he getting at?

His eyes glittered with genuine admiration. "You're a badass, Jenna. You know that, right?"

"I . . ." She didn't feel like a badass. She felt desperate to build a better life for her and Tommy somewhere away from Catcher Creek. But Matt's praise felt good. Jenna wasn't sure anyone had ever admired how hard she worked and how many hats she wore. "Thank you."

"Does UNM hold a ceremony for people who graduate in summer?"

"A small one, along with an invitation to walk in the campus-wide one after the fall semester."

"Are you going to attend them?"

She considered demurring, then decided against it. "Yes, I am. I think I've earned that."

"Absolutely."

She gestured out the windshield. "We'd better keep moving. I don't want your sister waiting too long for us."

He nodded, reclipped his seat belt, and eased back onto the highway. "This doesn't sound like it should be a secret, but something you should be shouting from the rooftops. Your sisters would be proud of you. Why haven't you told them?"

No wonder he was such a great lawyer. Always bringing the topic back to the main point, not letting anything slip past his radar. "Because it means I'm leaving the farm. I have a job lined up working for the state as a software developer in their Santa Fe office. It's not my dream job, but it's another step in the right direction."

His eyebrows flickered up. "When is that happening?"

"September first."

"Wow." His expression turned thoughtful. "Amy's wedding, it's a thank-you for her help in saving the farm, but it's also a parting gift to your sisters, isn't it?"

"Yes." She hugged herself. Guilt gnawed at her every time she thought about breaking the news to Rachel and Amy, even though she knew full well that leaving was her only logical choice.

"I still don't understand why you've kept your schooling a secret all these years. How could they be upset with you for going after your dream?"

She picked at her fingernails. "It's not Amy I'm worried about. If anybody will understand, it'll be her because she left town to pursue her dream of being a chef the same week she graduated high school."

"Rachel . . ."

Helping Matt understand meant sharing with him the unflattering details about her past. Not exactly the stuff a lady should be talking about with a man she was interested in romantically, but it was too late to start pulling her punches now.

"I might owe Amy for saving our farm, but it's Rachel to whom I owe everything else. For the longest time, it was Rachel and me against the world. Our mom was bipolar and iffy about taking her meds, and our dad was good for nothing all the way around. When Amy skipped town, I was twelve and green with jealousy. Before she left, it'd never occurred to me that someone could pick up and walk away from Catcher Creek. After she opened my eyes to the idea, not a day went by that I didn't dream about escaping."

She knew he understood the general flavor of her family

history already, having renegotiated their oil rights contract the year before in the wake of her parents' deaths, but the two of them had never had a serious, private conversation like this. They'd never talked specifically about her life and her dreams.

When she paused, his focus shifted briefly from the road to regard her. "Did you ever go through with it—running away?"

"No. I was too chicken. And lazy. Running away would've meant getting a job to support myself, and why bother with that when I had a free ride courtesy of Rachel?"

"Ouch. Hard on yourself much?"

Ouch was right. It wasn't a pretty picture. Real life rarely was. "Just telling it like it is. I'm not going to pretend to be someone I'm not, especially to you. And glossing over my trip to rock bottom would be a disservice to Rachel. She's nine years older than me and handled all my raising up, which was no easy task because by the time I started high school, I was already wild."

"Miss Soon-to-Be College Graduate, wild? I don't see it."

She laughed, although it wasn't at all funny. Wild didn't begin to describe her teenage years. "It was only by the grace of God and Rachel that I didn't end up dead or in jail. Since the day I was born, she worked her fingers to the bone on our farm to make sure I had a roof over my head and food in my belly. She's the reason I didn't drop out of high school. She made me do my homework, got me out of bed so I wouldn't be late for school. And I repaid her efforts too many times by getting brought home in a patrol car, drunk or high."

"Drugs even?"

She was determined to own the choices she'd made, even the ones she was the least proud of. "Pot mostly. But sometimes harder stuff." And, boy, her knees had been chafed from praying that Tommy wouldn't be born with problems because of it. She'd given it all up cold-turkey the day she'd found out she was pregnant, but there'd been a couple times in those weeks before she'd known . . .

Even now, it dropped a rock in her stomach to think about it. His first year, she'd anticipated every one of Tommy's doctor appointments with vomit-inducing anxiety. But he'd been smart and healthy and happy since the day he'd greeted the world.

"And then, fresh out of high school, I got pregnant. When I dropped that bomb on her, she told me everything was going to be okay, and it was." Even now, six years later, the emotion of that day, that conversation, crashed through her, potent and painful. She teased the cuticle of her thumb, fighting the welling of love and melancholy. "She won't understand why I have to leave."

Matt was silent for a beat. Then, "Why do you have to leave?"

That was one secret she wasn't prepared to divulge—not even to Matt. She'd tell Rachel. While Amy and Kellan were on their honeymoon, she'd sit Rachel down and explain every last sordid detail of the disaster that had brought about Jenna and Tommy's need to move from Catcher Creek as soon as humanly possible.

Before Carson brought about the reckoning he'd threatened when he'd left.

But she wouldn't tell Matt or Amy or anyone else. The fewer people who knew, the safer she and Tommy were, and in the end, that was all that mattered.

Time to throw one of Matt's verbal U-turns back at him. "You mentioned at the saloon that most of your relatives live in the Santa Fe area. How many generations does your family go back in New Mexico?"

The quirk of his lips told her he knew exactly what she'd

done. The question was, would he play along? He tapped the top of the gear shifter. It had to be killing the lawyer in him not to press her back to his topic of choice.

Finally, he nodded in acquiescence. "My great-great-grandfather on my dad's side moved his family from Maryland and settled in the mountains outside of Santa Fe right before the Civil War broke out. He wanted everyone out of the line of fire without leaving the country altogether. I know that seems unpatriotic, like why didn't he support the North and fight? But honestly, I'm not sure what I'd do in his position. Self-protection or sacrifice. It's a complicated choice."

Not for Jenna. She admired that kind of circling the wagons. Protecting family was her number-one mantra in life too. "I like the way your great-great-grandfather thought."

"When my grandpa was alive, he used to tell stories about the pioneer days, as he called them. Stories passed down from his father. I loved hearing about how the Roenicks and the other families who made the trip with them transformed from mercantile factory workers into bona fide cowboys and cowgirls. They built ranches from the dust up and eventually a synagogue."

Pride colored his words. And how could it not, with such a rich family history? "My family still lives on the same property my great-great-grandfather staked more than a hundred and fifty years ago and worships in a new synagogue built on the original location. There's a lot to be said about growing where you're planted."

Envy tugged at her heart. She'd grown where she was planted, yet her experience had been far different. Maybe because Catcher Creek's population had never exploded like Santa Fe's, but small-town life had smothered Jenna since she was old enough to notice that every single person she came across knew her name, her family history, and everything else about her—the good, the bad, and the ugly.

As she'd aged, she'd started noticing the ugly in other people too. The crime and the small-minded ignorance. The way people turned a blind eye to her mom's depression and her dad's gambling. Everyone stood aside and watched her family sink. And then after what happened to Carson . . . well, after that, there was no beauty left in Catcher Creek at all that Jenna could see.

She cleared the lump from her throat. "I had no idea the Jewish community had such deep roots to Santa Fe. That's incredible."

He scowled. "Sorry. You just told me you and Tommy were moving and then I put my foot in my mouth. I'm not trying to make you feel guilty for wanting to leave your hometown."

"Don't worry about it. I'll always have roots and family in Catcher Creek. And I'm excited about starting my career. Nothing to feel guilty about."

That was the God's honest truth. Except that she couldn't shake off the regret. Even with a future as bright as hers was looking, the unfinished business of her past wouldn't lie down and die.

Two hours and a pit stop later, the Rocky Mountains began. The road snaked a path through the rising elevation. Santa Fe unfolded from the darkness one light at a time until the string of homesteads lining the road gave way to a bustling city. Unlike Catcher Creek, which rolled up the welcome mats early, even on Friday nights, Santa Fe was alive with activity and cars.

It was nearing midnight when they stopped for coffee at a convenience store. Jenna poured from the pots that were the fullest with the hope that they were also the freshest while Matt walked the aisles with a basket, dropping in snacks. Loaded with goodies, they drove the remaining few blocks to Tara's flower shop.

Carpe Diem Flowers sat in the parking lot of a supermarket and shared a flat, Southwest-style roof with a dry cleaner and sandwich shop. Behind the glass walls of the shop, all the lights were on. The doorway and aisles were crammed with plant stands and signs that looked like they belonged outside during operating hours.

Matt parked his SUV out front. He met Jenna on her side and took the tray of coffee cups from her. A pretty thirty-something woman with a slick, black pageboy haircut and a one-sleeved green shirt looked up from a spread of flowers on the counter. She gave a wave as she trotted toward the door to unlock it.

She shared Matt's rich brown eyes and was blessed with a willowy figure that was soft around the edges in a way that looked carefree and happy. Up close, it became clear to Jenna that the one-sleeved shirt was actually an emerald-green tank top and an elaborate hummingbird-and-flower tattoo cascading down her left arm. Bold. And totally forbidden by Jewish laws, Jenna recalled reading somewhere. It seemed as though Tara took a carpe diem approach to life as well as her flower shop. Jenna admired that.

"Tara, hi. I'm Jenna." She held out her hand. "Thank you again for doing this."

"Oh my gosh, you're adorable." Tara's words were filled with genuine delight. She bypassed the offered hand and embraced Jenna in a sincere hug. "And young." She pulled back and lifted Jenna's left hand. "And single. You're single, right?"

Unfortunately. Thanks to your brother. "Definitely single. Painfully single."

Tara raised on tiptoes to look her brother square in the

face. "Do you hear that, Matt? This adorable, young woman is single. Painfully so. Isn't that terrible?"

Matt kissed her hair and handed her the tray of coffees. "Almost as terrible as you, sister dearest."

Jenna's chest shook in a silent chuckle, even as her cheeks heated. She walked to the flower-prep counter so Matt wouldn't see her blush.

Tara moved next to Jenna, sliding the coffees onto the counter with a wink. "It certainly makes the male population of New Mexico seem downright stupid, if you ask me."

Amen to that.

Tara was a riot. When Jenna moved to Santa Fe, she'd have to invite her out for drinks or maybe they could get the kids together for a playdate. "I don't date much. My son keeps me busy."

"Ah." Tara's eyes shifted briefly to Matt and her expression blanked. "You're a single mom."

Jenna would've sworn she heard a strain in her tone.

Matt, wearing an odd smile that didn't seem a hundred percent genuine, walked to the counter and cracked a couple knuckles. "Jenna's a great mom. She has a five-year-old son named Tommy who's a lot like Brittany. A real spitfire. And as smart as they come, like his mama."

Even his words, though effusive in their praise, lacked his usual spark, but held an undercurrent of some unspoken message to Tara. Jenna fingered the delicate pink petal of a peony and decided to ignore the underlying weirdness that had descended on the conversation.

Matt and Tara were doing her a huge favor tonight, and repaying their generosity by seeing tension where there most likely wasn't any didn't fit with her agenda. "Aw, thanks. I agree about Tommy, by the way. He's a sweetie and a spitfire. Matt was showing him some slick moves on the dance floor tonight. How old are your kids, Tara?"

Tara picked up a bundle of white roses and arranged their heights. "I have a five-year-old girl, Brittany, and an eight-year-old boy, Len. But enough about me," she added with a wave of dismissal. "We've got a lot to do tonight, so we'd better get to it. I can fill you in on all the details of my family and some pretty embarrassing stories about Matt as a kid once we're working. You said the bride's colors are pink and white with a shabby chic look. I can't manage sweet peas this late in the summer, but peonies and rose will do the trick. And these stephanotis for the bridal party's updos will look beaut—"

Tara's face puckered. She backed away from the table and sneezed about twenty times in a row. With a hand over her nose and mouth, she ran to the desk for a tissue. She blew her nose loudly, then sneezed at least a half dozen more times, then blew her nose again. When she returned to the flower table, her eyes were bloodshot and watering.

"Are you okay?" Jenna asked.

"Tara is allergic to flowers," Matt said dryly.

"What? But you're a florist!"

Tara wiped her eyes with the back of her hand. "Geez, Matt, you could at least paint an accurate picture." Her watery eyes met Jenna's. "I'm allergic to everything God put on the Earth. Dust, pollen, perfume, animals, nuts, gluten, soy. You name it."

"Except tattoo ink," Matt muttered with a bemused smile.

Tara took his jab in stride. "Except tattoo ink and loud music. The only way I could go through life without stuffed-up sinuses, weepy eyes, and itchy skin would be to sit alone in a sterile room. And that is not acceptable to me. Other than the food allergies and bee stings, which might actually kill me, nothing's going to stop me from doing what I love, least of all my own body. And what I love most is creating beautiful pieces of art using flowers."

Go, Tara. "That's why you named your flower shop Carpe Diem?"

"Damn straight. I almost named it Screw You, Immune System, but that didn't quite have the same ring to it." She blew her nose again and tossed the tissue like a basketball into the trash can. After wiping a tear from her eye with the back of her hand, she picked up a set of shears. "Time's a-wasting. Let's get to it."

Jenna sipped her coffee and tucked in close to Matt, listening while Tara launched into a motor-mouthed explanation of their game plan for the night.

Chapter Five

Matt awoke to find he was still sitting upright on the tattered sofa in the back room that he, Jenna, and Tara had collapsed on sometime around three. Jenna was asleep with her head propped against his shoulder, her hair fanning over his shirt and her body heat seeping through his clothes into his skin.

He turned his nose into her hair and luxuriated in her honey-almond scent, fantasizing about hauling her onto his lap and waking her with a kiss. He bet she'd feel just right in his arms, as she had while they were dancing.

A look over her head revealed Tara sleeping on the opposite end, curled over the sofa's arm and snoring through her open mouth. It had probably been hell on her allergies to spend a whole night in the shop, and he bet her nose would be impossibly stuffy for days to come.

The air glowed a faint yellow-orange from the lights still shining in the main part of the store. Through the walls, he could hear the hum of activity from the dry cleaner next door, but he didn't need to look at the cheap plastic face clock hanging on the wall to know it was just about six o'-clock. As it had his whole life without fail, his internal alarm clock woke him at almost precisely the correct time, no matter what time he needed to get up.

Tara had insisted on setting the alarm on her phone anyway because she and Matt had both been born as stubbornly independent as cats, way more than any of their other siblings. Their mom swore it was an inherited trait, passed from their pioneer ancestors.

Now that he thought about it, Jenna had a stubbornly independent streak in her too. She'd blown him away last night with her confession that she was about to graduate college and leave her family home in pursuit of her dreams, in Santa Fe, of all places. That took gumption, big-time.

The more he learned about her, the more he found to love. He couldn't remember ever wanting a woman more. But he already had three pictures in his wallet of smiling, precious kids he'd thought he was going to have the privilege of fathering until he and their mothers had broken up. The pain of those breakups had dulled over time, which was probably why he'd let himself get so close to Jenna and Tommy. But now, with her snuggled against him, he fought to remember the heartache.

He forced himself to evoke the pain of saying good-bye to each of those kids, knowing he'd never see them again. That's how it would feel if he and Jenna didn't work out. One more chance at having a family slipping through his fingers.

The truth closed around his heart like an iron fist.

Jenna would have to go on haunting his dreams because his spirit couldn't survive another loss. What he needed to do, what he would do as soon as the wedding was over, was go hunting. Take his horse and a shotgun into the mountains for a long weekend to clear his head. He'd always called it hunting, as his father had when he'd gone off in the mountains alone, though Matt rarely did much shooting, and even less killing. But it was as good an excuse as any for beating it out of town and allowing the solitude of nature to settle his soul.

After that, he really ought to get serious about opening his legal clinic. Jenna was moving to Santa Fe, so Matt's best move was to relocate to Catcher Creek. He could buy Vaughn's old house, open his clinic in the heart of New Mexico's oil country, and maintain a three-hour buffer between him and the most tempting woman he'd ever known.

The tinny peal of a rap song sounded from Tara's phone, rousing her. She smeared her hands over her face, then turned off the alarm. Jenna squirmed, nuzzling her face deeper into his arm, but slept on.

Tara offered him a sleepy grin across the top of Jenna's head. "Hey."

"Morning." He tested his left knee by straightening his leg. Despite standing on it all night, it wasn't any stiffer than it usually was at the start of the day since that truck had plowed into his bike eleven years ago and turned him into roadkill. He bounced his foot in a small, controlled rhythm, careful not to jar Jenna as he loosened the joint.

"Those three hours of sleep went fast," Tara said through a yawn.

"Thank you for doing all this. Losing sleep and being away from the kids. I appreciate it, and I know Kellan and Amy do too."

"You're welcome, even though I'm positive we're not doing this for Kellan and Amy." She worked a frog out of her throat, blew her nose, then leveled a way-too-serious stare at him. "I like her, Matt."

Right. Of course. Because six in the morning, in Jenna's presence, on a day they were going to need to work their asses off, was the perfect opportunity for Tara to lay into him again, as if they hadn't beaten this particular dead horse a million times over the past few years. Well, he didn't have to play along.

"She likes you too," he said instead, wishing he didn't sound like a snarky teenager.

The remark earned him a belabored sigh. "You've got to get over—"

"I'm not talking about this. Not here. Not now."

Tara lifted her palms skyward. "I'm just saying."

"I already know what you're saying. And you know what I'm going to say back. We really ought to start numbering our arguments. Then we could call out 'Fight Number One' and be done with it. Think of the energy and time we'd save."

Jenna squirmed again. Her eyes fluttered open.

Looking affectionately exasperated, Tara pushed up from the sofa, brushed imaginary dust from her legs, then walked to Matt's end of the sofa and crouched.

"You deserve this," she whispered close to his ear. "You deserve to be happy." With another pointed look, she headed to the bathroom.

Absolutely obnoxious, the way she needed to always have the last word. He was the same way, but still. Sometimes Matt hated being the youngest. The eternal little brother. Everyone in the family thought they had a right to tell him how to live his life. Sometimes, he swore that when they looked at him, they still saw that gangly, awkward kid with the glasses and the too-big ears.

Matt knew what he needed to be happy. He knew how to take care of himself, and exactly what he deserved and didn't deserve, meddling big sisters be damned.

Jenna pulled away from him, taking her warm softness with her. Bummer.

"Good morning. Sorry I crowded you. You make a good pillow." Her voice was thick with drowsiness, her hair tousled. The cheek that had been resting against him was rosy. His body stirred to life.

"I didn't mind. You made a good blanket." *And the award for the most awkward compliment ever paid to a woman goes to Matt Roenick.*

Jenna grinned and smoothed a hand over her hair. "Is Tara ready to hit the warehouse?"

They'd completely tapped out the store's refrigerator and still had two mega arrangements to create, so the plan was to make a quick trip across town to the only wholesale flower supplier in Santa Fe and pray they had what Tara needed. "Just about. If we leave in the next five minutes, we should have enough time to swing by a coffeehouse before the wholesaler opens at six thirty."

"Perfect." She stood, stretching her arms over her head, and Matt had to agree—she looked perfect. Especially the creamy backs of her thighs where the dress pulled up during her stretch. Not that he was trying very hard, but all night long, he hadn't been able to get his eyes off her legs.

She'd taken off her boots almost as soon as they'd arrived in the shop, claiming achy feet. She'd doffed her socks as well. Her choice had been a torturous one for a leg man like him because now free of boots and socks, her thin, tan, gorgeous legs seemed to stretch for miles and ended in pretty, white-tipped toenails that matched her fingers.

Who knew he had a thing for nail polish? He'd certainly never given it much thought before. But now, he couldn't stop imagining polished fingers wrapping around him and polished toes tangling with his legs while he rose above her.

Swallowing a growl, he pushed off the sofa, snatched her boots and socks from the corner, and delivered them to her. Then he walked away before he was tempted to sit back down and watch her put them on. A man could only take so much.

In a matter of minutes, they'd locked Carpe Diem's door and assembled at Tara's van.

"Toss me the keys. I'll drive," Matt said.

The look Tara shot him would've wilted a lesser man. "You think I'm going to let you drive my van? Because, what, you're a man? Out of my way."

It had been worth a try. He much preferred being a driver to being a passenger. Apparently, Tara felt the same.

Jenna stood there grinning like crazy.

He offered her a mock-defensive scowl in return. "What? You gonna tease me now too?"

She shook her head. "My big sisters won't let me drive either. Rachel still reminds me about what a terror I was behind the wheel when she was teaching me to drive. As if I'm still that young and irresponsible."

He opened the passenger door for her. "That's the story of my life. My family still treats me like I'm a kid." Not only was he the youngest, but he was the only sibling who wasn't married or had kids of his own. "Drives me bat-shit crazy sometimes."

Jenna paused halfway onto the seat and touched his cheek. "Despite that, you've got a great family. I look forward to meeting your parents tonight at the wedding."

Tara angled forward, a mischievous twinkle in her eye. "After I tell them about you and Matt's teamwork to fix this flower emergency, I'm sure they'll be dying to meet you too."

Bat. Shit. Crazy.

He didn't bother to scold Tara with a cranky expression, just closed the passenger door and crawled in the backseat. "Let's move it, Tara. I need some coffee."

By nine o'clock, without a minute to spare, they'd returned to Carpe Diem to fashion flower toppers for the arch Kellan and Amy were going to stand under during the ceremony and the wedding party's table at the reception. They'd then transferred the arrangements, bouquets, corsages, and boutonnieres from the shop's fridge into the back of Tara's minivan.

Time was flying way too fast. The wedding might not be until three o'clock, but the photographer would be there to take pictures of the bridal party at one. Which meant he and Tara needed to put some extra pressure on their gas pedals to make it to Catcher Creek in time for a beautician to stick flowers in Amy's hair, better known as—he'd learned at about 2:00 A.M.—her updo.

He programmed directions to Catcher Creek into the minivan's GPS, then jumped into the driver's seat of his SUV and jammed it in gear.

Jenna's purse chimed. She pawed through it and came up with a cell phone. "It's Kellan, returning my text from earlier. Amy's feeling better. That's a relief."

"Excellent. I'm glad she got over whatever it was fast. You ready to ride with me again, darlin'?" he asked, cocking a brow in her direction as he navigated out of the parking lot.

"I'd be your passenger any day. I wouldn't even fight you for the keys." She paired the remark with a set of bedroom eyes that heated him all the way down to where it counted.

Yow. Guess it was his fault for opening the door to flirtation with his question, but it was going to be a long day for his fraying willpower. He was still going to allow himself to dance with her tonight at the wedding reception, if she'd have him, but that was a safe, public place and they'd be surrounded by people. Until then, he was not under any circumstances going to let himself touch any part of her or even allow his attention to linger on her figure too long.

Irritated by how turned on he got by simply telling himself he wasn't going to think about her body, he flipped on the radio, checked for cross-traffic, and pointed them south.

After the windy drive down from the Rockies, it was a

straight, flat shot to Highway 40, which would take them on into Quay County.

He blazed over the blacktop like a rocket, with Tara's minivan tailgating him. Every so often, the van's speed would plummet before eating up the ground between their vehicles again. He could easily imagine her having sneezing fits, being trapped in a closed area with so many flowers. What a ridiculous way to live, ignoring what her body was trying to tell her.

Jenna spent the first part of the drive on the phone with the cake lady, the event rental company, and who-knows-who-else, making arrangements and confirming arrival times. The hairstylist was going to meet them at the civic center, the DJ was all set, and between Rachel and Kellan's mom, Tommy was taken care of.

An hour and a half into the drive, she tossed her phone into her purse and shook out her arm.

"We good to go on this wedding?" he asked.

"Finally. I don't think there's anything more I can do from the road, which is good because my mind is toast."

"How about some music?" Anybody who loved dancing as much as she seemed to was probably a huge fan of music, though they hadn't listened to much on the way to Santa Fe because they'd been deep in conversation and he'd kept the volume on his radio extra low on this drive because she'd been on the phone.

He found a bouncy pop station on the radio playing songs from the 1980s and immediately felt the tension melt away from her. Before long, they were both singing along at the top of their lungs. For the most part, he kept it together, fighting to be gentlemanly, but at the first notes of Jenna singing along to "Hungry Like the Wolf," he couldn't stop his affectionate cringe. She had a terrible voice. And by terrible, he meant dying-donkey bad.

Lucky for him, she knew exactly how she sounded and didn't mind being ribbed about it. Didn't let it stop her either. She belted each and every song right along with him until the original German version of "99 Luftballons" came on.

They hummed and mumbled through the first verse before dissolving into laughter.

Matt poked his tongue in his cheek and tried to get a grip. He couldn't remember a time he'd had such good, clean fun with a woman off of a dance floor. In his center console, his Kenny Chesney ringtone started up, which meant one of his friends was calling. He hadn't put on his earpiece and so turned the radio down and hit the speaker button.

"Hello?"

"Matt, it's Kellan." Odd. Why was Kellan calling him and not Jenna?

"Hey, man. I've got you on speaker. Jenna and I are only an hour away, and my sister's following us in her van. Plenty of time to get the flowers everywhere they need to be. What's up?"

"My brother. He's here." His voice had grown thicker with every word.

Matt met Jenna's bright eyes. She gave a fist pump, grinning. She leaned toward the phone. "That's fantastic, Kellan. I'm so happy for you."

"That's why I'm calling," Kellan said. "Jake drove, but his car broke down in the Sandia Mountains and it'd take a taxi at least an hour to get to him. How close are you?"

The Sandias stretched along the east side of Albuquerque. Jake would be stuck on Highway 40, the same road Matt, Jenna, and Tara were on. "About the same as a taxi would be. But if a taxi ran late, Jake might not make it to the ceremony in time. Jenna and I will pick him up. I'll send Tara ahead to the civic center with the flowers."

Blinker on, he slowed the SUV onto the next off-ramp.

Kellan released a huge huff of air into the phone. "My brother drove from L.A. for my wedding." He said it like maybe giving voice to it again would make it seem more believable.

Matt had never met Jake and he didn't understand a lot about Kellan and Jake's history, but he kind of hated Jake on the basis of all the circumstantial evidence he'd been presented. No way should a man have that much gratitude in his voice for his brother doing what every brother *should* do in the first place. But to each his own. Kellan was happy and his wedding was going to go off without incident. All was well.

He came to a full stop at the bottom of the ramp. There wasn't any traffic at all out here in the middle of nowhere, so he wasn't worried about blocking the lane for any other cars. Tara followed suit, probably wondering what the heck was going on.

"You're going to have a fantastic wedding, man. The greatest. Amy's feeling better, we've got your flowers, and we're going to bring your brother. Nothing to worry about. You just relax and enjoy yourself, okay? We've got you covered."

"You're the best, Matt. Jenna, you too."

After a few more words of consolation and thanks, Matt scribbled down Jake's cell phone number and a description of the location, then ended the call.

He punched in Tara's number and filled her in on the latest development. "You got this, sis? You know where you're going?"

"Believe it or not, this isn't my first wedding as a florist."

Always the smart-ass. "You two get the groom's brother and I'll see you at the reception hall in a few hours."

"Thank you again. Now go forth and updo." He tossed the phone into the center console and turned left onto the road under the freeway, then back up the ramp in the opposite direction.

"Wow," said Jenna. She sat with a rigid spine, blinking hard. "Jake drove. I didn't see that coming."

"Neither did Kellan, by the sound of it. Can't wait to find out what Jake's story is as to why he missed his flight."

They blasted by the turn-off to the route leading to Santa Fe, headed west toward Albuquerque. Even though Matt's speedometer read seventy-five, it felt like they were crawling along in comparison to how fast the numbers were clicking higher on the clock. After what felt like ages, they started to climb in elevation. The plants evolved from scrubby bushes to squat, mangy desert trees, and the road grew twisty.

After they passed the mile marker Kellan had given them for reference, tense silence filled the car as they concentrated on every turnout and shoulder looking for Jake.

"There he is," Jenna said as they took a hairpin turn.

Sure enough, a sporty black coup sat in a turn-out. Matt pulled in behind it. A man who looked like a younger, tougher version of Kellan leaned against the side, two ripped, bulky arms crossed over his chest and a murderous expression carved on his face. His black hair was cropped short, about the same length as the facial hair that was desperately in need of a shave.

With the black ribbed tank top and nylon workout pants, he looked more MMA fighter than cop, but that look probably came in handy for a SWAT officer. "He looks pissed," Matt said out of the side of his mouth.

Jenna chuckled under her breath. "I've only met the guy once, but Jake's always pissed, as far as I can tell. In his defense, it's nearly a hundred degrees outside. I'd be ticked off too if my car died in the middle of nowhere during the summer heat."

Matt opened the door and hopped out. Jenna did the same.

Jake pushed away from the car and started their way. "Jenna, am I glad to see you. And you must be Matt?"

"Yeah. Nice to meet you, Jake." They shook, and Matt's initial impression of the guy softened. His angry eyes were red-rimmed and sat above dark bags, and his overgrown facial hair looked even scragglier up close. Whatever had led to Jake Reed being stranded on the side of the highway in the middle of New Mexico had to be one doozy of a story. "Grab your stuff and let's get you into some air-conditioning."

A dry, sardonic laugh burst from him. "Jesus, that's the best thing I've heard in days. Thanks for the lift. My piece-of-crap car isn't used to this kind of heat, I guess."

It didn't look like a piece-of-crap car to Matt. It looked like it might be worth more than Matt's annual salary, but if it couldn't last through a twelve-hour drive, maybe it really was a pile of junk under that slick exterior. God knew Matt had met many a lawyer and oil executive in his day who matched that description.

Jake grabbed a stuffed backpack from his passenger seat and collapsed on the backseat of the SUV. Jenna handed him a fresh water bottle.

He snapped off the lid and drank deeply. "Kellan said you two were off getting flowers. For the wedding?"

"I got jilted by the original florist, but Matt's sister Tara saved our butts," Jenna said.

Jake shook his head. "It's always something, isn't it?

When I got married, the cake lady sent the wrong cake. She sent us this one with strawberry filling and Heather, the girl I was marrying, hated strawberries. We didn't find out it was wrong inside until we cut it. That was probably a sign, like a bad omen, that Heather and I were doomed."

"How long were you married?" Jenna asked.

Jake broke out in a self-deprecating smile. "We put up with each other's shit for a whole three months before bailing. I'm not that guy, you know? Husband material."

Matt wouldn't touch that comment with a ten-foot pole. "How'd you end up making this drive? I bet it was a grind."

He rubbed his eyes and lounged back. "I missed my flight and this was the best I could come up with."

"No offense, but you don't look so good," Jenna said.

Jake sniggered. "Yeah, I bet. Haven't slept in a few days."

"Kellan said you had a work emergency."

"Worse than that, but it was all I could think to say." He took another noisy hit of water. "Nick, my partner, is in the hospital. Dropped right in the middle of an operation. A thirty-five-year-old man in prime shape and he had a fucking stroke right there next to me in a crapper of an alley while we were closing in on a suspect."

Matt looked in the backseat through the rearview mirror. Jake stared at the water bottle in his folded hands, looking frustrated and tired.

Jenna twisted and set a hand on his knee. "Is he going to be okay?"

"I don't know. He survived surgery, but he's still in a coma. All his family lives in Wyoming so I stayed with him until his folks got there."

Matt swallowed hard, feeling like a douche bag for being so critical of Jake before knowing the real score. Amazing how easy it was to get on a high horse and forget that other people had their own stuff going on. "I'm really sorry about all that. I have an older brother who's a cop, and we're always worried about him being safe around all the scumbags and criminals, but to get taken down by a stroke? That's the worst kind of irony."

"You should've seen the look on his mother's face when she first walked into the hospital room. I've never seen anything like it before, and I've seen some heartbreaking shit on the job. I almost cancelled coming to the wedding. Nick and I have been partners for five years, you know? How could I leave him and his family and take off for a party? Didn't seem right."

Into the stretching silence, Jenna asked what Matt had been afraid to. "What changed your mind?"

"Complicated."

In other words, mind your own business. Matt was all for that, but Jenna had other ideas.

"We can do complicated," she said. "We've got two hours to kill before we get to the civic center."

Matt gauged Jake's reaction through the mirror, prepared to step in the middle of the conversation if he got snappy or rude to Jenna. Jake squirmed in his seat and scratched the thick stubble on his neck, but the seething look he'd had when they'd picked him up didn't return. "All right. Fine. I didn't invite Kellan to my wedding. I wanted to give him a big screw-you for all the bad blood we'd worked up through the years, but, uh . . . I'd do it differently if I had to do it again. I think being at his wedding makes up for that, at least a little."

"It makes up a lot," Jenna said gently. "When Kellan called asking us to give you a lift, he was choked up that you'd made an all-night drive to be with him."

The plastic bottle crinkled as Jake drained it of water.

After a few silent beats, he released a heavy sigh, thick with burden. "I've never been a best man before."

The vulnerability implicit in his admission hit Matt in the gut. Whatever conclusions he'd jumped to about Jake, he'd been dead wrong. Here was a guy much like him, dealing with personal demons and doing the best he could to be a good man.

Matt cleared his throat and tried to sound casual and optimistic. "Being a best man is easy. I was a best man at my college roommate's wedding and one of my brothers'. The only tricky part is the speech. I tried to recite it from memory the first time and that didn't go so hot. There's no shame in using your notes."

Jake cursed. Matt's eyes flew to the mirror. Jake was gripping the door handle like he was considering ripping it open and making a break for it.

The truth hit Jenna at the same time it did Matt. "You didn't write a speech, did you?" she asked.

Another curse. "I thought something would come to me, but then with what happened to Nick, I . . ." He shook his head, his eyes back on his clasped hands. "What am I supposed to say about Kellan? It's not like the two of us have spent much time together in the past twenty years." He closed his fingers into a fist around the empty water bottle, crushing it.

To Matt's way of thinking, there was only one thing to be done in a crisis like this. "Jenna, could you reach under your seat? There should be a pad of paper there."

He grabbed one of the pens he kept stashed in his center console. Over the years, his car had morphed into a rolling office since most of his business was conducted from the road. He preferred to meet homeowners dealing with oil issues at their houses, where they were most comfortable and he could look at the land in question.

He clicked the pen, then tossed it to the backseat along with one of the candy bars left over from the all-nighter at Carpe Diem. "Okay, Jake. Brace yourself. It's time to get mushy."

Chapter Six

Matt, Jenna, and Jake hightailed it from the parking lot into the lobby of the Tucumcari Civic Center with thirty minutes until showtime with the photographer.

Jenna had phoned Rachel and Kellan with an E.T.A. fifteen minutes earlier and confirmed that Jenna's bridesmaid dress and boots were waiting for her in the bridal suite down the right-hand hallway from the ballroom, along with the hairdresser. Vaughn and Kellan were waiting with Matt and Jake's tuxedos in the groom's suite down the hall on the opposite side of the ballroom.

Tara emerged into the lobby from the ballroom's double doors. Her hair was in disarray behind the red bandanna she'd fashioned into a headband and her cheeks were flushed from exertion. Her tank top was covered in pollen and petals, and her red, swollen nose and eyes dripped with moisture.

"Well?" Jenna asked. "How'd you do?"

Tara flashed a thumbs-up and a watery smile. "It's ready. We did it."

She was on her way to hugging Jenna when she noticed Jake and pulled back. "Oh."

Jake squared his shoulders and gave her a once-over. "Oh, yourself."

Matt had no idea what *oh* meant, and neither Jake's nor Tara's expression was giving much away.

"Who's this, Jenna?" Jake asked.

Jenna fumbled through an introduction. "Um, Tara, this is Jake. Jake, this is Matt's sister, Tara."

Jake crossed his arms over his chest, his gaze raking over her tattoos. "So you're the new flower lady that saved the day?"

Tara wiped her drippy nose with the back of her hand. "That's me."

"Your clothes are a mess and your face is leaking. What, are you allergic to flowers or something?"

Tara planted her hands on her hips and looked about as confident as a woman could with puffy sinuses and a shirt covered in flower debris. "Maybe I am. And you must be the best man who almost missed his brother's wedding."

"That's me." Jake's eyes gleamed and his face morphed into either a scowl or a smile. With Jake, it was impossible to tell.

Matt wasn't sure what was going on, but he was getting some weird vibes from the two of them so he stepped between them. "Tara, you said you're done with the flowers. Are you hitting the road soon?"

She tore her gaze from the staring contest with Jake. "No. Ira called. He's taking the kids to his house for the rest of the weekend so they can swim in his complex's pool. Kellan invited me to stay. Mom and Dad are stopping by my place to pick me up a dress for tonight and one of the bridesmaids gave me the key to her hotel room so I can shower and primp."

Their parents were coming to the wedding because they'd sold a handful of horses to Kellan over the years and, from what Matt could tell, he'd pretty much invited everyone he'd ever crossed paths with to his special day.

Tara swung her attention back to Jake, who had yet to take his eyes off her. "You need to shave. You can't be in a wedding looking like that. It'll offset all my beautiful flower arrangements."

Jake narrowed his eyes.

Behind them, a door clattered. Matt twisted to see Kellan approaching, dressed to the nines in a tux and fancy new black Stetson. "Jake."

For the first time, Jake's focus left Tara. He strode over the carpet and met his brother halfway, his hand outstretched in greeting. "Sorry I'm late, man."

Kellan got that look in his eyes and arms like he was about to grab Jake in a hug, but he jammed his left hand in his pocket and slapped his right one into Jake's in a vigorous handshake. "I'm just glad you made it. Is everything okay at work?"

"Yeah." Shrugging, Jake swatted the air. "With the LAPD, it's always something. Nothing you want to hear about on your wedding day."

Good on you, Jake.

"You got my monkey suit ready?" he asked Kellan.

"Absolutely. The groom's suite has a shower so you can get cleaned up. That is one ugly beard you've got going."

Jake scraped his fingers from his cheek to his neck, and this time Matt could tell he sported a grin and not a scowl. "It wasn't a beard when I left L.A. I feel like a fuckin' werewolf sometimes."

Kellan rocked onto the heels of his shiny, black boots, affection radiating from his eyes. "I know what you mean."

Tara patted Matt's arm, wiggled some fingers at Jenna, and whispered, "I'm going to go get ready. See you soon."

Jake's chin flicked once, briefly, over his shoulder in

Tara's direction as she walked away. "I'd better get busy if the pictures start in a half hour. Is the suite this way?" He motioned to the hall Kellan had emerged from.

"Yeah. Go ahead. I'm right behind you."

Jake afforded Matt and Jenna a one-finger wave. "Thanks for the lift and everything else." Without waiting for a response, he turned his back to them and walked away.

"Matt, Jenna." Kellan's jaw was tight as he bridged the rest of the distance between them. He snagged both their shoulders for a group hug. "I can't thank you enough. I don't know what to say."

Matt slapped his back. "It's nothing. Happy to help."

Jenna kissed his cheek. "You make my sister happier than she's ever been in her life, and that's thanks enough for me."

"Still, I owe you."

"No, you don't," Jenna and Matt answered at the same time.

Kellan pulled away from the hug, smiling. "The photographer's starting with the groomsmen and me and Amy, so you have enough time to get ready, Jenna. Don't worry about Tommy. My mom and Mr. Dixon are getting him dressed and ready at the hotel. I'm going to make sure Jake's finding everything he needs. You coming, Matt?"

"In a sec."

The moment Kellan disappeared and they were alone, Jenna and Matt's eyes found each other.

"We did it," he said, and before he could think better of it, he raised his hand for a high-five. 'Cause that was the smooth thing to do with a hot woman—high-five her like she was one of the guys. Doofus.

Before he could lower his hand, she set her palm on his and curled her fingers down. "You're the one who made it happen. You saved the day."

She looked up at him from beneath her lashes, the same soft expression she'd had the night before when she'd wanted a kiss. He twisted away from her grip. "Like I said, I'm happy to help."

Unfazed, one corner of her lip kicked up. "Want to know something else?"

He was almost afraid to ask. "What?"

Her coy grin blossomed into a full-blown smile. "Your sister has a thing for Kellan's brother."

"No way. They were totally rude to each other. Plus he's scary-looking." And he had a completely opposite worldview from Tara, who thought all women should be surrounded by flowers and beauty.

"I think she likes the rough ones."

Matt pressed his hands to his head with a groan, fighting to deflect the unwanted knowledge from sinking in. "I don't want to think about that. She's my sister. Bleh. More brain bleaching needed."

"You'll survive." Chuckling, Jenna wrapped her arm around him, then ran the pad of her thumb over his lower lip.

He swallowed hard and thought about the pictures in his wallet. He thought about how he'd coached Brandon's little league team that one year. He, Brandon, and Lauren had been playing house for two years and his transition into coaching had felt so good and right. A dream come true. The next season, after he and Lauren broke it off, he showed up to watch a game and Lauren asked him to leave. Too confusing for Brandon, she'd said.

That's when he knew, once and for all, he was done with single moms. Because Lauren was absolutely right. It wasn't fair for the kids to have him hanging around after he and their mom split. But standing here with Jenna, her soft, small hand warming his face, her flirty eyes bidding him nearer, it was so easy to forget everything he stood to lose.

His dad's favorite saying came to him. No one ever said doing the right thing was easy. He turned the words over in his mind. What he was doing, leading Jenna on and flirting with her as he'd been, was wrong. It had to stop here and now. Time for him to man up and do the right thing.

Gathering her in his arms, he pressed his lips to her forehead. "You are . . . incredible."

She stiffened, then pushed back and searched his face with mournful eyes. "But that's not enough, is it?"

"You've got it backward. It's that I'm not enough." For one feverish moment, he thought about telling her why. Stupid idea because the last woman he'd told had sworn it didn't matter to her right up until she broke up with him because she didn't think their futures meshed—a.k.a., she wanted children and he couldn't give them to her. End of story.

It was the one fact about his life that would never change. And there was no use praying about it or wasting time and money seeing any more doctors about it, because there was no cure. Matt's infertility was in his goddamn DNA.

"You're more than enough." Closing her eyes again, she grazed his jaw with her closed lips. "You're all I want."

He'd heard that before too. "I bet that's not true. I bet you want more kids."

"Of course. But we don't need to get ahead of ourselves. That doesn't have anything to do with you kissing me right now."

Impossible not to wince. And she must've seen it because she dropped her arms and put some space between them. He braced his hands on his hips, grinding his teeth, fighting to get a grip. "I can't be with you and I'm sorry that

I've led you to believe otherwise. That was unconscionable of me."

Instead of looking offended, though, her expression remained soft, imploring. "Is it because we practice different religions? Because that doesn't matter to me."

In the months since he'd met Jenna, he'd contemplated that difference, even used it as an excuse on occasion when he was trying to convince himself that they were wrong for each other, but an excuse was all it was. Not an insurmountable problem or a deal breaker. Nothing that love couldn't have conquered had he not been a broken man. "No. That's not it. I wish that was all it was. It's just me, and I . . . I can't. I'm sorry."

She nodded as though digesting his rejection. The world stilled as they studied each other in silence. He hoped he didn't transmit any of the overwhelming frustration he felt. He hoped he looked strong and committed to his choice.

Finally, she drew herself up tall. "I won't pressure you anymore. But please understand I care about you. A lot. And I think you and I would be great together. I want you to know that whatever it is—whatever you're not telling me— if someday you decide to trust me with it, I won't let you down and I won't hurt you. You can take that to the bank."

Her words slayed him. All he could do was push his tongue against the roof of his mouth and stay standing. *No one ever said doing the right thing was easy.*

She cupped his cheek and it was a wonder that he was holding it together enough not to nuzzle deeper into her touch.

"Jenna—"

Her thumb slipped over his lips. "Shhh. You think about what I said, okay?" She brushed a kiss across his jaw. "I'll see you at the wedding. You're going to save a dance for me, right?"

"Of course."

Nodding wistfully, she turned and walked away.

In a daze, Matt headed toward the groom's suite, not releasing the breath he'd been holding until he heard the door to the bridal suite open and close. He stopped moving and wiped the back of his hand over his cheek and lips, where his skin still tingled from her touch.

He'd wanted Jenna Sorentino from the minute he'd laid eyes on her. From her toes to the wavy tips of her dark blond hair, and every little bit of her in between. Eight months later, the feeling had exploded into a fierce, unrelenting need.

He'd thought he was being strong, denying himself of Jenna. Self-preserving and strong, like a man should be. But if that was the case, then why was he still standing there shaky and breathless. Why did he feel so damn weak?

There was no denying it. Amy made a stunning bride.

Jenna froze in the door of the bridal suite and clamped a hand over her mouth as tears threatened. She'd never seen her sister look so beautiful.

Amy walked her way, arms outstretched. Rather than hug her, Jenna joined hands with her and held her arms open so she could thoroughly admire the way she looked. The sweep of her hair lent a perfect balance to her figure, lengthening her neck and highlighting her slender, strong arms and shoulders. As it had been when she'd first tried it on, her wedding dress was a head-turning knockout. An off-the-shoulder scoop neck in cream and lace, it hugged in all the right places, accentuating the curviness of her figure.

Kellan would be scraping his jaw off the ground after he saw her. Too bad Jenna would still be getting ready when he and Amy glimpsed each other in their fineries for the first time. Hopefully the photographer would capture the look on his face because it was going to be priceless.

She and Jenna had shopped for the dress together in a marathon day trip to Albuquerque with Kellan's credit card, along with his blessing to buy whatever made Amy happy. It wasn't an exaggeration to say Rachel had been relieved to stay at the farm and watch Tommy. Shopping—especially dress shopping—was as torturous a notion to her as getting a pedicure.

Though Amy looked stunning, her skin was paler than usual, and Jenna was fairly certain it wasn't because of the makeup. Maybe she wasn't as over her stomach ailment as she'd led Kellan to believe. In support of her theory, the glass of champagne someone had poured for her sat untouched on the glass coffee table. Only Lisa, Sloane, and Rachel were taking advantage of the bottle Jenna had paid the staff to stock.

Rachel, beaming ear to ear, nudged Jenna's arm and gestured to Amy with her champagne flute. "She cleans up well, doesn't she?"

"Does she ever," Jenna said. "And so do you."

Rachel's impossibly straight brown hair had been twisted into a flower-dotted updo much like Amy's. Marti, Catcher Creek's premier hairstylist, had skillfully arranged it. However, on Rachel the style looked rather silly. As frivolous as the ruffle lining the bottom of the strapless pink country dress Jenna and Lisa Binderman had chosen for the bridesmaids. And yet her freckled, tanned skin glowed healthy and vibrant against the delicate fabric. She'd even accepted the application of mascara and eye shadow.

"Rachel looks like a whole new woman," Amy added. "I almost didn't recognize her."

Rachel huffed. "Why are you saying that like it's a good

thing? I'm pretty damn happy with the old me. Don't make me get offended or this ridiculous hairdo is coming down."

Jenna swiped Amy's champagne flute from the table, pushed it into Amy's hand, and stepped between her and Rachel. "Hey, you two. It's Amy's special day—no bickering allowed."

"Fine, but can you blame me for getting cranky at all the people telling me I look so much better than usual? It's insulting." Rachel hitched the dress higher over her bust and squirmed in discomfort, sloshing her champagne over the lip of the glass. "I'm still not convinced my boobs aren't going to pop out of this thing at any minute."

Jenna grabbed a tissue and dabbed at the champagne collecting on the flute's base. "Your boobs are going to be fine. Even if they do pop out, it'll only lend a little extra excitement to the night. And need I remind you that the only person whose opinion of your looks matters is yours?"

"And Vaughn's." Rachel's shoulders rose and fell with her deep sigh. "What if he likes me better like this, dressed up like some damn princess instead of . . ." She shook her head, then guzzled the remainder of her drink. "Instead of the regular me. I don't think I could bear it."

Jenna snagged the bottle and refilled her flute. "Oh, sweetie. He fell in love with a tough-nut, no-nonsense cowgirl. Do you know what I would give to have a man look at me the way I catch Vaughn stealing lovesick puppy glances at you? Do you think he'd rather have himself a high-maintenance princess, even if you do look good as one?"

Rachel grunted, unconvinced. "At least we get to wear boots."

Keeping with the rustic country chic theme, Jenna and Amy had decided to accessorize the bridal party's formal wear with boots—chocolate brown with elaborate pink stitch work for the ladies and shiny black for the men. Being that the majority of the bridal party lived their daily lives in boots, everyone was more than happy to oblige.

Only Jake, they'd discovered, had never had the pleasure of stuffing his feet into a pair of leather western boots. In fact, Jenna wasn't altogether sure Kellan had told his brother there'd be a pair of boots waiting for him along with his tux. Ought to be an interesting conversation in the groom's suite right about now.

Amy draped an arm across Rachel's shoulders and squeezed. "If Vaughn tells you he loves your dress, it's probably only because of how much skin it shows and how fast he figures he'll be able to get it off you tonight when you get home."

A mischievous smile threatened to spread over Rachel's lips. "There is that."

Crisis averted. Jenna gestured to Amy's still-full glass. "You're not drinking your champagne. Still queasy from the tequila? I'm so sorry I made you drink that last night. I thought it would help, but it only made things worse."

Amy waved off her apology. "It wasn't the tequila. Well, it was in a round-about way, I suppose." She looked around at the other women in the room—Marti the hairstylist, Lisa Binderman, Sloane Delgado, and Tina, Kellan's mom—as though she had more to say about the tequila incident, but not with so many people around. "Go get your shower over with so Marti can do your hair."

Time for some unspoken sisterly communication. Jenna leveled a look square at Amy, eyes narrowed. *What aren't you telling me?*

Amy's eyes grew wide and flashed to the room full of people, as if to say, *Now's not the time or place.*

"Should I be worried?" Jenna whispered.

A hint of a smile flashed over her features as she gave her head a brief shake. "It's all good."

Maybe for Amy, but nothing was crueler to Jenna than someone letting on they had a secret to share but not just yet. And now she was contending with both Matt's and Amy's unspoken secrets. Torture, plain and simple. Thank goodness death by impatience wasn't possible or Jenna would've succumbed years ago.

Amy handed her glass of champagne over. "Here. Take this with you into the bathroom and get a move on. Your shower travel kit's in there already."

The shower felt heavenly. Jenna hadn't realized how grungy she felt until the hot water hit her skin. Stifling a moan of pleasure, she allowed herself to stand under the stream for a solid minute she probably couldn't afford before beginning the arduous process of soaping, scrubbing, and shaving.

With Matt's and Amy's secrets nagging at her, as well as all the last-minute wedding prep she'd be doing in the next two hours until the ceremony, her mind whizzed with disparate thoughts. If only she had a waterproof pad of paper and pen to jot it all down so it wouldn't crowd her mind.

She'd finished shaving her legs and was in the middle of a final rinse when curiosity about whether Rachel had brought Tommy's tux led her train of thought in an entirely horrible direction that had slipped her mind in all the hubbub of the flower and best-man emergencies.

The Parrish family would be at the wedding. Every single one of them, save for Carson. And the secret she'd vowed to take to her grave was in imminent danger of exploding into public knowledge tonight—because Tommy was the spitting image of his father.

She sagged against the white tile wall, the bite of cold making her wince as much as the epiphany.

She'd known Carson her entire life, and when she looked at Tommy, she saw Carson's essence through and through. For the longest time, she'd rationalized that maybe the image of Carson in her mind was wrong. Memories were faulty, the victims of time, distance, and experience. Besides that, a lot of people looked radically different as children than they did as adults and it was quite possible that Tommy and Carson looked nothing alike.

But the older Tommy got, the more obvious the resemblance. In March, Carson's mother, Patricia, had cornered Jenna and Tommy at the church donut table after the service, remarking about how handsome a young man Tommy was and how familiar he looked, though she couldn't place how.

That night, Jenna had stolen away in a panic to the storage cellar beneath the farm's big house, rifling through Christmas decorations and old quilts until she'd found a bug and rodent-eaten cardboard box filled to the brim with yearbooks. She'd emptied the box until she found Catcher Creek Elementary School's yearbook from her kindergarten year, then flipped to her class page to take a good look at Carson at Tommy's age, hoping to quell her fear.

The photographs of the students in their kindergarten class were faded, but Carson's picture was clear enough to make her stomach turn. Tommy looked exactly like his father at age five, from the goofy grin, sandy blond hair, and shape of his head to the layout of his features and his lanky body.

Sitting on the floor of the dusty, stuffy storage cellar, Jenna had allowed herself a good, long pity party, complete with tears, about her past and the unfairness of life. She'd cried until the hollowness of solitude had wrapped around her like creeping ivy. Then she'd continued to sit there, watching particles of dust whip in the air, until self-preservation won out over despair. She and Tommy would leave Catcher Creek, as had been her plan all along, and until that day arrived, they would keep far away from the Parrishes.

Yet, though she was painstakingly careful not to take Tommy to downtown Catcher Creek except when she couldn't avoid it and though she'd never returned to First Methodist Church since that fateful Sunday in March, Jenna knew with fatalistic certainty that it was only a matter of time before Lou and Patricia Parrish or Carson's sisters realized who Tommy resembled.

She hadn't anticipated Amy's wedding or what that would mean for her secret. In ninety minutes, give or take, Tommy would be paraded in front of the Parrish family as a ring bearer. They'd have the entire ceremony to watch him and put together the pieces of the puzzle—and there was nothing Jenna could do to stop it.

She closed her eyes in prayer that she would get through the night with Tommy's true parentage protected. The alternative was too overwhelming to bear. If the truth came out, she and Tommy would have to pick up and leave town immediately, in a middle-of-the-night, desperate-woman-on-the-run type of move. Away from her support system, she had no idea how she'd take care of Tommy and still get through her last month of college.

Stumbling out of the shower, she wrapped a towel around her middle and drained the champagne. Then she did the only thing she could think of. She found her phone in her purse and called her best friend, Carrie. "Hey."

"Hi. Didn't expect to hear from you this weekend. Shouldn't you be getting ready for your sister's wedding?"

Jenna sat on the closed toilet lid. "I am, but I needed a break."

"Uh-oh, what happened?"

Nothing wrong with a little white lie when the truth was too dangerous to share. "Just bummed I don't have a date for this thing."

"What about the hot lawyer?"

She and Carrie had had many talks about Matt, from PMS-fueled bitch-fests to diabolical strategy sessions. "He's not ready for a relationship right now. He tried to let me down easy today."

Carrie sighed into the phone. "What is it with this guy?"

Jenna didn't have the slightest idea, but even if she did, she would never divulge Matt's private life to her friends. "No clue."

"I'm sorry, chica, but I think it's time for you to give up on this particular fish and go back out in the sea."

Jenna fiddled with the tag on the towel. "I'm not sure about the merits of comparing men to fish. I think they're more like—"

"Peacocks? Donkeys? Hyenas?"

Jenna laughed despite herself. "I was thinking more like elephants."

Carrie gasped. "Hold on a sec. That sounds to me like you've seen this Matt guy naked. And he's . . . he's hung like an elephant! This changes everything. Honey, you can't let this one slip away."

"What? Sorry to disappoint you, but no. I haven't seen him naked and I have no idea how he's hanging." Not actually true because she'd felt his arousal while they'd waltzed and caught a glimpse when she'd woken on Tara's couch, so she knew firsthand that he was hanging just fine, thank you very much.

"Damn. You know that's one of my top twenty things I want to do before I get married, right?"

"Sleep with a well-endowed man? Yeah, I'm aware of

that." As far as goals went, Carrie's might be shallow, but it had merit.

"Just once," Carrie pined. "One magic night of hedonism is all I'm asking. I mean, how are we supposed to know if the adage 'size doesn't matter' is true or merely a cruel urban legend perpetuated by teeny-weenie men?"

That was a conundrum. Jenna tried, but she couldn't hold back a giggle, as usual when their conversation plunged into the gutter. "I'm already feeling better. Thank you."

"I'm here for you anytime. You know that. Okay, I'm off my magic wang soapbox—for now. Tell me, why are men like elephants?"

Jenna indulged in one more laugh. Nothing like a magic wang soapbox to put her problems in perspective. "Okay, so Tommy and I were watching this show on elephants a few years ago. Did you know male elephants don't live with the pack of females or their kids? They can't even live together in a herd of males because all their macho maleness makes them too aggressive. It's the female elephants that run the show, feed the young, and protect the herd. And men . . . well, they only come around when they want to get laid."

"That's a really jaded view of dating and relationships for someone who's about to watch her sister get hitched."

"I know."

She wasn't entirely convinced of the accuracy of her analogy, and if pressed, she could come up with lots of examples of men who were the doting, stick-around types, her soon-to-be brothers-in-law included. But it made her feel stronger to think of herself like one of those powerful elephant matriarchs, wise and unflappable, protecting her own and dismissing the male gender as nothing but baby-making love machines. After all, she'd done more than all right for herself and Tommy without Carson's support, or any man's, for that matter.

"Forget about the hot lawyer," Carrie said. "He can't be Kellan's only single friend at the wedding."

She had a hunch where Carrie was going with the conversation and grinned, the last of her anxiety evaporating. "He's not."

Carrie always did think outside the box. Besides her wicked sense of humor, it was one of the things that made her such a great study partner and friend. She wished she could've invited Carrie to the wedding, but there was no way she could've gotten away with it without explaining where she knew Carrie from.

"So, do your thing. Shake your moneymaker and show Mr. No-Commitment what he's missing. Didn't you tell me Tommy was leaving the reception early with a babysitter?"

"Yeah . . ."

Carrie hummed, intrigued. "I think it's time for mama to have some fun."

Jenna stood and drew a heart on the fogged-up mirror. She was definitely overdue for some fun. It'd been six months since her get-your-rocks-off fling with a guy from her computer-engineering lab. That had been a nice distraction, with a lot of screwing and not much talking, but the whole time, that hollow, lonely feeling had dogged her. When the relationship had run its course, she'd been right back to wishing for something more substantial.

Something with Matt.

"I'll see what I can manage and report back tomorrow."

"See that you do," Carrie said in an overly formal voice. "If I can't live vicariously through my best friend, then what good are you?"

Jenna swallowed a comeback about how, since Carrie was single and kid-free, Jenna should be the one living vicariously through her. For all her big talk about big men, Carrie was just like every other woman Jenna knew, herself included—an old-fashioned girl at heart, waiting for Mr. Right to come along and love her forever.

After connecting with Carrie, Jenna felt more grounded and able to face Matt, the wedding craziness, and the Parrishes. Wrapped in a robe she'd found hanging on the bathroom door, she stepped from the bathroom into the main room of the bridal suite. Rachel and Amy were alone and sitting close together on the sofa.

"Where did everyone go? I thought Marti was going to style my updo."

"She is," Amy answered, "but I sent her to make sure Kellan's hair was behaving itself. Lord knows he can't get it to lie flat. Really, though, I wanted to get you two alone to tell you the good news."

Good news? Excellent. Good news was the best kind of secret. And, bonus, Amy hadn't kept them waiting long at all to spill the beans. Jenna sank onto the sofa on the opposite side of Amy from Rachel, her heart rate picking up speed in anticipation.

Amy sat up straighter, curling her hands over her knees. "As you know, the tequila shot I drank last night didn't sit well with my stomach."

Rachel snorted. "That's putting it mildly. The way you sounded in that bathroom, I thought an alien was trying to break free of your body."

The look Amy gave Rachel could've leveled a building. "Thanks for the poetic reminder, Rach. Really."

Rachel didn't take the hint to zip her trap. "Are you telling us you have good news about puking up tequila?"

Amy's wedding dress rustled as she jagged sideways on the sofa with a little hop to face Rachel. "I swear, you are the most literal person I have ever known."

And they were off. Jenna shot to her feet and wedged her posterior between her sisters. "Time out. You two can argue while I'm getting my hair done. Spill it, Ames—what's your big secret?"

It took rolling her tongue over her teeth and a deep sigh for Amy to collect herself. "Back to my story. After that one time getting sick at the saloon, I felt better until the morning when I couldn't hold down breakfast."

That kind of intermittent nausea could only be one of two things, Jenna figured. And the anxiety attack option didn't involve sitting your sister down for good news. She clapped a hand over her mouth as reality dawned on her, trying desperately to let Amy finish her story.

"Kellan insisted on dragging me to urgent care, hoping that whatever was wrong, we could get some medicine. Not only so I could function at the wedding, but because we're leaving on our honeymoon tomorrow. Imagine how stupid we felt when the nurse told us—"

"You're pregnant!" Jenna hadn't meant to beat her to the finish line, but she couldn't contain her joy any longer.

The smile stretching Amy's lips told Jenna she didn't mind Jenna stealing her glory. "I'm pregnant. And not just pregnant—I'm nine weeks along."

Rachel rocked back, her eyebrows high into her forehead. "Well, I'll be. You haven't had your period in two months and it never occurred to you that you might be knocked up?"

Jenna put her mom skills into practice with a searing knock-it-off look that'd been known to put grown men in their places. Luckily Amy was now floating on cloud nine, complete with a dreamy, faraway expression, and didn't register the bite in Rachel's admittedly logical question. "I thought it was wedding stress. You know how I get." She hummed and drew her shoulders up, hands around her middle. "Kellan and I are so happy. I can't believe I have to wait seven more months to meet our baby."

Rachel slipped her arm behind Jenna and rubbed Amy's shoulder. "Congratulations. I can't wait to meet him either. Or her. That's going to be one spoiled baby, I'll tell you that right now."

Amy hugged her belly tighter. "No doubt about it."

Jenna pulled her into a tight hug. "Rachel's right. Congratulations, sweetie. Even if means you won't be toasting your wedding with champagne, this is still the best news ever."

"You don't think the alcohol I've had will hurt the baby, do you?"

Jenna shook her head. "No way. You threw up all the tequila before it could hit your system."

Amy pulled back, a shadow of worry on her face. "I've had more than that. A glass of wine here and there to relax. Kellan likes the way I get silly from drinking."

Rachel groaned. "T.M.I., for God's sake."

Amy angled around Jenna and poked Rachel's shoulder. "Stop acting like a prude. You know what? I bet you have the dirtiest mind and busiest sex life among us. In fact, I bet you're into all kinds of kinky stuff. The loud-mouthed, judgmental ones always are."

Rachel snorted in protest, even though her cheeks pinked. "You're getting me mixed up with politicians."

Time to swing the conversation back to neutral territory. She squeezed Amy's hands. "Sweetie, before I found out I was pregnant with Tommy, you know I was no angel, but he came out fine. Of all the things you could be thinking about right now, that one's not worth your energy. The OB-GYN's going to tell you the same thing. Here's what I want to know—when are you going to start telling people?"

"Kellan should be telling his mom and brother right

about now, and then . . ." If possible, her smile grew even wider. "We're going to make an announcement at the reception."

Full-steam ahead must be Kellan and Amy's relationship theme because nothing they did was gradual or cautious in the least. "Oh, my. That will certainly be the icing on the cake of what was already bound to be the most perfect night ever. The good people of Catcher Creek will be wagging their tongues about your wedding for years to come."

A knock sounded at the door; then Marti poked her head of bottle-blond hair in. "Everybody decent?"

"That's negotiable," Amy answered. She poked Rachel's shoulder again and whispered, "Kinky beast."

Rachel grabbed Amy's finger and twisted it until she squealed.

"You wouldn't hurt a pregnant lady, would you?"

"You better watch it, little sister, or I'll advise Kellan to smash that wedding cake right on your nose."

"He wouldn't dare!"

Hopeless was what her sisters were. Jenna stood and scooted out of the line of fire. "Glad you're back, Marti. Time for me to get ready for my close-up." She took a seat on the chair Marti patted. "Amy, Rachel, you'd better get moving for the pictures before you ruin each other's hair and makeup."

Chapter Seven

The wedding-party photographs went off without a hitch, even though it took all of Jenna's best kid-wrangling skills to keep Tommy from bouncing off the walls or getting his suit dirty and wrinkled. At the rate he was going, they'd be lucky if his boutonniere survived until the end of the wedding ceremony, much less the reception.

When the photographer announced, *finally*, that they were done and could release the smiles they'd plastered to their faces and regroup before the ceremony, Amy and Rachel headed back to the bridal suite, while Kellan and his groomsmen chatted up the arriving guests. Jenna tucked into a corner of the lobby, keeping one eye on Tommy as she took the opportunity to skim her checklist before showtime.

"Yo, little man," Kellan said. "You're looking so fine in that suit that you're making the rest of us guys look bad." He squatted to get eye level with Tommy. "It's not fair. Nobody can compete with cuteness this extreme. But wait, you've got something on your jacket. Let me get that." He stuck his finger in Tommy's armpit.

Giggling, Tommy buckled over as Kellan doubled his efforts with a finger to Tommy's other pit. The next time Jenna glanced up from her list, Kellan had Tommy upside down while Tommy retaliated by tickling Kellan in the back of his knee. Petals from his boutonniere sprinkled to the ground. Oh well.

"Your boy's gotten so big since the last time I saw him. And so handsome."

"Thank you." She marked her place with her finger before looking up to see who it was. When she did, her insides clenched. Mrs. Parrish.

"He reminds me of my boys when they were young. Full of spit and vinegar."

Jenna swayed. The room exploded into a vacuum of space, the sounds far away and floating—the cascade of water from the fountain in the atrium, conversations, the click of heels—and she had no anchor.

"Mommy, I broke my flower," Tommy said, running her way with a handful of petals.

"It's okay, buddy. Flowers aren't meant to last forever." Heart pounding, she took the flower remnants and gripped his shoulders. He squirmed beneath her touch and stepped behind her as though sensing the shift in the atmosphere.

Mrs. Parrish got down low at Tommy's level and beamed at him with the wide-eyed, exaggerated enthusiasm of someone who wasn't used to being around kids. "Hello, young man. We need to have your mommy bring you to my store. I keep candy there."

He buried his face into Jenna's dress. "I'm not allowed to take candy from strangers."

"What a smart answer!" She stood and aimed her too-bright smile at Jenna. "You know, when you were a girl, your daddy brought you into the shop all the time. You loved the cinnamon candies. Neither of your sisters had a tolerance for the heat of them, but you used to strut around, a sassy little thing, flaunting your special treat. How about you bring Tommy around to the shop sometime soon? I could use a fix

of the little ones, since none of my own children have seen
fit to provide me with any grandbabies."

"Sure. Of course," Jenna said, choking on the lump in
her throat.

"Such a sweet lad." Mrs. Parrish reached out to Tommy.
He dodged her hand and bolted toward Rachel, who was
walking their way.

Rachel took his hand, then leveled a pointed look at
Jenna and Mrs. Parrish. "Sorry to interrupt, but Jenna and
Tommy are needed in the bridal suite because the cere-
mony's about to get started."

Inching toward the hall, Jenna offered Mrs. Parrish a
conciliatory smile. "Thanks for coming. I'd better not keep
the bride waiting." Heart pounding, she hastened after
Rachel and Tommy through the hall, not breathing until
Tommy disappeared through the bridal suite door.

Though she'd never claim to feel this way as a rule, today
Jenna was grateful that five-year-old boys had the attention
spans of puppies hopped up on caffeine. Because nobody
expected Tommy to remain standing with the wedding party
for the duration of the ceremony. Amy wanted him to try to
last, but Jenna and Mr. Dixon—Amy's sous chef and the
honorary grandpa of everyone at Sorentino Farm—had
created a carefully constructed backup plan involving Life
Savers hard candies for when his wiggles got distracting.

As they'd practiced at the rehearsal, he walked with
measured steps down the aisle while holding the ring pillow,
then stood between Jake and Vaughn. During his walk,
Jenna kept one eye on him and the other on the Parrishes,
who beamed at him and whispered to each other, hopefully
about how precious and cute he looked—not how familiar.

She didn't detect any gleam of awareness in any of their eyes, but that didn't mean her secret was safe.

Jenna's anxiety must've been palpable because Rachel elbowed her and told her to relax because Tommy was doing great. Tommy took his place between Jake and Vaughn and smiled proudly at Jenna. She shoved aside her fears and nerves and gave him a thumbs-up as the opening strains of "Here Comes the Bride" filled the air.

Amy appeared from around the corner, so radiant and glowing that she seemed to float on Mr. Dixon's arm. She smiled at the rows of standing people, then her gaze found Kellan's and she burst into silent, effusive tears.

Amy hadn't even managed to make it all the way down the aisle at Mr. Dixon's arm before Tommy's distracted bouncing of the ring pillow against his knee devolved into whacking himself in the head with it. Thank goodness Jake had the foresight to rescue the rings and transfer them to his pocket.

Mr. Dixon handed Amy off to Kellan's arm with a kiss on her cheek, then, after exchanging a smile with Jenna, took Tommy's hand and led him to a seat.

Thanks to Tommy's inability to stand still, the Parrishes only had a couple minutes to study him, but Jenna remained off balance and nauseous until Amy and Kellan were standing in front of the minister and the people in the audience had settled in to give their full attention to the bride and groom.

She recited the alphabet backward to R and gradually felt her spirit snap back into alignment with her body. Only then did she process how beautiful a ceremony she'd helped orchestrate.

The atrium was a tropical oasis, with floor-to-ceiling windows behind a massive waterfall fountain dropping into a dark pool lined with fauna. Tara had floated pink flowers and candles in the pool and lined the edges with flower petals. One of the arrangements Jenna, Matt, and Tara had created cascaded from the arch behind the minister in a burst of glorious excess that coordinated exquisitely with the bouquets, boutonnieres, and flower-adorned updos of the wedding party.

Amy and Kellan couldn't take their eyes off each other. Amy's hormones were probably going haywire because she wept through the whole ceremony. Jenna wouldn't have put it past Kellan to have planned for Amy's high emotions because he conveniently produced a handkerchief from his pocket to intermittently dab at her tears and runny nose as the ceremony wore on. It was a romantic, intimate gesture that spoke volumes about Amy and Kellan's rock-solid relationship and chased Jenna's nerves away.

Her focus drifted over the groomsmen. Jake stood next to Kellan, looking every bit of the odd man out. Jenna didn't think she'd ever seen a man more uncomfortable in a Stetson, suit, and dress boots. He squirmed a lot and scratched the beard he'd chosen to keep. Though he'd trimmed it neater, it still carpeted his neck and disappeared behind the tie he'd probably be ripping off the first chance he got.

As opposed to Jake, Matt wore his suit like he was born for it. The cut highlighted his tapered physique and dark eyes and hair. She'd never before seen him in a cowboy hat, but damn did she love the hint of swagger it added to the way he held himself. Would she ever get over how devastatingly handsome he was? If he never changed his mind about giving a relationship with her a chance, she hoped on high she could eventually find peace with having him in her family's life and give herself a break from *what if*s and daydreams.

Carrie was right. It was time for Jenna to move on. Have

a little fun. She was twenty-four and on the verge of
wonderful changes in her life. A new job, a new city, a new
home. Time to take a page from Tara's book, flip the prover-
bial bird to the things holding her back, and seize the day.

Jenna easily found Tara in the audience. She'd changed
from her green tank top to a purple, knee-length cocktail
dress that flaunted her pale skin and lent vibrancy to the
colors of her tattoos. She sat next to two people in their
fifties she assumed were Dan and Cynthia Roenick. They
had a dignified air about them, like wealthy patriarchs. Dan
was an older, stouter version of Matt, but with skin that was
several shades more tan—a cowboy tan, it was called
around ranch country.

Jenna couldn't help but wonder if Tara had done as she'd
affectionately threatened, filling in her parents about the
closeness with which Jenna and Matt had worked together
to solve the flower emergency. Given how enthusiastic Tara
had been about Jenna and Matt's teamwork, Jenna wouldn't
be surprised if Mr. and Mrs. Roenick were expecting the
two of them to be engaged by the end of the year.

When the minister called for the rings from Jake, the
room hushed. Amy and Kellan's vows captured everyone's
full attention. Though they'd written their own, Amy had
been uncharacteristically coy about the content. This was
the first time Jenna had heard them. She had to concentrate
to catch all the words through Amy's blubbering, but was
deeply moved by the deep, unyielding love pouring from
every word. They vowed to cling to each other during hard
times, through their whole lives, forever. They pledged
patience and understanding, to never let anger get the better
of them and to never keep secrets from each other.

On the surface, the vows seemed straight out of a rule
book for marriage success. Except that Jenna knew life was
more complicated than the beautiful words would admit.

Sometimes patience did more harm than good. Sometimes you had to get mad for the other person to hear you. Sometimes secrets needed to be kept.

Her focus strayed to the audience, to the blandly smiling Parrishes. During Jenna and Carson's final confrontation before he'd left town, he'd intimated that his parents were as guilty as the rest of them for what had happened to him. What part had Lou and Patricia Parrish played in those terrible events? At the very least, they were guilty of a cover-up, and at the worst . . .

Patricia noticed Jenna staring and smiled. Jenna startled and attempted a smile in return, but her pulse sped.

At the worst, she was looking into the eyes of attempted murderers.

Jenna shifted her attention to Amy and Kellan as they sealed their union with a kiss. She clapped with the rest of the crowd, filled anew with joy for her sister—except for the dark corner of her mind that couldn't shake the sensation that all her years of careful planning weren't enough to protect her and Tommy.

Fours weeks. All she had to do was lie low for four more weeks and then they'd be out of this town for good, out from under the prying eyes of the community. She followed Amy and Kellan up the aisle, conjuring a visual of herself as an elephant matriarch—unflappable, tough, and singularly focused on the protection of her family.

She and Tommy were going to be okay, more than okay, and she was going to emerge from under the shadow of her secrets fighting strong. Nothing was going to go wrong and no one was going to stop her now.

The reception was a wonderland of flowers. Even though Matt had witnessed Tara's genius at Carpe Diem, a vision of the final outcome of their efforts had eluded him. Every table burst with blooms of pink, white, and green arrangements that looked like they'd been the plan all along. He couldn't have been prouder of his big sis.

At the long bridal party table set apart from the other tables at the head of the ballroom's dance floor, Jenna was seated between Jake and him. The arrangement was awkward as hell, given the painful, humiliating *It's not you, it's me* conversation he'd had with Jenna before the ceremony, but now both he and Jenna had their game faces on.

The reality of their relationship moving forward was sure to hit him hard once the dancing got going, but for the time being, they were united in their focus on getting Jake through his best man speech, which the DJ had informed them was coming up next.

"You're going to do great," Jenna whispered to Jake.

"Don't sweat it, man. You've got this," Matt added. He leaned behind Jenna's back and lightly socked Jake's shoulder.

Jake nodded without looking up from the table, his blank expression drilling a hole in the floor as if he were a prizefighter sitting in a corner, waiting for the bell to ding. It took the DJ two attempts to get Jake's attention to pass him the microphone. Jake took it in hand and met Jenna and Matt's supportive smiles, panic radiating in his eyes.

"Seriously, man, you've got this. Just read your notes," Matt whispered.

With grim resolve, Jake stood and faced the crowd. From his inside jacket pocket he pulled a folded paper that crackled into the mic as he opened it. Silence descended over the room. For nearly everyone in attendance, today marked their first glimpse of Kellan's brother, and for some, their first time learning Kellan had a sibling in the first place.

Jake stared at the paper, his Adam's apple bobbing in a

swallow. "Thank you all for coming out tonight for this wonderful celebration of my brother and his new bride. Isn't Amy beautiful? When we—" Applause and hoots cut off his hastily spoken words. His shoulders twitched like the sound surprised him.

Jenna pressed near Matt's shoulder, crowding him with her good smells and warmth—and an extraordinary view down her dress that he pointedly avoided. "We should've written in the pause."

They'd prepped Jake about taking a breath after he read that question to let people clap their agreement, but it seemed he was way too nervous to do more than exactly what the paper indicated. It was a great speech, though, and no one was expecting an Oscar-worthy performance. "He's doing fine. Tricky part's over."

Once the cheers subsided, Jake scanned the speech until he found his place. "When we were kids, Kellan and I used to play cowboys and robbers in the streets of our neighborhood. We'd sneak rubber bands from people's newspapers and turn sticks into rubber band guns."

Kellan tipped back in his chair, his expression distant, his smile fond, as though he were picturing the memory like a movie in his head. "I forgot about that."

Jake swiveled to look at Kellan over the paper. For the first time, Matt could see in his face a tinge of kidlike vulnerability. "I didn't forget."

Kellan held Jake's gaze and offered a nod full of apology and regret. Jenna braced a hand on Matt's knee. Matt went completely still. He rolled his eyes to their point of contact and curled his fingers into the table to keep from covering her hand with his like he was desperate to.

And then Jake did the most amazing thing. With a smile, he reached over and squeezed Kellan's shoulder. It was as though the whole room let out a collective exhale. Or maybe it was only Matt and Jenna.

Jake turned forward again, his hand still on Kellan's shoulder. "I worshipped my big brother. He was three years older than me and always the coolest kid on the block. And here he is today, a real, honest-to-God cowboy with a great life and a great woman to share it with." He silently read the next lines, then leaned into the mic for the punch line that he, Jenna, and Matt had spent a solid half hour crafting. "But Kellan, there will always be one way I'm cooler than you. You might've grown up to be a cowboy, but I'm the one who gets to carry a gun and catch the robbers."

The whole place burst into cheers. He flashed a pleased smile at the crowd, then at Kellan. When the din subsided, he let go of Kellan's shoulder and gripped the paper hard, concentrating. "Uh . . . where was I? Oh! One thing I've learned since the days he and I played make-believe is that life is all about change—some good, some bad. You learn to go with the flow of jobs, apartments, and people in and out of your life. That is, until you find that special someone you can't imagine giving up, no matter what changes life brings."

Matt had written the end of the speech and, though he wasn't usually boastful, he had to admit it had come out damn good.

Jake lifted his champagne glass. It wasn't written into the speech, so Matt took it as a sign that he was relaxing into the idea of being in the spotlight. "It reminds me of a quote I once heard." *About five hours ago*. "True love is not about finding a person you can live with, it's about finding the person you can't live without. I think we can all agree that my brother has found that person in Amy. Cheers to the happy couple."

Amid the *awww*s and claps of the crowd, Jake was treated to a gigantic bear hug from Kellan.

The quote was one Matt had heard at a wedding once. He remembered it because then, as now, it had filled him with so much frustration that he couldn't look anyone in the eye lest he give himself away. That was what he wanted. To be the person a woman couldn't live without. What would it be like to be so wanted that a woman would be unwilling to live without him, despite his flaws and damage?

Jenna leaned into him again, her champagne flute up in a request to clink glasses with him. "Nice work, speechwriter."

He shook off his darkness and raised his glass, touching it to hers. "Don't leave yourself out of the credit. You were the one who pulled that childhood story out of him."

"I never once, in my wildest dreams, thought I'd need to write a best man's speech, but we didn't do too shabby."

He sipped the champagne, then said, "When it all came down to it, you threw your sister the best, most perfect wedding Catcher Creek has ever seen. Kudos."

"I'll drink to that."

The DJ took the mic from where Jake had set it and directed the crowd to gather for the first dance. While people stood and moseyed to the edge of the square, Kellan broke from the kiss he'd been laying on Amy. He got the DJ's attention, then took the mic.

"Before Amy and I get started on our dance, I'd like to say a few words. I wasn't planning to, because, uh, public speaking isn't my strong suit. But here it goes. I'd like to thank you all for joining Amy and me on our big night. We appreciate it. I'd like to give a special shout-out to three people who made this all possible: Matt Roenick and Tara Weiss for stepping in at the last minute with all these beautiful flower arrangements, and most of all, my new sister-in-law, Jenna Sorentino, who planned today down to the last detail. Thank you, Jenna, for everything. I love you and I'm really honored to call you my family."

Jenna covered her heart with both hands and smiled at Kellan, misty-eyed.

After the applause died down, he continued. "With everybody Amy and I love in one place, we're moved to share our big news with you and kick this celebration up another notch." He took Amy's hand and pulled her into an easy embrace. "We found out this morning that Amy's pregnant."

Matt flinched as his insides quaked. *Double whammy.* It was hard enough watching one person after another in his life get hitched. He hadn't seen that second blow coming. Working hard to keep a neutral smile on his face, he joined the rest of the reception guests in clapping.

"Isn't that wonderful?" Jenna asked, beaming at him.

He nodded, but couldn't muster the strength to look her in the eye.

Always a groomsman, never a groom was exactly the kind of self-pitying muck he'd disavowed after the last of his siblings wed. He resented the bitterness that crept through him like a blood-borne poison with each of his friends' and family members' joyous milestones. He hated feeling like a whiny asshole because he couldn't have what he most wanted in life.

First-world problem. Get over yourself. You've got money, a life full of family and friends, and your health.

Hell, if he were really trying to get some perspective, he'd focus on being grateful for clean drinking water and freedom of speech. But it was hard to stay focused on gratitude for the many blessings he already had when every other week he was invited to wedding after wedding, first birthday parties and brisses, bar mitzvahs, and school talent shows for his nieces or nephews.

Geez, he knew a lot of happy couples with kids.

Choking back a sardonic bark of laughter, he watched Kellan and Amy take the dance floor for their first dance as newlyweds and fantasized about snapping his champagne flute in half. Something a nice guy like him would never do.

The thing of it was, he was tired of being nice. He was tired of smiling and saying *congratulations*. Tired of the private shame that came with being jealous of other people's happiness.

What he needed right now was to get some air.

"Excuse me," he muttered to no one in particular. He twisted his way through the crowd toward the exit. Someone tapped him on the shoulder. He turned to see his dad.

"Are you okay?"

Just great. His dad had sought him out to check in with him because of the pregnancy announcement. That was another thing he was sick and tired of—his parents' pity. What he wouldn't give to go back in time and stop himself from confessing to them how every new baby announcement hit him like a fresh trauma. A cruel reminder of his defectiveness as a man.

But he'd had to tell them because they weren't getting what it was like to be surrounded by his ridiculously fertile brothers and sisters. Or what it did to him inside when some unsuspecting member of their extended family would joke, *Just you wait until you're a father. Then you'll know what I'm talking about.*

He'd had to explain to his dad why he went hunting every year instead of attending the family's Father's Day barbecue.

"I'm fine." Though he kept his eyes locked on the dancing couple, in his periphery he watched his dad swab a hand over his mouth.

"Look, son, the way modern medicine is changing so

fast, it's only a matter of time before the scientists and doctors figure out how to—"

Matt gripped the champagne flute harder. "Stop, Dad. Please."

"You can always adopt."

That's what they all said, his family. And they were right. He could adopt. But that option added a whole new dimension to the vicious cycle of hope and loss he'd experienced over and over. What if he fell in love with a baby and something went wrong with the paperwork? What if the birth mother changed her mind? He wasn't sure he was made of strong enough stuff to survive any more dashed dreams of fatherhood.

He couldn't stand there any longer under his father's watchful, pitying scrutiny, surrounded by hope and happiness. With a smile as brittle as his self-control, he put his back to the dance floor and started walking. His dad made to follow.

Matt held up a hand. "I'm sorry. I need some space."

Dad nodded and stopped midstride.

Matt lowered his eyes to the ground, rolled his shoulders back, and kept moving as the DJ invited the rest of the wedding party to join the bride and groom. Damn it, all evening he'd been looking forward to dancing with Jenna. It was the one way he could be close to her without risking himself.

Missing this dance meant one of the bridesmaids would be left without a partner, but he couldn't face his friends right now. Someone was bound to see through his façade, Jenna or Kellan most likely, and he wasn't willing to taint everyone else's fun with his personal pain.

He couldn't get his hand to uncurl from around the flute so he carried it with him out of the room and through the lobby doors.

Smokers stood in clusters around the planter boxes out

front. He barreled past them, to the shadows on the side of the building, his stride lengthening as he neared the Dumpsters and cinder-block wall surrounding the parking lot.

Anger lit his nerves like a fuse. Winding back, he growled as he launched the flute at the wall. It shattered with a satisfying crash that went a long way toward diffusing his rage.

He braced his hands on his knees and sucked in deep gulps of air. The grief was sharp tonight, even more so than in the days following his diagnosis. Sharp and raw in a way that had caught him off guard.

"Guess you really hated that champagne, huh?"

Matt startled and spun in the direction of the voice.

A man, bigger than him, slouched against the chain-link fence enclosing the Dumpsters, his hands wedged in his jeans pockets and his clunky, black work boots crossed at the ankles. He was as big as Jake, but less beefy, and while Jake gave off a vibe that he was pissed off at life in general, this man had the same look as the bullies Matt had feared growing up, the type who had taken pleasure in beating up the scrawny Jewish kid in glasses.

But Matt wasn't scrawny anymore, not by a long shot, and he'd donated the glasses to charity after laser surgery had fixed his eyes. He could take on a knuckle-dragger like this guy any day of the week and might even best him.

Matt took a few careful steps back. Not because he was intimidated, but to better size the man up. "Rough night," he said by way of explanation.

"Yeah, I'm having one of those myself." The man pushed away from the wall and into a swath of light that gave Matt a good look at his high-and-tight haircut.

A soldier, younger than Matt by a few years, if he had to guess. And judging by the Semper Fi tattoo below the sleeve of his gray T-shirt, a Marine.

All the fight drained out of Matt. He was tough, but he

was also smart enough to know he probably couldn't best an active-duty Marine in a brawl.

The Marine nodded toward the building. "How's the reception going? Sounds like a typical Catcher Creek party." It was said sarcastically, like he'd long outgrown his countrified roots.

A conversation with a jaded soldier wasn't exactly what Matt had expected when he'd stormed outside, but it only took a second for him to decide to roll with it. He ignored the sarcasm and instead offered a genuine answer, which was more his style. "Reception's going great. Everyone's having a lot of fun."

"Oh, yeah, I can tell. That's how come you're out here smashing glass. What, were you in love with the bride or something? 'Cause if that's the case, you'll need to rein it in before Kellan Reed kicks your ass to Mexico."

Hearing Kellan's name had Matt doing another about-face. "I'm sorry. I should've introduced myself. Matt Roenick. I don't remember you from the wedding."

The Marine took his offered hand in a firm shake. "That's because I dodged out at the last minute. Carson Parrish, but my friends call me Lynch."

Parrish rang a bell, but Matt couldn't remember where he'd heard it. Then again, he only knew perhaps a quarter of the wedding guests by face and even fewer by name. "How do you know Kellan?"

Lynch shrugged. "From way back. My family owns the only feed and grain store in Catcher Creek, so I got an invitation by default even though I haven't been in this town for going on six years." There was venom in his tone, like he and his demons hadn't done the water-under-the-bridge thing yet. "Never RSVP'd, and I'm sure no one expected me to actually show up, but I'm assuming my whole family is inside that building right now doing the YMCA or whatever stupid dance the DJ's calling."

"You're not sure if your family's here or not?" It was a prying question, but Matt couldn't get a read on the guy's motives for lurking outside the building.

His expression cracked into a hard smile. "I wanted to surprise people, but I think I'll save it for another day. It's weird, coming home after being gone so long, like I don't belong. I'm not the same person I was when I left, so I didn't expect all the old shit to come rushing back at me like it has." He squinted into the darkness. "I need more time to get my bearings before I do what I came here to."

Matt nodded. "I know exactly what you mean." That was no lie. He knew all about feeling like an outcast around the people and places you grew up—different, defective. And he knew a hell of a lot about how all your old shit could slap you upside the head when you least expected it, hence tonight's broken champagne flute.

The difference between him and this Lynch guy was that while Matt worked really hard to stay positive, Lynch had a world-weary edge to him. Like he'd seen and done too much in his life to appreciate the beauty of the world anymore. Like the best parts of himself had been defeated.

"So I 'fessed up. Your turn. What's with the smashed glass?"

"I . . ." Matt was suddenly acutely embarrassed by his tantrum. "I lost perspective for a minute there about what was important."

"Man, the only thing that's important in this life is looking out for number one. If you want something for yourself, make it happen. If something or someone's pissing you off, bulldoze over them. No regrets. Because when it comes right down to it, nobody's got your back. It's all about you and what you can do for yourself."

Man, this guy was a cynic. Matt was starting to see why his friends called him Lynch, and had to wonder what his enemies called him. He was everything Matt didn't want to become, but feared himself inching closer to each day. Matt wanted to believe in people, and in the inherent goodness of the world. Like Lynch, he wanted to bulldoze over what was holding him back, but rather than act like the world was out to get him, as Lynch seemed to, Matt understood that his greatest enemy was himself.

When had he started letting grief and fear dictate his choices? He knew the answer. His decision to stop dating and keep Jenna at arm's length had everything to do with the three kids whose pictures he still carried in his wallet. Was he strong enough to risk the possible pain of losing another kid he'd dreamed of being a father to if things didn't work out between him and Jenna?

Five minutes ago, he would have answered no. But now, all he could think about was how to keep himself from turning into this Lynch guy. His gut was telling him that Jenna was his salvation. She'd blazed a trail through his toughest resistance, straight to his heart with her smile and the way she'd felt in his arms when they'd danced, the way they'd sung along to the radio together and worked as a team to save Amy's wedding.

She was smart and funny and resourceful and gorgeous. He wanted her so damn bad. Worse than he'd wanted any woman before—and not in a way that was polite or friendly or half-assed, like he'd been telling himself he was at peace with. He wanted all of her: her secrets, her body, her love.

He wanted to go all in with Jenna and Tommy, even if it meant he might get hurt.

Was she inside wondering what'd happened to him? He'd let her down by skipping the wedding party dance, and he'd let down Kellan and Amy too. It was time to focus on the blessings that were right in front of him, instead of the parts of his life that hadn't gone according to plan. It was time to bulldoze over what was keeping him down and crush his demons once and for all.

No more hemming and hawing, no more stewing in bitterness, no more being Wade-in-Slowly Guy. "Talk to you later, man. I'm going to get back in there."

"Yeah? You going to get another champagne glass to smash?"

Matt waved off the joke. "Nah, I'm done with that. There's a woman in there I need to find."

Chapter Eight

Tommy didn't precisely stay by Jenna's side like a perfect angel during the reception, but that was a good thing because his little-boy energy kept him bouncing around the room at a fast enough pace that Patricia Parrish didn't have a prayer of cornering him again since the incident in the lobby.

Still, eight o'clock was slow in coming. It wasn't until Jenna had Tommy by the hand in the parking lot, surrounded by balmy summer air, that she felt the rock budge from on top of her chest.

On Tommy's other side walked Charlene Delgado, who'd been sitting for the Sorentinos since Jenna was a baby. A grandmother now, she was an early-to-bed, early-to-rise type and didn't mind taking Tommy home with her so Jenna could stick around to the end of the reception. The nominal sitting fee she charged was worth every penny.

As they crossed the parking lot to Charlene's car, Jenna's relief about Tommy's departure was only tempered by concern about Matt. Something had shifted in his mood after Jake's speech. Okay, yes, during the speech she'd been a bit handsy with Matt's knee, but she chalked that up to nerves. He couldn't take that personally. It wasn't like she'd leaned over and laid a big kiss on him like she'd wanted to after they'd clinked glasses.

Discomfort about her over-friendliness didn't explain the tense exchange between Matt and his father before he'd stalked from the ballroom during the first dance. What could've possibly happened at the reception to put them at odds with each other? Nothing added up.

Now that Tommy was taken care of and there was nothing left to do at the reception but dance and visit, Jenna could afford the time to look for Matt. He might not want any kind of relationship with her, but she couldn't flip the switch on caring about him that quickly. She knew she wouldn't have peace of mind until she made sure he was okay.

Once she'd strapped Tommy into the booster seat in the back of Charlene's car, she kissed him good night. "Be a good boy for Miss Charlene, okay?"

He rubbed his eyes and wrinkled his nose. "Mommy, I'm always a good boy for Miss Charlene because she lets me eat licorice before bed and I don't even have to brush my teeth!"

Oh, God.

Charlene twisted in the driver seat, grinning like she was daring Jenna to challenge her sitting techniques. Jenna snapped her gaping mouth shut and smiled back, having learned over the years that Charlene chafed at childcare advice of any kind.

The kicker was, Jenna wasn't in a position to sweat the small stuff because there weren't a whole lot of other people in town she'd trust with her baby overnight. Making a mental note to brush his teeth the minute he was back home in the morning, she gave Tommy one last kiss, thanked Charlene for the umpteenth time, and shut the door.

She waved until the car disappeared from view, then turned her face up to the stars, closed her eyes, and inhaled. She'd done it. She and Tommy had made it through the afternoon and evening without any conflict. The wedding and reception had gone off without a hitch, and she had two more hours of dancing before the DJ packed up. Plenty of time to figure out what was wrong with Matt and scope out Kellan's single friends, as per Carrie's suggestion.

She opened her eyes again and jolted at the sight of Matt jogging across the parking lot toward the building's entrance, a determined look on his face.

She trotted after him as fast as her strapless dress would allow. "Matt!"

But he'd opened the door and the blare of music drowned out her voice. She hooked a thumb behind the material across her bustline to secure the dress and picked up her pace, slipping through the door closing behind him.

"Matt," she called again, tapping his shoulder.

He whirled to face her, his hands coming to her waist. Gone from his eyes was the torment that had haunted his features since that afternoon, replaced by a smoldering intensity that left her fighting for air.

"What were you doing outside?" he asked.

It took a shake of her head to clear it enough to remember what she'd been doing before looking into his dark eyes. "Saying good night to Tommy and his sitter. Listen, are you all right? I saw you leave before. You looked—"

His mouth descended over hers, hot and demanding.

She drew herself up, shocked stiff, her fingers splayed over his chest. His hand found her jaw, giving him the control to tip her head to the angle he wanted. His lips were firm, his tongue insistent. He smelled fantastic, as she'd noticed when they'd walked down the aisle together—clean like shaving cream, the really good stuff that cost a pretty penny and made her want to smear her nose and lips across his cheek and inhale.

Or kiss him senseless.

Giving herself over to what she'd longed to do month after month, she wrapped her arms around him and took his tongue inside her. A masculine rumble of satisfaction vibrated from his throat, curling her toes in her boots.

This wasn't the Matt she knew best. The gentleman with the fears and private pain who could compose speeches about love after pulling an all-nighter to create flower arrangements to help save a wedding. Instead, this was the man she'd danced the waltz with, the one who knew exactly what he wanted from her body and how to get it.

A blaze of heat rocketed through her. What a crock that she'd thought the passion between them would be easy and comfortable, leisurely even. She wanted to devour him. She wanted to rip his suit off, push him to the ground, and fuck his brains out until they'd made up for all the time they'd lost being apart and all the years she'd wasted with lesser men.

Something had happened during the reception that she didn't understand. Whatever it was, it'd given him permission to let go of what was holding him back. She had every intention of pressing him for details about what that something had been, but not right now while she was locked against his hard, lean body, with his hands and mouth commanding her attention.

She didn't care that they were in the lobby, surrounded by people she knew. Let them look and gossip to each other. She'd wear the badge of the wicked, loose-morals Sorentino sister the rest of her life if it meant Matt would keep on working magic with his lips and tongue, as if he were starved for the taste of her.

Finally they came up for air. Their lips brushed as they panted into each other's mouths and looked into each other's eyes.

"I was wrong before," he said between breaths.

"About what?" She'd already figured what he meant, but wanted to hear him say it.

"That you and I shouldn't be together. That's bullshit. I want you." One of his hands left her waist to splay over her backside. "All of you."

Time would tell if he truly wanted all of her—including her heart—but for tonight the confession was enough. She slipped a finger behind the knot of his tie and tugged. "I'm yours for the taking."

His body tensed, radiating torrid, male need. He drew her lower lip into his mouth and ran his tongue across it. "Right now."

The terse demand sent a shot of arousal through her. Right now sounded just exactly perfect.

She looked around the lobby. Mr. and Mrs. Parrish were watching them with wrinkled noses, judging. Others darted glances, smiling knowingly, and no doubt filing away the juicy news of Matt and Jenna's heated embrace for later.

Matt seized hold of her chin and forced her attention back to him, his eyes relentless in their hunger. "Right now, Jenna."

She licked over her lower lip, tracing the path his tongue had taken. Sweet sundae, she loved the way he tasted. "Guess we'd better find ourselves an empty room."

The tension on his features cracked into a wicked grin. He took her hand and started down the dark, empty hallway leading to the groom's suite.

She watched the play of his body as he moved and came to a maddening conclusion: he had far too many clothes on.

His torso was buttoned into a concealing shirt, vest, tie, and jacket, with his lower body hidden behind pants and a belt. The second they were alone, Jenna needed to get her hands on his skin.

She'd only ever touched his face and arms. She wanted to feel the hard, hot expanse of skin on his chest and back. She wanted to lick her way down his stomach and up his legs. She wiggled free of his hand, reached under his jacket, and pulled his dress shirt from his pants, then his undershirt.

He quickened the pace, lengthening his stride so that she had to shuffle double-time to keep up. When he reached for the doorknob to the groom's suite, her fingers finally hit the skin of his stomach and skittered over the ridges of his abdominal muscles. Sucking in a sharp breath, he spun and pushed her up against the hallway wall.

His mouth found hers, consuming her, demanding surrender.

Her hands groped between them, tugging material out of the way and unfastening buttons until she hit skin again. Her fingers and palms rippled over the unyielding flesh of his stomach, then higher, slipping around the curved base of his pectoral muscle. She couldn't wait to get him naked and use his body as her own personal playground.

He must've thought she had the right idea about getting skin-to-skin because his hand left her ribs and slid low on her skirt, bunching it in his hand, working the fabric higher as their kisses turned wet and desperate.

Pinning the fabric between their bodies, he grabbed a firm hold on the back of her thigh, lifting her leg and wrapping it around his hip. His lips left hers to lave a path down her neck, then chest, along the hem of her dress.

"I've got to get you in that room," he growled into her skin. "Get your fucking clothes out of my way."

She loved this new side of him—the gruff seducer, oozing raw, primal need. Loved it even more than the smooth, easygoing gentleman part of his personality, or maybe because of how deliciously at odds his two halves were.

He released her leg to reach sideways, opening the door. They stumbled in as a unit, clinging and kissing. From inside the room came a squeal of surprise.

Tara, on top of the console table behind the sofa, bolted upright, clutching her dress in front of her naked chest like a sheet. Jake was completely nude and probably the brawniest naked man Jenna had ever seen, like a beefcake lumberjack. Not her style, but really darn studly nonetheless. He'd frozen midthrust between Tara's legs, his thick arms popping veins while holding her hips in place against him, making no move at all to cover himself or her.

A gentleman, he was not.

Jenna had never considered herself a voyeur, and didn't care much for porn, but Tara and Jake locked together was pretty hot.

Matt released a yelp of agony and clamped his hands over his eyes. All Jenna could do was smile. Guess she'd been right about Tara's attraction to bad boys. She couldn't blame her; after all, Jenna planned to spend the rest of the night exploring some dirty fantasies with her own closeted bad boy.

Tara pushed a tangle of hair from her face, not looking the least bit scandalized that she'd been caught in the act. "Oops."

"Really, Tara?" Matt scolded, his eyes still hidden behind his hand.

Tara's gaze slid to Jake in a bold appraisal before returning to Jenna and Matt. "Hey, we weren't doing anything you weren't about to."

"Except that you forgot how to lock the door."

Jake's lips contorted, like he was battling a smile. "Where's the sport in that?"

A strangled noise bubbled from Matt's throat. "You're talking about my sister, not a sport."

"Since you brought her up, let me tell you something about crazy chicks." His lips lost the battle as a broad, shit-eating grin broke out over his face. "The sex is unbelievable."

Tara gave him a hard shove that nearly knocked him off balance. "Hey, I'm not crazy."

He grinned down at her and yanked her hips toward him. "What? I dig your brand of crazy."

Matt groaned. "Not enough brain bleach in the world."

Tara slung an arm around Jake's neck and whispered something in his ear too quiet for Jenna to hear.

Time for Jenna and Matt to take a hint and leave. She pushed Matt backward, out of the room. "Have fun, you two."

"How about you do the world a favor and use the lock this time?" Matt hollered as Jenna gave him a final shove that sent him in the hallway.

"Jenna," Tara called, her tone beseeching.

She turned and met Tara's suddenly serious eyes. In a quiet tone heavy with worry, Tara said, "Matt's my only little brother. Don't break his heart, okay?"

The way she asked it went beyond normal sisterly caring, evoking her memory of Matt's tormented admission that he wasn't enough for her. Soon—very soon, in fact—she was going to need to know what secret plagued him, and why Tara acted as though one of the strongest, most capable men Jenna had ever known had a fragile constitution.

She took hold of the doorknob and gave Tara a solemn nod. "I won't. Promise."

She shut the door and headed for Matt's open arms.

Nice guy Matt was back. The fire in his eyes had extinguished. He tried to give her what she assumed was supposed to be an apologetic smile, but more closely resembled a grimace. "I could've lived my whole life without seeing that particular train wreck in progress."

Jenna busied her fingers with Matt's still-knotted tie. He might've lost his mojo, but he wasn't weaseling out of having down-and-dirty sex with her tonight. "Then I won't bother to say I told you so about Tara liking them rough around the edges."

His face contorted into a full-blown scowl. "Not helping."

"How about this?" She plunged her hands in his hair and pulled his face to hers. "Let me see if I can make you forget everything else but me."

She kissed him, working her lips over his until he opened his mouth and let her tongue in. Then she kept on kissing him, deep and wet, until his erection made its presence known.

"You're going to do me tonight, Matt." She stroked her knee up his leg. "You can't take it back now. I want you too badly."

His eyes were dark again, simmering with arousal. "You thought I was going to change my mind?"

"I didn't know what to think."

His hands strayed from her back until they clutched her backside. "You remember last night while we were dancing, you told me you wanted to know all my secrets? Here's one. For months now, I've been going crazy wondering what you sound like when you come." He jerked her high against him, forcing her up to the balls of her feet, rubbing her against his hardness as though to prove how she'd affected him. "What you look like. How you taste."

Oh, my.

Clinging to his neck for support, she dropped her head

back as he bathed her collarbone with kisses. "You have? For months?"

His answer took the form of a roguish smile. After another wet, reckless kiss, he dragged his lips to the pressure point at the side of her neck and locked his teeth on her flesh with enough pressure that a *zing* of pleasure rocketed all the way down her legs.

"Harder," she said breathlessly.

He upped the pressure until the pleasure swirled perilously close to pain. Hot damn. She dug her nails into his shoulder and let her knees buckle.

After debating the merits of unzipping his pants and hoisting her dress up right there in the hallway, she croaked in a strained voice, "The bridal suite."

They needed a room with a lock because no way was she going to let anyone interrupt them again, especially not Tara and Jake, should they emerge from the groom's suite unexpectedly.

He scraped his teeth and tongue along her shoulder, then straightened to grin down at her, smoothing his hand over the path his teeth had taken. "Bridal suite it is. Does it make me a sick puppy that I like seeing my teeth marks on your skin?"

Jenna refastened his collar. "No more of a sick puppy than I am for getting turned on by being bit."

With a chuckle, he released her and got busy putting his tux in proper order. "You think we can make it all the way across the lobby without every single wedding guest figuring out what we're up to?"

She wiggled, realigning her breasts in the dress. "I don't care. Do you?"

After a few fumbles with his tie, he pulled it off and stuffed it in his jacket pocket. "Do I care that everyone knows I'm the lucky man who's earned the attention of one of the world's most beautiful women? Not on your life. I was just trying to be a gentleman about your reputation."

"Then we're golden because my reputation in this town's already shot to hell." And good riddance too—both to Catcher Creek and to the pressure of adhering to the archaic standards of propriety most of the women in town held each other to.

"I've always wanted to date a bad girl."

"Really?"

"Only if it's you." He shrugged out of his jacket and held it out to her. "To hide the bite mark."

She shook her head. "Let them look. Maybe later we can add a hickey to the other side to balance it out."

"You really are a rebel. I like it." He hooked the jacket on his index finger, slung it over his back, then took her hand and started toward the lobby. "Let's get this walk over. I need you naked and underneath me."

Chapter Nine

If any of the people milling about in the lobby noticed Matt's and Jenna's disheveled appearances, cat-eating-a-canary grins, or Jenna's bite mark, they weren't saying. Of course, the way gossip worked, no one would come right out and mention it, but if Jenna didn't care what people said behind her back, then neither did Matt.

A few more steps and he would've had Jenna through the social minefield, into the relative seclusion of the dimly lit hallway leading to the bridal suite. Too bad Rachel cut them off, throwing her arms up and looking exasperated.

"Where were you two? We've lost half the wedding party. Lisa and Chris are off dealing with their kids, you two were nowhere to be found, and no one's seen Jake in a while either. What if he left without telling Kellan good-bye? I wouldn't put it past him to disappear like that."

In a rare turn of events, Matt was at a loss for words. *Actually, Jake's banging my sister in the groom's suite* wouldn't do. Neither would *Well, I was throwing a tantrum out by the Dumpsters until I decided I should be screwing your sister instead.*

What kind of hedonistic wedding was this, anyway? Crazy.

Perhaps Jenna's thoughts mirrored his because her throat clearing sounded suspiciously like a snort of laughter. "I'm positive Jake wouldn't leave without telling Kellan and Amy. He doesn't have a car, remember? As for Matt and me, we were seeing Tommy off with the babysitter."

Great answer. At least one of them could think on the fly.

"And Jake's probably getting some fresh air or something," Jenna continued.

Heavy on the *or something*. He grinned at Jenna as though in support of her theory but choked at the red half-circle bite mark in plain view on her neck. It was even more obvious now that they were standing under one of the lobby's recessed lights. He draped an arm across her shoulders, close to her neck at an angle to cover the mark.

Jenna's flimsy answer satisfied Rachel, thank goodness. "Well, you missed the cake cutting. Here's the kicker. The cake bites Amy and Kellan exchanged made Amy sick. Right before she was supposed to toss the bridal bouquet, she had another bout of nausea and ended up tossing her cookies— er, cake—into one of the champagne buckets instead."

"Oh, no. Is she okay?"

"Fine. You remember how it is to be pregnant. You used to yak while running the tractor in the fields, then keep on truckin'."

Jenna wrinkled her nose. "Lovely image, Rachel. Thanks."

Matt could totally picture that. Jenna with her gumption and farm-girl toughness. Pregnancy-induced queasiness would be nothing but a minor inconvenience to a woman like her. He bet she'd been beautiful while pregnant, too.

The visual in his mind of Jenna ripe with child sent a pang of longing knifing through his heart. Tomorrow, he'd come clean to her about his genetic defect and plead his case for the future he could offer her. Tonight, though, was all about crushing his fears to dust by embracing opportunity and going after the woman he wanted.

"You two headed back in to the reception?"

Jenna shook her head and shifted toward the bridal suite hall. The bite mark, previously obscured by Matt's arm, came into full view again in all its reddish-purple glory. "Oh, we've got a few more things to do. Details." She swatted the air. "We'll be back in a bit."

She threaded her arm around Matt's waist and started walking.

"What details? Everything's done but paying the DJ," Rachel called after them.

Jenna picked up the pace, tapping her wrist as if she wore an invisible watch. "No time to explain."

Matt tried out his best apologetic grin on Rachel over Jenna's shoulder, but his acting skills were crap tonight. With a quick prayer that the room was empty, he wrenched the bridal suite door open, piled in after Jenna, and kicked it shut.

Empty.

A freakin' miracle. He flipped the lock, pressed Jenna against the closed door with his hips, and smiled at her. The delight dancing in her expression sent him over the edge. The next thing he knew, they both dissolved into laughter.

"How did Rachel not notice your neck?"

Jenna dabbed at the corner of her eye. "Rachel's never been particularly perceptive, which is hilarious to Amy and me because she's a photographer by hobby. And she's really good at it! It doesn't make any sense."

Matt was pretty much done talking about Jenna's sisters. Or talking in any capacity, for that matter. Impatience had never been an issue for him until tonight, but now he couldn't dam his flood of need. He took her chin in hand and angled his lips over hers, sinking into her soft sweetness. She slung an arm around his neck and kissed him back, complete with a little purr in the back of her throat.

Matt was dizzy with the headiness of his desire, as if he hadn't fully grasped the depth of his feelings for Jenna until he'd given himself permission to pursue her.

She broke the kiss and tugged on the top button of his shirt, concentrating all her focus on unbuttoning it. He watched her white-tipped nails work, mesmerized by them and by the way her hair tumbled haphazardly from the pins of her updo as she peeled his shirt and jacket off.

Her fingers smoothed a path over his chest, tracing the edges of his muscles. He flexed his abdominals and relished the reverence in her eyes. He'd never thought he had much of a male ego, but damn if it didn't roar like a beast in response to Jenna's admiration.

She was the most incredible beauty he'd ever witnessed. And she wanted him as badly as he wanted her. Remarkable.

So full of adrenaline and testosterone his hands were unsteady and damp with sweat, he shed his undershirt, pants, and boxers, working until he stood before her, naked and hungry to crush his bare flesh to hers.

No more wading in slowly. It was time to take what he wanted. Blindly, he slid his hands along her back for the dress's zipper, but couldn't find it. "Zipper?"

Her hot, hungry gaze was on his erection as her hands continued exploring his chest. "On the side. Left."

Fighting to ignore the feel of her fingernails scoring a path down his abs, into the hair below his navel, he found the hidden zipper and pulled it open. Then fingers closed around his dick.

Sensation ripped through him. He closed his eyes and

rode it out, but he would not be swayed from his quest to get her naked. He smoothed his palms down her sides, along her gorgeously rounded hips. Lower, until the hem of her skirt was bunched in his hands.

He stilled again as she gave him a slow, tight, skin-stretching tug.

Fuck.

He rolled his neck, calming his mind. This whole impatience, full-speed-ahead mantra wasn't going to be very fun if he couldn't keep his shit together long enough to make love to her for any respectable length of time.

She tugged again. He grunted through it, then countered the move with a slow, wet, tongue-tangling kiss meant to distract her from her torturous ministrations. She released his dick long enough for him to get her dress up over her head and toss it to the pile of his clothes while she pulled off her boots.

She wasn't wearing a bra, only a lacy, white thong. Her small, perfect breasts were pink-tipped, rounded swells of creamy skin framed by tan lines in the shape of a strapless bikini top. Intrigued, he tugged the strap of her thong and found another bikini-like tan line. Blood pounded straight to his dick at the sight. When had she ever been in a teeny bikini in the middle of the New Mexico desert and how soon could he be treated to a private fashion show?

She reached for him again, but he was faster. Taking her wrists in hand, he pinned her arms over her head. "Stay," he commanded, his voice a dry rasp that sounded distant to his ears.

An open-mouthed, blissed-out smile spread on her lips. "I don't think so."

With a twist of her wrists, she slipped away from him before he could tighten his grip. Then her hands were back on him, running X-rated experiments on his body—a flick here, a squeeze there—coiling pleasure tight and deep in his belly until his eyes rolled back in his head.

Two could play at this game.

He closed his hands over her breasts, lifting, twisting her nipples between his thumbs and index fingers. He ground his molars together, fighting the urge to take more from her, faster, though that seemed to be exactly what she wanted because she moved her hands to his head and jerked his lips to her breast. He drew her nipple into his mouth with a hard, decisive suck that made her knees buckle.

He wrapped a hand around her ass and the other around the back of her knee, securing her against him as he feasted on her upper body to his heart's content. About the time he gave the left side of her neck a bite mark to match the right, they toppled to the ground, Jenna on top. She pushed to her hands and knees over him.

"Now I've got you where I want you."

She crawled down his body and between his legs.

Holy hell, she was going to put her mouth on him. His hips arched and his eyes closed in anticipation. His hands went to her hair. Rather than the soft, wet heat of her lips around his girth, though, her next touch was to his inner thigh.

To his scars.

They were so much a part of who he was, he no longer saw them when he looked in the mirror, but he revisited the horror of the injuries he'd sustained in the eyes of every woman who saw them for the first time.

Lifting his head, he braced to see pity in her expression before meeting her gaze. But in her face, all he saw was strength and wonder.

"So you wear your scars outside, hmm?" she said.

He blinked. No one had phrased it quite like that before. "Some of them."

She sat on her heels, tracing an arched, pink divot to the crease of his hip. "Sometimes I wish I could, too. I think people would be more understanding."

What scars did she mean? From her crappy childhood? From Tommy's dad or her parents' deaths? She was the most extraordinary woman he'd known. If she had scars, they must be deep down inside her. "There's a fine line between understanding and pity."

"You'll tell me about them someday soon?"

"Tomorrow."

She nodded, appeased. Her interest shifted to his erection. His excitement had dimmed, so he took himself in hand and stroked. With a cluck of disapproval, her hands clasped around his wrists and she scrambled up his torso until she had his arms pinned over his head. Setting her lips close to his, she whispered, "Stay."

She was throwing his words back at him and it was sexy as hell, even if he wasn't in the mood to cede control. "Not a chance."

The next second, he'd flipped her to her back and settled his knees between her thighs. He lifted their joined hands. Straddling her breasts, he pinned hers over her head again.

Their eyes met and held. A current of erotic challenge crackled in the air. Whatever he had thought sex with Jenna would be like, it paled in comparison to this intense, down and dirty intimacy. A vision of his future with her opened up. They'd never be bored. With her, he could explore his every fantasy, his every sexual whim, as she could hers. A thrill rippled through him at the idea that Jenna might be the one and only woman he fucked for the rest of his life. It would be ecstasy, pure and simple.

"You still want my dick in your mouth?"

She ran her tongue across her lower lip. "Feed it to me."

Exactly what he wanted to do. Yeah, life with Jenna would be sweet indeed.

Leaving one hand over both her wrists, he took hold of his shaft at the base and surged forward until the heat of her mouth closed around him.

He pumped into her, not too deep, aware that she was helpless beneath him—her body pinned by his, her hands by his hand. The tip of her tongue pressed along a groove on the underside of his shaft, matching his rhythm, keeping her grip tight.

"God, Jenna. You're so fucking perfect."

He transferred his free hand to the back of her head and supported her neck. She responded by taking him deeper on his next thrust, deeper still on the next. He released her wrists and sunk his fist into the carpet as pleasure gathered force inside him. She wrapped her hands around his hips, grabbing his ass cheeks, urging him down her throat.

One day soon, he was going to come this way. But not tonight. Tonight, he hadn't even gotten to the good stuff yet. He backed his hips up, wincing at the divine friction of her lips grazing his shaft as he pulled out.

Kneeling next to her, he looked in awe at her body. Arousal looked magnificent on her. Nipples tight, her body supple, her lips rosy and moist. He trailed his thumb across her lower lip. When the tip of her tongue flicked him, he barely resisted the urge to feed his dick to her again. With a growl, he splayed a hand over her flat waist, scratching his fingernails over the strip of hair above her pussy until she curled her hips under as though trying to coax his fingers to move where she really wanted them.

He indulged her, sinking his middle finger into her folds. The breathy whimper she made in response left him greedy for more. He dipped his finger lower and curled it inside her wet, hot body as he kissed her, open-mouthed with tongue.

His finger pushing deeper, he ground the pad of his thumb over her clit in tight, slow circles until she whimpered.

Briefly, he thought about adding more fingers, but decided against it. He wanted it to be his dick that stretched her first. He wanted that initial tightness gripping him even though it would probably take him over the edge too fast.

He ended their kiss and slipped his finger out of her. "Sofa," he breathed. "Right now."

He grabbed his discarded pants and stood, then pulled her up into a hug. She kissed a path along his jaw as he rummaged for his wallet. From it, he pulled out a condom, dropped the pants again, and scooped her into his arms.

The sofa was plush blue material and low to the ground. He set her on a cushion and dropped to his knees between her thighs, then pushed her legs wide and let his eyes drink their fill of her while he rolled the condom on. He planned on giving her long, slender legs a proper worshipping later, but right now, he only had eyes for her pussy—pink, swollen, and ready for him.

"You like what you see?" Her voice was thick and low with arousal.

The question had him scrambling to find words and remember how to speak them through his haze of arousal. "You're so beautiful," he croaked. It was the truth. He'd never seen a more beautiful or provocative sight in his life than Jenna Sorentino in the throes of passion.

She offered him a half-lidded smile in return and slid a foot around his waist to his back, urging him closer. "I need to know what you feel like inside me."

They were about to solve that mystery together. Lightheaded with anticipation, he took his dick in hand and guided the tip inside her. He watched it disappear inch by inch, moaning along with her at the profoundness of their joining together—finally, after all these months, after so much angst and denial and loneliness. He reached around her hips and took hold of her hands, interlocking their fingers. Her limbs trembled and twitched, as if her need for him made her vibrate from the inside out. He liked that.

She was as tight and hot as he'd fantasized. When he'd seated himself fully inside her, he sucked in air through flared nostrils, struggling to regain composure. Nothing else felt this good. His orgasm wasn't even going to feel as good as the act of burying himself inside Jenna for the first time.

With their eyes locked on each other, he rocked his hips back, then thrust. Her eyes fluttered closed, her lips parted. He waited for her to meet his gaze again, then fucked her with long, even strokes. She caught on to his rhythm right away and moved in synchronicity with him, together and apart, the friction of flesh driving them ever closer to release.

Every deep thrust elicited a grunt or moan from her that made him long to kiss her. When he could no longer stand not to, he got his feet under him and lifted. Taking hold of her hips, he rotated her with him as he moved onto the sofa, turning them lengthwise. He settled his body over hers so that their stomachs touched and their faces were close enough for him to drop his lips onto hers.

He shifted her knees up close to her ribs, tilting her so that the fluttered series of short thrusts he transitioned into tickled her G-spot. Her mouth dropped open with a strangled cry. "And I thought you were good at dancing," she said with breathy wonder.

He might've smiled except he was a man on a mission now. The need for release was building steadily inside him, intoxicating in its breadth and potency. If he didn't focus, he was going to explode and he was nowhere near ready to.

Before he lost complete hold of his faculties, he withdrew

and bathed her neck and breasts with kisses. "Time for the main event."

Her hands settled in his hair, stroking lazily. "I thought that was the main event."

He grinned down at her. "Not in my world."

He stood and took hold of her legs, dragging her lower body up over the arm of the sofa until her butt rested on it. He kissed a path from her ankle to her inner thigh, then hooked her leg over the back corner of the sofa, her other leg over his shoulder.

Her body's center was dark pink and open and so delectable that his mouth watered in anticipation of tasting her. Curious if she was looking forward to it as much as he was, he looked past her sex and met her languid gaze.

One corner of her mouth curved up. "You had me wondering if you were going to do this."

"Are you kidding? This is my favorite part." Keeping his eyes locked with hers, he put his mouth on her, letting his breath fan over her.

She released a shaky exhale and seemed to settle into the cushion. "Good, because I come so much easier this way."

Most women did, in his experience. He traced a pattern over her clit with his tongue, then flicked, enjoying the way her whole body clenched in response. Smoothing a hand over her outer thigh, he brushed a kiss to her folds. "Then let's keep it easy tonight."

Done teasing and tasting, he got down to the business of coaxing her body to a state of ecstasy. She moaned loudest when he put a little angle on the flicks, so he stayed with that motion, always gauging her responses and adjusting his.

He kept a hand loosely over his dick, stroking occasionally to keep himself hard and in the condom. She came like a massive ocean wave he could see building from far out, quietly gathering momentum until it crashed, loud and powerful. She writhed against his face and he stayed with her, stroking himself in earnest until he was rock hard and ready.

She scooted back, her legs open with the unspoken knowledge of what he needed. He sunk himself into her, his thrusts impatient. She clung to him, arms around his neck, legs around his waist, whispering dirty, sweet nothings about how good he'd made her feel, how huge he was inside her, how badly she wanted him to come.

He buried his face in her neck, giving in to the sensations until release crested once again inside him. "Do you want to try to come again?" he asked. That would be fantastic, but if so, he needed to slow down and pick a position that didn't hit him so intensely.

She fluttered fingers over the nape of his neck. "No. I just want to bring you pleasure now."

"No problem there."

Only a few thrusts later, he captured her mouth in a demanding kiss as he gave himself over to pulse after pulse of sweet release. They collapsed together, panting. Matt couldn't stop smiling. He rolled to his back, pulling her atop him, and wove his fingers with hers, feeling lighter and happier than he could ever remember. Fear and self-doubt could go pound sand. If she'd let him, he was going to make her the happiest woman in the world, of that he was certain.

She drew lazy circles on his shoulder. "What do we do now?"

"Well, first I'm going to dance with you at the reception until they turn on the lights and make us leave."

She backed her face up to beam at him. "I like that plan. And then what?"

He traced her bikini tan lines with his finger. "And then

I'm going to take you to my hotel room and spend the rest of the night making up for my stupidity in thinking that letting you go was the right thing to do."

"And then . . ."

"And then I'm going to beg you to make room for me in your life."

She levered onto her elbow, her hair falling in a tousled cascade around her face to frame her sated smile. He cupped her breast, relishing the delicacy of her skin. She was so pretty, she made his chest ache.

She tapped the end of his nose with her finger. "Baby, you've got yourself a deal."

The first light of morning streamed through the sheers-covered windows, turning Jenna's bedroom creamy gold. Matt was asleep, sprawled facedown into Jenna's pink pillow, his arms and legs stretched to all four corners of the double mattress. His feet hung off the bed. Her very own sleeping giant, complete with a low rumbling snore.

Jenna had planned from the beginning to hitch a ride back to the farm with Rachel and Vaughn after the wedding reception ended so she could help out with the morning chores. Livestock were notoriously unsympathetic about late-night revelry. Before leaving the reception, she'd let Rachel know she no longer needed a ride, and would be late to help in the morning because she was staying with Matt.

In typical Rachel fashion, she'd accepted the news with dry wit—"About time you two figured it out"—before hurrying through the civic center lobby doors to meet Vaughn, who was pulling his truck around.

Despite that their feet were tired from dancing, Jenna and Matt had fast-walked across the parking lot to the hotel, anxious to be alone again in Matt's room. It was a blessing and a curse that they saw Jake at the hotel check-in counter exchanging harsh words with the front desk worker who'd given his room away because he hadn't checked in and the hotel had been overbooked. Jenna had known instantly how Matt would handle the situation, and had watched with an incongruous mix of pride and disappointment when he handed Jake his key fob.

Jenna's cottage at the farm was more than a half hour away, but she used the drive wisely and had them both breathing hard and half undressed by the time they burst through her front door. Sometime after two, they made it onto her bed and let exhaustion sweep them into slumber.

Now that it was morning, all Jenna wanted to do was stay in bed with Matt. Without rolling from her back for fear of rousing him, she turned her head to check the time. Three minutes until the alarm sounded; then she could no longer deny the coming day or her myriad of responsibilities. Three more heavenly minutes snuggled close to Matt, who was buck naked under the sheet draped across the swell of his ass.

If she worked the covers down with her feet, she might be able to give herself a view to go along with the mental image of the backside that she was presently visualizing. She pointed her toe. The sheet slipped several inches lower, revealing the swell of his butt along with skin knotted with old scars that shone silver and pink.

She'd forgotten about that because she'd been so wrapped up in passion, but now her curiosity was tickled. She flexed, then pointed her toe, tugging the sheet lower until it fell away from his butt to rest on his upper thighs. As she'd discovered with her hands the night before, his backside was gorgeous in its masculinity—defined by hard, rounded muscles and a slight fuzz of dark hair—but it was also covered by a web of scars, some divots, others flat, and a few raised and ropey.

She wanted to touch them, to understand what he'd gone through that had left such angry marks on him. She wanted to know how much more scarring the sheets hid.

She spread her toes and caught an edge of sheet between her big toe and second toe, then gave a jerk of her leg sideways. All that remained under the sheet were his feet. She lifted her head a shade to look.

"Hey." She'd been so intent on her task, she startled at the word.

Matt sounded like he had about a pound of sand stuck in his throat. He wiggled his arm free from under her pillow and slung it over her ribs. His hand cupped the underside of her breast.

"I was trying not to wake you."

"My body has a good internal clock. I bet your alarm's about to—"

The radio burst to life with a fast song in the throes of a banjo solo. Jenna groaned and slammed a hand over the snooze button.

Matt poked his tongue into his cheek like he was trying not to smile. "That radio station has obviously never heard of the banjo rule." He rolled her nipple between his fingers, then gave it a gentle tug.

Pleasure fanned from her breast through her body. "I'll have to write them an e-mail." Her voice was throaty, and it had nothing to do with the early morning wake-up.

In a sudden burst of motion, he shifted, caging her beneath him. The whole length of his body was hot and hard. He opened her legs with his knees and her mouth with a kiss that was demanding, needful. She clung to his back and gave herself over to it.

When he tore his lips from hers, his breathing was labored and his eyes had darkened with desire. Through a lopsided smile, he said, "That was one of the best nights of my life."

She nuzzled his shoulder, drinking in the scent of his skin. "Mine, too."

"The only way I could be happier right now is if we made this official." He brushed his thumb over her cheek, his smile firmly intact.

She had no idea what he was talking about. Official? They'd spent the night dancing and screwing. He'd kissed her in front of both their families. How could they make it any more official?

"Jenna Margaret Sorentino, would you be my shiksa girlfriend?"

She nearly chuckled, the question was so surprising and endearing. "I've been waiting months for you to ask me that. Of course I'll be your shiksa girlfriend, Matthew . . . I don't know your middle name."

"Joel. Matthias Joel Roenick." He punctuated the words with a slow rotation of his hips that rubbed his erection against her folds with a tease of light pressure that made her crave more.

"Matthias?" The words rode out of her throat on a breathy moan. She wrapped her legs around his and stretched her arm to her nightstand, groping in the drawer for a condom. They'd have to make this a quickie because she had promises to keep to Rachel, who'd probably been up and working the farm for a couple hours already.

"Matthias Roenick was my great-great-grandfather's brother, who came out west with him."

She flicked her favorite pink toy out of the way, scrambling to close her fingers over one of the condoms she knew was in there somewhere. "You and your pioneer spirit."

"What are you looking for in there?"

"Condom."

He stretched over and his eyes widened, presumably at her toy collection. But hey, a girl had to pass the lonely nights somehow. He sucked in a breath through his nose, the wheels of his mind clearly turning.

"What?"

He shook his head. "I was trying to figure out a way to justify it, but there's no way we have time to play with these right now, which is really too bad because I'm already having visions about all the things I could do to you with them."

She liked the way he thought, liked it even more that he wasn't threatened by the discovery that she was fully capable of taking her pleasure into her own hands. With one last reach, her fingers closed around a condom. "I can't wait to find out about those visions next weekend."

His shoulders deflated. "Damn it, I hate the way that sounds. I'm going to go crazy without you this week."

She tore the top of the wrapper off, but he grabbed it from her and tossed it on the nightstand, out of reach. *Okay . . .*

She couldn't even recall what an unsheathed man felt like inside her. She hadn't had unprotected sex since Tommy's conception. The idea of going condomless with Matt turned her on like crazy, but not until they'd discussed it properly. In each other's arms with the clock ticking down on their time together wasn't the right moment to swap STD test results and discuss birth control. "You have something different in mind?"

He kissed his way down her stomach. "I thought I'd show you more of my pioneer spirit."

"Did you now?" She looked at the time and tried not to care. Rachel would understand her tardiness this once.

He stretched his legs back and dropped to his stomach between her thighs, continuing the trail of kisses. "Oh, yes. Especially with that brand-new challenge you issued me."

"What challenge was that?"

"I know it's nowhere near the official window of time, but I figured before we got to that"—he motioned to the condom—"I'd see if my mouth could make you hear banjos and like them."

She threw her head back with a husky laugh. He kept surprising her and she loved it. The point of his tongue did a three-sixty loop around her clit that made her forget all the reasons she'd set her alarm in the first place. She curled her toes into the mattress and lost herself in the sensations evoked by Matt's clever, capable tongue.

He must've been paying close attention to her every nuanced reaction because he brought her right to the edge of release, but no further, before sheathing his erection in the condom and thrusting into her.

Unlike the night before when she'd been too lost in lust to care, this time when she gripped his ass, she felt the ridges of his scars and realized how little about Matt's life she knew. Maybe this week apart would be good for them. They could talk on the phone and learn about each other in a whole different way from what sex allowed.

Matt was as deft with intercourse as he was with oral sex and, even though she rarely came this way, she found herself digging for release. She wanted to make it happen with him, not only because she wanted him to see that she could, but because she wanted their sexual encounters to be special, set apart from her other experiences. He must've sensed her concentrated effort because he withdrew and rolled her to her hands and knees, taking her from behind. His hand reached around her hip to swirl her clit, relentless in pursuit of her orgasm.

No doubt about it, he was the most skilled lover she'd ever had—and the most compatible. The idea of spending the rest of her life making love with him turned her on like nothing else. He'd always be like this, sensitive to her needs, insatiable. And he was so deliciously big, with a body to die for, and more alpha male than she'd expected, demanding and—

From out of the blue, she came undone, dropping her head to the mattress, pulsing around him. His hand slipped away from her clit. Gripping her hips, his thrusts grew faster. She breathed into the sheet, taking it, taking him, whatever that meant, whatever he wanted. She'd never felt like this before, with her heart and body open and full of feeling.

He slammed himself balls deep, grinding into her and sending ripples of pleasure through her as he grunted his release. She smiled into the sheet, dreaming of a million more mornings like this one.

He withdrew and gave her a gentle push that tipped her sideways on the bed, gave her ass a playful smack, then stepped away to clean up.

"Challenge met," she purred as she ogled his back.

He looked up from the tissue he'd wrapped around the condom and smiled her favorite dimpled smile. "You heard banjos?"

"And then some. Maybe even harpsichord."

He mock-frowned at her. "I was with you on the banjo

part, but you can't fool me—it's never the right time for harpsichord. Ever."

Chuckling, she rolled to her back. How in the heavens was she going to get her noodly legs to function enough to be any help to Rachel?

Matt flopped onto the bed next to her and kissed her forehead. "How about I stay around Catcher Creek today? Tonight after Tommy goes to sleep, we can do this again before I hit the road."

She bit her lip, considering. She had study group tonight and she wasn't quite sure why she hesitated to tell Matt. He already knew her secret, but she supposed old habits died hard.

She mentally shook some sense into herself. "I have virtual study group every Sunday night at eight, so that won't work unless you stayed super late. But that's not a good idea because neither of us has gotten much sleep the past few nights and I don't like the thought of you making a three-hour drive in the middle of the night while exhausted."

"I hate to admit it, but you make a good point."

"How about you plan on staying next weekend with me and Tommy at Kellan's house? We'll still be there house-sitting."

"When does that start?"

"Today. After I get Tommy from the sitter's house at nine, we'll come back here and do more chores, then plan on being at Kellan's ranch before nightfall. His dog, Max, will be wanting his dinner by then. The ranch hands and his fore-man are taking care of the livestock, but Kellan wanted someone around at night to keep Max company." She slid her fingers over his arm and took his hand. "Even though tonight won't work, you'll still spend the day with us, right?"

He hesitated. "Are you sure it's the right thing for Tommy? You and I are pretty brand-new."

A hollow space opened up inside her. Had he just insinuated what she thought he had? Was he hedging his bets? She took her hand back and pushed to a seated position. "I don't understand. Tommy already loves you. He talks about you all the time. Heck, you cut up his chicken at the rehearsal dinner and taught him the Watermelon Crawl."

"I know, and I really like the little guy, but everything changes now, doesn't it? Now that we're dating, I don't want to confuse him."

She drew a steadying breath and took his hands, hoping to make him see the fallacy of his logic. "That's like heading into a relationship expecting it to fail," she said gently. "It's no different than a wedding pre-nup. I'd never introduce Tommy right away to a new boyfriend I'd been set up with on a blind date or a guy I met online, somebody I needed to vet first. But it's different with you. I'm sorry if it scares you, but I'm in this to try for forever." A new humiliating possibility occurred to her. What if his reluctance wasn't about a fear of commitment, but about a disinterest in it? "Please tell me this wasn't about the thrill of the hunt for you."

He seemed genuinely appalled. "Hey, it's not like that with me."

"But?"

"But nothing. No hidden agenda. I've dated women with kids before, so I know the drill. That's what they all said. They didn't want me to confuse their kids or get their hopes up or anything until we . . . you know."

What they all said? she wanted to ask. *How many is all?*

She had no delusions that a good-looking, hot-blooded sex god of a man like Matt wouldn't have a dating history.

But acknowledging the existence of a trail of ex-girlfriends was vastly different from lumping her into the same general group as them.

"You know the drill?" she asked instead. "Are girlfriends like boot camp, or are we more of the fire-drill variety?"

He winced. "Fine. Not the best choice of words." His thumb depressed each finger, cracking each knuckle in turn. "Look, I'm trying not to push you too fast. I have a history of making that kind of mistake, okay?"

Again with being roped into the same corral as his exes. Buzzing with frustration, she couldn't get her brain to stop repeating Matt's voice in his SUV, spouting from memory the most romantic line she'd ever heard a man say.

True love is not about finding a person you can live with. It's about finding the person you can't live without.

Zap, like lightning, she was furious and frustrated. All of a sudden the happiness her two sisters had found seemed nigh impossible. How had they managed to find men who were crazy about them when the reality of modern dating was so completely FUBAR?

Whoa there, girl. Your scars are showing. She threw the breaks on her toxic line of thought and aimed her face at the ceiling, closing her eyes. Stupid daddy issues. A part of her would always be that girl who was ready to battle, to fight against being ignored or shoved aside or minimized. It was such bullshit that she had to keep dragging that anchor when she was a self-sufficient single mom on the verge of being a college graduate forging a new career as an engineer. A goddamn engineer, for Pete's sake.

Large, strong hands cradled her cheeks. She opened her eyes to see Matt looking down at her, his face close enough to kiss. His gaze burned with intensity. "Jenna, I'm all in. You said you were waiting for me to notice you, but my mind and my heart have been stuck on you since the first time we met. You, me, and Tommy—it's what I want. But I just . . ." He gave a tight shake of his head, distress infusing his features.

Like a second jolt of lightning, Tara's plea for her not to break his heart came back to her. "My mind and heart are stuck on you too." She spread her palms over his collarbone. "Which is why it's time for you to tell me why you're so afraid of us."

Chapter Ten

Matt's jaw tightened, his eyes grew sharp. "That's a fair question. You're right—I am afraid of us, and it has to do with the injuries I promised to explain today. But is now the right time? Rachel's expecting you."

"This is more important."

Nodding, his lips a stiff, thin line, he stretched to his back next to her. "When I was in my early twenties, I was gung-ho into long-distance road cycling. Seventy-five or a hundred-mile routes were my norm, sometimes farther. One Sunday when I was twenty-two, I was hit by a truck near San Ysidro. Not hit so much as run over."

"You were badly hurt."

His brows flickered as he huffed. "The bike caught somewhere on the truck's undercarriage and it dragged me along the road until the driver realized what he'd done. I was impaled by the bike frame. Most of the skin on my groin, left leg, and lower back sloughed off."

Aching for what he'd gone through and trying not to visualize the accident or what it'd done to his body, she reached for his hand and took a firm hold of it.

"I blacked out and when I came to three days later, I was in a hospital ICU. They'd patched me up during a fifteen-hour marathon surgery, then induced a coma so I could heal. For the first week after I was brought back to consciousness, my family and I spent every waking moment thanking God I was alive and hadn't lost any limbs or suffered brain damage."

Jenna didn't see what his accident had to do with his fear of relationships, but she was horrified at what he'd lived through and profoundly grateful that he had indeed lived.

"But then, once I was stable and off the heaviest pain meds, a urologist paid me a visit."

He sat and swung his legs off the bed.

Jenna stared at his scarred backside, her heart sinking. A urologist? Clearly, something had gone terribly wrong during the accident, but she'd spent a lot of quality time with his goods in the past twelve hours and knew they were in excellent working order. "You were injured . . . down there? Worse than your skin coming off?"

He grabbed a sheet of paper from the pad on her nightstand and crumpled it. "According to the doctor, my groin looked so messed up and the procedure to fix the area was so delicate that before the plastic surgeon did his thing, the urologist was called to draw sperm out to save in case they weren't able to put me back together down there."

He attempted to make a basket into the trash can under the window, but missed. Shaking his head, he ripped another paper, crushed it in his palm, and attempted another shot.

Jenna scrambled up and knelt behind him. She wrapped her arms around him and pressed her lips to his shoulder. "They obviously put you back together just fine. So what was the problem?"

"The problem was that there was no mature sperm to take. Lo and behold, I was born with a freak genetic anomaly called Sertoli-cell-only syndrome—SCO. It's permanent and untreatable." He threw the paper at the trash can again. This time, it went in. For the first time since he'd said the word *urologist*, he looked her in the eye. "I was a mangled piece of raw meat after that collision. I was impaled, of all the nasty things, so who would've guessed that the accident's most monumental, long-term effect on my life was finding out I could never father a child?"

Oh. Wow. Reaction was everything. He twisted his neck and looked at her, studying, gauging. Giving her no time to craft the perfect expression, or even decide what it was. "There's more to life than having children."

He rotated his neck. "Okay, yeah, except I want children. I want a family. I know that sounds petulant, like I'm dwelling on the one thing in life I can never have, but even beside that, my situation has made dating"—he swirled his tongue in his mouth as though searching for the right word—"challenging. I mean, when is the right time to bring up something like that? The first date, the tenth? There's no good way. I've dated women who swore it didn't matter to them right up until it did."

"Fathering a child and being a dad are two totally different things. Just because you can't do one doesn't mean you're barred from doing the other. Any kid would be lucky to have you as a dad. My kid would be lucky to have you as a dad."

His expression was distant, like he'd heard it all before and didn't believe a word of it. He slapped his hand over the wallet on the nightstand and flipped it open, then tossed three pictures of children on the pillow.

"Who are they?"

"Brandon, Stephy, and Jordy. Stephy and Jordy are siblings. I had long-term, monogamous, live-in relationships with their moms when I was in my twenties. Stephy and Jody's mom left me to get back together with the kids' biological father. And Brandon's mom and I just weren't meant to be for a lot of reasons. When each of the relationships didn't work out, I had to say good-bye to these wonderful, innocent kids who I'd fallen in love with and thought I was going to be a dad to. It destroyed me, knowing I'd never see them again."

Jenna was getting it now, his hang-ups about relationships, why he hadn't asked her out months ago. This was the storm she'd seen in him, the reason Tara had warned her against breaking his heart. People were so fragile. Even big, strong men like Matt who seemed to have the world on a string were made of glass. As she was. As it turned out her parents had been, and her sisters. Carson, too.

Matt fingered the edge of one of the pictures. "I've got this fight going on inside me. I'm an optimistic, happy person. Always have been and that's who I'm determined to be. I never want to forget about what a beautiful place this world is or how lucky I am to be alive, but sometimes it's hard not to turn cynical. I have triggers and when they hit, it's like a battle zone inside me."

"Last night at the wedding. You got upset at your dad after Kellan's announcement that Amy was pregnant. Was that a trigger?"

"Yes, big-time. My dad knew it, too, and he was trying to console me, but I'm so tired of everyone in my family looking at me with pity. I went outside to get away from all the happiness and celebrating. That's when I realized I was letting fear and bitterness get the better of me."

"That's why you kissed me."

He rolled his gaze from the photographs to her. "It wasn't why I kissed you. I kissed you because I've wanted to since the moment I first laid eyes on you. But the epiphany I had last night broke the chains that were holding me back from going after what I really wanted. Who I wanted." He swallowed. "I want you in my life. I hope forever. But I've learned the hard way that what I want only goes so far."

He gathered the photographs in his hand. "You have to do me the courtesy of telling me up front if you can't handle the fact that I could never give you children if things worked out between us. If there's any part of you that thinks it'll be an issue down the road, you've got to let me go. Please. I know that's a lot to ask, but I'm not sure I could survive losing you and Tommy."

This wasn't supposed to be happening, making decisions that would ripple out for the rest of her life with a man she'd never even been on a date with. She was all in. She'd said it; she believed it. But she wanted more kids, siblings for Tommy. Could she be okay with adoption? She'd like to think she would be, but she'd never given it much thought.

Her instinct was to suggest they take it slower than this. One step at a time. But he was right. If she let him into Tommy's life as a father figure, she didn't take that lightly, either. Nor did she take it lightly that Matt was placing his heart in her hands for safekeeping.

And so she would think about children with Matt, even though she was ninety-nine percent sure she already knew her answer. His experience might dictate his fears, but her experiences had informed her choices, too.

She hugged him with all her strength. "I promise I'll think about it, but I'm smart enough to cherish what's right in front of me instead of making plans for what I don't have and might never get anyhow."

"I'm so sorry to dump that all on you, but I can't . . . I don't—"

She cut off his struggle for words with a kiss and she kept on soothing him with her lips and stroking his body with her hands until she felt his shoulders relax and his posture ease. "I'll think about it, I promise. But give me today with you, please. It won't scar Tommy to spend time with one of his favorite grown-ups. You're around our family a lot normally, so he won't think anything of it. Would you do that for me? I'm not ready to let you go."

He crushed another paper in his hand and tossed another basket that banked off the rim and went wide. "I don't know if that's a good idea. You have a lot to consider."

True, but that wasn't going to happen until after her full day of chores and mommy business and study group were over. She walked her fingers up his arm. "You could help with the farm chores this morning."

A sardonic smile accompanied his eye roll. "Now there's a tantalizing offer."

She stretched her palms across his pecs, copping a feel. The muscles bunched. "Are you flexing for me?"

"You seem to like it when I do that. You want me to stop?"

"Heck, no." She squeezed, awed enough by his bulging muscle that she nearly busted out with some country twang—*dayam*. "What was I saying? Oh, and after the farm chores, I could really use a big, muscly man to help move all our stuff into Kellan's house."

"You'd better watch it or there won't be enough room in your bed for me and my giant ego." Despite his words, he relaxed then flexed again, making his pecs jump. How could she possibly think of farm chores at a time like this?

As if reading her mind, his attention shot to her night-stand drawer. "Do you hear what I hear?"

She cocked her head, listening. The room was silent save for the buzz of the tractor engine in the distance. "The tractor?"

Her legs were swept out from under her as she was

tossed on the bed. Matt looked her over, his dark gaze raking over her body. "I think I hear more banjos . . ."

Under the late afternoon sun, Kellan's ranch was quiet, save for a handful of workers near the feed sheds and office buildings in the distance and the faraway hum of farm machinery. Grazing cattle dotted the hillsides and pastures.

His rustic wood, two-story house sat in the middle of rolling desertscape and fields of dry, wild grass and shrubs amid his booming cattle business. Matt had been there plenty of times over the years, for parties, meetings about oil rights deals he was helping with, and the like, but he had to admit that the idea of spending the next weekend there with Jenna and Tommy felt weird.

Oh well. Kellan wouldn't care, and as long as Matt and Jenna made use of the guest room for their recreational activities, Matt shouldn't care either. By next weekend, he'd probably be so desperate to be near Jenna again that he wouldn't remember his own name, much less whose house they were staying at.

Matt pulled his SUV into the gravel yard between the stable and the house, lining it up next to Jenna's car. They'd driven separately because he'd be leaving for Santa Fe later that evening, as soon as he could make himself say goodbye and face the week alone. He smiled at Jenna, who was still in the driver's seat. She made big eyes at him and tipped her head toward the house.

Matt followed her line of sight. Jake sat on the porch steps, a cell phone next to him. He watched Matt's SUV and Jenna's car with dull eyes. His hair was a mess and his beard had returned to the mangy look it'd had when they'd picked him up in the Sandia Mountains. Deep scuff marks cut into the dirt below his feet as though he'd been sitting in that same spot for a long time, shuffling his shoes.

Intrigued, Matt left the groceries he, Jenna, and Tommy had picked up from town on their way over in the back of his car and walked across the yard while Jenna unbuckled Tommy from his booster seat.

"Hey, Jake. I thought you were headed to L.A. today."

"Change of plans."

Matt took a seat on the porch step next to him. "Is everything okay?"

Jake swallowed and rocked back, his heavy expression focused on Tommy, who was bounding toward him.

"Uncle Jake, what're you doing here?"

Jake gripped the porch stair as though bracing for impact.

Matt leapt up to intercept Tommy. Snagging him around the middle, he twirled the little boy, setting him down in the opposite direction. "Hey, buddy, why don't you go see if Kellan's dog is sleeping in the barn?"

Tommy looked from Matt to his mom, then at Jake, clearly sensing that something was up. Thank goodness he had enough sense to go along with Matt's suggestion and took off skipping toward the barn.

Jenna propped a hip against the side of the house. "Are you hungover?"

Jake scratched his fingers through the hair on his chin. "I wish. Hell, I'd be drunk right now except I couldn't find any liquor in Kellan's place. The man's a fucking saint." He squeezed his hands together, hunching into his elbows, eyes on the ground.

Matt and Jenna shared a look of concern. Not counting the fact that he'd walked in on the guy banging his sister, Matt liked Jake. He'd driven through the night to make his brother's wedding, pulled off a great speech along with the rest of the best-man duties, and kept his personal troubles under wraps so as not to darken Kellan's big day.

He eased onto the top porch step and mimicked Jake's posture. "What happened?"

"My partner died. His sister called this morning. He didn't make it." Sniffing, he wiped the back of his hand across his face and shook his head.

Oh, man. That was brutal. Jenna made a sound of pain and frustration. Her arm fell around Jake's shoulders in a hug that he didn't return.

"His last word was calling my name. Back in the alley. I turned around and he was on the ground, eyes rolled back, the freakiest expression on his face. And now he's gone."

"I'm so sorry," Jenna said.

Jake indulged in more head shaking. "His family's taking him to Cheyenne to be buried. I got a message from my department that the squad's holding a service too, but I already told his sister I'd be at the memorial in Cheyenne. To represent, you know? I don't know if I have it in me to do both."

Matt and Jenna nodded in tandem because that was what Jake seemed to need, even though Matt couldn't possibly relate to what he was going through, having never lost anyone close to him. The only grief he felt was for a dream of fatherhood, as if a dead dream could possibly compare to the loss of a life.

Tommy and Max came running up, the dog far older and grizzled than Matt recalled. Nevertheless, it matched Tommy's stride, woofing and hopping with glee, too excited to keep all paws on the ground.

Jenna met them before they'd reached the porch and knelt, petting Max and accepting sloppy dog kisses on her chin.

"How'd you end up at Kellan's ranch?" Matt asked.

"With Kellan on his honeymoon, this seemed like as good a place as any to crash while my car gets fixed for the trip to Cheyenne. Tara gave me a lift on her way out of town. I figured I'd get one of Kellan's workers to let me in, but the door lock was easy enough to jimmy. You country people are the worst when it comes to home security, by the way."

So he and Tara had spent the night together, which Matt could've lived without knowing, but oh well. "Don't I know it. If your car's not ready by next week, then I'm sure Kellan wouldn't mind if you took his truck."

"Yeah, I figured that, too. What are you and Jenna doing here?"

"Jenna was going to house-sit for Kellan to take care of his dog, but it looks like now she doesn't need to."

Jake cursed under his breath and hung his head lower. "I don't want to interfere with your plans, Jenna."

Jenna took a break from petting Max to give a wave of her hand. "I don't mind. In fact, it'd really help me out if you could keep an eye on Max this week. I've got a lot going on and work is always easier to do at home."

"What?" Tommy threw his hands up and drilled Jenna with a look of pure, childish outrage. "I want to stay at Uncle Kellan's house. That's not fair." He stomped his foot. "You're so mean."

Jenna braked so hard her boots turned up the earth below them. "Excuse me?"

If Matt were Tommy's dad, he'd have grabbed him by the scruff of his shirt and hauled him behind the barn for a private talking-to about respecting his mom. But all he was at liberty to do was watch along with Jake.

He wished he could've seen the look on Jenna's face that accompanied her next words. "You've got about two seconds to apologize before life as you know it gets a whole lot harder."

The stubborn kid narrowed his eyes at her and stomped his foot again.

"He's dead meat," Jake whispered.

Matt nodded, expecting Jenna to make a move toward Tommy, but she folded her arms over her chest and shifted her weight to one hip. "What gets taken away first?"

Just like that, Tommy's posture deflated. "My Transformers."

"That's right. And what's next?"

Tommy's eyes morphed from dragon to puppy dog. "Not dessert. Please don't take away my dessert."

An index finger speared toward the house. "Then you'd better apologize to Uncle Jake and Matt for your outburst, then get your butt in the car. Uncle Jake's going to stay at Uncle Kellan's house for a few days. It's a grown-up decision, so you're going to have to live with it."

"I wish I was a grown-up."

"Someday, sweetie. Now do as I said and apologize."

Tommy trudged to the porch stairs and mumbled the most insincere apology Matt had ever heard. In his periphery, he saw Jake's body shaking and looked up to see him in the throes of silent laughter that looked suspiciously like crying except for the pained smile on his lips. He swiped at his watering eyes.

Matt held his hand out, palm up, to Tommy. "Give me five, buddy. Sorry it's not going to work out like you want, but you can't sass your mom."

Tommy slapped Matt's hand, his hangdog expression lengthening. "I know. Now my Transformers are going in a time-out. At least I still get dessert. Bye, Uncle Jake. Max likes to sleep in the kitchen so don't forget to leave a light on for him." He shuffled to the car, his head hung so low that he couldn't see where he was going and bumped into the car door.

Jake snorted in amusement at Tommy's blunder, then stood and wiped his eyes. "Jenna, I don't want to disappoint Tommy. I can get a hotel room."

Shaking her head at his request, she bridged the distance to the porch. "Giving in after a tantrum like that wouldn't do him or me any favors. Besides, I was serious about this helping me out. I've got a lot on my plate this week." She threw her arms around Jake. He didn't exactly hug her back, but he didn't balk either. "We're family now, Jake. Don't forget that. Whatever you need, you let me know, okay?"

"Thanks." His voice was gruff with emotion. Rubbing his head, he turned away, climbing the stairs with heavy footfalls like he needed a moment to regroup.

"Are you following me out?" she asked Matt.

He shook his head. "Thought I'd stick around, unload the groceries, that kind of thing." Jake might not consider himself a people person, but there were times in every man's life when being alone wasn't the wisest choice. Fully aware that Tommy was watching from the car, he made do with pecking Jenna's cheek. "I'll stop by your place tonight before I head to Santa Fe."

"I'm looking forward to it."

Matt waved the pair away, grabbed the groceries from his car, and set them near the front door, then joined Jake where he'd resettled on a wicker porch chair.

They sat in silence, staring out at the expanse of land that stretched as far as the eye could see in every direction, dotted with buildings that were part of Kellan's beef business—a double wide trailer that looked like office space, a large building Matt thought might be the slaughterhouse, and a smattering of worker bunkhouses and storage sheds. Other than that, all he could see was high desert prairie, a maze of fences, busy workers, and grazing cattle.

Sitting there, Matt's mind inevitably wandered into the

unsavory territory of his conversation with Jenna that morning. He'd laid everything on the line for her—his heart, his secret, his future—and put the ball in her court. What would she choose once she had the time to mull over everything they'd discussed?

Thinking about kids and the future was a lot to ask of a woman before they'd really spent much time together romantically, but he had to know where Jenna stood before he fell even more deeply in love with her. More than anything, he didn't want her to feel like she was settling by being with him. He didn't want to be with someone who felt like she was sacrificing her dreams if she chose to be his wife. That wouldn't be fair to either of them.

"No offense, man," Jake said, cutting into his ever-darkening thoughts, "but I'm not really up for company."

Matt nodded. He wasn't the best company right now either, it turned out. "Didn't figure so. But I have a proposition."

Jake scowled. "Shoot."

Matt propped a boot up on the porch rail. "That's exactly what I was thinking. Are you in the mood for some hunting?"

"Now?"

"Yeah, now. Why not? It's hot as hell, but I don't mind. Do you?"

Jake tipped back in his chair. "Heat doesn't bother me. What do you want to hunt?"

Matt shrugged. "The rabbits will be out around sundown to feed, so will the coyotes. As long as we stay on Kellan's land, we can pretty much shoot whatever we want. I figure we can ride out and see what we find."

"Ride?"

Here's where he might lose Jake's buy-in, but Matt didn't feel like walking and trucks were too noisy. "On horses."

Jake snorted and dropped the chair back onto all four legs. "Horses aren't my gig."

"You'll like it, I swear. I'll set you up with a good, even-tempered horse. Kellan's got lots of horses to choose from."

"What if I hate it?"

Matt smiled. "Then I guess you won't have to eat barbe-cued rabbit for dinner."

"Say I do go along with this crazy-ass plan. I have my department-issued piece"—he flipped the hem of his shirt up to reveal a black pistol in a black nylon belt clip—"but that doesn't cut it for hunting game and it doesn't help you out any. Where are you going to get rifles or shotguns on such short notice?"

Matt lowered his boot and leveled an *Are you kidding me?* look at him. Only a city slicker would ask a question like that. "You haven't spent much time in the country, have you?"

Chapter Eleven

Jenna passed the rest of the day in two places at once. Half her mind remained in the present with Tommy while the other half was stuck on the conversation she'd had with Matt that morning. She'd been serious when she'd told him that she knew better than to pine for what she didn't have at the sacrifice of the blessings she already had in her life, but she'd always assumed she'd have more kids.

Not that Matt had intimated that they wouldn't have kids. Quite the opposite, actually. It was just that they couldn't conceive them biologically, and so the issue weighing heaviest on her mind was about adoption, which she'd never given much thought to. Adoption was a scary idea filled with problems and concerns that were borne mostly out of her ignorance on the subject, but they were concerns nonetheless. There was something satisfying about the idea of adoption, though. Giving a loving home to children who needed it was a worthwhile argument to consider.

It wasn't like pregnancy had been the most glorious feeling ever. With Tommy, she'd been sick and bloated for months, feeling like a whale, even after she gave birth. It'd taken her nearly six months to lose the baby weight and feel normal again. She would miss nursing, one part of her body's transformation she'd loved. And she'd really miss feeling a baby kick and move inside her.

Though she diligently considered the many facets of the issue throughout the evening, her mind kept looping back to how screwed up it was that she and Matt had spent only one night together, yet she was already having to think about what she wanted in a forever sense. It was too much, too fast. But wasn't this what she wanted? Matt, however he came. She'd told him he could take it to the bank that he could trust her with his secrets and she took that promise very seriously.

Matt had texted her that afternoon that he and Jake had decided to go on an evening hunt on Kellan's land, so he'd be later to her house than he'd expected and would call when he was on his way. Killing cute, innocent animals as a way of dealing with grief was the most screwed-up thing Jenna had ever heard, but she wrote it off as guy logic, which would be a waste of energy trying to understand.

At seven thirty, she tucked her curious little guy into his bed with lots of kisses, hugs, and promises to answer the rest of his questions about the wedding and Jake in the morning over breakfast. She closed his door, then gathered dirty laundry and toys in her arms as she walked to the living room. Cringing at the disaster her cottage had become while she'd given all her focus over to the wedding, she managed a quick tidying of the areas in the living room that were in view of the webcam in preparation for her virtual study group, which started at eight.

She reawakened her computer and found her notes from last week's lecture on microcontroller architecture in her desk drawer. Midterms were next week, which seemed impossible given that the two summer-school classes had only started a month ago, but these accelerated summer courses were fast and intense.

Those were two words she could use to describe her and Matt's relationship, now that they'd decided to make a go of it. Situations like this were probably how the adage *Be careful what you wish for* got started.

Then again, Jenna had a terrible habit of overcomplicating issues. Maybe the situation with Matt was simpler than she was making it. Maybe her choice to give up the dream of having more children of her own came down to the fact that she couldn't imagine standing in front of Matt and telling him that he wasn't enough. Not because she pitied him, but because she cared about him so darn much. Besides that, she didn't like what it would say about her if she'd willingly give up the love of a great man who'd be a great father to Tommy because bringing one healthy, beautiful baby into the world had left her wanting more. How greedy would that be?

It wasn't like the world was teeming with men she was perfectly compatible with, who would also love her son, support her career, and had solid careers of their own—and who loved to dance. Yeah, Matt was one in a million. One in a billion, more like it. She'd be a fool to let him go.

She pulled up the video chat forum on her computer with ten minutes to spare and spread her notes and index cards on the table. How was she supposed to focus on studying with so much else happening in her life?

Headlights shone in the driveway at the same time she heard the rumble of a car engine. Her heart flip-flopped. Matt. He'd forgotten to call first, but no big deal. At least he'd come after Tommy was in bed so they could give each other a proper parting kiss . . . or perhaps a quickie to tide them over for the week. If she was a couple minutes late to study group, then no big deal.

She lighted to the door. Out of habit, she peeked through the blinds of the window. The vehicle was a hulking black truck she didn't recognize, and that put her instantly on alert. Who would dare come around without calling first after dark on a Sunday evening?

She looked again. It was tough to see beyond the glare of the headlights, but sitting in the driver's seat she could just make out the silhouette of a man.

She double-checked that the front door was locked, then flipped the blinds closed and jogged to the bookshelves on the far side of the room. Standing on her computer desk chair, she grabbed the shotgun from the top shelf, behind the row of books. She could call Rachel and Vaughn for backup once her gun was loaded, cocked, and ready for action.

Her heart pounding like crazy, she jumped down and darted to the kitchen for the shells that were in a locked box on the shelf above the refrigerator, cursing herself for child-proofing her emergency defense system so completely that it wasn't much good for defending her and Tommy unless the emergency was happening in slow motion.

A knock sounded on the front door. A light, friendly knock—two raps with a knuckle, like a neighbor might do. But she wasn't taking any chances. Shaky with adrenaline, she fumbled with the combination lock on the box of shells and had to start over twice.

Finally, the lock gave way. She grabbed two shells and loaded one after another into the shotgun, then cocked it. The knock came again, louder and less polite this time.

She didn't have a peephole. So few people came to Jenna's house, it'd never been an issue. Looking out the window adjacent to the door was good enough. But she wasn't about to look out the window and put herself face-to-face with the unexpected visitor. She stuffed her cell phone in her pocket, ready to call for help if need be, then pointed her gun at the door and crept closer.

"Who is it?" she called.

"Open up, Jenna."

The man's voice was unfamiliar. A brand-new fear crawled up her spine to hear her name from a stranger.

She stood on a chair to look through the blinds without opening them. When she saw who it was, the shotgun fell from her hands. A strangled gasp was all she was capable of as her soul, her very life, drained out of her. The shotgun landed on the ground with a deafening bang.

Flinching in shock at the unexpected sound, she stumbled, falling with flailing arms and legs from the chair. She landed hard on her back with the wind knocked clean out of her.

"Jesus Christ, did you just try to shoot me?" he hollered.

She lay on her back, staring at the ceiling and gasping for air, too terrified to move. Holy fuck. Holy, holy fuck.

The doorknob rattled; then the door burst open. "Oh, shit! Did you shoot yourself, Jenna?"

He dropped to his knees next to her, looking over her body with wide eyes and his hands out in front of him as if he was scanning for injuries through the air with his palms.

"You're too pale. Can you talk? Were you shot? You better tell me or I'm going to start stripping your clothes off, looking for blood."

He touched her shoulder and she nearly jumped out of her skin. Please let this be a hallucination, a nightmare, anything but real. His face was fuller than she remembered, with a hint of facial hair below the skin of his clean-shaven face. Laugh lines bookended his lips and he wore a military tattoo prominently on his arm.

"Say something, damn it. You're freaking me out."

She shook away from his touch and swallowed back the dinner climbing up her throat. "Carson."

He sighed and rested on his haunches. "I told you I'd be back."

Jenna's life would never be the same again. Nothing was going to happen the way she wanted—not her plans for the future with Matt or what she hoped for Tommy—and there wasn't anything she could do to stop the inevitable as it came at her like an avalanche.

All she'd wanted was to get out of town before this happened. She'd been so close. Weeks away. She thought about the pictures of Tommy hanging on the walls and her desk, on the bookshelves and TV stand. Photographic evidence of him was everywhere.

Not to mention the possibility that the shotgun blast had woken Tommy. He was a deep sleeper, but still. If he woke, he might come to investigate. And then what?

Her mind howled. She'd been so close to finishing her plans. So very close. And in the blink of an eye, it was over. She had no idea what the next five minutes would hold, much less the next days, months, and years.

She couldn't tear her eyes from him as she stood, nor he from her. He tried to help her, but she refused. Once she was up, they just stood there staring at each other, Jenna trying not to throw up and Carson thinking God-only-knew-what.

"Did you really try to shoot me?"

Jenna flexed her fingers. She swung her focus to the shotgun, then to the smattering of holes in the wall below the window. "No, I . . ."

The sound of Jenna's cell phone made both of them jump. It sat on her desk, glowing and vibrating as Matt's ringtone played.

Oh, God. Matt was on his way here. She couldn't have him walk in on this. Even if she could convince Carson to go away before he found out about the truth about Tommy, she needed time and space to figure out what she was going to do before she could even think about what to tell Matt.

Which meant she had to answer the phone. First, she had

to get Carson out of the house before he saw Tommy's pictures. He was already looking around, taking stock of the place.

She took her phone in hand and pointed it at the door. "Wait outside for me. Please."

His eyes continued giving the room a once-over. He pointed to the toy bin next to the sofa. "You have a kid."

Her stomach lurched. "Yes. And we're not going to wake him up with this conversation. Wait on the bench outside and I'll be right there."

She opened her arms wide and was walking his way to usher him toward the door when the video chat chimed from her computer. She turned and saw Carrie smiling into the camera. "Hey, Jenna. I hear you in the room. I'm early so we could chat about the wedding."

She backtracked to get in view of the webcam. "Hi, something's come up here. I can't do study group. I'll tell you more later."

The ringtone sounded again. The last ring before it flipped to voice mail. She pressed the *accept call* button. Carrie was saying something with a baffled expression, asking a question maybe, but Jenna couldn't hear her.

Jenna looked at the camera on the top of her computer and pointed to the phone. "Got to take this call. I'll talk to you soon."

She closed the computer lid, aware at how rude that was to Carrie. She'd have to make up a worthy excuse for her bad behavior later, but she was in full damage-control mode now and nothing was going to slow her down, not even good manners.

"Hi. I'm just finishing something up," she said into the phone. Carson stopped at the door and squatted, bringing the shotgun up with him as he came. Her throat constricted, seeing him armed like that in her house. He had to be at least fifty pounds of muscle heavier than he had been when he'd left Catcher Creek and he had a dangerous edge to him now that the sweet-natured misfit Carson she'd known never had.

"Jenna, are you still there?"

She shook her head, chasing the disparate thoughts away. "I'm here. Listen, can I put you on hold for a sec while I free up my hands?" At Matt's hesitant assent, she muted the call.

Carson looked natural with a gun in his hands. Most Catcher Creek men did, as rural as their town was, so it shouldn't have bothered her, but it did. It scared the hell out of her because it got her remembering his fury before he'd left town. Violent fury that had wanted to burn the whole world down. She'd realized in that final confrontation between them that the boy who'd been her best friend was lost forever.

He opened the chamber, popped the spent shell and removed the second one, which he pocketed. Then he propped the shotgun between the chair and the window and looked her way. "You gonna take that call or what?"

She released a ragged exhale, blinking. She'd forgotten about Matt on the line. "Yes. Wait outside. I'll be right there."

"I'm not leaving until we talk. I want you to know that. You and I have unfinished business that's six years overdue."

Boy howdy, did they ever. And if there was any way she could bargain with God to let her live the rest of her life out without finishing that business, she'd give just about anything. "Okay, I know. Just, please. Outside."

Nodding, he walked out and stood just beyond the door, inspecting the spot below the window where the shotgun spray had hit from the inside. He glanced her way. "Not too much damage. Nothing a little putty and paint can't fix."

She nodded. Whatever. She wasn't going to be in this

house much longer anyway. As soon as she could get Carson off her property, she'd start packing.

Wow. That was it, wasn't it? Tonight, she was going to have to grab Tommy and run—her backup plan if Carson ever returned. She'd reasoned it out years ago, but never thought she'd have to go through with it. Funny how life was. She was close to making the move anyway. But close didn't cut it, not with her worst-case scenario unfolding before her eyes. The thought of abandoning all her plans and running away to Santa Fe got her heart racing all over again in panic.

With a hand on her chest, she shut the front door, took a few calming breaths so Matt wouldn't hear any hint of strain in her voice and unmuted the phone. "Hey, good-lookin'. Sorry to make you wait like that. How's Jake?"

Matt sank into his chair, staring at the blank touch screen on the phone long after his call with Jenna had ended. She'd asked him not to come over. Straight up told him to leave her alone tonight. And with his work schedule and her school, it'd be next weekend before he saw her again—if he saw her again. The calm he'd found by hunting with Jake was evaporating.

It'd been a great afternoon. In minutes flat, he and Jake had rustled up more than enough firepower to hunt with. The rifle from Kellan's truck, the shotgun that had been hanging over his fireplace, and a backup from Kellan's foreman, who'd also pointed them to the ranch's impressive stash of ammo. Jake's amusement at the ease with which they'd armed themselves for the hunt had been enough to get Matt out of his head. It was nice to see Jake's grief lift a little, if only briefly.

The relief from Matt's troubles had shattered the moment

he'd heard Jenna's tense, distant voice on the line. Then again, what had he expected? He'd dropped a bomb on her that morning, forcing her to decide now whether she could be with a man like him for the rest of her life without regret.

Judging by her shuttered emotions and request that he not stop by to see her one last time for the week, he could predict what her choice would be. Darkness simmered inside him, but he tried to take solace that this was happening now rather than a year or two down the road. Though he was already falling hard for Jenna, he and Tommy hadn't bonded yet to where he'd suffer devastation at the loss. Sure, he was already half in love with the little guy, but who wouldn't be? The kid was adorable and smart and full of gumption like his mom.

Jake stretched his legs out past the railing of Kellan's back deck, his dinner plate on his lap with nothing but bones from their dinner of barbecued rabbit. "What's up? You headed to Jenna's place?"

Matt set his phone on the railing ledge and poked at the rabbit's foot sitting there. He'd cleaned and saved it as a gift for Tommy, but now he wondered if he'd ever get the chance to give it to him.

"No." He cleared his throat. "She said she has a lot to do tonight, and now that the wedding's over, she's tired."

Jake tossed a bone off the deck into the darkness. "Sounds like a lame chick excuse to me."

Kellan's dog, Max, trotted to the edge of the deck, his eyes following the trajectory of the bone. If the poor thing had been a few years younger, he probably would've lit off after it, but instead he sank to his belly next to Jake's chair.

Matt ground his molars together. "Yeah, it does, doesn't it?"

Jake dropped his hand onto Max's head and gave him a rough scratch between the ears. "How long have you and

Jenna been together? I don't remember seeing you around last Christmas when I was here."

"That's around the time I met Jenna and her sisters, but we just decided to start dating last night at the wedding."

Jake snorted. "Dating. That's one way to put what you two were up to at the wedding. Maybe she thought you were rushing it so she wants to slow things down. That sounds like some kind of wacky logic a chick would dream up."

Matt didn't want to get into the nuts and bolts of his and Jenna's situation with Jake, but the man had a point. Jumping into the sack with Jenna might not have been his brightest move, not because they were rushing it, but because if he hadn't known how sublime their chemistry was in bed, it might've been less painful to absorb the breakup he was more certain by the minute was coming. Maybe then he wouldn't feel as raw and ready to shatter as he did now, waiting for her to issue her verdict.

He forced the dark thoughts away. "I can't believe you'd bring up what happened at the wedding between me and Jenna after what we walked in on. What I should be doing right now is kicking your ass in defense of my sister's honor."

Jake's lips twitched into a jocular smile, but his eyes remained heavy with the dark grief. "I could use a good fight right now, if that's what you want. I might even let you get a few hits in."

Jake was clearly kidding, but Matt sensed the truth in his offer, as well as the pain. He'd lost his partner today. Probably his best friend. Matt could see how sparring might help take away the hurt for a few minutes, as hunting had.

That was the thing about grief. You constantly had to invent new ways to cope, even if it only got the rock off your chest for a few minutes at a time. Too bad Matt wasn't in the mood to show up at work the next day with black eyes and bruises. "Sorry. Fistfighting with an LAPD SWAT officer is right there at the top of my list of things not to do. Ever."

Jake chortled. "Smart man." He winged another bone into the darkness. Max stood, ears up. Jake stroked his back until the old dog lay down again. "Just so we're clear, I'm not sorry about your sister and me. Nobody's honor was compromised or any bullshit like that. There's nothing wrong with two people giving each other what they need, and I definitely needed a distraction from what was going on with . . ." He swallowed, narrowing his eyes at the dark horizon. "With Nick. You probably don't want to hear me say it, but there it is anyway."

All Matt could do was nod. Nope, he definitely didn't need to hear that, but he took comfort in the revelation that he could count on Jake for honesty. That was rare in a friend.

"I liked being on the horse today," Jake said. "I didn't expect to, but it was cool. Wouldn't mind doing that again if I got the chance. Tara said your family breeds and trains horses, so you grew up in a place like this ranch, I guess?"

"Kind of like this, but Circle R Ranch is at a higher elevation so there's more greenery. Kellan's land is set up for cattle breeding, grazing, and beef processing. My family deals in horses so our property has more fences, corrals, and stables, that sort of thing. Another difference is that Kellan's ranch is quieter than my family's because besides breeding horses, my parents run a therapeutic riding center for people with disabilities, so the ranch is always crawling with people and cars. My house is on the property, but a mile away with its own entrance road. One of my older brothers and his family live on the ranch, too, closer to my parents' house."

"I've never heard of horse therapy. Is that like a kind of physical therapy?"

"Physical therapy, mental therapy, all that stuff. Being on a horse is good for the soul."

Jake pressed the bottom of his shoe against the rail and rocked the chair onto its back two legs. "I can see that. That's why you took me out today, isn't it?"

Matt shrugged. "Partly. I like to ride and hunt when I'm down or something's bothering me. You get the benefit of working with a horse, plus in order to hit anything you're trying to shoot, you have to clear your mind."

"If you love horses so much, why didn't you stay in the family biz?"

At the time he'd made his career choice, grief over his SCO diagnosis had been fresh. Being around his family with their pitying attitudes and unwanted advice had made him feel even worse, as had watching all the children and their families coming for equine therapy. "I'm happy as a lawyer."

Jake dropped the front two legs of the chair down with a thunk. "You're a lawyer? How did I miss that? Please don't tell me you're a criminal defense attorney, because if that's the case then we might have to brawl after all. Those dicks make my job harder than it has to be."

"Oil law."

"Okay. I'll give you a pass on that one." He grinned and smacked Matt's shoulder as though to make sure Matt knew he was kidding around, but Jake wasn't the first law officer he'd met with an aversion to attorneys. Cops and lawyers didn't exactly mesh in temperament or personalities.

Come to think of it, the two of them probably looked like the world's oddest pair at the moment—a city cop and a country lawyer. But Matt genuinely liked Jake and got the impression the feeling was mutual.

"How did you decide to become a cop?"

Jake set his plate on the rail ledge and took up his beer bottle. "My dad pushed me to it."

"Oh yeah? But your dad isn't in law enforcement, is he?" Matt thought he would've remembered Kellan mentioning it if that were the case.

Jake huffed. "Not quite. More like a criminal. Went to prison when I was young, he and my mom. All I wanted out of my life was to be the opposite of them in every way, and so I figured what's more opposite from a career criminal than a police officer? When I was going through the academy, I figured out that being a generally pissed-off, fearless son of a bitch worked in my favor. The job was a natural fit."

"I thought there was a saying about an angry cop being a dead cop, or something like that."

"It depends on what you do with the anger. I learned how to control it right away. I also learned to embrace my first training officer's philosophy that when you have the skills, size, and temper to do harm, you also have to be man enough not to."

Matt liked that philosophy. If a miracle happened and Jenna and he worked out and he got to help raise Tommy, that would be a lesson he'd want to pass on to him.

Thinking about becoming a family with Jenna and Tommy made him restless for the solitude of a long, dark drive to Santa Fe. He set his boots on the ground and picked up his phone. "I'd better hit the road. Got to be up early for work tomorrow morning."

Jake stood too and offered Matt his hand to shake. "Hey, thanks for staying today. That was cool of you."

They shook. "You bet. I'm always up for a hunt. Maybe if I come down to Catcher Creek next weekend we can do that again."

"Sounds good to me. I'll probably leave for Cheyenne

next Monday. Hey, don't forget your rabbit's foot." He tossed it to Matt. "It might give you good luck with Jenna."

He needed a whole lot more than luck for things to work out with Jenna. "Thanks."

Matt idled his car under the entrance arch to Kellan's ranch, where the dirt road met the blacktop. The entrance to Jenna's property was to the right, only a couple miles away. He wanted so badly to pop in and remind her of how good they were together. But she'd said she needed time and he owed her that much with the choice he was asking her to make.

It hurt like hell to know she was close, yet out of reach. But like his dad said, doing the right thing wasn't easy. It was damn depressing how often Dad's words rang true in Matt's life. For once, he didn't feel like doing the right thing. He wanted to break rules. Be selfish. Take. It wasn't the man he had been raised to be and went against everything he stood for, but tonight he wanted to fight for Jenna's love, brazenly. He wanted to show her everything she stood to lose if she cut him out of her life.

He looked left, toward the highway. It was nearing eight o'clock and he had a three-hour drive to get home after forty-eight hours of barely sleeping. The prudent thing to do would be to hit the highway while he still had a semblance of energy, rest up for work, and call Jenna in the morning.

"Screw it."

No more wade-in-slowly guy. He sent one last look in the direction of the highway, eased his foot off the brake, and turned right. He needed one more kiss from Jenna, a real kiss this time instead of that peck on the cheek from earlier. Tired of playing it safe, he was going to go after what he wanted, consequences be damned.

Chapter Twelve

The last time Jenna had seen Carson, his face had been swollen and damaged, his body and spirit broken. Since that day, Carson had transformed into a taller, broader version of the lanky farm boy he'd been. Shorter hair, clearer eyes, fighting strong. Clearly, his time in the Marine Corps had hardened more than his body.

Under the yellow glow of Jenna's porch light, they each staked a territory outside. Jenna stood in front of her kitchen window, jumpy with nerves, while Carson paced with measured steps along the white picket fence at the edge of the mangy-grass front yard, his face a web of shadows.

"You've changed," she said in the tense silence.

"You haven't."

He wasn't really seeing her then, if he thought she hadn't changed. Jenna doubted there was another person in Catcher Creek who had undergone such a radical overhaul as she had since finding out she was pregnant.

That was what made the past so hard to reconcile. She'd relive that night with Carson on the sleeping bag in the bed of his truck a thousand times over if it meant she ended up with Tommy. It felt shameful to wish things had gone down differently with Carson when Tommy's conception was inextricably woven into everything that had gone wrong in the weeks that had followed.

Carson's steps faltered with a crunch of gravel and weeds. Huffing, he whirled to face her, gripping the fence behind him. "I thought I knew what I'd say when I saw you again. Hell, I had six years to think about it. But now, looking at you, being here . . ." He shook his head.

She felt the same way. Having spent so much time figuring out how to avoid this very confrontation, she'd never given much thought to what might actually happen if it came to pass.

"Is there any chance you and I can agree to let the past go? We could call each other friends and be on our way."

He rapped his knuckle against his forehead. "You think that's why I'm here? To grant you a pardon? God, hearing you talk like that, I hate you all over again."

His hatred didn't surprise her in the least. Two weeks after Tommy's conception, when he'd demanded she meet him at an abandoned barn, she'd shown up and seen it in his eyes that he was furious with her. At the time, she'd had no idea why her best friend hadn't returned her phone calls or answered his door for two long weeks after she'd shared her body with him and he'd shared his secret with her. She hadn't understood the wild hurt in his eyes when it was she who'd felt neglected and used.

Yet at the first sight of his broken, beaten body, she'd set aside her hurt feelings and rushed to him, only to have him shove her away and accuse her of unspeakable betrayals. The argument that followed had been the worst she'd ever experienced—unmatched in its vitriol and volume.

Tonight, she knew intuitively that there was nothing she could say to convince Carson he was wrong to accuse her.

"I know you're not going to believe me any more now than you did then, but I kept your secret. I've kept it to this day."

In her mind's eye, Jenna could see the two of them in the bed of his truck, gazing at the stars. *I'll tell you something about me I've never told anyone, but it can't get out. Not even to my family.*

She remembered holding her breath, her body tingling. Even as a teenager, she'd loved being privy to people's private business. *You're my best friend. You can tell me anything*, she'd said.

She'd taken his hand. The attraction she'd come to feel toward him because he was a good-looking guy had gotten jumbled up inside her with the platonic love of being long-time friends who shared a bond. Maybe daddy issues were to blame. She'd grown up so lonely and neglected that of course she craved attention. She'd slept with nearly every other guy in her class, yet Carson never acted like he wanted her, and men who ignored her drew her in like magnets. It was embarrassing, how naïve and needy she'd been. How starved for love. She hugged herself more tightly as the memory flooded through her.

"Enough with the lies, Jenna. You were the only person in the world who knew. I trusted you, and only you, then not more than two days later, I was ambushed behind my parents' store. They waited for me to lock up and head for my car. I really think their intention was to kill me." He smashed his lips together. "I think they thought they had killed me."

"Who?"

"Stop pretending you don't know. How do you live with yourself, lying like that?"

"You were my best friend. I loved you." What more could she say?

He released a bitter laugh. "That's the bitch of this whole

thing. All these people swore they loved me—you, my parents, my brothers and sisters—right up until they found out who I really was. No more lies, Jenna. Tell me why you betrayed me. Tell me how you live with yourself or I'm going to take my vengeance out on you the same way I'm going to take it out on everyone else who tried to destroy me."

Whatever kind of vengeance he had in mind, she had no doubt he planned to take it out on her, no matter what her response. But she had to try to make him see the truth. "I didn't tell anybody. Not a soul, whether you believe me or not." Desperation rose inside her, constricting her throat. "Tell me the names of the men who did that to you. Don't make me face another day in Catcher Creek wondering which of the people I've known my entire life have the hearts of murderers."

"You're going to stick to your story, then? Fine. Bucky Schultz, Kyle Kopec, and Lance Davies. Go ahead and act surprised."

It was the first time she'd heard the names of the boys who assaulted Carson. Punks, every last one of them. Punks a few years older than she and Carson, and whom they'd partied with and considered friends. Lance brought the pot, Bucky the booze, and Kyle the ideas that never failed to land them in trouble with the law. Her sister, Amy, had even dated Bucky briefly. All three had joined the rodeo circuit by the time Carson and Jenna had graduated high school, but they still called Catcher Creek home. She had distinct memories of partying with them that fateful summer.

Jenna had no idea if they were presently in town or not, but their families were. "What are you going to do to them?"

That garnered a hard smile. "I'm going to hurt them like they hurt me. And then I'm going to tell everyone the truth—about my parents' cover-up, about you and your betrayal, about how the hate in this place has been allowed to fester. No more secrets. I'm proud of who I am. I fought for this country and now I'm ready to fight for myself. Nobody's pushing me around anymore."

Jenna pulled at her hair. "Can you hear yourself? You've got as much hate in your soul as they do. What happened to you?" She heard her tone rising to a shout, but couldn't stop it. "Where's the boy I knew? The boy who saved me from bullies and from myself too many times to count? I want him back."

Her voice broke on that last word. They could've been parents together. They could've grown up into better people together. But their connection had arrested the day he first confronted her and she couldn't see a way out of the hurt.

Carson stabbed a finger in the air between them. "Whoever I was, you destroyed him."

"I would never betray you like that. Why are you so sure they beat you up over your secret? Maybe it wasn't about that. It could've been a dare or robbery gone wrong, some kind of misunderstanding."

His nostrils flared. He stood legs apart, hands clenched, red in his eyes. "You don't get it, do you? There was only one reason Bucky, Kyle, and Lance tried to kill me. One reason my parents refused me medical help so their friends and customers wouldn't find out. One reason I was left for dead, then shipped out of my home. Shunned by my own parents."

"How can you be so sure?"

"They carved it into me, Jenna." He ripped his shirt off over his head and spun away from her. "They fucking carved it into me."

There, scrawled across his flesh in ragged lines of scar tissue were the letters *FAG*. His whole body moved with the force of his labored breaths. The word rippled with the flex of his muscles. She gasped and swayed, a hand to her mouth, aching for what he'd been through. No wonder he was so full of hate.

With his back to her still, he braced his hands on the fence and sunk into his arms. "What do you think it was like for me, coming out to my parents like that? What do you think it was like for me in the Marines, denying who I really was so I wouldn't get kicked out of the service, defending myself against every bigoted prick who wanted to take a shot at me anyway?"

Tears sprang to her eyes. It must have been horrible. Pain piled onto pain. It must have felt to him like the world was ending over and over. How had he borne it?

"My dad found me half dead behind their store. He took one look at my back and he . . ." He hung his head. "I wished I'd have stayed unconscious instead of having to listen to my parents debate the pros and cons of taking me to the hospital. Eventually, they decided it'd be bad for business if the truth came out. My mom called her sister, who's a nurse. She did what she could and as soon as I was healed enough to travel, they shipped me out."

Jenna didn't think she could stand to hear any more. She reached out, walking forward, needing to touch his pain, to let him know he wasn't alone if he didn't want to be. He hated her, but she'd never stopped loving him as a friend and brother. As the father of her child.

He must not have sensed her approach because at the first touch of her fingertips on his back, he flinched and pulled away. Spinning to face her, he clamped a hand over her wrist. "Don't you dare touch me. Don't you *dare* pretend sympathy for me after what you did."

"I didn't do anything. You left me all alone and I couldn't

find you. I had no idea who'd hurt you because you hadn't told me. All I knew was people in this town were capable of such unspeakable violence that no one was safe. I've lived in fear since the day you told me you were almost killed. I was afraid they'd come after me, too." *Afraid they'd come after our son if they realized who his father was.*

She stopped fighting his grip on her arm. The tears that came were hot and angry. "I trusted you. I trusted you with me, but you left."

Until the words were out, she hadn't realized how betrayed by him she felt. Not only by his accusation, but his abandonment. It flooded through her now as fresh as if it'd happened yesterday. All that hurt and fear she'd endured back then. The shock that he could so easily and fervently believe her capable of betrayal. That day had scarred her as deeply as her parents' deaths, as brutally as her childhood of neglect. Maybe he hadn't ever really cared about her, for him to think the worst of her on the turn of a dime.

Sneering, he released her and fumbled back. "I trusted you, too, and look what it got me." He prowled to the far edge of the picket fence. "But the joke's on you and this town because I'm not that weak-ass wimp I was back then. That boy I was, the Carson you knew, I think Bucky and his friends really did manage to kill him like they wanted to."

He sounded like a victim. This hulking Marine sounded like a weakling. Weaker than the Carson she'd known. Maybe he was right, and Bucky and his friends had killed that boy. "They might have hurt your body, but you're the one who let them mangle your spirit."

He spun around in slow motion, rolling his head on his neck. "Well, fuck you, too, Jenna." He enunciated every word like a bullet. "You're the one who allowed that to happen to me. Who did you tell—Bucky? Your sisters? One of the girls in school? You never could resist a juicy bit of gossip."

No, she couldn't. Especially back then.

I think I might be gay, he'd told her the night of Tommy's conception in the back of his truck. It hadn't been much of a surprise. She'd found gay porn under his bed one day when she'd been looking for his stash of pot. She doubted she would have had much of a reaction even if she hadn't found evidence, because she'd been so high that night. Pot and pills and tequila. She'd been buzzed, lying there next to Carson. Would've vibrated right into the atmosphere if she hadn't been holding his hand.

You're not sure? she remembered asking him.

Not really, okay? It's all so fucked up. I mean, how do you know for sure?

And then she'd said the fateful words. *I can think of a way.* With that, she'd taken his hand and cupped it over her breast. His touch had made her higher than the drugs. It was the ultimate rebellion—screwing her best friend. Screwing the boy who'd ignored her every flirtation. He wouldn't reject her this time if she helped him figure things out about himself.

If she'd only known.

She shook herself back to the present. "I never told anyone you might be gay."

"There was no might about it. I was. I am. And of course you told someone, you lying bitch."

Carson stepped toward her and she responded with a step back. A new awareness tingled over her spine. He could hurt her tonight. His eyes radiated violent potential. She couldn't afford to argue with him anymore, not even to defend herself. Time to be smart and let self-preservation win out over taking a stand for the truth about what had really happened.

Around the corner, propped against the house, she kept a rake. She took another step back, then another, until she could see the rake in her periphery. Three feet away.

Carson inched toward her, spitting hate and fury. "Six years I've been working up to this, training, getting strong. I'm a fucking soldier, and there ain't nobody going to mess with me anymore. I'm going to weed the poison out of this small-minded Hicksville. It's time for me to get biblical. You all are going to pay the price of your sins."

All that mattered now was Tommy. His safety, his future. She ruminated on her son, gathering strength. If she'd ever doubted her resolve to keep the truth about Tommy from Carson, she didn't any longer. The bitter, vicious man before her was beyond reason, beyond humanity. What would he do to her, to Tommy, if he learned the truth she'd hidden from him?

Holding her breath, she lunged for the side of the house, grabbing a firm hold on the rake. She jabbed the tines in Carson's direction.

He appeared around the corner, fingers outstretched, nostrils flared. When he saw the rake, his eyes narrowed on it and he gave a snorting laugh. "A rake? Real nice, Jenna. You think I'm going to hurt you?"

Her heart hammered against her ribs. "Yes."

Grinning malevolently, he smoothed a hand over the hard ridges of his abdominal muscles. "I'm going to hurt you, all right, just not like you're assuming. But let me just tell you that it feels damn good to be on the right side of fear for a change. Tell me, how does it feel, knowing someone who's bigger and stronger than you could do anything he wanted to you and you'd be powerless to stop him?" He took another step nearer. "You feel pretty helpless right now, don't you?"

His words sent a fresh chill through her bones. She brandished the rake in front of her.

"Yeah. You're terrified of me. I can see it in your eyes." His smile turned to a sneer. "That's how I felt when Bucky, Kyle, and Lance surrounded me. Now you know." With stone-cold eyes, he pulled his shirt on and fished truck keys from his pocket. "Brace yourself, Jenna. It's almost time for Judgment Day in Catcher Creek."

When Jenna opened her front door in response to Matt's knock, she was winded, her cheeks flushed. Dressed in the same clothes she'd worn that day, she shook her disheveled hair away from her face and gave him a smile that didn't reach her eyes.

"Hi." She said it with a bit too much exuberance, like she was forcing cheeriness because she was hiding something.

Matt's defenses were instantly on alert. *Steady, man. You already laid your heart on the line for her, so you might as well stay the course.* He offered her his best smile. "Hi. You told me not to come, but I couldn't help it. I need one more kiss from you to last me the week."

"Oh. That's sweet."

He'd heard corporate litigation attorneys speak with more convincing sincerity. "Am I interrupting your Sunday night study group?"

"No. Not at all. I didn't join the group tonight. I'm too worn out from the wedding to study."

Awkward silence descended over them. Rather than invite him in, she maintained a hand on the doorknob and another on the frame. A full-body block of the entrance. Hard not to take that personally since just that morning he'd been in her bed and his skin still carried her scent.

She blinked and looked past him, her eyes shifting,

scanning the darkness. He cocked his chin over his shoulder and followed her line of sight, seeing nothing but rolling hills and scrub grass.

On his way to her house, he'd passed a truck leaving their property. It hadn't looked like Vaughn behind the wheel, but it was hard to tell in the glare of the headlights. It could've been one of the farm workers pulling a late night or one of Vaughn and Rachel's friends. Other than that, the night had been quiet, the roads empty. "Expecting someone else?"

She swallowed, her expression blanking. "No. I thought I saw something move, like a coyote."

Right. Something was definitely going on. Clearly, she didn't want him here. It'd been a mistake to push her like this. But here he was, so there wasn't anything left for him to do than kiss her like he'd been determined to and hit the road. "Is Tommy asleep?"

"Yeah." She rubbed her upper arms.

He held his hand out. "Do you have time to join me outside for a minute, so we don't take a chance of waking him?"

After an inhale, she placed her hand in his, gripping it tight, and allowed him to coax her out past the concrete slab in front of her door, into the sultry summer night.

It hit him that this might well be his last opportunity to fight for Jenna's love. She may have already made up her mind about him, but rather than sinking into offended self-pity about the emotional wall she'd erected, he owed it to his renewed sense of optimism and hope to do his best to remind her how great they were together.

He pulled her up against him and wrapped his arms around her, rubbing her back and kissing her hair until the stiffness in her spine yielded and she melted into him. Her cheek and palm rested on his chest. He tightened his hold on her, rocking them a little.

She sighed deeply and melted into him even more. "How did you know I needed this?"

Relief swept through him. It was possible he'd read her body language wrong. Maybe she'd had a tough night with Tommy or was worried about her midterms or something. Maybe he was a big, fat narcissist for thinking her emotional world revolved around him. "I needed it, too. I'm going to kiss you now, okay?"

She turned her face up and smiled, though her eyes were shiny with wetness.

The plot thickens . . . He skimmed a finger along her jaw. "Do you want to tell me what's going on?"

"No." She gave a slow blink and dabbed at her eyes with her fingertip. "I want you to kiss me."

Fair enough. He pressed his lips to hers, tender and sweet in a kiss that went on and on. He wished he didn't live and work so far away. But in a way, he recognized the distance as a blessing because it'd force them to take their relationship slower than his heart was telling him to go. Asking Jenna to think about children may have catapulted their thoughts into the distant future, but Matt knew there were no shortcuts to a forever kind of love. They had a lot they still needed to figure out about each other—quirks and habits, the little things that made up a person.

By the time Jenna moved to Santa Fe in late August, they'd be ready to speed things up. She could meet his family and they could talk about when it'd be okay for Tommy to see that they shared a bed.

That was, if Jenna decided she could accept his infertility. That was one hell of an *if*, too.

Dark thoughts crowded closer to the forefront of his mind. He pushed them away. He was here to make the most of his one last chance to woo Jenna and he had one more card up his sleeve.

He ended the kiss and loosened his hold on her. She watched him with a dreamy smile, looking tons more relaxed than when he'd arrived.

"Is that what you needed?" she asked.

"Yes. Big-time. But there's one more thing I'd like to do before I hit the road."

Apprehension clouded her features. "I'm not sure I'm good for much tonight. I'm pretty wiped out."

Oh, geez. He had a robust libido, but he wasn't sure even he'd be up for more sex after their marathon love fest the night before. "Then it's a good thing that wasn't what I had in mind."

On his phone, he scrolled through the music library on his phone until he found the perfect song. He slid the volume button to high and set the phone on a nearby rock. As the first notes of a country waltz poured from the speaker, he offered her his hand. "Dance with me?"

She swayed where she stood and her expression relaxed again. She set her hand in his and allowed him to bring her into closed hold. "Do you have any idea how many things I love about you?" she asked.

Enough to give up your dream of having more babies? But now wasn't the time to dwell on problems. All he wanted was a dance.

He stepped her back, waltzing in basic steps around the perimeter of her fenced yard. Nothing fancy. It was too dark and he didn't want to take the chance of stepping her into a hole or tripping, and frankly he was loving the way she felt in closed hold, hand to hand and face-to-face.

"This morning, you asked me to think hard about what I

wanted, and if it bothered me that if we worked out, we couldn't have more children."

His stomach dropped. Oh, man. He just wanted to dance with her. Not this. Not now. "Yes. And I know you haven't had enough time to think about it yet. It's okay. I wasn't trying to pressure you by coming back here tonight."

He looked past her to double-check that the ground was even, then spun her in a triple turn so he could regain his faltering composure.

Back in closed hold, she strummed her fingers on his shoulder. "That's not what I meant. I thought about it all day. I don't need more time to think."

Her declaration caught him by surprise. He lost his rhythm and missed a step, tripping over her foot. So much for him being a competent dancer. Apologizing, he dropped his hands from hers and stood, cowboying up to handle with grace whatever she said next.

Smiling, she stroked his cheek. "I don't think I've ever seen you misstep, Mr. Smooth."

He didn't feel smooth at the moment. He felt exactly the opposite—vulnerable and anxious. "I'm not going to lie to you," he said. "I want you in my life in a bad way. I'll re-spect your decision, of course. But—"

She cradled his cheeks with her hands and cut his words off with a kiss. Not a *good-bye, I have to let you go* kiss, but one full of passion and promise. His heart started to beat again. She wouldn't kiss him like that if she had bad news, right?

"Do you remember before Amy's wedding, I told you that you were all I wanted?"

"I remember." That had been a pathetic moment of self-pity for him. He'd be eternally grateful that he'd met that

Lynch guy in the parking lot and recognized that he didn't want to become such a jaded, pessimistic man.

"It's true. I don't need to be pregnant again. I really don't. I was watching Amy last night. All that barfing and weepiness. Been there, done that. I'd rather have you. It would be an honor to have you as my man."

He looked into her eyes, for any hint of reservation, any reason for him to wonder or worry that she'd change her mind someday. He couldn't find one. Gathering her in his arms again, he kissed her. "I'm going to fall asleep tonight with a smile on my face, thinking about you and me. What do you say about getting a babysitter for next Saturday night so I can take you out?"

She fiddled with the collar of his shirt. "Let's plan on it, but I don't think I can hold off until next weekend to see you. How would you feel about me and Tommy coming up to Santa Fe to spend time with you this week? I know you have to work, so during the day, Tommy and I could start apartment hunting and checking out his new school, things like that."

Even though her suggestion took him by surprise, he kinda loved that she was having as much trouble as he was with taking things slow. Wade-in-slowly guy reared his prudish head with a warning that rushing things with Jenna wasn't a good plan, but Matt was getting better and better at ignoring him. "Whenever you want. I have a house on my family's ranch, a lot like your setup. My mom and dad would love to help you entertain Tommy while I'm working."

Her smile turned radiant. Thank goodness she'd gotten over whatever melancholy had been plaguing her when he'd arrived. "Tomorrow? We could meet you at your place when you get off work."

"Tomorrow is good." He brushed hair away from her

face and tucked it behind her ear. "I'm going to make you happy, Jenna. As happy as you've made me."

She cocked her head toward his phone, from which another country ballad was playing. "I know you need to get home, but do you think we could dance one more time before you go?"

He took her hand in his and straightened to proper dancing posture. "Do you think I could ever deny you anything?"

He swept her into a two-step, his soul buzzing with joy.

Chapter Thirteen

"Hold up, did I hear you right? You're at the clueless lawyer's house?"

Jenna watched Tommy climb up a maze in the play area of the fast-food restaurant where they'd stopped for lunch after a morning of apartment hunting in downtown Santa Fe. Hard to fault Carrie for her bewilderment after their last conversation the night of Amy's wedding. "We're on our way there. And it turned out Matt wasn't clueless."

"He gave you the royal kiss-off at the wedding, remember? So what changed? Help me understand because you're not that girl with the self-esteem issues who hangs around a guy who treats her like garbage. We've seen those girls at the UNM campus and it's not a pretty sight."

Jenna pushed a cold, limp French fry around the tray. What Carrie didn't know was that Jenna was that girl—at least she had been. Born to a house of neglect, to a father who'd escaped his wife's mental illness by gambling and drinking and staying gone for days at a time. It was impossible to live through a childhood like that with one's self-esteem intact.

It was why she'd gotten pregnant, why she'd drank and

partied. Because even the wrong kind of attention was still attention and she'd been starved for it. A ride in the back of the sheriff's patrol car or a night spent in a stranger's bed had been better than feeling invisible, as she had at home.

Tommy had snapped her out of her spiral of recklessness and regret, and had granted her a huge dose of awareness of why she did what she did, but that insecure girl who was used to feeling unseen and unwanted would live on inside her forever like a scar on her soul. Probably, that was why she'd pined so long for Matt, a man who hadn't given her the time of day for months. In a sick, twisted way, that dynamic was her comfort zone.

She might've had all the wrong reasons for wanting Matt, but she was grateful she hadn't given up on him because it turned out that he'd been ignoring her because of his own fears. It turned out he had as much baggage and scarring from his past as she did hers. All it had taken was a shot of courage for him to open his heart to her.

It was nobody's business that Matt had been gun-shy because he was nursing a broken heart for three kids he'd wanted to be a dad to, but hiding the truth about his medical condition from Carrie seemed pointless. Everyone close to them would eventually know once she and Matt decided it was time to adopt. "He has a genetic issue that makes him infertile and he was worried that would be a deal breaker for me."

Silence on the line. "Oh. Damn. I didn't see that coming."

"Neither did I. The hardest part was thinking that far into the future to decide whether it was a deal breaker or not. I mean, I'd never given adoption much thought before. But he's worth it. I really like him, Carrie. Actually, I think I'm falling for him."

"Okay, wow. That's fast."

"Yes and no. It feels like I've been waiting for him forever."

"And by forever, you mean, what, a year? Less than that?"

"Come on, Carrie. Cheap shot."

"I'm sorry. It's just that I don't want you to get hurt."

Jenna rotated her jaw, which had grown uncomfortably tight. "I won't. And I know you have a right to be skeptical, especially since he pushed me away for so long. But we're past that now and we're going to give this relationship our best shot."

Carrie sighed, resigned. "Well, I look forward to meeting him." A heavy pause ensued, then, "Please don't hate me for sounding like a harpy, but you're going to have to tell him you're going to school. I know you've got some weird hang-up about your sisters finding out, but—"

"I already told him."

"You are serious about this guy."

Jenna rolled her eyes with affectionate exasperation. "Yes, I am. And before you go there, I know I need to tell my sisters about UNM, too." Tommy sprinted by, grabbing a handful of fries as he passed. "No running with your mouth full," she hollered after him.

He skidded to a halt at the base of the slide and jammed them in his mouth, chomping noisily.

"What are you waiting for?" Carrie asked.

"I just need a little more time to work up to it. The plan always was to talk to Rachel as soon as Amy's wedding was over."

"And yet, you're spending the week after the wedding in Santa Fe. That doesn't sound like coming clean to Rachel. It sounds like running away from your issues."

She had no idea how right she was. "I know. Let me get through midterms and then I promise I'll sit Rachel down and tell her everything. Maybe you could lay off the stern best friend act until then, okay?"

"I care about you is all, but I'll give it a rest. So you're staying the week at Matt's house?"

"Yes." Jenna felt the defensiveness ease in her chest. Carrie had waved off her apology about flaking on study group, probably because she thought Jenna's distractedness had to do with Matt. Jenna didn't want to lie to Carrie, but correcting the assumption would've involved Carson's confrontation and that was one truth that was going to stay buried for now. "But he knows I need time to study and he'll support me on that. In fact, would you have time for a one-on-one webcam with me tonight? With the midterms coming up next week, I bet I missed a lot of good notes last night at study group."

"That would be great. If you want, I can ask my parents to babysit Tommy during computer lab on Wednesday. They already watch my sister's boy, who's four," Carrie offered.

Usually, Charlene Delgado watched Tommy on Wednesdays to spare him from having to make the weekly errand run for the farm to Albuquerque, as Jenna told everyone. One of the many little adjustments she was going to have to make sooner than she'd anticipated was finding reliable, trusted childcare in the Santa Fe area, but this week was complicated enough without adding childcare worries to the mix.

"Thank you. If they'd be willing, that would make my life easier."

They made plans for that night and ended the call. She and Tommy weren't supposed to arrive at Matt's family's ranch until that night at five, when Matt got off work, but after performing her morning chores alongside Rachel, Jenna had been too twitchy and anxious to run down the clock in Catcher Creek, deciding instead that she and Tommy could get a head start on apartment hunting.

She'd let Rachel in on her plans to stay at Matt's house, not giving her any other reason except that she didn't like the idea of not seeing him for a whole week. Rachel had been nonplussed, reiterating her words from the night of Amy's wedding that it was about time she and Matt figured things out.

Jenna didn't have it in her to feel guilty for taking advantage of Matt's generous spirit. Was she staying at his house for the wrong reasons? Yes. She was woman enough to admit that fear of Carson's return had her skipping town. But was she using Matt? Absolutely not.

She was still riding high on the newness of their connection, and it was the absolute truth that she didn't like the idea of being apart for the workweek. Sure, if she didn't have Tommy's safety to consider, she would've put off overnight visits at least until they had a few dates under their belt, but as a mom, protecting her son was her number-one job. More important than her sisters or school or a new relationship.

Matt understood about family first and self-protection. They'd talked about their philosophies before the wedding, about his ancestors coming to New Mexico and the challenge of choosing whether to fight or run when the shit hit the fan. What her choice boiled down to was that she needed somewhere safe to regroup and make plans. What better place to do that than at her boyfriend's house?

Several times that day, she'd picked up the phone to call Vaughn and alert the sheriff's department to Carson's return and the possibility that he might hurt the men who'd tried to kill him, but she couldn't figure out what to say that wouldn't put her in the position of fielding questions from

Vaughn and his deputies that she couldn't risk answering. As far as she knew, Bucky, Lance, and Kyle were off touring with the rodeo and out of danger, but she couldn't just sit helplessly by knowing a potentially violent man was loose in Catcher Creek.

With her eye on Tommy through the glass, she slipped out the fast-food restaurant's door and dropped coins in the grimy, clunky pay phone. Using her cell phone as a reference, she dialed the sheriff's department's dispatch desk. When Irene answered, Jenna lowered the timbre of her voice. "I have an anonymous tip that something bad's going to go down in Catcher Creek soon."

Keeping the tip general, she told Irene that Carson Parrish was in town and was planning to commit violent acts against the Kopec, Schultz, Parrish, and Davies families, while skirting Irene's clarifying questions about who she was and how she'd come about the information. She felt better after ending the call. Maybe Carson would be arrested. Maybe he'd get spooked by the police buzzing around him and leave town. A girl could dream.

She and Tommy hung out at the fast-food restaurant playground until he was worn out and bored, then checked out another couple apartment complexes within a few miles of the state building she'd be working at.

She'd never before had to pay rent, and everything in her price range was dinky, run-down, and dark. Despite all those detractors, the complexes she'd decided to take a closer look at boasted pools, which Tommy had informed her was a consideration of the utmost importance. His buy-in to the move would make the relocation go all the more smoothly, so she'd indulged him on that point.

She had a solid list of possible apartments going, and several more she wanted to check out, but Tommy had had enough. "Can we *pleeease* go to Matt's house? I can't take this anymore."

He said it with such earnest panache, Jenna couldn't find it in her heart to get upset with him for asking her about it again even after she'd commanded him to stop begging.

"Almost, buddy. You're being very patient today and I appreciate it. Matt still has three hours before he gets home from work and I don't have a key to his house, so we've got to hang in there for a little while longer."

"We can sit outside or walk around. He told me there were so many horses at his ranch that I couldn't count them all. I want to try, Mommy. Can't we just go already?"

She was as restless with curiosity as Tommy to check out Matt's family's ranch, but the thought of having a potty emergency or inadvertently running into Matt's parents without knowing if Matt had given them a heads-up about Jenna's arrival had her dragging her feet. "Soon. I have one more stop I'd like to make first."

Using the GPS on her cell phone, she found Carpe Diem with no trouble. She pulled into a spot out front, and through the window could see that the woman behind the counter wasn't Tara. It made sense that Tara would have employees, even if it hadn't occurred to Jenna.

"This stop might be faster than I thought. This is Matt's sister's flower shop, but it looks like she might not be here." She unlatched her belt, got out, and opened Tommy's door. "Do you remember Tara from Aunt Amy's wedding?"

Tommy already had his seat belt undone. He bounded out of the car. "She's the one with all the pictures on her arm. What do you call those again?"

"Tattoos." She took his hand and led him toward the store. Maybe Tara was in the back room. Since they'd made the trip, it was worth asking.

"Can I get a tattoo someday?"

Jenna cringed. "When you're thirty, sweetheart. Then we'll talk."

"What? That's ridiculous! I'm not going to be thirty for a really long time."

She loved the way he said *ridiculous* like he was an old soul in a kid's body, outraged by the innumerable indignities of youth. She had to work to keep a grin from her face as she opened the door for him. "I know. Life stinks like that."

She followed Tommy in. The woman at the register smiled in greeting. She looked to be around Jenna's age, with straight brown hair falling around her shoulders. On the counter was an open textbook. Ever the nosy one about books other people were reading, Jenna did some eyeball stretching to look at the page of differential calculus equations. Nice. Calculus had been one of Jenna's favorite classes.

"Is Tara here?"

"I'm afraid not. She's making a delivery and isn't expected back for an hour. Is there something I can help you with?"

An hour? Must be quite a delivery. "No, thank you. We're friends of the family and were in the area. I thought we'd stop by and say hi. Another time, perhaps."

"May I have your name so I can tell her you were here?"

"You can tell her Jenna and Tommy," Tommy said. "Are those suckers?" He pointed to a glass jar of rainbow-colored lollipops next to the register.

The woman chuckled. "They sure are. You may have one if it's okay with your mom." She raised an eyebrow in Jenna's direction.

Jenna nodded. Keeping Tommy away from sugar was like trying to keep flies off a horse's ass. Impossible. His sugar radar was more highly developed than that of anyone else she knew. Thank goodness he was an active kid who never stopped moving. If only she could get him to brush his teeth without a fight, then she might feel a more worthy opponent in her battle against sugar.

She'd made him get milk with his lunch and no dessert, even though the ice-cream sundaes at the fast-food restaurant were dirt cheap and darn tasty. A lollipop wasn't so bad and might keep his mouth too busy to pepper her with questions about Matt's ranch on the way there.

After he selected a green lollipop, they bid the woman behind the counter good-bye and set off to Matt's family's property in the eastern outskirts of the city.

In the directions he'd given Jenna the night before, Matt had explained that he had his own entrance to the property three-fourths of a mile past the main gate. Jenna was impressed by the privacy that having his own road afforded him. Her cottage sat a quarter mile from the big house, which doubled as an inn three seasons out of the year, but her family's farm boasted only a single, unpaved road that forked to the separate houses. With the dust kicked up by a vehicle's tires, anybody standing on the big house's front porch or in Jenna's yard could see if someone was coming or going.

Matt had given her the code to his entrance gate, which probably meant his road was paved to boot. Her property didn't even have a gate. Just an old wooden arch over the turn-off from the main road. It seemed excessive to shell out money for a locked gate, especially since only the newly rich did that in Catcher Creek. Coded entrance gates were interpreted as even more antisocial and snobby than locked front doors.

The urban landscape of Santa Fe gave way to a winding mountain road cutting through a wide valley between two mountainous ridges. She slowed the car after passing the winery Matt had mentioned as a landmark and did a double take when an elaborate, stained-wood and wrought-iron gate appeared to her left, a sign above it declaring it the Circle R Ranch. Behind the gate, a long, tree-lined drive ended in a glimpse of sprawling buildings, white fences, horses, people, and cars.

Sweet sundae, Matt's family was loaded. She'd only seen ranches this luxurious in reruns of *Dallas*.

As he'd described, a second unmarked gate appeared three-quarters of a mile later. The lack of signage didn't detract from the opulence of the sculptured wrought iron and thick, espresso-stained wood. Jenna punched in the four-digit code Matt had given her and watched the gate swing slowly open.

In her rearview mirror, she saw Tommy's eyes grow wide. "We need one of these, Mommy."

"Someday, sweetie. An apartment with a pool is the best I can do right now, but someday." Maybe they'd be able to claim this gate as their own eventually, if she and Matt worked out like she hoped.

She kept her speed at a crawl, taking in the gorgeous green landscape surrounding the single-lane road that wound through the property. There wasn't a whole lot of green grass in Catcher Creek, save for alfalfa fields, and she couldn't wait to run barefoot with Tommy on Matt's ranch, then lie in the grass and stare up at the sky. Even the smell of horses and ranch life was tempered by the scent of lawn.

Matt's house appeared after several minutes, tucked behind a hill near what she assumed was the back edge of the property, judging by its position near a ridge overlooking an expansive high-desert valley. With the hill, the ridge, and its distance from the main highway, Matt's house seemed purposefully positioned to be secluded. No other buildings, roads, or people were visible as far as her eye could see. She liked that a lot.

The house itself was larger than she expected—two-storied and made of light stained wood like a modern log cabin, complete with a wrap-around porch that ran around the entire circumference of the house. Jenna was entranced. Already, she felt like she could be happy here for the rest of her life with Matt and Tommy and whatever other kids they adopted.

What caught her by surprise was the appearance of Matt's SUV under a carport to the left of the house, and in front of the house, Tara's minivan. Why hadn't Matt called to tell her he was home early?

Baffled and trying not to jump to any conclusions, she pulled her car alongside Tara's van. Before she could get both her legs out of the car, Tara jogged out the front door. Not seeming to notice that Jenna had arrived, she headed for the open back doors of her van. When she spotted Jenna, she wobbled and her eyes grew wide. "Oh! Hi there. Just a sec." She spun toward the house and cupped her hands around her mouth. "Matt?" she hollered. "Jenna's here."

"What? No!" came Matt's panicked reply.

Jenna got Tommy out, feeling awkward. Matt didn't sound happy.

Tara grinned at Jenna. "He didn't mean that. It's just that you're early."

"I know. We let our excitement get the best of us and couldn't stand to wait any longer." Tommy bounded out of the car, toward the house.

Tara snagged Tommy's shoulders to prevent him from getting any closer to the house. "Whoa there, partner. Just bear with us for a moment."

Matt skittered through the front door, looking winded. "Hiya. Hey, Tommy. You're here." He loped down the porch steps and held his hand out for Tommy to slap. "Gimme five."

They high-fived, then Matt ruffled his hair, then met Jenna's gaze. "Okay, you have to leave now."

Chapter Fourteen

"What?" Jenna asked Matt, searching his happy, anxious expression for a sign about what he meant.

Her favorite dimple appeared as his smile broadened. "I got off work early because I have a surprise for you." He dug into the pocket of his khaki shorts and brought out a set of keys, which he twirled on his finger. "You can wait at my parents' house. I'll drive you."

Before she could protest or ask any more questions, he'd swept Tommy into his arms and planted a big old kiss on her lips. "Trust me on this," he whispered. "I promise it'll be worth it."

Delicious tingles skittered over her skin. The reality of dating Matt was so much better and more romantic than she'd ever imagined. Every day she fell more in love with him.

The drive to Matt's parents' house took only a few minutes, much to Tommy's disappointment since he'd been allowed to ride without a booster seat, which was a rare occasion indeed. Matt pulled up in front of a long, two-story ranch house that made his own large house look diminutive in comparison. Across a gravel courtyard, inside a massive covered arena stood a cluster of adults surrounding a child on a horse that was being led in a slow walk. That must be the therapeutic riding school, Jenna reasoned.

Jenna got out of the car, helped Tommy out, then stood admiring the house's wood and stone exterior. "This is where you grew up?" she asked when Matt joined her.

"Yes. It's pretty impressive, isn't it? My grandparents built it. There was a time that three generations of Roenicks lived here."

"Are your grandparents still alive?"

"Both my grandfathers died more than a decade ago. Not long after that, my bubbies decided to move to town together. My parents offered to build them a cottage on the ranch or a private suite attached to the main house, but they wanted to be within walking distance of a Starbucks."

"There's nothing wrong with that logic." There wasn't a Starbucks or fast-food place within more than thirty miles of her family's farm and there were many times she'd wished for the modern convenience of having one nearby.

A large, colorful mosaic hanging over the front door caught Jenna's attention. Amid swirls of tiles in every color of the rainbow were various images—a tree, a Star of David, birds—and beneath them in letters formed from onyx black tiles were the words TIKKUN OLAM.

Jenna gestured to the mosaic. "You weren't exaggerating that your family was into the whole tikkun olam idea."

With a snort of laughter, he broke out in a white-toothed smile. "Yeah. It's no joke to them. Don't worry, they're not going to drill you about it—yet. They'll wait until they're sure you won't be scared away."

"Oh, ha, ha."

His eyes went wide with mock-seriousness. "What? You think I'm kidding?"

She bumped her shoulder with his. "I guess I'll start working on my answer."

"I'm glad you're not expecting to get scared away."

"Never."

He tipped his head toward the stable to the left of the house. "Mom won't be inside. She's probably running the show out with the riding classes."

On their walk to the stable, they nearly collided with Matt's mom, who was beating a hasty path from the tack room with her nose in a clipboard. She looked up and saw Matt, Jenna, and Tommy just in the nick of time to grind her boots to a halt, smiling warmly at them. "Beg your pardon for nearly bulldozing over you. I get in work mode and forget to look around."

Though she still carried an air of dignity and old money about her, the glamorous fashion statement she'd made at Amy's wedding had given way to cowgirl chic. She wore a radio clipped to the belt of her Wranglers, no-nonsense brown boots, and a blue and white western-style shirt.

"Mom, you remember Jenna from Amy's wedding?"

"Of course! Matt told us you were coming for a few days." She offered her hand and when Jenna clasped it, she sandwiched Jenna's hand between both of hers and gave it a hearty squeeze. "We were delighted to hear it."

"Likewise, it's wonderful to see you again, Mrs. Roenick."

"Call me Cynthia, please. Only my doctors call me Mrs. Roenick."

Matt wrinkled his nose, smiling. "You still do that?"

"You bet your bottom dollar I do."

Matt looked Jenna's way. "Mom thinks it evens out the power differential for doctors to have to address their patients formally."

"I figure they owe it to me since I have to call them by their surnames, which is a crock because I'm the one hiring them to do a job and not the other way around. Besides, my primary physician is a fine-looking man so having him call me Mrs. Roenick reminds me that I'm married."

Jenna chuckled. That was awesome.

Matt groaned. "What a terrible joke, Mom. It gets worse every time I hear it."

Cynthia winked at Jenna. "I love watching my boys squirm."

Jenna chuckled at that. "I can tell." She squeezed Tommy's shoulder. "This is my son, Tommy. I'm not sure if you two met at the wedding."

"We didn't have the pleasure." Cynthia squatted and offered Tommy her hand to shake. He timidly leaned in to Jenna's thigh, but shook her hand. "Very nice to meet you, Tommy. You can call me Ms. Cynthia, okay?"

Tommy nodded, wide-eyed.

"Tommy has a sweet tooth as big as Brittany's," Matt said.

Cynthia stood and crossed her arms over her chest, maintaining eye contact with Tommy. "Oh, my. That's serious."

Tommy nodded sagely.

"You've come to the right place, sir, because I have a magic cookie jar."

"Magic?" Tommy whispered.

"Magic because it's never empty," Cynthia said.

Jenna felt Tommy's shoulder relax against her leg.

"Matt, would you like to show them where the cookie jar is?"

Matt rattled his key ring. "I was hoping you could give them a tour while I finish with a surprise I have in the works at my house."

Cynthia beamed. "That would be my pleasure."

"Then I leave them in your capable hands." He kissed Jenna's nose and added, "I'll be back for you in forty-five minutes, tops."

Jenny nodded, feeling relaxed and confident with the choice she'd made to use Matt's ranch as her safe haven. These were good people. Nothing could touch her while she was here with Matt and his family, not even the demons from her past.

They watched Matt drive away; then Cynthia offered Tommy her hand to hold. "All right, sir, let's see about that cookie jar. I'll teach you the magic words on the way."

A half hour later, Tommy had put the magical refilling cookie jar to the test, as had Jenna. Jenna's own mom had lived a tormented life, plagued with bipolar disorder. By the time Jenna had been born, farm living and her poor mental health had beaten her down pretty hard. The only time there'd been cookies in the house had been when Rachel had bought them or Amy had made them, and there had never been any magic to their days, just scraping by and coping and treading water.

When her mom was in a good mood, life couldn't have been sweeter. But that wasn't all that often. Jenna lived for those days, even though she never knew when her mom's mood would turn on a dime. All that unpredictability wore on her and her sisters.

It'd worn out their dad before Jenna's birth, hence his escape through gambling, drinking, and doing God-knows-what for the long stretches of days and nights he'd be gone. Jenna had vivid memories of her two parents being unable to tolerate each other for even a few minutes. It was hard to believe the two of them had spent enough time in the same room together for her mom to get pregnant with her.

All three kids had worked out their own ways of escaping, too. Rachel immersed herself in farm work, Amy in cooking, and Jenna in books and school. And secrets. Then, as a teenager, drugs and drink and friends.

Matt's mom's house was a lot like the home Jenna had set up for Tommy. On a far grander scale and with top-of-the-line appliances and furnishings, true, but homey and bright and easy to be in. After maxing out on cookies, Cynthia had taken them to the barn to meet Mrs. Carrots, a calico cat who had appeared at the ranch one day from out of the blue. She'd accepted the food they left out and let everyone pet her and seemed thoroughly domesticated— until anyone had tried to pick her up or trap her in a cat carrier. They'd finally stopped trying and let one of the grandkids give her a name.

Two months later, Mrs. Carrots had become the proud new mother of four. Tommy was instantly smitten. The moment Cynthia set a kitten in his waiting hands, he looked at Jenna with pleading eyes and asked to keep it. While she was mentally rephrasing *Not a chance in hell* to make it kid-friendly, Cynthia stepped in and broke it to him that all four kitties had homes waiting for them already.

"That's for the best, buddy, because our new apartment probably won't allow cats. But we can visit Mrs. Carrots and her babies a lot while we're here, okay?"

When they walked out of the barn, Tara was waiting for them with the side of her minivan open. She waved them over with a big smile. "Matt's ready for you."

Jenna's pulse sped. She wasn't usually a fan of surprises, but she had a feeling this one was going to be great.

Cynthia hugged them both good-bye. "I already suggested

to Matt that you all come to our home for dinner on Wednesday night. You two discuss it and let me know."

Tommy squealed. "We could see Mrs. Carrots again and eat cookies!"

Jenna smiled and took his hand. Her little guy was already settling in and making himself at home. That pleased her. She'd be back from her computer lab on the UNM campus by dinnertime and truly hoped they could make it. "I'll talk to Matt, but that sounds great to me. Thank you."

When they were loaded in Tara's car and driving once more, Tara asked, "Having fun yet?"

"Definitely. Your mom's great. I can see so much of her in Matt and you."

"Wait until you meet my oldest sister, Leah. She's Mom's spitting image."

"I'm looking forward to it."

"Just so you know, Tommy and I swung through Carpe Diem on our way to the ranch. We left a message that we'd stopped by with your employee."

"That's ironic with me already being here. The woman you met was Evie. She's not an employee, though. We met a few years back and started a coalition of women small business owners called Destiny by Design, or, as we affectionately call ourselves, The Alpha Chicks."

"Nice. What was she doing at your store?"

"Everyone in the group helps each other out by watching each other's stores when our employees call in sick, things like that. Evie owns a salon."

That took Jenna by surprise. "She was reading an advanced calculus textbook."

Tara snickered. "That's her dating strategy. She likes her men young and smart so she keeps enrolling in college classes. It works because she gets asked out a lot by her classmates—and she's halfway through her second bachelor's degree."

"That's . . . ingenious? Diabolical? Offensive to feminists everywhere? I can't decide."

"I know, right? Neither can I. Were you just stopping by the store to say hello?"

With a glance at Tommy to make sure he was distracted and not listening in, Jenna said in a quiet voice, "Actually, I wanted to talk to you about something you said at the wedding, about me not breaking Matt's heart. I promised you I wouldn't, and I wanted you to know that I take that seriously. He and I had a big talk and he told me about his infertility. I'm okay with it, by the way. It's not like pregnancy was all that fun, if you know what I mean."

She nodded. "I'm glad he told you right away. It's only fair. He's taken it hard. Of all of us, he was the one who always knew he'd be a father. When we played house as little kids, most of the other boys preferred to be the doggie or the baby, but he liked pretending to be the daddy, even though he was almost always the youngest kid around. We all wished he wasn't so preoccupied with the idea, but you know how when you're dieting, all you can think about is food that's bad for you? And because you're denied it, it becomes an obsession? That's what being a father is like for Matt."

That made sense to Jenna. She might feel the same way if she were in his situation. She certainly was that way about junk food when she was dieting. "It's overwhelming to think that far into our future when we're only now starting to date, but I'm going into this relationship planning on forever."

Tara flashed a smile. "Good. I mean, I know it's none of

my business, but you've got my blessing, for what that's worth."

"Thank you."

Tara strummed her fingers on the steering wheel. "Any word on how Jake's doing? It's not like he opened up to me or anything after getting the call about his partner's death, but I could tell it devastated him. I thought I'd give him a day or so before calling to check on him."

Jenna tried to keep her expression blank, but she was tickled by the possibility that Jake and Tara hadn't seen the last of each other, and might even start a relationship. "Matt, Tommy, and I stopped by Kellan's place yesterday and you're right, he seemed pretty devastated. He's going to stay at Kellan's until it's time to drive to Cheyenne for his partner's memorial service next week. After that, I'm not sure what his plans are."

"Mmm."

Jenna wasn't ready to drop the topic of Jake yet. She didn't exactly fancy herself a matchmaker, but it gave her a thrill to have the inside scoop on a potential fledgling relationship. "Last night he and Matt went rabbit hunting."

Tara raised her brows. "Like on horseback?"

Jenna nodded. "I didn't get many details out of Matt, but yes, on horseback. Matt said Jake really enjoyed himself."

"Interesting. I'm trying to picture Jake on a horse and I can't see it. Hunting on horseback is Matt and our dad's go-to coping mechanism for stress or whatever's bugging them. Did they catch anything?"

"They did. Matt shot three rabbits and Jake two plus a coyote."

"Matt saved me a lucky rabbit's foot," Tommy added. Maybe he was listening more carefully than Jenna had given him credit for. Sneaky kid.

"Cool!" Tara said. "Well, I'll be darned. I'll have to ask Jake about it."

"Do you think you might see him again?" Jenna asked before she could think better of it. She bit the inside of her cheek as she waited for Tara's reply.

Tara offered a coy smile. "I'm not exactly in the market for a long-distance relationship. Life's complicated enough without trying to make a relationship work with a man who's nine hundred miles away. But he's, um . . ." She held up a finger and cocked her head in Tommy's direction as if to tell Jenna that they'd need to wait because what she really wanted to say about Jake wasn't kid appropriate. "I'll tell you more later."

Jenna died a little, wanting to know what Tara was going to say. They arrived at Matt's house to find him leaning against the closed front door, his legs crossed at the boots and his arms crossed over his chest. When he saw them, he jumped upright, looking nervous and happy. Tara put the van in park but didn't turn off the engine. "There you go— front-door service. Enjoy your night."

Gah. Now Jenna was feeling a little panicked that Tara was going to withhold the juicy bit of information she was eager to hear. "You're not coming in?"

"No. This is between you and Matt. And I need to get back to my shop in time for the after-work rush."

Jenna opened the door for Tommy. He ran to Matt, who squatted and collected him into a hug. Jenna walked around to the driver's side of the van and crooked an elbow through the open window. "What were you about to say about Jake? He's what?"

Tara gave a throaty laugh. "Jake Reed might not be long-distance boyfriend material, like, *at all*, but—forgive me for being crass—"

"Crass works for me."

"—let's just say he's welcome in my bed anytime."

They shared a smile. "So it's like that, is it? Good for you. We moms deserve some good loving as much as the next girl, as my friend Carrie says."

"Damn right we do."

They hugged through the window. "Speaking of good loving, have a great time tonight."

Matt's house smelled of baking cheese and marinara sauce. Jenna detected it wafting through the open windows before she'd hit the porch. Dinner was a wonderful surprise. What a sweet guy he was. "Did you make us lasagna?"

Matt was in front of her, his hand on the doorknob to open it. "Good nose you've got there. I must admit, though, I didn't make it. I mean, I can cook. I'm pretty good at it, but I didn't have time today. This is from Ciotta's, down the street from my office."

"So then, is that the surprise?"

She wasn't sure she'd ever seen him smile so big. "Not even close." He turned the knob, then stopped and stepped aside, taking Tommy with him. "Why don't you go in first?"

The door was already unlatched so she pushed it open. The interior of his house matched the modern-day log cabin look of the exterior, with wood-paneled walls, exposed beams, and photographs of bears and other wildlife on the walls. Straight ahead, on a decorative foyer table, sat a mammoth yellow and purple flower arrangement. That must've been the reason for Tara's visit.

More flower arrangements dotted the living room, from end tables and the coffee table, to the thick wood mantel above the fireplace, adding a nice contrast to the blue plaid sofas and window dressings. "Flowers," she breathed. "A lot of flowers."

"Keep looking," Matt prompted.

She turned toward the right, the direction of his kitchen. On every horizontal surface sat a vase of flowers in every shape, color, and size. She couldn't help but touch and smell every arrangement she passed, paying special attention to the shabby-chic arrangement divided into three mason jars on the kitchen table, with a big blue ribbon tying the jars together—her favorite arrangement by far.

Matt came up behind her, threaded his arms around her waist, and kissed her neck.

"They're all so beautiful," she said, rubbing his arm. "You didn't have to do all this."

He brushed his lips along her earlobe. "You said you'd never been surrounded by flowers. I wanted to be the man who did that for you."

She turned in his arms, searching his eyes. She probably should have felt worse about the heartache he'd endured in his other relationships that hadn't worked out, the pictures of the kids in his wallet that still brought him grief, but all she felt was gratitude to the other women who hadn't had the good sense to hang on to him.

"I don't know how to express what that means to me. Thank you."

He kissed her. "Notice that there aren't any stargazer lilies in the arrangements. I told Tara specifically not to use any."

All she could do was gape at him, awed. "You remembered about Philomena and the stargazers?"

"I might be a guy, but I'm also a lawyer." He tapped his temple. "Details."

"I'm sure your extraordinary memory for detail will

come back to bite me someday, but right now, I'm extremely impressed."

"There's more upstairs!" Tommy called. In her surprise at the flowers, she'd forgotten to keep tabs on his whereabouts.

"We'll be up in a minute. Did you figure out which room is yours?" Matt called.

"I think so," Tommy called back. "Is it the one with two beds?"

"That's the one." He kissed Jenna's hair. "I wasn't sure if you wanted Tommy to know we were sharing a bed yet, so you have the option. The room he'll stay in has two twin-sized beds. I keep it like that because the only guests I ever have stay over are my nieces and nephews."

She splayed her hands over his chest. "Thank you for being so amazing. I don't know what I did to deserve you. I feel like the luckiest woman in the world."

He twirled a strand of her hair around his finger, glanced behind them as if making sure the coast was clear, then put his lips close to her ear. "If you feel like that now, just wait until tonight when I can pamper you in the manner in which I want you to become accustomed."

Oh, she liked the sound of that. She pressed her lips to his in a brief, enticing kiss, to leave him craving more.

He crooked his finger, tugging the lock of hair still wrapped around it. "And by that, I mean I want you naked."

"I figured as much." She laid another kiss on him.

He released her hair and trailed his finger down her chest, tugging the V-neck of her shirt down until he saw cleavage. "And on my bed." He settled his roving finger into her bra between her breasts. "And on the floor. Then on that chair in the corner of my room. And possibly on the balcony."

She closed a hand around his pectoral muscle, letting her

thumb trace its curve. Damn, she loved his body. "Definitely on the balcony."

His mouth quirked into a charming smile. She rolled to her tiptoes and pressed the tip of her tongue into his dimple. This was going to be a great week. One thing was for sure: she may have had to wait eight months for Matt to gather the courage to tell her how he felt, but he'd been worth every single minute of waiting and wanting.

Chapter Fifteen

Matt loved that Jenna and Tommy were staying with him. The flower idea had come to him in a burst of genius first thing that morning during his shower. It'd been a long time since he'd felt inspired to orchestrate a grand romantic gesture and he couldn't have been more pleased with the result or Jenna's reaction.

From the kitchen table, he listened to the murmur of Jenna's soothing mommy voice as she tucked Tommy in bed. He loved the sound of a woman and child in his big, drafty house where before there had been only silence and emptiness.

He wanted to be in that room with her when she tucked Tommy in, he really did, but he couldn't. Not quite yet. Old fears died hard, apparently. Tucking kids in was his specialty, a skill honed with his nieces and nephews, Brandon, Stephy, and Jordy, but he'd have to build up to the idea that he could let his guard down around Tommy without too great a risk to his heart.

In front of him on the table were the transcripts from two depositions he'd meant to get through that day at work but had been too distracted with excitement over Jenna and Tommy's arrival to concentrate on. It worked out perfectly that Jenna needed to study tonight before they enacted their balcony fantasy. Her computer was already set up across the table from him and he'd been warned against interfering with her and her friend Carrie's webcam-assisted study session. No problem there considering the ream of paperwork he needed to plow through in time for work the next morning.

Jenna snagged a soda from the fridge, then assumed her seat across the table from Matt.

"Did Tommy settle in okay?"

"He's still pretty amped about being here, but he'll settle down fast. He's been keeping me on my toes since the day he was born, but one thing I'll say about him is that he's an excellent sleeper."

"That's a great attribute for a kid to have. Tara's always struggling to get her kids to go to sleep."

Jenna wrinkled her nose. "That would cramp my style. After Tommy's asleep is my prime study time."

"Speaking of which, hi there," said a woman's voice through the laptop speaker.

"Carrie, hi. You're right on time," Jenna answered.

"I e-mailed you a copy of the notes from last night's study session so we can go over them, but before we get started, I want to meet him. Is he there?"

Jenna smiled hopefully at Matt over the top of the laptop screen, but he was already setting his pen down and standing. Though he'd met a lot of Jenna's acquaintances at Amy's wedding, he'd gotten the distinct impression that she'd erected an invisible wall between herself and the people of Catcher Creek, probably in preparation for her move. He was curious about who her real friends were and welcomed the opportunity to meet Carrie, if only via webcam.

Standing behind Jenna's chair, he waved into the webcam.

Carrie was a tousle-haired brunette with an easy smile, cute. He could only imagine the stir she and Jenna would cause if they walked into a bar together for a night of letting off steam and dancing.

Carrie steepled her hands and studied him. "You have designs on my best friend."

Straight to the point. Matt admired that. "I do. Big designs."

Carrie gave up the stern father look and grinned. "I liked your style today with the flowers."

Jenna's skin flushed the most adorable shade of pink from her cheeks to her chest. "You're not supposed to tell him that."

"Word travels fast among you ladies." He kissed Jenna's temple to let her know he didn't mind that she'd been bragging to her friends about his gesture.

"I've seen pictures and everything," Carrie said.

"Ah, the glories of a smartphone," Jenna muttered bashfully, thumbing through a stack of blank index cards.

"I like him, Jenna," Carrie said. "You were right."

Matt almost asked Jenna what she was right about, but thought Carrie might be more open to telling him. "What was she right about?"

Carrie's grin widened. "She told me you were worth waiting for."

Oh, man, he loved that Jenna was thinking that way, so much so that she'd told her best friend. Jenna twisted her neck to look up at him through her thick lashes. The sight hit him like a zing to the heart. That look meant she wanted to be kissed. He used to fear that look, but now he couldn't get enough of it.

He leaned in, but before their lips touched, Carrie cleared her throat. "Okay, lovebirds. Time to start studying before this single girl gets irrationally jealous."

He leaned in farther anyway and pecked Jenna on the lips. "Fine. I'll leave you two to it." He wagged a finger at Carrie. "I'm going to be here, too, getting some work done, so no funny business."

"Wouldn't dream of it. I'll get her on track for her midterm in no time so she can get back to making lovey-dovey eyes with you."

With a squeeze to Jenna's shoulder and a wave to Carrie, he walked back to his side of the table and resettled in front of the stack of deposition papers. Over the next forty-five minutes, he put a big dent in his stack of papers, which was saying something because Jenna was distracting as hell. Watching her sharp mind work intricate computer programming tasks and her luscious lips spouting complicated words and phrases of computer terminology he'd never heard before turned him on in a major way.

On a whim, when he reached a stopping point in the deposition he was reading, he swiped one of the index cards from the stack she was using to make flash cards. She watched him take it, her eyebrows bunching together in puzzlement, but Carrie was reading aloud from her notes and he could tell Jenna didn't want to interrupt her. He offered her a sly grin and retreated to his end of the table.

On the index card, he wrote, *I never knew studying could be so sexy.*

He folded it into a paper airplane and sailed it her way. Apparently, the hasty design wasn't all that ingenious because instead of gently tapping her on the shoulder, it dive-bombed her keyboard. Carrie blinked and stopped talking.

Jenna glanced his way with scolding eyes. He mugged an innocent expression while he fake-studied the top paper on his pile.

"Anyway, back to what you were asking. I think the answer is on page two-twenty-five," Carrie said.

All seemed back to normal until Carrie started quoting from the textbook. He watched Jenna's hand creep to the pile of index cards and slip one off the stack. She scribbled something, a smile fighting to break free of her serious study face. Matt waited with bated breath.

Holding the card between her fingers, she flicked it in his direction.

He snapped it up and stared, a heavy heat coiling in his body. What a dirty girl.

Rather than a note in reply, she'd drawn two stick figures complete with goofy, generic happy faces going at it, missionary position.

He tried to catch her eye, but her focus remained riveted on whatever Carrie was saying. With a flourish of his hand, he reached across the table and grabbed another card.

The drawing's wrong. When I have you under me, the look on your face is more like . . . And he added his own X-rated stick figures, doggie style. On the woman's face he drew slits for closed eyes, a circle for a mouth in mid-moan with a trail of hearts streaming out from it to show how good she was getting it from stick figure stud. Drawing wasn't his forte, but he had to admit he'd nailed this one, so to speak. Grinning with amusement at his own stupid joke, he folded the card into a football and flicked it in her direction. It tumbled into her lap.

Jenna had split her computer screen, with Carrie's web video phone on one side and a black screen on the other side filled with what looked like programming code—not that he knew the first thing about computer languages. She unfolded the index card without breaking stride in her heated discussion with Carrie about something called synchronization primitives.

She glanced to where the note sat in her lap and her tongue poked into her cheek. Either absentmindedly or on purpose—he couldn't decide—she fluttered fingers over the fading bite marks he'd given her Saturday night.

A minute later, an index card spun through the air in his direction.

I want to dance with you naked. Beneath it were stick figures in closed hold. On the male figure, she'd drawn round, cartoonish butt cheeks.

"Is that what my butt looks like?" he asked in a mock-offended whisper that earned him a reprimanding glare. Then again, that glare was tempered by teeth tugging her smiling lower lip into her mouth. He wasn't a fervent body-part namer, but was seriously entertaining the idea of naming her rosy, plump, talented lips Helen, after Helen of Troy for their ability to drive men crazy and make them do stupid-ass stuff.

Case in point, he swiped a card. She wanted to dance with him in the buff, which was a great idea. They'd have a fantastic time twirling around his master suite with nothing on but their smiles. It'd give new meaning to the Tush Push line dance. Fun, but not what he had in mind. Not tonight, anyway.

I want to lick chocolate sauce off your nipples. He drew his best, most junior-high-school-crude pair of knockers covered in dark liquid. They looked like a two-scoop ice-cream sundae floating in front of a stick figure woman. Close enough.

Her comeback: *I want to leave teeth marks on your ass.*

"Cheeky," he whispered.

She arched a brow at him, but continued to jot notes on a spiral pad of paper.

I want to . . . He drew a stick-figure woman on her back, her stick legs bent like a triangle, and the circle-shaped head of a man between her legs. Yeah, his face was going to spend some major quality time with her pussy tonight. Let's see what she thought about that.

Without folding his masterpiece, he slid it across the table to her.

She recrossed her legs and did a little arch of her back that told him she was feeling it down there like he was, heavy and low down, aching to be touched.

He had to adjust his erection in his pants when he read the next message she'd dashed off for him.

I want to suck on your nipples until you beg me to move my mouth to your dick.

That could be arranged.

I want you to keep . . . The pen froze on the page as he considered his next move. He almost wrote that he wanted her to keep her eyes open to look at him when she came. And he did. That would be magnificent and sexy. But he was beyond romance at the moment. He tapped the pen against the paper, considering. Screw it. Time to write what he really wanted.

He crumpled the paper and started over.

I want to fuck you without a condom.

Take that, wade-in-slowly guy. It wasn't the writing of a poet, but, damn, did penning the words make his dick even harder. He'd had his annual check-up a few months ago, so he was clean and ready to go. And getting pregnant was no issue, he thought with his usual flare of irritation. This was all on her. Whatever her wishes were, he'd abide by them. But, God, he hoped she was game for it.

He stood and deposited the note on her keyboard, then stood behind her laptop screen and waited for her reaction.

She sucked in a sharp breath, then rolled her eyes up to meet his stare. Arousal was written all over her face.

Tonight, he mouthed.

The slow nod she gave sent a ripple of electricity through him. Yeah, this was happening. There was no way he'd be able to concentrate on his work now, so he decided to stop pretending to. With Jenna watching, he stripped his shirt over his head, draped it on a chair, and flexed for her. Totally egotistical, but whatever. He worked hard at the gym and knew Jenna enjoyed his physique.

As he'd hoped, her gaze raked over his body with bold admiration.

"Okay, I'm not Helen Keller. I can hear and see what you two are up to," Carrie said.

Jenna snapped her focus from Matt to the computer and folded her hands demurely on the table. "Sorry."

"No, you're not. But that's okay. We have a great start on the test prep. Matt? Are you there?" She'd pitched her voice to carry.

"I'm here." He scrambled to pull his shirt back on and jogged into view of the webcam. "Hi again."

Carrie speared a finger at the camera. "Our girl here has to study. She has a lot riding on this class and the midterm's next week."

He liked the way Carrie was looking out for Jenna. It was impossible not to feel a measure of guilt. He was supposed to be supporting her studying, too, but he'd acted no better than a hormone-fueled teenager tonight. "I know. I'm sorry. I promise to behave next time."

She nodded. "Thank you. We have a computer class on Wednesday at the UNM campus. Pinky promise me you'll make sure she gets there." She poked her pinky finger up to the camera.

Uh, okay. Time to roll with it. He pressed his pinky to the camera on Jenna's computer. "I pinky promise. She'll be there." Who was going to watch Tommy during her class?

He'd have to ask her about that later. "Thank you for looking out for her, Carrie. It makes me feel better knowing she has friends who have her back."

"Hello? I'm sitting right here," Jenna said, "and for both of your information, I'm a grown adult who's managed to get this far in my education all by myself."

"Only because you won't tell your sisters," Carrie said. That caught Matt's interest. Carrie seemed as uncomfortable with Jenna's lies of omission as he was.

Jenna slapped her palms on the table. "Carrie, I love you but you're turning into a harpy."

"I know. But I'm only turning into a harpy because I love you, too, sweetie. I just want what's best for you."

"Thank you for that."

Carrie sighed and pulled herself straighter. "Okay, you lovebirds. Go be ridiculously happy together. I have a date with a French boyfriend named pinot noir." She waved. "Nice to meet you, Matt."

Matt smiled, genuinely. Carrie was good people. "Likewise."

Jenna shut the laptop, splayed her hands over the closed lid, and rose, leveling him with a heated look that might've singed a lesser man. "No condom?"

"That's what I want." In fact, the more he thought about feeling her grip around him as he thrust, flesh on flesh, and the more he considered the idea of what coming inside her would feel like, the shorter his breath got and the faster his pulse. "I'm clean. Recently tested. You?"

"I've been checked and I'm good." She came to him, pushing her breasts against his chest, her hands fluttering on his neck. "Get your shirt back off and come with me."

Then she walked out the kitchen door, into the night.

He fancied himself a smart man, and so he ripped his

shirt over his head and followed. Out of habit, he touched the porch light switch, but then thought twice about that choice and left the lights off. It was a clear night and the moon was a sliver. The stars would be brilliant.

She was waiting on the porch, staring over Aldra Valley, his private sanctuary. The stars were, indeed, breathtaking. A million glittering jewels from the edge of the world and up to infinity. Over the years, depending on his mood and the tenderness of his grief, he either took comfort in how small the stars made him feel or he cursed his insignificance to God. Tonight, with Jenna, he felt like he owned the universe.

The wild grass on the valley's slope behind his house crackled and shook in the slight breeze, sending up their sharp, beautiful baked grass scent. He loved the land, the freedom of wide-open spaces stretching out before him and the wide-open sky above him. It was the greatest feeling to know he had this place to offer Jenna and Tommy.

He took her hips in hand as he came up behind her. "I want to give you the world," he whispered into her hair. "My whole world, Jenna. Will you take it?"

She turned in his arms, walking him backward. Her eyes were fathomless orbs of darkness, but her parted lips were dewy and glittered in the light from the heavens.

She pushed him back, into a porch chair. He went, wondering what her plan for him was, eager to find out. Maybe the nature he offered her had turned her wild, too. They could lose themselves in the universe tonight, make it whatever they wanted.

She lowered to her knees and unlatched the button on his jeans.

Drunk with the knowledge of what she was about to do, he was lost about whether to help with the zipper and boxers, thread his hands into her hair, or grip the armrests for dear life. Ultimately, there was nothing for him to do but take whatever she was going to give him. Slouching in the chair, his fingers twitching idly, he watched her mouth close over him.

Chapter Sixteen

If Matt hadn't had his heart set on condomless sex, he would've let Jenna finish him off in her mouth. She was so damn skilled, he was ready to blow almost immediately. But now, all he could think about was how it was going to feel when their bodies joined.

He knew he was close when he couldn't stop his hips from thrusting into her mouth with a reckless lack of control. "God, Jenna. You're so good at that. But I need you to stop."

She dropped her head all the way down, deep throating him and pulling back off with a slow suction that had him hissing through his teeth. "Why should I stop now?"

He cupped her chin with his hand, touching his thumb to her moist, swollen lips. "Do you have any idea how hot it makes me, thinking about my come inside you?" He sat forward, his cock pushing up over his stomach, and felt the moisture at the tip smearing across his abs. "I want to go to work tomorrow dreaming of you walking around with panties wet with my come. Fuck, Jenna, it makes me so damn crazy to think about that."

With a carnal smile, she extricated her chin from his hand. "I love it when you get like this. Aggressive and growly, so demanding. It turns me on something fierce." She bent low and licked the moisture from his stomach, then the tip of his cock. If she liked aggressive, he could give her that, no problem. He wrapped his hands around her head and shoved his cock down her throat. She took it like she was greedy for it as deep and hard as he wanted to give it to her.

When he couldn't take anymore, he backed her face off of him, hooked his hands under her arms and pulled her to standing with him. After a hard, wet kiss to let her know how ravenous with desire she made him, he moved past her and grabbed the cushion off the bench swing.

Tugging her along by the hand and with his cock straining out from his open pants, he descended the porch stairs, If they were going to do it in the great outdoors, then they were going all the way—in the grass, under the stars, out in the open.

A ways from the house, in the thick, soft grass, he tossed the cushion down. Turning to Jenna, he took hold of her shirt and pulled it off over her head, then made short work of the rest of her clothes. He felt between her legs, to the wetness there. Good. She was ready for him. "Lie on your back."

He memorized the look of her open, beautiful body under the glow of the night sky as he shoved his pants and boxers to the ground and dropped to his knees. He kicked her legs farther apart and buried his face in her pussy.

He loved going down on her more than anything. Just this once, though, he wanted so badly to ram himself inside her—rough, quick, and dirty. But she didn't come easily with intercourse and he'd never be the kind of man to sacrifice her pleasure for his own. Though his body was growing impatient, he forced himself to slow down and take care of her.

When she was breathing hard and straining with need,

her back arching and her body swollen and ready for him, he kissed his way up her stomach to her breasts, positioning his cock at her entrance. She curled her arms around his shoulders and brushed kisses along his jaw.

The feel of his cock head touching Jenna's hot, wet body and her arms and lips caressing him, brought him right to the edge of ecstasy. He looked out over Aldra Valley, then out at the millions of stars above them, shimmering on Jenna's skin, and the thick, dried-sage desert air wrapping around them like sanctity itself.

"Matt," Jenna breathed, nuzzling his neck. "You make me so happy."

He raised up to his elbows and looked into her eyes, brimming with tenderness and arousal. Holding her gaze, he sunk his cock into her. *May this be the first time of thousands*, he thought as their hip bones touched. They held themselves together, kissing and breathing into each other until Matt's body took over control and began to move.

Their lovemaking built to a crescendo until the movement had no ending or beginning, transforming into a blur of need and love, sweat and flesh, and sweet, sweet friction under the wild New Mexico sky until he didn't even want to come. He just wanted to hang there suspended in time and the bliss of being Jenna's lover.

Holding her tight, he rolled to his back, with Jenna on top to better access her clit. He worked her body with unyielding purpose, his fingers coaxing sensation from her clit, his hips thrusting up hard and fast, straining to hold back until she could drop over the edge of release with him.

Her inner muscles clenched. With a ragged gasp, she fell forward, gripping his shoulders with her fingernails. Her pussy pulsed around him and he finally let go. He grabbed her hips and pumped every last drop of himself deep inside her. He wrapped his arms around her, pulling her flat against his chest, and closed his eyes, content in the knowledge that he was the luckiest man in the world.

Long after their climaxes, they remained in each other's arms, staring at the night sky and talking about the future. Jenna didn't think she'd ever been happier in her life. She stretched her toes out in the cool grass and indulged in a deep, cleansing sigh. "I love it out here."

"Me, too. I've been meaning to ask you about something you mentioned at dinner. You said that apartment you decided on is available on the first of August. That's next week. Are you serious about that?"

Thinking about moving to Santa Fe put a smile on her face. She'd be away from the danger of Carson uncovering her secret and close to the man she was falling in love with. Double bonus. "I am. In fact, I'm going to tell Rachel about college and my new job this weekend."

That was the only tricky part for Jenna. She dreaded that conversation, which was why she'd put if off for so long. But there was no getting around it, even though the thought of it twisted her stomach into knots.

"You're not worried about Amy coming back from her honeymoon to find you gone?"

"Amy's going to be too busy being pregnant and a newlywed to give my life any more than a passing thought."

He looked unconvinced, but dropped it. "All right, then. What can I do to support you?"

Despite her sudden rush of anxiety, she grinned. Could he be any more perfect a boyfriend? "That depends on what your plans are for this weekend."

He shrugged. "I usually mountain bike on Sundays with my buddies Ken and Liam, but I was thinking that if you were serious about moving up here next week, then we should spend this weekend at your place packing. We could join the Sunday barbecue with your sister and friends, and then, whenever you're ready to make the actual move, I'd drive down after work and we could gather a crew of guys to help you with the big stuff."

"Lisa Binderman's hosting the barbecue this weekend since Kellan and Amy are out of town. I'd love to go."

"Then it's settled."

"One more thing, actually. Bunco is this Thursday night at Patricia Parrish's house. I was thinking of going. Then, I'll already be there to talk to Rachel about UNM and my move to Santa Fe on Friday."

She loathed the idea of spending another evening in the company of Carson's mother and the other matriarchs and town gossips, especially now that she knew Kyle Kopec had been involved in Carson's beating. Kyle's mother, Gayle, was a regular player and Patricia Parrish's best friend. But Jenna was dying a slow death not knowing what Carson's plan for vengeance was.

Why hadn't he made his move yet? What was he waiting for? Had he paid a visit to his parents yet? If so, to what end? If there was any surefire way to get a read on the situation, Bunco would be it.

"Would you take Tommy with you?" Matt asked.

"Rachel usually babysits him when I go to Bunco. I'll need to check with her to make sure that's still okay, but I'm sure it is."

"Well, you leaving on Thursday will give me time to take care of something I've been planning on doing."

"Oh? Do tell."

He wrapped a strand of her hair around his finger, then let it go. "I've been saving and planning for something almost since I became a lawyer. It's nothing like you going to college and becoming a computer engineer, and it's not a secret to my family or friends, but I've had this dream for years and I've never been able to get myself to pull the trigger."

She drew a patter through his chest hair. "Tell me about it."

He took a deep breath. "My favorite part of my job as a lawyer is the pro bono work I do on the side. Helping families get a fair shake against big oil. I've helped save family farms and houses and send kids to college. It's fulfilling in a way the corporate litigation isn't."

"You saved our farm."

He shrugged off the praise. "It wasn't all me, but I helped and it felt great to be able to do that. My dream is to quit my job at the law firm and open up a low-cost legal clinic."

"Wow. Cool."

"Yeah. I'm really excited about it, but it's a risk—a huge risk—financially. I don't need to make a killing to survive, financially. I mean, I live on my family's land, so there's no mortgage, and I don't have many needs. I didn't get into law to get rich. Since I haven't had a family of my own, my career is everything I am, my whole identity, and giving it up to go for this dream, I'll be honest with you, it's scary."

"What tipped the scale for you to decide to finally go for it?"

He stroked her hair. "You did. When we were dancing during the rehearsal dinner, you said I was a wade-in-slowly kind of guy. You were absolutely right, but I hadn't been able to see that in myself. I didn't use to be that way. I was always cautious and a planner, but at some point my caution transformed into cowardice against taking chances. I forgot what it was like to want something and go after it full-speed ahead."

"Something changed for you at the wedding."

"Yes. It finally hit me how much I was missing out on because I was afraid to take a leap of faith. I wanted you in my life so badly, for so long, and yet I let fear keep me from telling you how I felt. It's the same for me with this job change. You've given me the courage to pull the trigger and go for it. Not only because of how happy you've made me, but because you're living your life boldly, going for the dream career you want and you're not letting anything stop you. I want to be like you. I want to be as brave with my life as you are with yours."

Her heart swelled with pride. "That's the best compliment I've ever been given. I bet you have the clinic all planned out, too. I bet you even have an office picked out."

He grinned. "I do. Actually, I'd narrowed it down to two locations. One in Santa Fe and one in Catcher Creek. You moving here makes the decision a no-brainer, even though the timing is ironic."

"How so?"

"Because I have your and Tommy's futures to think about now. I know you and I have a long way to go to being a family, but I feel like we're headed that way. I want to be able to provide for you, but giving up a great job in this economy seems outrageous."

She splayed her hands over his chest and snuggled closer. "Not to me."

"It wouldn't bother you if I got poor all of a sudden?"

She chortled. "You know it wouldn't. Look at me—I'm giving up free housing on thousands of acres to move into a tiny apartment in the city. Who's the crazy one now?"

"Going after your dream isn't crazy."

She pushed up on an elbow and tapped the end of his nose. "Are you hearing yourself? It's time for Mr. Conservative to do a little dream following of his own."

She rubbed over the hair below his belly button and felt his cock grow until the tip touched her hand. When it came to sex, they were both insatiable. She loved that aspect of their relationship.

"With you in my life, I feel like I can do anything." He pinned her beneath him and kissed his way across her collar. "Tomorrow, would you and Tommy meet me for lunch downtown? I'll show you the storefront I have my eye on for the legal clinic."

"Sounds wonderful."

He covered her breast with his hand, tugging on the nipple. "And then Wednesday, I'm going to take off work. I'll watch Tommy so you can go to your computer lab. Would that be okay with you? I know your friend Carrie's parents offered to watch him, but I think some guy time with him would be great." He curled his head down and circled her nipple with his tongue.

Love for him crested inside her. "Guy time. He'll love it."

"Good." He moved to her other nipple and drew it into his mouth. "We need to take my bubbies to Torah study in the morning, but there's a playground at the synagogue we can hang out at. Then, I was thinking he and I could go horseback riding and have a picnic lunch, if that's okay with you."

"Whatever you want. I trust you implicitly with him. I am a bit jealous he gets to meet your bubbies before I do."

"They're a crack-up. After my grandpas died, they moved into a condo together. Neither one of them has a verbal filter worth a damn. My parents invited us to their house for dinner on Wednesday, so I'll make sure the bubbies get an invite."

"Sounds like a great plan. I can't wait." She wrapped a hand around his hardened cock, reveling in its thick, heavy length. "Sounds like we've got everything worked out except how we're going to spend the rest of the evening."

He stroked her hair as her favorite lazy, lopsided smile spread on his lips. "Actually, I'm crystal clear about my plans for you tonight."

"Is that so?"

He captured her mouth in a sweet kiss, then rose to his feet and offered her his hand. "I think it's time I introduced you to my bed."

She let him pull her up to standing and into a tight embrace. She looked over his shoulder at the moonlit wilderness, thinking that there was no more perfect place in the world for her and Tommy than this peaceful, magical land, alongside the man who called it home. It was all in her grasp—this place, Matt's love, her future career—and all she had to do was make it through one more quick trip to Catcher Creek before she could escape that town and the ghosts of her past once and for all.

On Wednesday, Matt sent Jenna off to school early. Her class didn't start until one, but he figured she could use the extra time to study, so he and Tommy waved her away after breakfast.

Chauffeuring the bubbies was uneventful. They were delighted that Tommy laughed at all their jokes, and he was delighted when Bubbie Roenick produced a peppermint candy from her purse. There were a couple other kids at the temple's playground and Matt moved off to the sidelines with the other kids' dad, like it was the most natural thing in the world to stand there with other parents and watch their kids play. Matt was in heaven.

After packing a picnic back on the ranch, Matt and Tommy drove the mile road to the stables near his parents' house to select the horses they'd take on their ride. Though Matt had woken up early from his excitement about their picnic, Tommy was decidedly more jazzed about visiting Mrs. Carrots and her kittens.

They were grooming Hershey and Toby when Matt's

mom popped her head in, waving a bag full of cookies. "Hi there. I brought you a fresh supply of snickerdoodles since I heard all about Tommy's sweet tooth. Is it just you boys today?"

"Yes, Jenna had to go to Albuquerque."

Tommy brushed Toby's flank with erratic circles. "My mom's going to school. She doesn't think I know, but I figured it out."

Mom grinned, amused. "You're pretty smart like that."

Puffing out his chest, Tommy shrugged. "Not really. She has books all over the living room and sometimes I open my door and lay in bed and listen to her talking about school with her friends. She doesn't ever mention it, so I don't think she wants me to know. Don't get me in trouble, okay?"

"You don't have to worry about that. Your secret's safe with us," Matt said.

The night before, Jenna had agreed with Matt that it was time to tell Tommy a modified version of the truth about her schooling. His little mind didn't need to know all the details or that Jenna had been working toward her degree for four years. Someday, Matt would make sure Tommy understood how hard his mom had worked to give him a good life and follow her dreams, but for now, all he needed to know was that she was going to school and when she finished next month, they were having a big celebration.

He could tell that, for Jenna, the idea of telling Tommy even that much was scary for her. She'd kept the secret for so long, it was hard to get out of that mentality, he supposed. She'd committed to talking to Tommy about it on Thursday, since Wednesday was busy from morning until Tommy's bedtime.

"School?" Mom asked.

"We can talk about it later." Behind Tommy's head, he gestured to his ears, then pointed to Tommy, hoping to convey that there was more to the story that Little Big Ears didn't need to know.

Mom nodded her understanding. "She'll be back in time for us all to have dinner together tonight, I hope? I'm making my famous bleu cheese burgers."

Score. "Yeah, she should be back before six. I love those burgers. Good call."

"It was your father's idea. So what are you two gentlemen up to today?"

"We're taking Hershey and Toby on a ride through Aldra Valley to my super secret picnic spot."

"Sounds like a great way to spend the afternoon. Don't forget sunscreen."

"We didn't," Tommy chimed in. "But I wish Mrs. Carrots and her babies could come with us."

"It's not safe out in the big, wide world for her little ones yet. There are a lot of scary predators out there for tiny, defenseless kittens."

"That's what a mommy cat is for. She's their defense shield," Tommy said in a matter-of-fact tone. "If they had a daddy cat, they'd be even safer."

Mom's expression lengthened. "Matt, could I speak to you in private for a minute?" When she got that tone, every one of her kids, grandkids, and employees knew a lecture was coming. Matt was so sick and tired of being given a talking-to like he was still a kid. His mom's eternal baby boy, without a family of his own. The accident hadn't helped him escape that image, either, setting back any strides toward independence he'd made in college. He'd had to regress by necessity, counting on his parents for help bathing and feeding himself. He hadn't been able to drive for months. After that, the dark place that the news of his infertility had catapulted him into only made the situation worse.

He followed Mom out of the stable and around the corner. "Mom, please don't spoil my good day."

"That's not fair. What makes you think I was going to do that?"

Matt sucked his cheeks in and counted to ten silently. "Sorry. What's up?"

"I know you're happy to have Jenna and her son here—your father and I like them a lot—but don't you think this is too fast? You're basing your decision on your legal clinic location on your girlfriend of the moment."

Matt ground his molars together, shaking his head. Wow. Girlfriend of the moment. How could Mom think that? He'd phoned his parents that morning to share the good news that he'd put in an offer on the storefront in downtown Santa Fe the day before, and here she was throwing the news back in his face. "You said you weren't going to spoil my day."

She pressed her lips into a thin line. "Your father and I worry about you. You can't fault us for that."

"I know. And I love you for it, but it's gotten to the point where I feel like I'm damned if I do, damned if I don't in your eyes. Jenna's not my girlfriend of the moment, so please don't talk about her like that. And if I want to make a choice to build a business in the city I was born and raised in, I don't think you need to criticize that, despite the assumptions you're making about my motivation."

She wrung her hands together. "Matty, you've gone through so much and been hurt so many times. Watching you . . ." She shook her head. "It's hard, son. That's all. It's hard to watch and be powerless to help your baby with what he's going through."

He bet it was. It still didn't give her and Dad the right to hand over judgment of him all the damn time. Despite the lawyer part of him pushing him to keep battling until he won the argument, he knew deep down that there was no sense driving himself crazy trying to persuade his parents to change their mind-set.

Only time would prove to them that he could manage his own life just fine. Eventually, they'd figure out that his relationship with Jenna wasn't a passing fancy and nothing he could say would speed up their acceptance of that.

The shitty thing was a part of him still agreed with his mom. He was rushing into things with Jenna. And, yes, he did have a history of being hurt—badly. After all the heartache he'd been through, he couldn't escape the nagging fear that all he and Jenna had done was build a house of cards. Because the truth was that he hadn't been bold enough to tuck Tommy into bed either Monday or Tuesday. When it came right down to it, he didn't need his parents introducing any more insecurity into his mind—he was doing a bang-up job of that all on his own.

"I know, Mom. It's okay. Thank you for caring about me so much. I love you. Tommy and I need to get on our picnic. We'll be at your house at six tonight for dinner."

The trail was wide enough that Matt and Tommy were able to ride side-by-side as they descended into the valley. The sun was shining bright and hot, a smattering of white clouds dotted the sky, and Tommy was in a fantastic, chatty mood. Still, Matt stewed. He couldn't stop thinking about his conversation with his mom, considering that maybe she had a valid point about him rushing into things with Jenna and Tommy too fast.

"Was that your mommy?" Tommy asked.

"Sure was. And you met my dad the day you got here.

He was the old guy with the big ears and black cowboy hat. Remember?"

"He was nice. I'm like one of Mrs. Carrots's kittens," Tommy announced.

"How do you figure?"

"They don't have a dad either."

Matt's mouth went dry. *Keep it cool, man.* "How do you feel about that?"

Tommy fiddled with the rein, looping it around his middle finger. "Daisy's dad takes her camping. They make s'mores."

Fair enough. It wasn't like he'd expected a heartfelt speech from the little guy about the lack of a father figure in his life. "Have you ever been camping?"

"No. My mommy says we'll go someday, but she doesn't know when. She's really busy."

I would take you. I'd take you all the time, as much as you wanted. We would roast s'mores and fish and shoot targets with BB guns and tramp all over the countryside. "You're right." He cleared his throat. "She's really busy, and that's why you and I have such important jobs."

Tommy looked his way, squinting at the glare of the sun. "What jobs?"

"Keeping her happy. That's what a man's job is, you know. Keep the women in his life happy."

Tommy screwed his mouth up, thinking, then his whole face crinkled in a cringe. "Does that mean I have to eat broccoli now?"

Matt chuckled. How could he not? The kid was adorable. If he'd been Matt's kid, he would've gathered him into a bear hug and made some sort of secret rewards deal for eating his veggies without complaint.

Panic struck his heart like lightning. His parents were

right. He was rushing things with Jenna and if things went south now, it would be the worst heartbreak of his life to lose her and Tommy. He wanted to be Tommy's dad so badly it stole his breath clean out of his lungs. He and Jenna were so very new and new meant fragile. Shit. What had he done? He felt like a man on a high-wire with no safety net below him.

Heart pounding, he kept his fingers laced tight over the horn of his saddle and broadened his smile. "Aw, now, how can you think like that? Broccoli's delicious. I bet your mom makes it real good."

Tommy sighed and melted over his saddle, exasperated as only a kid could be. "Okay, fine. I'll eat broccoli, but no asparagus. Bleh." They rode in silence while Matt talked himself down from the panic attack.

After a few minutes, Tommy added, "You could be my dad, you know. If you wanted."

Matt's chest tightened painfully again. Yeah, he wanted.

Above them, the clouds stretched and morphed. The long grass rustled in the wind and the trees grew denser as they descended into the valley. He had to choose his response carefully. For all he knew, he was the first man Tommy had ever voiced that invitation to. Not something a man could take lightly. *It's not up to me* would make Jenna the bad guy if things didn't work out. *We'll see* was glib and didn't address that tagged-on qualifier Tommy had added. *That would be great* might inflate his expectations.

He wiped sweat from his forehead with the back of his hand and released a slow exhale. He refused to let fear rule his life any longer. He refused to be cynical like that Lynch guy at the wedding even if it meant sticking his neck out with nothing but a prayer to guard against it getting cut off.

"Thank you," he said. "I don't think I've ever gotten a better offer than that. You are one special kid, that's for sure.

The tricky part is that your mom and I don't know what's going to happen in the future; there are a lot of grown-up choices we have to make that aren't easy. But I'll make you a promise. When I figure out what's going to happen, I'll tell you right away, okay?"

He held still and silent, awaiting Tommy's reaction.

Tommy scratched his cheek. "What about s'mores?"

Matt's breath came out in a huff of anxious laughter. "You sure are single-minded about sweets, buddy."

"I know," Tommy replied heavily, like that was his burden to bear.

"I'll see what I can do about the s'mores situation. Maybe tonight we can rustle up some supplies after dinner, if it's okay with your mom." After a second's hesitation to let the panic pass through him, he threw his arm around Tommy and gave him a giant, one-arm hug and a kiss on the hair. "Have you ever sung 'The Cowboy Lullaby'?"

"Aren't lullabies for babies when they're going to bed?"

"You're right about lullabies being sung before bed. But my nieces and nephews are older than babies and they still love me to sing them 'The Cowboy Lullaby' when they stay the night at my house. I figured you and I could practice right now so you'll be prepared tonight. We can sing it to your mom when we tuck you in tonight."

"Does it have a horse in it?"

"And boots and spurs, too. It's a real cowboy song from back in my great-great-grandfather's pioneer days. It starts out like this." He took another fortifying breath, smiled at the little boy who was hanging on his every word, and started to sing. "*When the prairie moon shines in the prairie sky, that's when cowboys sing a lullaby . . .*"

Chapter Seventeen

The best, most logical way to stay on the pulse of Catcher Creek gossip was not by grabbing a beer at Smithy's Bar, as many of the men in town claimed. They could have their delusions about saving the world one brew and bowl of pretzels at a time, but football scores and steer prices didn't delve into the heart of the town or the people in it. If one wanted to be privy to the private matters that happened behind the closed front doors of the homes and ranches scattered over the Quay County countryside, then you had to devote the fourth Thursday of every month to Bunco.

At its heart, Bunco was a big ol' excuse for ladies to get together and dish on friends, family, and neighbors wrapped in the guise of a dice game with rotating tables of players. Jenna was the youngest player by several years, but she'd signed up with the Bunco powers-that-be the week after her twenty-first birthday and had been one of the town's most devoted participants ever since. She enjoyed the occasional win and getting out of the house away from her schoolwork. And she loved the gossip.

Sure, Jenna had a reputation as a gossiper around town, but not with secrets of any grave importance. She liked to know the private business of people, but nothing harmful, just tidbits about who'd been seen playing grab-ass at church or who was sporting a gaudy new hair color. Indulging in secrets like that hurt no one. It was no different from watching a celebrity gossip show on TV.

Though she was having the time of her life with Matt in Santa Fe, there was information she couldn't get any other way but to return to Catcher Creek in time for Bunco. Information like, what was Carson waiting for with his vengeance plot? Had he contacted his family yet, and to what end? What were his plans for Bucky, Lance, and Kyle's families? She had a good feeling that tonight she was going to get the answers she needed, especially since Bunco was being hosted this month by none other than Patricia Parrish herself.

After dropping Tommy off with Rachel and Vaughn, she swung through the grocery store for a prepackaged platter of veggies and ranch and a bottle of wine, then headed to the Parrishes' house on the east side of town.

What she hadn't mentioned to Rachel was her plan to spend the night on the sofa in the big house, rather than in her cottage. She couldn't take a chance on Carson cornering her alone again. Friday and Saturday night, Matt would be with her; then, on Sunday, she was leaving Catcher Creek in her dust once and for all. Jake would be leaving for his partner's memorial service the next day, so Kellan's dog would have to stay with Rachel because it was high time for Jenna to move on.

It was a solid plan, but also one that hinged on her getting Rachel alone to come clean about college and her move to Santa Fe, which terrified her to no end. She'd have to worry about that tomorrow. Tonight, navigating the Bunco minefield was going to take all her concentration.

The Parrish family owned a modest spread, with a pair of old horses under a lean-to and chickens running through the yard. Jenna pressed the doorbell, painted a smile on her face as the knob turned, and stepped into the fray.

"Why, Jenna, hello! Marti told us you'd be here. Don't just stand in the doorway, come on in." Patricia took the wine and veggie platter off her hands and ushered her into the room full of women standing amid the Bunco-prepped card tables.

"There she is," Gayle Kopec said, wrapping a wineglass-holding arm around Jenna's shoulders. "That was some wedding you threw last weekend. When my Kyle gets married, we'll have to send his bride to talk to you for advice. Maybe you can lend her a hand, like a wedding planner would."

Not if my life depended on it, Jenna thought, offering Gayle her most saccharine smile. "I didn't realize Kyle and Brenda were engaged."

Patricia twittered by. "Not quite yet, but my cousin Madge saw him at a jeweler in Tucumcari buying a ring last week. We think he's going to propose at the rodeo on Wednesday. I can't wait to see my boy in action. Makes me so nervous to watch him on those bulls, but so proud at the same time, if you know what I mean."

The rodeo. Of course. That was what Carson was waiting for. He wanted a big display and there wasn't anything bigger or more well attended in Quay County than the annual rodeo. Bucky, Kyle, and Lance would all be there. The local boys' heroic homecoming.

The thought gave Jenna chills. If Carson got his way, if he chose to levy eye-for-an-eye vengeance onto Kyle, would Kyle survive to propose to his girlfriend? If Carson came in with guns blazing, would he be arrested—or worse? Had he taken collateral damage and civilians into account when planning his attack of revenge? God, she hoped so. But with so much hatred in his heart, she doubted he was thinking clearly about the consequences of his actions. She made a mental note to lodge another anonymous call with the sheriff's department to tip Vaughn off to the potential trouble.

The last player to arrive was Charlene Delgado, who, besides being Catcher Creek's best babysitter, held the dubious unofficial title of the town's number-one gossip maven. With Charlene present, the games got under way. Jenna found herself sitting across from Carson's sister, Kate, and next to Patricia and Marti.

The sound of dice crashing onto the room's tables did nothing to deter the conversations. Patricia tapped the score-keeping pencil on the table and squinted thoughtfully in Jenna's direction. "Your sister Amy had some big news at the wedding. I'd make a smart comment about the bride wearing white except that I know I'm excessively old-fashioned about matters such as that."

"Oh, now. Sinning women have been wearing white on their wedding days for centuries. It's not like Amy Sorentino invented the cover-up," Marti said.

"I think it's romantic that Kellan announced it like that," Kate added. "Did you see how in love he was? I didn't think he had it in him to settle down until Amy came along. Now, I've never seen him so happy."

"I'm happy for them," Jenna said. "Kellan's a good man, the best."

"What about you?" Marti said. "The rumor going around is that you were kissing a man at the wedding reception. Wasn't it you who told me that, Patricia?"

Patricia stiffened and rolled the dice, as though attempting to conceal that same disapproval she'd worn on her face after Jenna and Matt had kissed in the civic center lobby. "I only mentioned it because I didn't recognize the man from town. He was in the wedding party, though, and I wanted to know if you knew who he was."

"So who is he?" Marti pressed.

As much as Jenna loved learning other people's secrets, she considered herself the most tight-lipped of the bunch. She'd learned after much practice that there was an art to making the women in town feel like she was sharing her personal business without actually revealing anything private. "His name is Matt Roenick and he's friends with Kellan from way back."

"Where's he from?"

Jenna rolled the dice. Two ones. "Santa Fe. His parents breed horses." That appeased the women. Horse breeding was a worthy occupation indeed. After scooping up the dice, she rolled again, got nothing of consequence, and passed the dice to Marti.

"Santa Fe is quite a haul from Catcher Creek. He must think you're something special. Will you be bringing him to the rodeo?"

Jenna wouldn't get within a hundred miles of the rodeo grounds, and she was going to make sure Rachel didn't either. She gave a noncommittal smile and shrug as she passed the dice to Marti. Enough about her and Matt. She was wracking her brain for a change of topics when Marti spoke up.

"Speaking of out-of-towners, I've been seeing a black truck I don't recognize parked in front of your house a few times this past week, Patti. Relatives visiting?" Marti asked.

Kate and Patricia froze, their eyes on each other. So they knew. Carson had been to see them, too. But to what end?

"Bunco!" Charlene hollered from the head table. Jenna startled and shot to her feet. Kate followed, along with two of the pairs of players who rose to switch tables. The volume of talking ramped up.

"Well?" Marti pressed. "Whose truck was that?"

"Yes, I meant to ask you about that earlier," Gayle said,

coming up next to Jenna to assume her old seat. "I saw that truck, too. In fact, you'll never guess who I thought was behind the wheel when I saw it coming down Main Street." She chuckled like she couldn't believe how crazy the notion was. "It looked like Carson."

Patricia blanched.

Gayle waved it off. "But I thought to myself, Patti would never keep something as big as Carson coming home a secret from her closest friends. Besides, it only looked like Carson in the face. This man was bigger, beefier. I figured he was one of your cousins' kids since the family resemblance was so strong. So who was it?"

The conversation had caught the attention of everyone in the room. Kate averted her eyes. Jenna followed her line of sight to a photograph on the wall of Carson in full military dress.

Like a mallet whacking Jenna on the head, her hatred of the Parrish family crashed down on her. They were still covering his presence up. Like he didn't exist. Like the shame of having him as their son rendered him invisible. As much as she hadn't wanted Carson to return to Catcher Creek, a part of her was glad about it. He was going to make his family take notice. She could well imagine the type of violent public shaming he was planning for Wednesday night.

In the wake of Patricia's silence and Kate's obvious discomfort, Gayle's face fell. "It's true, isn't it? That was Carson I saw. He's home. Well, I never. Why didn't you tell me?"

"Now, Gayle, don't be too hard on her," Charlene said, "He's been gone for, what, five years? No wonder she wanted to keep her boy to herself for a little while."

"Six." Patricia's voice was strained. She cleared her throat before continuing. "He's been gone for six. But he's not staying with us. I don't know where he's been sleeping."

"That doesn't make any sense. Why wouldn't he stay with you?" one of the other women in the room standing behind Jenna said.

Looks were shot in Jenna's direction, like they thought perhaps Carson was staying with her. Jenna backed away from her chair. She didn't think she could stand to play through until the Bunco game ended. Now that she was ruminating on how despicable the Parrish family was, how egregiously they'd wronged their son—if they hadn't had a hand outright in his attempted murder—she felt like the walls of the Parrishes' house were closing in on her.

"Jenna." Gayle set a hand on Jenna's arm. "You and Carson were best friends back in high school. Have you two gotten reacquainted since he's been back?"

This was the woman whose son had nearly killed Carson. The woman who'd raised a bigot, probably because she was one herself. She jerked her arm away from Gayle's touch and met Patricia's searching gaze.

In the woman's eyes, Jenna read panic. That's when Jenna knew—Carson hadn't just paid his parents a visit. Like he had with Jenna, he'd threatened them and given them a taste of what was to come. Had Patricia figured it out about the rodeo? She was probably worried about the effect it would have on her business. The idea sickened Jenna even more. Patricia looked like she was hoping Jenna would throw her a lifeline.

Too bad Jenna didn't feel like playing along. Lou and Patricia Parrish had made their choice. They'd been so worried about their business that they'd denied their son medical care and the loving support Carson had deserved when he'd come out to them. They rejected him so completely that he'd turned violent. They deserved to panic. They deserved to have their business suffer when the town figured out what they'd done. They were so damn worried about appearances and money, Jenna wanted to make them suffer tonight. Why wait until the rodeo?

A tendril of outrage unfurled inside her. Yeah, she wouldn't mind stirring things up. She and Tommy were out of there in a few days anyhow.

"Yes," she said to the captivated audience. "Carson came to see me last week. He's been through a lot, you know."

"You mean, overseas, during his deployment?" Charlene asked. "I've heard terrible stories about what the soldiers go through over there. They're all coming back with that PST, or whatever it's called."

"That's not what I meant." Jenna projected her voice. She wanted everyone to hear this next part. "I was talking about what he went through before he left Catcher Creek."

Patricia shot to her feet. "That will be quite enough. I don't feel right talking about him when he's not here. Why, I'm sure his ears must be burning." She made like she was headed to the kitchen, but Jenna cut her off.

"I've been meaning to ask you something, Mrs. Parrish. Something that's been on my mind for six years. Why didn't you take Carson to the hospital after Kyle, Bucky, and Lance tried to kill him? It was because you were ashamed, wasn't it?"

The room hushed graveyard quiet. God, it felt good, calling these hateful women out, spilling secrets that had no business staying buried.

"What is she talking about?" Gayle asked.

Patricia shook her head. "I didn't have a choice. Our business, our church . . ."

The last of Jenna's composure snapped.

She swept a hand toward the women in the room. "Y'all are unbelievable. Kyle, Bucky, and Lance tried to kill Carson and all you cared about was what your church friends would whisper behind your back? You were worried about losing business because, what—people would've stopped frequenting the town's only feed and grain store because of who the owners' son was? What the hell is wrong with this backward town?"

"That's enough out of you, young lady," Patricia whispered. "You're a guest in my house."

"And I'm about to leave, trust me, but you have to answer me first, Patti," Jenna spat. "When did you figure it out about Carson and who did you tell? Because someone told Bucky, Lance, or Kyle, and it sure wasn't me."

"Tell them what?" someone whispered.

Patricia's spine straightened. "I don't know what you're talking about."

Jenna swung her gaze to Kate. "It was you, wasn't it? Somehow, you figured out about Carson's secret and let it slip to one of the good old boys you were hot for back then." Kate's face blanched. "It really was you. I can see it in your eyes. Didn't you care what happened to your brother? You knew what would happen to him if you told the wrong people, didn't you? Or is that what you wanted?"

"You'd better watch your tongue, Jenna Sorentino. I had no idea."

"What happened to Carson?" Marti said. "What secret?"

Jenna made fists, then flexed her fingers out. Her pulse was pounding like mad, but it felt too good calling these women out for her to stop. "A couple weeks after high school graduation, Kyle, Lance, and Bucky jumped Carson behind the feed and grain store. They beat him to within an inch of his life."

A collective gasp vibrated through the room.

"You'll shut your mouth about my boy," Gayle said. "Kyle would never—"

"Oh, but he would," Jenna said. "He did. And, to me, that's not the worst part." She paused for effect, meeting the eyes of each of the other eleven women. "The worst part to me is that Lou and Patricia, after they found him, beaten and bloody, decided not to take him to the hospital. They decided not to press charges. They decided that the town finding out their son was . . ." Jenna screwed her mouth up with wanting to finish that sentence. But it wasn't her right to. Even if he never believed that she'd kept his secret, she'd never break her promise to him. Never. "They were more worried about their own bigoted asses than watching their son suffer."

"Bigoted? What are you talking about?" Marti asked.

"Mom?" Kate said in a quivering voice. "Is that true? Is that why you sent Stacey and me to Aunt Gretchen's house that summer?"

Patricia looked on her daughter with tear-filled eyes but didn't answer.

"When your husband brought Carson home, a bloody mess, what was your first thought? Were you disappointed that Bucky, Kyle, and Lance hadn't managed to kill him?"

Patricia lunged toward Jenna and, before she could back away, slapped her hard across the cheek. Jenna tasted blood where her teeth bit down on her tongue.

Gayle stepped between them, fury written all over her face. "My son would never beat up another person. You're fixing to get yourself in a pot of hot water out of which you cannot climb, Jenna Sorentino."

"Are you threatening me? What are you going to do?"

Gayle's nostrils flared and her lips mashed together like she was weighing her options.

"I never meant for him to get hurt." Everyone turned at the sound of Kate's meek voice.

"What did you do?" Patricia asked breathlessly.

"Kyle and I were dating, sort of. I mean, I wanted to date him, but he was the most popular guy in my class. He came to our house one day and it was just me at home. We started hanging out, watching TV and stuff. At one point, I went to the bathroom and when I came out, he was in Carson's room going through his stuff." Her face pinked. "He said he was looking for porn we could watch. And he found some under Carson's bed."

What had Carson been thinking, keeping his porn stash in such an obvious place? Of course Jenna wasn't the only one who'd stumbled across it. It seemed so obvious now. But would Carson believe her if she told him the truth or was he too far gone in his hate to care?

"We raised Kyle to be a good, Christian man," Gayle insisted, spearing a finger toward the ground. "He's respected on the rodeo circuit, a regional champion. He's going to ask Brenda to marry him and settle down in Catcher Creek to help us on the ranch." Emotion made her choke on the last word.

Patricia put her arm around Gayle and leveled a desperate look at Jenna. "I just wanted it all to go away. I want my old Carson back, before he turned . . ." She closed her eyes and swallowed.

A sharp, angry laugh bubbled up from Jenna's chest. "Before he turned violent? That's what you were going to say, right? Bitter and angry like he is now? Because, honestly, do you think Carson is going to let Kyle, Lance, and Bucky get away with their crimes? Do you think he's going to let you get away with yours? Why do you think he came back to Catcher Creek—to play nice with all the people who hurt him? You'd better watch your backs. All of you."

She stomped to the door and slammed it behind her.

On Friday night, Matt picked up Jenna and Tommy at a quarter to eight, fifteen minutes before Tommy's usual weekend bedtime, but Matt hadn't been able to get off work any earlier. She and Tommy nearly always went to the Catcher Creek Café on Friday nights for dessert, and he'd discussed it with Matt at length throughout the week, so there was no way he would've gone to bed without a huge tantrum.

Jenna prided herself on being the kind of mom who didn't give in to tantrums or care if she seemed cool in her kid's eyes, but if she changed her mind now about going to town, Matt would want to know why and, damn it all, Jenna couldn't think of a single viable excuse she was willing to share with him.

Tommy's world was going to be turned on its head soon anyway, with the move and starting kindergarten, and he'd been such a trooper with the drives to and from Santa Fe that it was tough to deny him anything as basic as a sweet treat and an extra hour of awake time.

She took comfort in the theory that Carson would wait until the rodeo on Wednesday to put on any public display. From Bunco she knew he hadn't paraded himself around town in an overtly public way so she wasn't all that worried about him showing up. What she was worried about was running into Patricia or Kate Parrish, Gayle, Marti, Charlene, or any one of the Bunco ladies or their families. She'd be happy living the rest of her life without coming face-to-face with any of them, especially Patricia.

She'd felt that slap tingling on her cheek for the rest of the night, long after she'd changed into pajamas and made up a bed on the sofa in the big house. She had no regrets about calling the women of Catcher Creek on their misdeeds, even though she was still a bit stunned that she'd been so forward. She was tired of sitting on the information like it was shameful. She'd never been one to court conflict, but it'd felt cathartic to stand up for the Carson she'd loved, that sweet boy who'd been her best and only true friend for so many formative years.

Downtown Catcher Creek was jumping, or what qualified as jumping for a town with only four thousand residents. The Catcher Creek Café was located on the corner of Del Zorro and First Street, right in the heart of the four-square-block downtown district that boasted a single stoplight.

They parked in the lot behind Catcher Creek Café and immediately spotted Rachel's truck.

Inside the café, the ice-cream counter was crowded. They were in the dog days of summer in the desert and the day's heat had finally cracked enough that people had ventured out of their air-conditioned homes. Many of the farmers and ranch workers headed for Smithy's Bar, but those who had families were at the café, kicking off the weekend with ice cream.

Jenna was proud to have Matt with them. She liked the idea of tongues wagging about how cozy she looked with her new man. She took his hand as they waited in line. Tommy raced ahead to peer through the glass at the ice-cream flavors.

They stood in line at the ice cream and pie counter, separate from the dining area, and scanned the tables for Rachel. Matt spotted her first, coming out of the hallway that led to the restrooms.

"Hey, you. What are you doing here? Where's Vaughn?" Jenna asked.

"He and I had plans to come here for dinner together, but he got called in to work a shooting in Devil's Furnace. He knew I'd probably just eat cereal for dinner without him there, so he made me promise I'd come get some dinner anyway. While I was here, I figured I'd drop off a slice of pie at his office because he'll probably be there doing paperwork late into the night. I thought it'd be a nice surprise."

"Rachel, you do so much manual labor every day, you know you need more nutrition for dinner than cereal. We've talked about this."

Rachel flashed a scowl. "There's nothing wrong with cereal."

It was no secret that Vaughn and Rachel had zero skills in the kitchen. Ever since Amy had moved in at Kellan's ranch and her sous chef, Douglas Dixon, had taken up with Kellan's mom, hot meals were a daily challenge for those two. Jenna and Tommy ate at the big house with them a couple times a week, with Jenna cooking, but they were left to fend for themselves most of the time and ended up eating out a lot. That was one aspect of moving Jenna didn't like. Rachel and Vaughn would be left on their own in the kitchen on days the inn's restaurant wasn't open.

"We're here for the ice cream," Tommy exclaimed.

"Nice. That sounds delicious," Rachel said.

"Did you eat dessert yet?" Matt asked. At her shake of the head, he added, "You should stay and have ice cream and pie with us before you hit the road for home."

Rachel surveyed the line for ice cream, then smiled. "You don't have to ask me twice."

They were waiting only a moment before the bells on the door jingled. Out of the corner of her eye, Jenna spotted Vaughn coming into the café, dressed in his sheriff's uniform and looking worn to the bone. She started to wave, but he warned her off, indicating with a finger over his lips that he wanted to surprise Rachel. Jenna was all for that. Little else warmed her heart as much as seeing Rachel happy and in love. After the decades she'd spent caring for Jenna, Amy, their mom, and the farm, she deserved it more than anyone.

Vaughn slid his arms around Rachel from behind and nuzzled her neck. Rachel didn't exactly squeal with delight like Jenna might have, but her whole being lit up. "What are you doing here?"

"My deputy took the shooting suspect to jail and I'm getting a head start on the paperwork. I saw your truck, so I thought I'd come and say hello before I anchored myself to my desk. Hey, Jenna, Matt. Hiya, Tommy."

"It's going to be hard for me to surprise you with this slice of pie since you're standing right here."

He took it from her. "Tell me you ate a real dinner."

"I did. Like I promised you I would."

He kissed her cheek. "Good. I hate the idea of you sitting at home alone eating cereal."

"How long have you two been engaged?" Matt asked.

Vaughn screwed up his face, thinking. "Three months. Right, Rach?"

"Sounds about right."

"Any wedding plans?" Matt asked. Jenna had been holding off on asking, figuring they were letting Kellan and Amy have their moment in the spotlight. She wagered they were going to wait until after the newlyweds had returned from their honeymoon before making the announcement about their wedding date, but she was glad Matt had gone down that road because she was dying of curiosity.

Vaughn and Rachel shrugged simultaneously. "Not so far," Vaughn said. "We move slow. Hell, it took me twelve years to figure out she was my person."

Rachel patted the arm he had wrapped around her middle. "I'm not in a hurry, though I wouldn't mind getting a ring on your finger."

Vaughn looked stunned by the pronouncement. "Yeah? That's news to me. I guess we'll have to work on that. What does your calendar look like next month?"

"Next month's wide open," Rachel said with a grin.

Vaughn beamed at Jenna and Matt. "See? There you go. Wedding plans."

Jenna was spellbound by the easy confidence they had in each other's unwavering love. She and Matt weren't there yet, but she felt their bonds strengthening with every passing day. The time together at his house had been good for them. In a few days' time, they'd be only a short car ride apart. No more three-hour hauls to be together.

She reached out to Matt, but just then, Tommy galloped to their place in line and grabbed Matt's hand, dragging him up to the counter to discuss flavors.

Rachel wagged a finger at Jenna. "Don't you dare get it in your head to turn it into a circus like Amy's wedding."

"I wouldn't dream of it."

Of course, she was going to need to figure out what day they were thinking of tying the knot. Jenna's graduation was in a month, on a Saturday. Her pulse quickened as she realized that, by then, everyone would know the truth about her schooling. She wished it didn't scare her, thinking of her secret getting out. After all, she'd nearly spilled Carson's secret to the world the night before.

Tommy and Matt returned to the line, and Tommy was so excited about the bubblegum ice cream—"it's candy and ice cream all in one!"—that he dragged Vaughn and Rachel by the hands to show them.

As soon as they were out of earshot, Matt leaned close and kissed Jenna. "How'd it go with your sister today? Did you tell her about UNM?"

The frustration she'd felt earlier that day at her failed attempt to get Rachel alone wrapped around her heart as she shook her head. "I'd planned on sitting Rachel down around lunchtime. Psyched myself up and got nervous and everything." She and Tommy had walked over to the main house, armed with a cartoon DVD to occupy Tommy's attention while they talked, only to discover that Vaughn and Rachel had gone on an all-day trail ride. "But I couldn't get her alone. Vaughn had the day off. He's working all weekend, so I was hoping you might be able to watch Tommy so I can talk to her."

A shadow of disappointment flitted across his face before disappearing. "Of course. I was thinking of taking him with me to visit Jake and Max tomorrow anyway, to give you a break so you can pack in peace."

"Tommy loves spending time with you. He's still talking about your picnic on Wednesday. He asked me if the two of you could go camping soon."

"What did you tell him?"

He looked anxious about her response. She smoothed a hand along his collar. "I told him that'd be up to you. I think he took that as a yes."

"It's a yes."

The bells on the door jingled again. The woman in line in front of them turned to look with a glance, then did a double take, her eyes huge. "Carson Parrish? Is that really you?"

Jenna's heart plunged to the floor. Her body tensed and it was all she could do to keep breathing. Maybe he hadn't seen her. Catcher Creek Café had a back exit down the hall from the restrooms. She could grab Tommy, fake a sudden bout of stomach flu, and leave. She didn't have her car, but they could hide out in Vaughn's office until they could catch a ride back to the farm.

There'd be questions from Matt, but those she could face. She'd even tell him the truth if it helped keep her and Tommy safe from Carson, Bucky, Kyle, Lance, and anyone else who might hurt them.

"It's really me. How ya been, Lanie?"

"Doin' real good," Lanie answered. "Hey, listen, it's great to see you but you can't be in here without a shirt on."

Jenna's mouth went dry. Shirtless? But . . .

"No shirt, no shoes, no service—is that right?" came Carson's glib response. "Don't worry. I'm not here to eat. Jenna, don't play the coward. I know you heard me come in."

She was vaguely aware of Matt watching her, Lanie, too.

Hands clutching her sides and her teeth chattering, she turned and looked into the steel-blue eyes of the last man on Earth she ever wanted to see again.

Chapter Eighteen

Carson was indeed shirtless, dressed in low-slung, faded jeans and wearing a hard, goading expression on his face. Behind him, café patrons stared blatantly at him. Or rather, they were looking at his back, whispering to each other.

It was a testament to how much Carson had changed that he was parading his scars in public, without care who learned his intimacies. Jenna couldn't imagine what that would be like, living with such an ugly word carved onto her skin, unable to escape the memory of being hurt or the reminder of how hateful the world could be.

How many times as a Marine had Carson needed to defend himself against bigoted fellow soldiers and his superiors? How many times had he been forced to either deny who he was or come out to friends and strangers alike every time he took off his shirt, whether in the barracks showers or at a doctor's office? Your past was always chasing you, no matter how badly you wanted it to leave you alone.

There was poetry in walking through the heart of Catcher Creek like that, turning the act of hate he'd endured into a fearless proclamation about who he was. She would have admired his boldness, if only she wasn't so scared of what he could do to her or Tommy.

"I paid a visit to Bucky and Kyle last night. They'd already heard I was here. And they'd already heard why. I got the impression you had something to do with that."

"Oh," she answered in a quavering voice. What did you do to them? She wanted to ask. Did you hurt them?

Matt must've sensed her agitation because he wrapped a proprietary arm around her waist. He studied Carson, then pulled his face back, blinking. "Wait . . . Lynch?"

Carson looked Matt up and down, moving his head in a slow nod. "Right, I remember you. The champagne killer."

Champagne killer? "You two have met?"

"Yeah, we met." He nodded in Matt's direction. "When you said you had a girl to see, you didn't mention it was Jenna."

Matt shifted, his hold on her waist tightening. "I didn't realize you two were close."

"Jenna and I go way back. In fact, we got reacquainted on Sunday night, didn't we?"

Jenna closed her eyes, grinding her molars together as anxiety set in. Of all the things Carson could've said to Matt.

Next to her, Matt stiffened and dropped his arm from her waist. "Sunday night?"

"Tommy wants to know if he can get a double scoop," Rachel said somewhere behind her.

Jenna's mouth flew open and she bit back a howl of fear at the sound of Tommy's name in Carson's presence. Light-headed, she couldn't wrap her brain around the idea that this was happening—everything was crashing down around her at once. If they would all just go away, she'd have the breathing room to figure out what to do.

She pivoted toward the ice-cream counter in time to brace her hands in front of her as Tommy bounded up.

"There are too many flavors to decide. Please, can I get a double scoop, Mommy?"

She fought to keep the panic off her face. Blocking Carson's view of Tommy with her body, she tried to smile. "I thought you were set on bubblegum."

His eyes widened in awe. "I was, but then I saw peanut butter cup."

"That's a difficult choice. Yes, you may have a double scoop. First, let's go wash your hands." Her heart hammered so hard that her ribs hurt. She reached for his hand.

He retreated, bumping into Vaughn's legs. "But it's our turn to order. Can we please buy our ice cream first? I promise I'll wash afterward."

Mechanically, she handed Vaughn a twenty-dollar bill. "Will you help him?"

But Vaughn was staring past Jenna, recognition settling on his face. "Carson Parrish. I got a tip that you'd come back to this town, but this is the first we've seen of each other. Where have you been hiding?"

A malicious grin spread over Carson's face. "If it isn't our old friend, the sheriff. Looks like you two are pals now. What's up with that?"

She and Carson had been hell-raisers together, both of them drowning their sorrows and pain in mischief and chemicals. As many times as Jenna had gotten herself brought home in the back of Vaughn's squad car, Carson had too.

"Yes. He's going to be my brother-in-law soon." Which was more proof that God had a soft spot for irony. Then again, Jenna could at least take some credit for Vaughn and Rachel falling in love seeing as how they'd first made eyes at each other across the doorway when Vaughn had delivered Jenna's drunk, drug-addled self to Rachel nearly every week.

The revelation caught Carson's interest. His eyebrows

bobbed in a flash of surprise. "That must have cramped your style."

It hadn't occurred to her, not for one second, that Carson believed she hadn't changed since the days they rolled together. If she could just get Tommy that ice cream, she knew she'd buy his compliance so they could escape without him throwing a fit.

She set the twenty on the counter. "Sweetie," she said to Tommy, "order whatever you want." She forced herself to meet Matt's hard stare. "Do you want an ice cream?"

He leaned into her. "Sunday night?" His tone was a harsh whisper. "Was he why you didn't want me to come over?"

She hated to lie to him, but what else could she say? *Yes, he was the reason, just not in the way you're assuming?* She shook her head. "Just . . . let's get Tommy an ice cream and get out of here. Please."

Vaughn repositioned himself even with Jenna, his right hand resting on his gun holster. "You go by Lynch now?"

"You like it, Sheriff? Let's just say I earned that nickname fair and square and leave it at that." Though Carson was behind her, she could hear the smirk in his voice.

"Lanie already told you that you can't be in here without a shirt on," Vaughn said. "I suggest you leave before I make you."

Jenna flicked a glance at Carson over her shoulder. His eyes narrowed and his grin disappeared. He rolled his shoulders forward, flexing his back muscles, then his biceps. "I learned a thing or two in the Marines, Sheriff Cooper. You can't push me around like you used to. I'm the one who does the pushing now."

Jenna swayed, dizzy.

"Mommy, look how big my ice cream is."

She scooped Tommy up and tried to angle his face out of

view of Carson. Everything had gone so horribly wrong, so fast. She never stood a chance.

"Who's he?" Tommy pointed at Carson.

Bile rose in Jenna's throat. She flattened her tongue against the roof of her mouth and tried to keep her soothing smile from faltering. "That's . . . that's Carson. He's somebody Mommy knows from when she was a little girl. Come on, sweetie. It's time to go."

"Hold on a second." Carson stepped sideways, blocking her progress. His focus was riveted to Tommy's face; then he blinked. His jaw tightened. "This is your kid?"

"Yes," Jenna breathed.

Carson paled, swaying as Jenna had not a few minutes earlier. "How old is he?" he ground out from behind clenched teeth.

The world seemed to freeze. Her heart beat loud in her ears and she stopped breathing. Then, as if someone had hit the *play* button again, her system jolted back to life. Panic gave way to steely resolve. Her vision tunneled and her mind cleared as her life came into stark focus. Everything she'd ever gone through, everything she held dear in her life, all boiled down to this one moment. Her sister didn't matter, and neither did Matt. Not school, and not what happened to her next. Only Tommy.

She squared her shoulders, set her chin high, and stared Carson straight in the eye, confident and capable. "He's four."

A ripple of confusion—or perhaps dawning awareness—passed through Matt, Vaughn, Rachel, and the diner patrons listening in. In Jenna's periphery, she watched Matt's focus toggle between Carson and Tommy, his face falling like he'd figured out the truth behind her lie.

Jenna let the gawking stares roll off her like rain, but when her whip-smart son piped up to disagree, she shoved his ice-cream cone into his open mouth and marched him out of the café.

God, she wished she had her car there instead of being at Matt's mercy to get them home. She nearly chickened out from facing him by getting in Rachel's truck, but if she did that, if she turned away from Matt now, he might never forgive her. At least if she and Tommy rode home with him, he might give her a chance to explain. Not that she had the luxury to care about salvaging their relationship now. Like an elephant matriarch, she had only one job and that was protecting her son at all costs.

Thank goodness Matt hadn't locked his car door. She didn't raise her eyes once to check if anyone had followed them out of the café, but kept her attention solely on her son, strapping him into his booster seat, praying that Matt appeared before Carson did.

Before she had Tommy's door closed, Matt was opening his. She could tell by the set of his lips in a flat line that he was upset. He didn't talk to her, just slid into the driver's seat and turned the engine over.

She took to her seat, keeping her face pointed straight ahead and her hands clasped in her lap to keep them from shaking too noticeably. She had no idea how to start a conversation with Matt, especially in front of Tommy, but it turned out not to be an issue because he never once looked at or spoke to her the entire drive to her cottage.

The tension in the car, coupled with the huge dose of sugar and a late bedtime, must've been too much for Tommy because, despite the massive double-scoop ice cream he held, his mood plummeted. What started as babbling questions about why Jenna had gotten his age wrong rapidly devolved into a tantrum about how fast the ice cream was melting all over his hands and pants.

Jenna passed back napkins from the stash in her purse

and tried to console him that she wasn't angry about his clothes getting messy because he'd be changing into his pajamas as soon as they got home, but all that did was turn his whining into out-and-out tears, complete with wailing. Matt had a death grip on the steering wheel and stayed silent, with splotchy red growing over the skin of his neck.

She couldn't be mad at Tommy for the tantrum. Her heart was breaking for the little guy. His life had to be so confusing to his young mind right now, with their imminent move to Santa Fe, starting kindergarten, and Jenna and Matt's new relationship. She wished more than anything that she could make it all stop and give him the stability he needed and deserved, but there was only one way through the upheaval to get to their new, peaceful life in Santa Fe, and that was to put their heads down and charge through it.

Matt pulled even with the walkway to Jenna's front door and idled the car, his focus on the horizon.

Over Tommy's whining, she said, "Please don't leave yet. Give me just a minute. Please."

His jaw rippled.

She nodded, unlatched her belt, and climbed out, then took hold of Tommy's ice cream-sticky hand and helped him hop out. "I'll be right in, okay, buddy? You can sit at the kitchen table and finish your ice cream, then play with your toys for a few minutes before you need to brush your teeth. Sound good?"

"All right." Head down and sniffling, he dragged his feet, then tripped and fell flat on his face on the grass. His ice cream rolled away, ruined.

Screaming and so mad that his face was bright red, he stayed facedown, kicking and screaming and pounding his hands on the ground. Jenna had known Matt for eight months, and every time Tommy had had rough patches, Matt had stepped in to help. Tommy looked up to him and listened to him so much better than he listened to Jenna. He was an expert at getting Tommy through his tantrums. Not tonight.

She looked Matt's way. His eyes were closed and he gripped the steering wheel so tightly that his knuckles were white.

Jenna pushed a strand of hair out of her face and tried to ignore the tears of despair she felt coming on. Rather than trying to save her imploding love life, she had to deal with Tommy. She'd begged Matt to wait, but he hadn't turned the SUV's engine off. She half expected him to drive away at any moment, even though she recognized how insulting to his integrity it was to think that.

She stood over Tommy, who was still crying and thrashing on the ground, and raised her face to the night sky. She loved being a mom more than anything and credited Tommy with saving her life—shocking her into adulthood—but she just needed a few minutes to catch her breath. She needed to figure out what to do about Carson and Matt and all the stupid, unfair turns her life had taken in the past week.

Nausea roiled in her stomach and she knew an onslaught of crazy tears was coming soon if she didn't calm down. She pinched the bridge of her nose. "Z, Y, X, W, V, U, T, S—" A lump constricted her throat.

"Arcuepee, Mommy."

She looked down at her son.

His face was red and streaked with ice cream, dirt, grass, and tears, but at least he'd stopped crying. "You looked like you didn't remember the next letter in your backward game and it's arcuepee," he said between crying hiccups.

She dropped her knees next to him, a hand on his leg. "You're right, buddy. R, Q, P. Thank you. Are you okay? Did you skin your knees or anything?"

He rolled into a butterball and stuck his knee up. It was scraped, but not badly.

"You want me to kiss it?"

"Maybe later. Right now I just want a Band-Aid and a new ice cream. We still have chocolate fudge Popsicles in the freezer, don't we?"

"We do. Do you remember where we keep the Band-Aids?"

"Uh, yeah. I'm not four, like you thought."

She fought to keep the sad smile off her face. "You're right. You're such a big boy. I made a mistake. Would you get yourself a bandage and an ice cream so I can talk to Matt alone?" She pulled out her phone and accessed his favorite game. "Here, for when you're done with your ice cream."

He stood, then took the phone with a glance at Matt's SUV. "I think he's mad at us."

"Not you, sweetie. He's mad at me. I messed up and I have to apologize."

"You mess up a lot, Mommy."

Sweet sundae, did she ever know it. She was doing the best she could as a mother. Falling short, but giving it her everything. Despite all her mistakes, despite everything that had gone wrong, Tommy was going to grow up to be a good, smart, kind person with a huge family of people who loved him. She took comfort in that, even if she'd never win a Mother of the Year award.

She stood and wiped the grit off her knees. "Everybody messes up sometimes. That's what saying sorry was invented for."

She kissed the top of his head and watched him walk through the front door. After a fortifying breath, she turned and marched to the SUV, then slid onto the passenger seat.

She still had no idea what to say to Matt. Better to stick with the basics, like she'd told Tommy. "I'm sorry."

He swallowed. "Carson is Tommy's father. That's why you lied about Tommy's age to him. Because you never told him he was a father and you were trying to lie your way out of telling him tonight."

So he had figured it out, and from the accusing tone with which he'd said it, he'd already made up his mind about what that truth said about Jenna.

"Yes."

Matt shook his head and cursed under his breath. "You said Tommy's father was out of the picture. You said he was a deadbeat dad."

"I never said that. You did."

"Yes, I did. And you didn't correct me. That's a lie of omission, Jenna. But still another lie in your long list of them. How do you live with yourself, lying to everyone like you have?"

She poked her tongue against her cheek. He wasn't giving her an inch. "Every lie I've told, I've had a reason for it."

"Oh, please. Give me a break. You robbed Carson of Tommy's first five years. You robbed him of his chance to watch his son grow up."

She pressed her hands together and met Matt's furious glare. "It's a lot more complicated than that." She'd tried to say it with a steady, confident voice, but the words had come out like a plea.

"Do you have any idea what I'd give to father a child? I've tried bargaining with God. I've seen every male fertility specialist out there. I've done everything humanly possible to become a father and you . . . you robbed a man of fatherhood. Blatantly. Callously. I can't think of a more despicable betrayal."

He started to tremble, as if his emotions were getting the better of him.

Silent tears streamed over her cheeks as she stared out the window. She didn't have the energy to fight with him or defend herself. There was nothing to say. He'd made up his mind. Besides, nothing mattered now except Tommy. Carson was going to figure out the truth, if someone in the diner hadn't told him already. He was smart. He'd put two and two together. She probably only had a matter of minutes to pack a bag, get Tommy in the car, and flee.

Matt was still ranting. "What is it—you're a compulsive liar? Is that your M.O.? You haven't told Rachel or Amy the truth about your school or new career or that you're leaving town next week. You didn't tell Carson he was a father. You lied to me about last Sunday night. What else haven't you told me? How am I supposed to trust you?"

"I don't know, Matt. I guess you can't."

He huffed. "You have a responsibility to let Carson be a part of his son's life. He could sue you for full custody and he'd have a pretty airtight case. You understand that, right? You could lose Tommy over this. You have to start working to make this right, whatever it takes."

Her stomach heaved. She hadn't thought about that angle before and it filled her with a fresh urgency to run. Through the kitchen window, she saw Tommy sitting at the table, the Popsicle held up to his mouth. She reopened the car door. "I'm sorry I hurt you. It wasn't my intention. Please know that. I have to go take care of Tommy. Are you coming in?" She knew the answer would be no, but she wasn't sure what else to say.

"No. I can't do this. I can't be with someone who treats fatherhood like it's expendable."

She figured that was coming, but it still brought fresh tears to her eyes. She sat half in and half out of the car, her hand on the door, and watched Tommy's silhouette. All she'd wanted was to be a family with Matt and Tommy, and it stole her breath how bad the timing of Carson's return had been. If only she'd had a few more months to build a stronger foundation with Matt, maybe they would've had a chance of weathering this storm.

She'd give it one last try to explain. Maybe Matt was done with his tantrum and was finally ready to listen. "The situation with Carson is complicated. I'd like the chance to explain it to you."

"No, it's not complicated. Carson deserves a chance to know his son, and I'm sure as hell not going to get in the middle of it. That wouldn't be fair to Carson and it'd be too confusing for Tommy. Did you know he already asked me if I'd be his dad?"

Jenna shoved aside the turbulent feelings that discovery evoked in her. She'd have to process that later, when the events of tonight weren't so raw. "What makes you so sure Carson wants to be a dad to Tommy?"

"Come on, Jenna. He's not the deadbeat you led us all to believe. He at least deserves the chance to decide for himself what his role in Tommy's life will be without you making that choice for him."

Stupid her for opening her mouth to reason with him. That was about as constructive as reasoning with Carson had been. Neither man was the least bit interested in hearing her side of the story. Both were self-pitying fools who only saw their own struggles reflected in her. But she couldn't waste energy worrying about Matt's feelings any more than she needed to worry about Carson's. She had enough on her plate without being their scapegoat.

She didn't need to be judged like this. She'd trusted him with her true self, like she had with Carson. Neither of them had handled her trust with care. They threw her faults back in her face and saw despicableness instead of just a girl trying to get by the best way she knew how. Was she really so unlovable that even the people who claimed to care about her thought the worst about her on the turn of a dime?

Feeling thin and brittle, she stood, shut the car door, and swiped at her tears before leaning in through the window. "It's a good thing we're breaking up because I can't be with someone so judgmental that they drop me the first time they get a real good look at my flaws." She braced her hands against the lip of the open window. "I'm sorry my scars are so much more repulsive than yours. You ought to take Carson out for a beer tonight. You two can commiserate about what a horrible person I am."

"You're not a horrible person."

Gee, thanks. Numbly, she moved toward her front door. A little boy could only be left in the house alone for so long and, besides, she needed to kick her act into gear to get them packed and on the road before she risked Carson showing up.

"Jenna . . ." Matt's tone was gruff and demanding, not regretful.

She had no intention of turning around. If he wanted to talk to her more, he could chase her into the house. She held her breath, every cell of her body praying for the sound of the car engine turning off, his door opening, and his footsteps on the walk. For him to fight for her.

The only sound was his engine purring, then the wheels crunching over gravel as he turned his SUV around and drove away.

Numbly, she watched the taillights of his SUV fade into the night, then roused herself with a sniff and a shake of her arms. She found Tommy on the floor of his bedroom playing with superhero action figures, his cheeks puffed and his brows furrowed as he made sound effects to add to the battle he was staging.

"Hey, buddy. Thanks for playing so good while Matt and I talked."

"Where is he?"

She stroked his hair. "He had to go home."

Tommy's shoulders dropped. "I wanted him to sing me the cowboy song before bed."

She gave him a big mama-bear hug, holding on tight until he'd had enough and squirmed away from her. "Let's get you in your jammies and ready for bed."

A good, honest mom would probably tell her child that they'd be leaving home that night, but Jenna couldn't bring herself to. Because then he'd perk right up and either start whining and fussing or asking a million questions.

It would be so much more efficient and easier on both of them if she waited for him to fall asleep, then carried him to the car. He was a deep sleeper and probably wouldn't wake up until she'd gotten them wherever they ended up going. Plus, a silent, drama-free drive would help her settle her mind and think clearly about her next move. What was one more little lie on top of all the others she'd propagated?

She laid Tommy's pajamas on his bed and left him to dress himself. Impatient and twitchy with pent-up energy, she jammed her textbooks, notebooks, flashcards, and study material in her knapsack.

The first thing she should do with the pay from her new job was get them both in therapy, especially if Carson threw Tommy's world out of orbit by wanting to be a father to him. Hell, Jenna should've been in therapy her whole life, now that she thought about it. She always felt well adjusted and normal until she stopped to give it serious thought. Or until someone like Matt or Carson reminded her that she couldn't escape the legacy left by the hurt, neglected child she'd been.

She sucked it up good for Tommy and was damn proud of the mother she'd grown into, but someday, she wanted to be able to relate to other people in the easy, natural way everyone else seemed to. She wanted to trust and be worthy of trust enough to build a life with a man. She didn't want to be alone forever, which meant she needed to start fixing herself. Just as soon as she handled the situation with Carson and got her and Tommy settled in Santa Fe.

She set the knapsack by the front door, then jogged to the bathroom and spread toothpaste on Tommy's brush. She got him started with that, then dragged a suitcase from the bottom of the coat closet into the living room and over-turned a basket of clean laundry into it.

The door squeaked open. Jenna's heart dropped to her knees for about the millionth time that night. In her haste, she'd forgotten to lock the door. *Please don't be Carson.*

Chapter Nineteen

Only after Jenna composed her features did she turn to see who it was. Rachel. Jenna released a shaky exhale of relief.

Rachel closed the door behind her, her eyes wide with concern. "What in the hell is going on?" She caught sight of the suitcase and her eyes got even bigger. She opened her mouth like she was going to give Jenna a piece of her mind.

Jenna waved her hands in front of her and tipped her head in the direction of Tommy's bedroom. "I'll tell you everything, I swear. But not yet. I've got to get Tommy to sleep. It's way past his bedtime." Frightening, how easily the lies were rolling off her tongue now. In for a penny, in for a pound, she supposed. But it still freaked her out how unscrupulous she could be when her back was against the wall.

Rachel gestured to the suitcase. "Where are you going?"

Jenna had no idea. A motel in Albuquerque, Carrie's apartment—anywhere but Catcher Creek. She dropped jackets onto the clothes in the suitcase, flipped the lid over them, and pressed her knees on it so she could zip it closed. "I don't know yet. But we can't stay here."

Rachel's consternation morphed into concern. Jenna didn't have time for concern. She had maybe twenty minutes until Carson showed up demanding answers or wreaking vengeance or both.

Pressing her lips together, Jenna listened for the sound of teeth brushing to make sure Tommy was doing what he was supposed to, then turned her focus back to packing. The clack of boot heels preceded Rachel's figure looming over her. She took hold of Jenna's arms near her armpits and hauled her to standing. "Whoa, there. Look at me, Jenna. Are you okay?"

It was the first time she'd stopped moving long enough that she could think past the whir of bright panic inside her. Fresh tears crowded her eyes as she released the air in her lungs with a series of dry, quiet laughs and sagged into Rachel's hands. Holy fuck, what had she gotten herself into? And what in the hell was she going to do to fix things now?

"No. Not at all."

"Tell me how running is going to solve anything."

"It's not, long term, anyway. But I can't deal with this tonight by myself."

Rachel drew herself up tall, her eyes glinting with big sister protectiveness. "You're not by yourself. You have me. I'll stay with you all night, okay? If Carson comes, we'll deal with him together."

So she'd put it all together about Carson, as Jenna expected everyone at the café had. Sure, Rachel had vowed to stand by Jenna's side, but would she still once she'd learned the truth about how Jenna had deceived her? Matt had called Jenna a pathological liar. Boy, was he right.

Even worse than the painful truth in his assessment was the dawning realization that the security she'd felt by keeping her secrets locked tight inside her had been an illusion. All she'd succeeded in doing was systematically alienating the people who meant the most to her. She might as well bite the bullet and alienate Rachel tonight, too, as seemed inevitable.

"We need to talk."

Rachel nodded. "Let's get Tommy to bed first."

Working together, they got Tommy in bed. He got sad again when he remembered how he'd wanted Matt to sing to him. Jenna tried, but her mind drew a blank on the words and melody of "The Cowboy Lullaby," despite that she'd heard him signing it to Tommy on Wednesday night. Rachel saved bedtime by whistling one of the songs she often whistled to Tommy when they ran the tractor together, which pacified him enough that he yawned and seemed to accept that it was time to close his eyes and go to sleep.

They crept out of his room and shut his door, then tiptoed to the kitchen.

Jenna cracked the top of a soda, while Rachel found the bottle of whiskey she kept in the pantry. They settled with their drinks at the small, round yellow-topped Formica table Rachel had found at a yard sale a few years back. Jenna wouldn't call herself calm, exactly, but with Rachel there with her, her panic had dimmed considerably.

Rachel rolled a sip of whiskey around her teeth before swallowing it. "Carson is Tommy's daddy, isn't he?"

Jenna decided right then and there that she wasn't going to tell a single lie anymore, especially not to her sister. If people took issue with the choices she'd made, then they could go to hell. "Yes."

Rachel nodded. "You're going to need to give me an iron-tight reason for why you kept this from him. Any man deserves to know he's a father."

"Not the first time you've lectured me about that, okay?" During Jenna's pregnancy and Tommy's first year of life, Jenna and Rachel had gone round and round about Jenna's refusal to name the father. But Jenna had known from the get-go that the safest course of action was to not share her secret with a single soul. Telling the truth took the power out of her hands and that was unacceptable where Tommy's safety was concerned.

"Fair enough, but all this time, I hoped Tommy was conceived in a one-night stand with some rodeo cowboy whose last name and phone number you didn't catch—or an older, married man. Someone who you had a real, honest-to-God reason to keep in the dark about him being Tommy's father. Not another kid like you.

"I mean, goddamn, Carson's in the military. You and Tommy could've been taken care of. We're talking medical benefits and child support. And Tommy could've known his daddy. He would've had grandparents in town to help you, so you explain to me how what you did isn't as cruel as it seems."

Jenna regretted a lot of things in her life, but her conscience was clear when it came to keeping Carson's parents away from Tommy or not using Carson for the benefits and money he would've provided. "I'll explain everything as soon as you stop throwing stones at me."

Rachel took another sip of whiskey. "All right. Go ahead."

Jenna stretched her chin up toward the ceiling, collecting her thoughts. Then she met Rachel's skeptical expression and started in on the whole, sordid truth. "Carson and I were best friends, but we weren't lovers. Then one night, a couple weeks before high school graduation, we slept together. Like, an experiment."

"An experiment? What do you mean by that?"

She swallowed. To tell or not to tell . . .

Screw it. Carson had already paraded through downtown Catcher Creek with his shirt off. "We had sex because he thought he might be gay and he was scared and confused about it. We were so high that night, so damn out of our minds and stupid and young, we decided that sleeping together might help him decide."

"And you didn't use a condom because . . ." Leave it to Rachel to zero in on the terrible choice rather than Carson's sexual identity.

Jenna set her soda can on the table a little too hard. "Because, I don't know. Take your pick of any ignorant teenage excuse that helps you make your peace with what happened—we didn't have a condom, I figured a gay guy couldn't get me pregnant, and he pulled out at the end, so that's like using birth control."

"That is the dumbest thing I've ever heard."

"Yep."

"So, then, how long was it after that before you found out you were pregnant? If that happened two weeks before graduation, and you told me, what, a month after graduation, then six weeks passed before you figured it out?"

"Thereabouts."

Rachel drained the last of the finger of whiskey she'd poured. She seemed to be getting agitated all over again, but there was nothing Jenna could do now about stupid choices she'd made six years earlier.

"You did some nasty shit to your body in those six weeks," Rachel said. "I remember the night after graduation, you were passed out in Vaughn's patrol car. It took both of us to get you into the house and you slept it off for nearly twenty-four hours straight. You better thank your lucky stars Tommy's okay, medically and developmentally."

"Do you think I haven't thought about that or that I haven't been saying prayers of thanks since the day he was born healthy and normal? I'm not perfect. Not even close and I never claimed to be. I'm having a real shitty week, Rachel, and you busting out with one of your patented lectures isn't helping any. I'm telling you all this so you'll understand why I made the choices I did."

"I still don't get why you didn't tell Carson."

"I was getting to that. That summer, before I found out I was pregnant, Carson was beat up. Badly. He almost died from the injuries."

Rachel gave a cringe of disbelief. "I don't remember that."

"Nobody does because Carson's parents covered it up. They didn't go to the police. And they didn't take Carson to the hospital. All they did was call one of his aunts who was a nurse to come to their house and patch him up."

"That's crazy. Why wouldn't they?"

"Because it was a hate crime, Rach. Bucky Schultz, Kyle Kopec, and Lance Davies beat him up because they found out he was gay. Carson's parents knew that and they didn't want the town finding out the truth about their son. Are those the kind of grandparents you'd want in Tommy's life?"

She could see the wheels turning in Rachel's head. Rachel wasn't naïve in any sense of the word, but she took people at face value and probably couldn't comprehend the type of evil that fueled that kind of hateful violence or Carson's parents' reaction. "If what you say is true, then Lou and Patricia Parrish are as guilty of a crime as the men who beat up Carson. But I know you and I know Carson being gay isn't the reason you didn't tell him he was a father."

Mark the date and time. Someone was assuming the best of her instead of the worst. Would miracles never cease? "Of course his sexuality wouldn't have mattered to me. The problem was, I only found out what happened to Carson because he confronted me."

Holding tightly to her soda can, she did her best to explain to Rachel about the fury and accusations Carson had lobbed on her that day. How he'd blamed her for what happened, then threatened her. How he'd refused to name the boys who'd hurt him. And how he'd vowed to return to Catcher Creek someday, bigger and stronger, to wreak vengeance on those who'd wronged him.

"And then he left. He left town that night and I never heard from him again," Jenna continued. Rachel listened with rapt attention, her second finger of whiskey ignored. "There I was, alone with the knowledge that there were people in this town who hated Carson because of his sexuality so much that they'd tried to beat him to death. I've seen guilt on the faces of every man and boy in this town since that day, and a couple weeks later, when I found out I was pregnant with Carson's baby, I didn't know what to do.

"If I'd have wanted to tell Carson, it would've had to have been through his family, and I've never stopped hating them for what they did to him. Worse than that, if word got around town that Carson had a son, who's to say those same men who hurt him wouldn't have lashed out at Tommy and me, or even our farm?"

Somewhere along the retelling of the story, Rachel's expression had changed to one of outrage at what had been allowed to happen to Carson coupled with acceptance of how Jenna had handled things. "You couldn't take that chance."

"Exactly."

"I wish you would've told me all this back then," Rachel said. "I hate thinking you were carrying that burden alone."

Reaching across the table, Jenna squeezed Rachel's arm and offered a melancholy smile. "You carried plenty of burdens alone over the years, so you know as well as I do all the reasons we tell ourselves why we can't share our heavy loads with the people we love."

Rachel covered Jenna's hand with hers. "That's the truth, but I wish it could've been different."

"What's done is done. I knew someday Carson would be back. Especially after word reached us that he'd joined the Marines, getting bigger and stronger, just as he'd threatened to. I was hoping Tommy and I would be long gone by the time he returned."

"Long gone?"

Time for more secret sharing. Jenna withdrew her hand from Rachel's grasp and wiggled the tab of her soda can. "It's always been my plan to leave as soon as I had the skills and job to sustain Tommy and myself."

"Where would you go? Santa Fe, with Matt?"

Tears sprang to her eyes at the mention of his name. "Not with Matt. Not now. And anyhow, you taught me not to rely on others, especially men, for my salvation—only myself. I will be going to Santa Fe, but on my terms, standing on my own two feet."

"What will you do there?"

Jenna popped the soda tab off and pressed the sharp edge against the pad of her finger. This was it. The other moment beside Carson's return that she'd been dreading for years. "There's something else I haven't told you. Something big."

Rachel threw up her arms and stood. "Goddamn, Jenna. You always were the one to give me gray hair. You got any ice cream here? I need to indulge in some stress eating."

"Only chocolate fudge Popsicles."

"Good enough. You want one, too?"

"No, thanks."

From the freezer, Rachel withdrew a fudge bar and returned to her seat. "Let me get a head start before you drop your other news on me."

Jenna waited until she had the plastic wrapper off and a

few good licks in before she started talking again. She'd mentally prepared for this moment over and over again, but now, under the weight of Carson's return and Matt's rejection, the urge to protect herself and Tommy eclipsed any delicacy with which she might have previously broached the topic. She was done with explaining herself. All she wanted was to pack Tommy up and get the hell out of Catcher Creek.

Good riddance.

"I've been going to college at the University of New Mexico to earn a degree in computer engineering."

Rachel choked on her ice cream, spluttering chocolate-colored spit on the table. "You what?"

"College. Me. At UNM."

Rachel set the fudge bar on the Formica, then gripped the edge of the table with both hands. "How long has that been going on?" Each word was measured precisely and said in a tone of great strain.

"Four years. I graduate next month."

Jenna wasn't sure she'd ever heard Rachel spew that many curse words in a row. She leapt from her seat and gaped at Jenna with crazy eyes. "What the hell, Jenna? Are you serious?"

"Yes. I'm so sorry I didn't tell you. I just . . . I don't know why I didn't. Not really." She could make all kinds of excuses like how she hadn't wanted to add to Rachel's financial or emotional burden or that she'd had low self-esteem and if she failed, she didn't want anyone to know, but those were only superficial reasons—and Jenna was done lying. Even lies of omission. "I liked it being a secret. It was something that was for me alone. Besides that, going to college was so wrapped up in the reasons I wanted to leave Catcher Creek, with Carson being Tommy's father, that I couldn't separate them in my mind."

"College?" She sunk back into her chair, her head in her hands. "I've always been your biggest fan. I wish you would've let me be proud of you about that."

Jenna puffed her cheeks full of air and released it in a steady stream. "I'm sorry. I started with UNM's correspondence program when I was twenty, when Tommy was a baby. I did it on a whim, thinking it would give me something to keep my mind sharp while Tommy slept. I knew even then that as soon as I could get a good job somewhere else, Tommy and I could get out of this town.

"I didn't tell you at first because, like I said, it was comforting to have a secret that was all for me. And then, after a while . . ." She shook her head. How could she explain? "You know how Jake didn't tell Kellan about his partner's stroke? He didn't want to worry Kellan or ruin his day. He kept the truth a secret for all the right reasons. That's the way it was for me with you about college, but it snowballed.

"The longer I went without telling you about me going to college, the more pissed and hurt I knew you'd be at me when you found out. It was never the right time. Mom's mental instabilities got worse and, more and more, Dad wasn't around. You had your hands full with the ranch. I couldn't find it in myself to hurt you more. Then Dad died and Mom turned suicidal and, God, Rachel, I just couldn't. I love you so much. But now, I'm about to graduate and I have a job lined up in Santa Fe with the state as a computer software programmer. It starts September first."

Rachel looked utterly flabbergasted. She poured herself another whiskey. "You're moving? What about Tommy's schooling? He's supposed to start kindergarten. What are you going to do about that?"

"I've already enrolled him in a school in Santa Fe."

Rachel rotated her jaw, her whole being radiating the exact same kind of hurt that Jenna had feared facing every time she'd thought about telling Rachel the truth. "Well, I'll be damned. I guess you've got it all figured out. I'm going to need some time to let that sink in."

There was one more thing, though, and Jenna was determined to get it all out in the open now. "I put a deposit down on an apartment already, and Tommy and I are going to be moving this week. I can't risk staying in Catcher Creek any longer now that Carson's back and the whole town knows the truth—or at least they will soon enough. Word spreads like a wildfire in this place."

Rachel swabbed her forehead. "I can't believe—"

A pounding knock sounded at the front door. Both Jenna and Rachel jumped out of their skin.

"Jenna!" It was Carson's bellowing voice.

Rachel straightened, her eyes wide. "Is that Carson?"

Jenna's gut twisted. Oh, God. She'd known this was coming tonight as much as she'd known Matt was going to break up with her, but she wasn't ready for this. She should be on the road to Santa Fe with Tommy, safely out of Carson's reach, instead of sitting at her kitchen table waiting for his wrath to strike. "Yes. That's him."

"Sounds like he figured it out about Tommy. I guess that means he's not as dumb as he looks."

"Carson's definitely not dumb."

Rachel stood, grabbed the fudge bar, and dropped it in the trash can. Her shock and disappointment of a few moments earlier was gone, replaced by iron-clad strength. "How do you want to play this?"

What an outrageous question. She didn't have any plays left. She and Rachel were two women alone in an old, run-down cottage with a sleeping child in the next room. If

Carson wanted to, he could probably bust through the side of the weather-beaten, termite-riddled wall or break the door down, dead bolt be damned.

The door rattled with three more loud poundings. "Get out here and face me, Jenna. And you better not shoot at me this time."

"Shoot him?" Rachel asked.

"Another long story." Jenna pressed her palms on the table and stood, drawing a slow inhale as she rose. She couldn't let go of the table, she was so off-balance with fear. "I don't know what to do, Rachel. I'm so scared right now."

Rachel strode around the table and pulled Jenna into a hug. "Everything's going to be okay. You and me, we've been through harder times than this. We're cowgirl tough, through and through, even if you don't feel like it now."

Everything's going to be okay. Rachel's same words of consolation and solidarity from when Jenna had told her she was pregnant. It was like Jenna couldn't stop screwing things up and needing her big sister to save her. She rested her chin on Rachel's shoulder.

"You know Carson a lot better than I do," Rachel said. "Is he going to get violent with us?"

Jenna pictured him the week before, hulking over her on the side of her house. She saw the shadowed, hard lines of his face, the fury in his eyes, the way his mouth had sneered when he'd called her a lying bitch. And all that before he'd figured out she'd hid the truth about Tommy from him. She shivered.

Even if she was ninety-nine percent sure she and Rachel could handle a confrontation with Carson on their own, she couldn't afford to be cavalier about Tommy's safety. "I think we should call Vaughn."

Rachel was already fishing her phone out, or so Jenna thought until a shiny silver revolver appeared in her hand.

"Jesus, Rachel. Is that loaded?"

She set it on the kitchen table, then plunged her hand back in her jacket. "Of course it's loaded." This time, when her hand came out, she was holding her phone.

Jenna's eyes shot to the back door, visible through the mudroom on the side of the kitchen. The door was locked, the dead bolt secure. Her eyes flitted next to the kitchen cabinet on which her rifle was stowed. Rachel wasn't the only badass in the family. There was no one tougher on the planet than a mom protecting her young. That was the way it was in nature and it certainly held true for cowgirls in the backcountry.

The rifle had misfired the last time she'd handled it, but Carson wasn't going to surprise her again. She pulled a chair over to the cabinet and stood on it to retrieve her gun, listening to Rachel on the phone.

"Hey, hon. I'm with Jenna at her house. Carson Parrish followed us here and he's in a right state. How fast can you get here?"

After the tedium of prepping the rifle with ammo the week before, Jenna had relocated the ammo to a coffee can in the pantry cupboard. While she was still standing on the chair, she grabbed the can and loaded two rounds in.

Carson pounded on the door some more. Both Rachel and Jenna flinched, but Jenna held steady to her rifle as she stepped to the floor.

"Yeah, that was him knocking," Rachel said into the phone. "No, he hasn't threatened us out-and-out and the doors are locked." She paused, her eyebrows flickering. "At least a half an hour? Okay, then. I'll keep my phone close and my Colt closer. See you in a bit."

"Goddamn it, Jenna! If you don't open this door in two seconds, I'm breaking it down."

Rachel shoved the phone into her pocket and took up her revolver, cocking it. "I'll be damned if I'm going to let him set a foot inside this house now."

Jenna pumped her rifle, cocking it. "He'd have to get through both of us first."

Chapter Twenty

Matt had needed to swerve off the single-lane dirt road leading from the Sorentinos' homestead to the main highway so as not to hit Rachel's truck as they crossed each other's paths. He hadn't even had the guts to look her in the eye. He couldn't. He'd never been more furious in his life. Betrayed. His breath came in fits and starts, as sporadic as his thoughts.

How could she? he kept repeating to himself as he navigated the last of the Sorentinos' road and bumped onto the main road leading to the highway. Jenna had stolen a man's opportunity for fatherhood without remorse. She'd played God. He could never love someone with such a lack of conscience.

This was what it'd felt like when he'd been in the accident—impaled by his bike frame, run over and dragged by a truck. When he'd discovered he could never father children. It felt like you could never trust again, because it didn't matter how good a person you were, how decent a man, how righteously you practiced your faith or tikkun olam, there were no guarantees that some random, sinister force wasn't going to take you down when you least expected it.

Karma was bullshit. Maybe Carson was right. There wasn't anything in this world a man could count on except himself. Jenna had taken his heart in her hand and crushed it. She'd crushed him. He would never be the same. He would never trust again like he trusted her.

Rage and adrenaline crowded his vision. His hands were shaking, and after one particularly harsh jerk of the wheel to keep his car in his lane, he pulled onto the shoulder and turned the engine off.

Breathing hard, and with sweat or tears or both streaming over his face, he shook the steering wheel and screamed.

He loved her. He loved Tommy. He loved the way the three of them were together. But all that time, there had been another man who deserved to be in his place. Were Carson and Jenna high school sweethearts? Had he been her first love? Carson had been with her last Sunday night, might've even been in the house while Matt was outside dancing with Jenna. Would they rekindle the flame now that Matt was out of the picture?

Stephy and Jordy's mom had left Matt to reunite with the children's father. To be a family again, like they always should have been, she'd explained. Matt got it. It had damn near killed him, but he'd seen where she was coming from. People naturally wanted to be part of a whole, nuclear family.

He would never have that. It was the one thing he wanted that he could never have. Every time he thought his grief over the loss had dulled, something like this came along— someone like Jenna—to remind him that grief never really did disappear. It only morphed into bigger, badder, more insidious forms.

He smeared the back of his hand over his cheek, dragging

tears and sweat along with it. This was going to hurt like hell, this breakup. He was going to need to do some serious grieving to get over losing Jenna—or at least the woman he'd thought she was. But he'd survived other heartbreaks, and so he'd survive this. He'd never, ever date single moms again.

He opened the SUV door and stepped into the warm evening. The spot where the sun had disappeared on the horizon glowed pink and orange. He stared out over the magnificent stretch of countryside, scrub trees and cacti, buttes and ravines. Rust and olive green and brown. The palette of his world.

He'd go hunting at the first light of dawn, and he'd go for as many days as it took for the pain of grief and betrayal to ease. He'd already planned to take some days off work to help Jenna move, so being absent from his job wasn't an issue. More than anything, he needed time on a horse and silence and the beautiful world around him.

He sucked in a deep, steady inhale, then released a loud whoosh of an exhale. Lacing his fingers together against the back of his head, he walked the edge between the blacktop of the road and gravelly sand that demarcated the high country wilderness.

Tommy looked just like his dad. How had nobody in Catcher Creek noticed before tonight? How had Jenna gotten away with such a flagrant deception? Not his problem now. Tommy would be taken care of, and that empty place in his heart that Matt had sensed when he and Tommy talked on their horseback ride last Wednesday would be filled by his biological father. That Matt could take a measure of bittersweet solace in.

After another long perusal of the sweeping expanse of land and sky before him, he opened the backseat door in search of one of the water bottles or energy drinks he'd stashed there, whatever his hand hit on first—a distraction to knock the last bit of outrage out of his system.

The first object his hand hit was Jenna's purse. He swore. Now what?

He wasn't returning to Jenna's house, that was for sure. He could drop it off at Rachel's place, but Jenna would see his car coming down the grade. Vaughn's office in town? What if Carson was still on Main Street? Matt couldn't face him right now any more than he wanted to face Jenna again.

What a coward.

He looked down the highway in the direction he'd come. He could mail it.

Then it hit him. Jake was at Kellan's place. He could leave it on the porch with a note. Even if Jake heard his car and came out to see what was going on, he didn't seem the type of man who'd ask prying, personal questions.

Jake's slick, black sports car was parked out front of Kellan's house. Tara's minivan sat next to it. Damn it. What the hell was she doing there?

Before he could second-guess the logic of his hasty plan, he rang the doorbell. After a long delay, Jake answered, clad in unbuttoned jeans with a gray T-shirt wadded in his hand. "Hey. Didn't know you were coming over."

He didn't mention Tara's van or ask about her because he wasn't all that keen on seeing the pity in her eyes when she put it all together about why Matt was handing off Jenna's purse for Jake to return. "I need a favor and I'm not in the mood to talk about why." He held Jenna's purse out.

"Uh, okay. What's with this?"

"It's Jenna's. She left it in my car. Can you make sure it gets back to her?"

Jake slung the shirt over his shoulder like a towel and folded his arms over his chest. "Why can't you do it?"

"I told you, I don't want to talk about it."

"Don't want to talk about what?" a female voice called. Sure enough, Tara, dressed in jean shorts peeking out from beneath a voluminous black ribbed tank top that looked suspiciously like it belonged to Jake, poked her head around Jake's arm. Her hair was damp and her skin looked freshly scrubbed like she'd recently taken a shower.

"Tara, please don't tell me you made a three-hour drive to hook up with Kellan's brother again."

Jake had the audacity to look amused by the insult. "What, you don't think I'm worth making a three-hour drive for?" He craned his neck to grin at Tara. "I think he just insulted my prowess."

"You want me to set him straight about it?" she asked.

Jake pretended to contemplate it.

Matt didn't mean to groan aloud, but he couldn't help it. Man, he hated being privy to the intimate details of his siblings' private lives. "Enough. Sorry I brought it up." He piled Jenna's purse on top of Jake's still-crossed arms. "Get this to Jenna, will you? I've got to get going."

Jake gripped the purse by its handles. "Let me get this straight. You want me to give your girlfriend her purse back?"

Matt backed down the porch stairs. In any other circumstance, he would've appreciated the disparity of macho Jake clutching a bright pink purse, but he was in no mood for joking around. "Just shut up and do me this solid, okay?"

"Did she dump you?"

God, he didn't want to answer that question. Luckily, he was spared by a sudden flurry of enthusiastic barking. A dog's nails clicked over the floor and Max appeared at Jake's side.

"I think a better question is why Tara's cooped up in a house with a dog. On a ranch, surrounded by animals." He shot Tara a glare. "Didn't you learn your lesson growing up on our ranch? Pets make you feel miserable. Why would you do that to yourself?" He shifted his focus to Jake. "If you cared anything about her, why would you put her through that?"

"I'm a grown woman, Matt. Stop being judgmental."

"Take a breath, dude. You sound like an uptight prick and I don't think you want to go there."

Jake was right. Matt didn't want to go there, even if his points were valid. Tara needed to take better care of herself before her immune system got too weak to fight back and Jake, as the man sleeping with her, should've cared enough to do right by her. But they were adults and even though Matt loved his sister, he had no right to harp on her. God knew he hated it when she harped on him. "No. Sorry. I'm having a bad day."

Jake squatted to ruffle Max behind the ears. "Yeah, I picked up on that. I was right about her breaking up with you, wasn't I?"

Matt's gut did a clench. "Not exactly, but she and I aren't going to work out."

"Well, shit."

"Tell me about it." Despair roiled through him, tightening his throat. He couldn't talk about it anymore, and definitely not with another guy while his sister looked on.

Tara squeezed past Jake and gave Matt a hug he was nowhere near equipped to deal with at the moment. He endured it until her grip eased and he could slip back without offending her.

"Come on in. I'll get you a beer," she said.

After everything that'd happened, to have his sister invite him in to Kellan's house like a gracious hostess while she was on a booty call was too much. "No, thanks. I've got to get home and pack."

"I bet you're going hunting," Tara said.

"You know me well."

Jake set Jenna's purse on the table just inside the door, then put his shirt on. "Hunting like we went hunting?"

"Yeah, but I'm drawing it out for the week. I already have the time off work, so I'm going to make an extended camping trip out of it."

"If I didn't have to get to Cheyenne by Wednesday, I'd join you."

Matt waved off the offer. "It's all good. I need time alone."

"Take it easy, okay? Maybe things will work out with you and Jenna. You never know. I'm sure whatever you did, she'll forgive you eventually."

Matt bristled. "What makes you think I was the one at fault?"

Jake and Tara looked at him like he was a moron. "We're guys," Jake said. "We're always the ones screwing stuff up."

"Amen," Tara said under her breath.

Matt opened the driver side door and looked at them over the SUV's roof. "Not this time."

"I don't believe that for a second. Not Jenna," Jake said.

"Like you know her so well?"

Jake shrugged. "I'm pretty good at reading people. What'd she do?"

If Jake was so curious, he might as well know the truth. Tara, too. "It turns out that she never told Tommy's father he has a kid. We were getting ice cream at the Catcher Creek Café and this guy, Carson, who she went out with in high school, or whatever, saw Tommy, recognized the resemblance, and called her on it. Can you imagine that? Tommy's five. Carson can never get those years of fatherhood back that he missed because of her. That's an unforgiveable sin in my book."

Tara gave a quiet gasp. She knew what fatherhood meant

to Matt. If anyone would understand his choice to end his relationship with Jenna over this, it'd be his family, who'd been his rock throughout his accident recovery and relationship heartbreaks.

Jake rubbed his chin, not looking nearly outraged enough to suit Matt. "She must've had a damn good reason for doing that."

"What? You're telling me there's an excusable explanation why a woman would keep a man in the dark that he's a father? It's inhumane. She cheated Carson and lied to his family, and to her family, to me, and to Tommy. There's no reason on the planet that would excuse that level of deception. I can't be with someone like that."

Tara crept closer, like she might want to hug him again. "Tara, please. I can't."

She looked stricken. "I know. I just . . . I'm so sorry."

All he could do was nod and look away.

"Did you ask her why she did it?" Jake said.

Matt drilled Jake with a scowl. "No, I didn't ask her because it doesn't matter. What I did was get the hell out of the way so Carson can get to know his son without me in the middle confusing Tommy and mucking things up even more than Jenna already has, all right? I'm sure Rachel's pissed, Carson's pissed, I'm pissed. Jenna made her choices and now she's got to deal with the consequences."

"But nobody knows why it went down like that?"

Matt ground his molars together. "Are you listening to me? The *why* doesn't matter. Here's a better question, what makes you care so much?"

Jake shrugged. "She and I are family now, like she told me the other day. And I think it sucks that nobody's listening to her side of the story. My whole life, nobody's ever listened to me, so I know what that's like."

Nobody in Matt's family paid much attention to what he had to say either. Call it youngest-sibling syndrome. He rallied against the compassion creeping into his consciousness. He didn't want to see Jenna's point of view. He wanted to keep being so mad at her that he didn't feel any pain. He opened his car door.

"When are you leaving on this hunting trip?" Jake said.

"At first light."

Jake shook his head and rubbed his jaw. "There's got to be a reason Jenna didn't tell anybody. Chicks don't want to raise kids on their own. I mean, kids are hard work and you always hear about guys paying child support through the nose." He gestured to Tara. "You get child support, right?"

Tara nodded.

"Yeah, so why wouldn't Jenna want child support? It doesn't make sense. What do you know about this Carson guy?"

Matt dug for a fault in Jake's logic but couldn't find any. "His family owns a store in Catcher Creek. He's a Marine . . ."

Jake's brows shot up. "A soldier, huh? I'm probably paranoid because with my job I'm around bad people a lot. Really shitty, violent offenders, day in and day out, but in my experience, sometimes soldiers go bad, like they can't adjust to the civilian world. Especially if they've seen battle. What if Carson the Marine isn't a good guy? What if he's bad news and that's why she didn't tell him? But now everybody's pissed and not talking to her. Who would keep her safe from this bad dude she didn't want around her or her kid if everybody threw up their hands and abandoned her?"

Matt hadn't thought about it from that angle. When he'd first met Carson, his intuition had sensed violence and volatility. Matt had thought him a bully. He hadn't seemed that way at the café, more like an average Joe with a chip on his shoulder who was having the carpet yanked out from under him. But what if he was a bully? What if he was worse than that—an abuser? Matt's mouth went dry. "You're absolutely right."

"No shit, I'm right." Jake backtracked into the house and grabbed something from the wall just inside the door. The next thing Matt knew, Jake had fastened a belt around his jeans, clipped a pistol to his waist, tucked a hunting rifle under his arm, and grabbed Jenna's purse.

"What are you going to do?" Tara asked him. Matt was wondering what his plan was, too.

"Matt and I are going to drive to Jenna's place to make sure she's okay." He stowed the rifle and purse in the backseat of Matt's car. "You can go back to hating her guts after we figure out what's going on."

Matt was confused about when dealing with Jenna's issues had become a *we* situation for him and Jake, but as he processed Jake's concerns, he grew more worried about Jenna's well-being—and kicked himself for flying off the handle without hearing her out. "I don't hate Jenna. I love her and that makes this whole mess even worse."

"I bet it would." Jake backtracked at a trot, lassoed Tara around the waist, and planted a kiss on her lips.

She grabbed a fistful of his beard below his chin. "Be safe."

"Jesus. You chicks and your safety bullshit. How about you assume I'm never playing it safe and stop worrying about it?"

"Easier said than done."

He grunted. "Are you still going to be here when I get back?"

"How long are you going to be gone?"

"No idea."

"Yes, I'll still be here."

He smacked her backside. Hard. "Good answer."

Matt winced and scrambled to find his mental delete button as he slid behind the wheel. Jake dropped into the passenger seat with a sigh as Matt turned the engine over. "Explain why you're coming with me, again?"

"Backup, dude."

Backup with multiple firearms and an active-duty LAPD SWAT officer. Hard to complain about that. If Carson was a bad seed, Matt and Jake were more than ready to take him on.

Jenna and Rachel took up positions on either side of the front door far enough away that they'd be clear of gunfire should Carson shoot at them. Jenna tucked her body behind the door frame leading to the kitchen, her torso at an angle that afforded her a clear shot should she need to take it. Rachel was similarly posed in the threshold to the hallway.

Looking across the living room at Rachel, Jenna felt her strength return in spades. With her sister as her partner, they'd defend this house and the peacefully sleeping child inside it. Like elephant matriarchs, they were women banding together, circling the wagons, protecting their own.

"I've been in a lot of situations with you over the years, Rach, but never one where we were both armed and dangerous."

Rachel flashed the barest of smiles. "There's no one else I'd rather be armed and dangerous with. Except Vaughn. And he's on his way."

"How do you do it? How do you give yourself over to a

man like that? You have total trust that he's going to come through for you."

"It wasn't always like that. Trust is a process. Don't go believing that we started out this solid. You know what we went through to get to this sweet spot. Like Jake said at Amy's wedding, 'True love isn't about finding someone you can live with; it's about finding someone you can't live without.' It took me and Vaughn a while to figure out that we couldn't live without each other."

Jenna had loved that quote when she'd first heard it, thinking it the most romantic idea in the world. But she didn't buy into the sentiment anymore. She could live without Matt. She was strong and capable and used to being alone. She'd live without him, no problem—it was just that she didn't want to. She wished she were an indispensible part of his life, but clearly he could live without her, too. Was she doing love wrong, like she did everything else?

It didn't matter now. What would Carson want with her and Tommy? Would he want parental rights? If he did, what in the blazes was she going to tell Tommy?

Rachel motioned toward the door. "You want to talk to him like this? Figure out what his intentions are?"

Jenna took a steadying breath, then called, "Carson, you're going to have to talk to us through the door, because we're not opening it. You're not going to open it either because Rachel and I have guns trained on it."

"Jenna might've missed you the last time she tried to shoot you," Rachel added, "but I don't miss and I doubt Jenna will again. Go ahead and tell us what you want."

The pounding stopped.

Jenna and Rachel exchanged anxious glances. In the yawning silence, Jenna whipped her head around to look at the pane of glass in the back door. She wasn't sure where to look. Carson knew about that door. The two of them used to sneak into this cottage as teenagers, when it was vacant after her dad had laid off the foreman because they couldn't afford his salary.

"Carson, you still there?" she called. Then she held her breath.

"He's five, Jenna. Your son. I asked around." Carson's muffled voice had a weary edge to it. Weary and hurt. "He's five. You lied to me about his age and I can only think of one reason why."

Holding the rifle in one hand, she silently lifted a kitchen chair and crept toward the front door, as she had the first time Carson came knocking. She balanced on it and peered through the crack in the blinds. She could see the tops of his knees from where he sat, elbows propped on them, head cradled in his hands and his back resting against the wall beneath the window.

He didn't look like a man on a rampage. He looked like a man who'd been stunned witless by news he'd never expected.

"Carson?"

"What are you doing?" Rachel hissed at her.

Jenna shot her a wide-eyed look. "It's okay." Toward the door, she called, "If I open the door, are you going to hurt me?"

"Damn it, Jenna. No. I don't hurt women. Not even lying bitches aiming guns at me. We have to talk about this face-to-face. I need you to look me in the eye and tell me the truth."

Standing with one hand on the dead bolt, the other on her rifle, Jenna whispered a prayer for strength and clarity. In her periphery, she saw Rachel assuming a position behind her. As Jenna turned the lock, she kept praying until peaceful resignation to her fate settled over her. She scrubbed a hand over her face, then rotated her jaw to loosen it, took one more cleansing breath, and opened the door to the night and looked straight into the barrel of Carson's gun.

Chapter Twenty-One

Jenna slipped her finger to the trigger of her rifle and planted her feet, lest she stumble back and give Carson an opening to get in the house. "I thought you said you didn't hurt women."

"I don't, but when I get guns pointed at me, I point mine back. Chalk it up to a strong sense of self-preservation."

Headlights rounded the corner of the hill leading to Jenna's cottage.

Carson's eyes shifted between Jenna and the approaching vehicle. "Who's this going to be?"

"Probably someone from the sheriff's department. We made the call when you showed up."

"You bitch. You just can't stop screwing me over, can you?"

The vehicle turned slightly, and Jenna recognized the shape and red paint job immediately. Her heart sank. Oh God, what was he doing here? Jenna didn't think she could handle any more hits. "It's Matt."

Matt parked next to Carson's truck. Jake was in the passenger seat. Both were armed, by the looks of it. Matt was halfway out of his SUV before the engine died. He and Jake assumed protected positions behind the SUV's doors.

"Police! Drop your weapon," Jake barked in a razor-sharp, authoritative tone Jenna had never heard him use before.

Carson swung his handgun toward the car. "Think again. Who the hell are you?"

"First Lieutenant Jake Reed, SWAT Division of the LAPD, and I'm not dicking around. Kneel slowly and set your gun on the ground. That's the last time I ask. Next time, I squeeze the trigger and let me tell you, son, you won't be the first person I've shot. You wouldn't even be the first person I've killed. I've had a shitty week, and I'd love nothing more than to blow that fucking gun out of your hand."

Jenna was like a lioness. Ferocious. Matt had never seen her equal.

Carson was bad news, but she and her sister were facing him down with so much ballsy courage, he couldn't help but be proud of her, even though he was terrified at the sight of Carson's gun. By the looks of it, Matt and Jake had gotten there in the nick of time.

As soon as he and Jake had rounded the hill to Jenna's house and seen guns, Jake had asked to take lead and Matt was more than happy to let him, given the guy's considerable experience with these types of volatile situations. Ensuring Jenna and Rachel's safety was his only goal.

"Jenna, disengage your firearm and set it on the ground. Rachel, you, too," Jake called.

Both Jenna and Rachel held steady, their guns aimed at Carson. "Like hell I will," Rachel said.

He glanced her way, clearly taken aback by her noncompliance.

She shot him a sidelong look and held her revolver steady. "He wouldn't be the first man I shot either."

Jake's expression took on an amused gleam. "That's how it is, huh?"

"Tell you what," Rachel said. "I'll let you shoot him first."

"You can both go to hell. I'm setting my gun down now," Carson said. He lowered into a squat, then set his handgun on the ground.

Matt couldn't wait any longer. He needed to get to Jenna's side and make sure she was okay. "I'll get his gun," he told Jake.

"Roger that."

Matt jogged between Jenna and Carson, picked up the handgun from the ground and checked to see if it was loaded. It was. He tucked his rifle under his arm and looked at Jenna. "Are you okay?"

She nodded.

He looked her over, just in case, but the wounded look in her eyes was the only injury he could see. And fear, plenty of fear. Gently, he took the rifle from her hands and unloaded it.

Standing in front of Jenna like a shield, he turned to Carson. "Are you going to play nice? Because if you want to get into it tonight, I'm all for that. Let's take it away from the women. It'd be fun to let you try to kick my ass. Say the word."

Carson stood again, shifting his weight restlessly, a hand braced on the back of his neck. "I'm just trying to talk to Jenna."

"Then you're going to have to talk to her over me," Matt said.

Carson huffed. "Or what, Champagne Killer? You gonna throw a glass at me?"

Matt raised the handgun, aiming it at Carson's middle.

"I'm pretty sure this nine-mil would do the job just fine. I don't recommend you test me to see if I'm bluffing."

Carson got the point. His head of steam cooled off and his shoulders lowered. "All right. Fine. Have it your way. But I need some answers and I'm not leaving until I get them." He angled a look around Matt at Jenna. "Why didn't you tell me? All this time I've had a son and I had no idea. You kept him from me. Is it because I'm gay? Are you as small-minded as the rest of them?"

Carson was gay? Matt blinked as the information sunk in. Matt had gone and gotten instantly jealous, thinking Carson and Jenna would want to rekindle their old flame and it turned out the guy was gay? What a stupid, immature idiot Matt was. Jenna had tried to explain and he'd been too hotheaded and self-absorbed to listen.

Behind him, Jenna paced in a tight line. "You were my best friend. The only reason you being gay had anything to do with why I didn't tell you is because you were gone and all I could think about was that a group of men in town hated who you were so badly that they nearly beat you to death. I was afraid they'd hurt Tommy if they found out who his father was."

Beaten? For being gay? Matt had never heard talk of a hate element in Catcher Creek, but most small towns had them. It disgusted Matt that there were still certain parts of the state he loved where being different put a target on a person's back. Carson stared at a patch of ground, looking as stunned by Jenna's revelations as Matt was.

Finally, Carson roused himself. "I still had a right to know."

Jenna threw up her arms. "You're not getting it. I was nineteen—just a kid—and the way I saw my choices laid out was that I could keep your identity as Tommy's father a secret and live here on the ranch, raising my child with the support of my family. Or I could've told your parents the truth, hoping you got the message, and left town for good in fear that whoever beat you up would come after us.

"For all I knew, whoever hurt you was powerful and untouchable by the law, and that your parents hadn't gone to the police or taken you to the hospital in fear of retaliation. Other times I wondered if your parents were in on the beating. What if they were the ones who told Bucky, Lance, and Kyle your secret? I didn't know who to trust or what to believe, so I made the best choice I could."

"I thought you'd given up my secret."

She shook her head. "Kyle found out all on his own. Kate spilled the secret the other night at Bunco. It turned out that he'd been at your house with Kate, and he'd gone through your stuff while you weren't there. He found . . ." She scrunched up her face. "Let's just say he found your stash under your bed."

Carson cursed. He slammed his palm on his forehead and paced to the edge of the yard and back. When he looked at Jenna again, his expression had shifted to one of regret. "You were the only person I told that I was gay. I thought you'd betrayed me. I thought—"

On shaky inhale, Jenna shook her head. "You thought the worst of me on the turn of a dime. You didn't even give me a chance to explain before you accused me of terrible sins and turned your back on me. Happens a lot to me, as it turns out." She drilled Matt with a look that spoke volumes about how badly he'd hurt her.

Matt swallowed hard and held her gaze. He'd never felt lower in his life. If he spent the rest of his days on earth trying to atone for the way he'd wronged her, it still wouldn't be enough.

"Do you understand now why I made the choices I did,

Carson? Why I didn't tell anyone, even my sisters, what happened that summer?" Jenna asked.

Nodding, Carson slumped against the side of the house. "I'm not supposed to be a father. I don't have that dream. A lot of guys do, but not me. I'm only twenty-four, for shit's sake. I can barely take care of myself."

The front door creaked, opening. Tommy stood in the doorway, squinting, his blankie wrapped around his shoulders like a shawl and his stuffed dog dangling from his hand. "Mommy? I'm scared. I heard noises."

All the guns disappeared, even Jake's. Matt slid the safety on his rifle and set it on the side of the house, out of view. Carson leaned against the house, watching Tommy with a hand over his mouth, stricken.

Jenna knelt in front of Tommy. Her smile had an obvious strain to it. "Mommy's fine. We were all talking and must have gotten a little loud. Sorry about that. You see? There's Aunt Rachel and Uncle Jake. Matt's here, too."

Though Jenna lunged for him, Tommy darted around Jenna's legs and ran to Matt. He threw his arms around Matt's legs. "You didn't tuck me in. I wanted to sing the cowboy song with you, but you didn't even say good-night to me."

Carson's gaze was riveted on Tommy. He slid to the ground, his eyes huge and brimming with moisture. Even if Carson wanted to be in Tommy's life, he sure wasn't equipped to take that step tonight.

Just like that, looking at Carson, feeling Tommy hugging his knees, and seeing Jenna standing stiff and tall like a lioness, Matt had an out-of-body experience. Tommy needed him. Jenna needed him. He'd fucked up in the worst way, twisting his father's philosophy about doing the right thing to fit his own agenda.

Doing the right thing wasn't about protecting himself by

turning his back on the people he loved. It was manning up and being whatever Jenna and Tommy needed so they could get through the challenges that lay ahead for them with Carson and with Jenna's move.

He knelt, arms wide open. Tommy hooked his hands around Matt's neck and held on tight. Matt lifted him into his arms. "Sorry about that, buddy. I love singing the cowboy song with you."

"Is that why you came back? So you could sing with me?"

Matt gritted his teeth, getting a grip on his surging emotions. It was shameful how ready he'd been to cast Jenna and Tommy aside. "Of course. That's our special song."

Over Tommy's shoulder, he met Carson's wide-eyed stare. He couldn't imagine what was going through Carson's head right now. He probably didn't yet understand the gift he'd been given in being a father to this precious little boy. That would take time.

If Matt could convince Jenna to forgive him, if they could overcome the damage they'd done to each other and forge a life, he'd have to share fathering Tommy with another man. He'd never seen that twist of fate coming. Not in his wildest dreams.

Even if Jenna couldn't forgive Matt, at the very least Carson was going to need help figuring out how to be a dad. There was going to be a time of transition, and Matt loved Tommy and Jenna enough to help them through it, even if it broke his heart in the long run.

Jenna stood in a wide, defensive stance, her eyes locked on Tommy and the lioness intensity glinting in her eyes. Behind the ferocity, he sensed her personal pain. He could only imagine how raw and hurt she was with all that'd gone down tonight. Matt's future hit him with perfect clarity. This family, however screwed up and unconventional it was, needed a leader. It was time to step up to the plate.

Matt buried his nose in Tommy's hair. He smelled like dirt and ice cream and little boy. "How about I tuck you back in bed and we sing our song?"

"I could show you my superhero action figures."

Matt tugged on the stuffed doggy's ear. "Let's do that tomorrow, okay? Ruff Ruff needs a good night's sleep. I think I just saw him yawn."

As if the word triggered it, Tommy yawned and burrowed his face into Matt's shoulder.

Matt walked toward Jake, who still stood alert in case Carson turned volatile again. Giving Jake a look that he hoped expressed how grateful he was that Jake had insisted they come back here, Matt handed him Carson's gun. Jake unloaded it and nodded back, clearly getting the message Matt was imparting.

Matt carried Tommy back to the house, stopping in front of Jenna. Their eyes met and held. Her jaw was tight and her eyes watery, but she radiated a toughness that held him in awe—like she was ready to fight the world rather than let it kick her any more while she was down.

Emotion tightened his throat. "I'm not leaving," he said. Jenna flinched, but otherwise her expression remained unchanged. "I've got this. And I've got you. And I promise I'll never let you down like that again." The iron will in his tone surprised him. So this was what it felt like to really be all-in. Whatever determination he'd felt before to make a relationship work with Jenna, it paled in comparison to the resolve pumping through his blood now.

Wrenching her face away, she hugged herself.

Matt swallowed. Rebuilding their trust would take time, he knew. Meanwhile, they all had a little boy to worry over.

He turned his focus to Carson, whose attention hadn't left Tommy since he'd come outside. Matt tipped his head toward the door. "I'm going to tuck Tommy in bed. You want to come? You might as well start learning 'The Cowboy Lullaby.'"

Carson's gaze shifted to Jenna as though seeking permission.

Jenna's statuelike expression cracked. Mashing her lips together, she nodded.

With a sigh, Carson focused on his feet and shook his head. "I don't think—"

But Matt wasn't letting him off the hook that easily. "I know you have a lot to process, but it'd be good for you to just stand in the hall and listen and start taking it all in." He shifted Tommy's weight to his left arm and hip, then offered Carson a hand up. "I'll help you through this, man. You and me and Jenna, we're in this together, okay?"

After a pause, Carson accepted Matt's hand up and stood. His eyes rolled around with a slow blink, like he couldn't yet believe the turn his life had taken tonight.

Tommy squirmed in Matt's arms to look at Carson. "You're going to listen to the cowboy song too?"

"Yeah, I guess I am," Carson croaked, his gaze flitting to Jenna and back. He cleared his throat and held the door open for Matt.

Once they were inside, Tommy rested his chin on Matt's shoulder and looked speculatively at Carson, as though sizing him up. "Matt's going to be my daddy."

Damn, he loved the sound of that. He wanted to ask Tommy what he'd think about him sharing the job with Carson, but it was too soon to know if Carson would do the right thing and embrace the gift he'd been blessed with. For Tommy's sake, Matt prayed he would.

"Oh yeah?" Carson managed in a ragged voice.

Tommy nodded against Matt's shoulder, his attention still on Carson. "Do you know how to roast s'mores?"

Carson cleared his throat. "Yes."

"Do you know how to ride a horse?"

"Yes. Do you?"

"Mm-hmm. My mommy taught me."

A stuffed suitcase and an equally full knapsack sat in the middle of the living room. Matt's gut twisted. Jenna had been ready to run. Alone. That's how afraid and overwhelmed she'd been. It was a hard pill to swallow to realize what a terrible position he'd put her in by walking away from her like he had.

"My friend Lizzy has two daddies and two mommies and two houses."

Maybe the little man was catching on to the reason for Carson's presence all on his own. "Does Lizzy like that?" Matt asked.

"I don't know. She likes to eat grass."

Matt wrinkled his nose at him. "That's gross."

"Sometimes I eat it, too."

Carson chuckled. Right then and there, Matt knew they were all going to be okay. It'd take time, but he and Carson and Jenna would figure out their new normal.

He set Tommy in his bed, then pulled the covers up around him. Carson hung back in the hall, his arms crossed, his expression unreadable. Matt gave him a reassuring smile as he knelt on the floor near Tommy's head.

Tommy snuggled Ruff Ruff under his chin. "Are you still mad at Mommy?"

The little guy didn't miss a thing, did he? A lawyer in training, perhaps? "Not at all. I'm mad at myself, though. Does that ever happen to you?"

"Sometimes. When I get in trouble."

"Makes sense. Are you ready to teach Carson 'The Cowboy Lullaby'?"

Tommy nodded and offered him a sleepy grin. "Kiss first."

Matt took his hand and kissed his forehead. Love, pure

and bright, shone through him. No matter what happened between him and Jenna or what choice Carson made about his role in Tommy's life, nothing could change the truth that Matt felt all the way to his core. For the first time in his life, he didn't just feel like a dad. He was a dad.

Jenna left the house quietly, so as not to alert Carson, Matt, and Tommy that she'd been checking up on them. Tenderness and anguish warred inside her after watching Matt put Tommy to bed, singing to him and tucking him in with hugs and kisses.

She still couldn't quite believe he'd come back. She'd wondered if she'd ever see him again, yet he'd returned with Jake as backup, guns blazing, and told her he wasn't leaving again. Did he mean tonight—or forever? If he did want to stay in her life, could she forgive him for his snap judgment of her?

Jake and Rachel were standing right outside the door. Jake's gun had been returned to its holster and Rachel's Colt was nowhere to be seen.

"Are you okay?" Rachel asked.

She didn't know what to think or how to feel anymore. "Not really." She looked to Jake. "Thank you for showing up when you did."

He shrugged. "Matt and I had a hunch."

Headlights flashed in the distance, coming down the hill toward Jenna's house.

"Who's that?" Jake asked. In a heartbeat, his gun was in his hand, pointed at the ground in the direction of the approaching car.

"Vaughn. I called him when Carson showed up," Rachel said.

"Good move." Still, he didn't reholster his gun until the

patrol car had pulled fully into Jenna's gravel turn-around and Vaughn was clearly visible through the windshield.

Vaughn's head was on a swivel as he exited his car, a hand on his holstered firearm. "Jake. I'm glad to see you here. What's the situation? Where's Carson now?"

Jake shook Vaughn's hand. "He's in the house, watching Matt put Tommy to bed."

Vaughn looked to Rachel and Jenna with confusion. "So he is Tommy's father, after all?" At Jenna's nod, he added, "You two sounded scared on the phone. You said he might be dangerous. Is it a good idea for him to be in there with Tommy?"

"Matt has things under control. Besides, Carson calmed down fast. He's not going to do anything stupid or reckless now," Jenna said. She'd seen in Carson's eyes that learning he'd fathered a child had knocked his anger clean out of him, and, as confusing as it'd been to see him in her house observing Tommy's bedtime routine, she couldn't deny the unexpected relief that the truth was out and she could stop fighting so hard to protect herself and her child.

"We confiscated Carson's gun," Jake added. He took it out of his pants, opened the slide, and took out the magazine to show Vaughn it was unloaded, then put it all back together and handed it to him, along with the ammo he'd put in his other pocket.

The radio clipped to Vaughn's belt chirped to life. Vaughn listened to the request for backup from the dispatcher, told her he was on his way as soon as he could, then replaced it on his belt.

"I don't know how I feel, leaving again. You had me really nervous when you called. I don't like people threatening you. Not at all." He kissed Rachel's hair. "But shit's hitting the fan in Devil's Furnace tonight. We arrested a drug dealer there yesterday and all these other lowlifes are fighting for dominance now. It's a real mess."

"We're okay," Jenna said. "It's fine for you to get back to work. Jake and Matt are here, and, anyway, Rachel and I were holding our own before they got here. Thank you for coming so fast."

"Of course. Anything for you two." He snagged Jenna in a one-armed hug, then nodded to Jake. "Thanks again for being here."

"Family's family, right?" Jake said.

Vaughn slapped his back. "You bet it is." He pulled Rachel into an embrace and nuzzled her cheek. The two of them weren't into public displays of affection, not like Kellan and Amy, and this rare intimacy made Jenna blush through her happiness for her sister.

"Good-bye," Rachel told him, stroking a finger over his cheek. "Give me a call in the morning, okay?"

Both Jenna and Jake stepped away, giving the two of them a modicum of privacy. After Vaughn had left, Jake turned to Rachel, grinning. "You didn't tell him to stay safe. Every chick I've ever been with has said that to me when I leave for work, especially when we get calls about bad stuff going down with shots fired, like Vaughn just did."

Rachel shrugged. "He already knows he'd better come back to me safe and sound. Some things don't need saying."

Her words hit Jenna hard. She and Matt had joked about things that go without saying on the night of Amy and Kellan's rehearsal dinner. And yet here she was, having to face up to a lot of things she hadn't thought needed to be said, but had ended up coming out anyway. That was the funny thing about the truth: if you didn't come clean, secrets would find a way out on their own.

The front door squeaked open. Matt walked out, followed by Carson.

Jenna, Jake, and Rachel walked their way and met them in the yard.

"Is Tommy okay?" Jenna asked.

"Fine," Matt answered with a lopsided grin. "That is one sweet kid."

"I know it," Jenna said. "He has his moments, but he's a pretty amazing little man."

"I thought I heard a car," Carson said. "Was someone else here?"

"Vaughn, briefly."

Carson nodded. "I guess he wasn't worried anymore about me and Jenna getting into it?"

Jake folded his arms over his chest. "We told him you weren't going to cause any more trouble. We were right, weren't we?"

His jaw was tight. "Yes."

"I gave him your gun, so you can talk to him on your own time about getting it back."

Carson's brows lifted on his inhale. "I suppose I had that coming."

Jake scratched his beard. "Rachel, it seems to me that Jenna, Matt, and Carson have a lot to talk about that doesn't involve you or me. What would you say to giving me a ride back to Kellan's place? I've got a woman waiting on me there."

Rachel raised a brow. "Dang, you don't waste any time. You just got to Catcher Creek a week ago."

Matt huffed. "He's talking about my sister."

That seemed to throw Rachel for a loop. "Tara? Really?"

Given what Tara had told Jenna last week about not wanting a relationship with Jake, she was as surprised as Rachel. Then again, maybe this was just another bed warming, one last fling before Jake left town.

Jake tipped his nose in Jenna's direction. "I'll be leaving for the memorial service on Monday, but I'll be swinging back through here on my way to L.A. How about I take Kellan's dog with me to Wyoming so you don't have to worry about house-sitting? You have enough on your plate."

"That would be really helpful, thank you." Jake was a stand-up guy. Looked like a thug, and she knew he and Kellan had a long way to go before their rift was healed, but the fact that Jake was coming back through Catcher Creek and was willing to look out for Kellan's dog spoke volumes. Of course, she had to wonder how big a factor Tara was in his decision to return.

She knew Jake wasn't into hugging, but she couldn't help herself. She threw her arms around him and squeezed as hard as she could. "Thank you for being here for me when I needed you."

He patted her back. "Likewise. You need anything from here on out, you give me a call, okay? You have my number."

He held his fist out to Matt and they bumped knuckles. "Take it easy, man."

"You, too," Matt said.

"You and me, hunting next weekend, all right? I look forward to beating your ass in the rabbit count."

"You're on. I'd like to see you try."

After hugs and thanks to Rachel, Matt, Jenna, and Carson watched in stoic silence as Rachel and Jake embarked on the quarter-mile walk to the big house where Rachel's truck was.

Once they were alone, Carson walked to his truck and put the tailgate down. "I guess Jake's right. We have a lot to talk about."

Jenna climbed into the truck bed and perched on the wheel cover, her knees drawn up. Though she was dying to know where she and Matt stood and what Carson expected out of a relationship with Tommy, the idea of talking more left her feeling weary to the bone. She was all talked out for one night, but there was no getting around this conversation. Matt hitched his hip on the tailgate.

Carson opened the back door of the truck and pulled a bottle of whiskey out from under the bench seat. "For emergencies—and this seems like an emergency."

He climbed into the truck bed and offered the bottle to Jenna. She nearly took it, but she had too many memories of her and Carson drinking in the back of a truck just like this for her to do so again tonight. "No, thanks. I don't drink anymore."

Carson's face registered shock at that discovery, but then he nodded. "That's probably a good plan. I can see why you'd stop. You and I used up at least six or seven of our nine lives by the time we graduated high school."

"Pretty much."

He held the bottle out to Matt, who took it, indulged in a brief swig, then returned it to Carson. She wished she knew what Matt was thinking about her, about them. She wished she knew what he'd meant when he said he wasn't leaving.

"Is my name on his birth certificate?" Carson asked in a pensive voice.

The question snapped Jenna's attention away from Matt. Carson rolled the whiskey bottle between his boots.

"No."

He sniffed, rubbing his chin. "Is there any reason I should doubt you about this—I mean, get a paternity test or something? Don't be offended by that, please. It's just that this is so crazy, I don't know where we go from here."

"I'm not offended. It's a legitimate request. If you want a paternity test, I'll support you about that, but I know with a hundred percent certainty that you're his father." In her mind's eye, she thought about the bewilderment in his eyes while he'd watched Matt put Tommy to bed. Was he asking about the birth certificate because he wanted a way out of the situation? Maybe. If he wanted to be part of Tommy's life, she'd welcome him, but he at least deserved the choice to walk away.

She swallowed and her heart rate picked up its pace. "You know, Carson, you could walk away from this right now and never look back. I'd never ask you for anything, no money—nothing. And I'd never breathe a word about you being Tommy's father. Let the people of Catcher Creek speculate. Nobody else has to know and the people who do know won't think any less of you."

Staring vacantly at the floor, Carson took a hit of whiskey. In her peripheral vision, she saw Matt shift. She quelled the urge to look at him, to see if his expression gave away his thoughts. She'd probably disgusted him all over again with that offer. He, of all people, wouldn't understand why a father might walk away.

"I'm not going to beat around the bush, Jenna," Carson said. "I almost didn't come here tonight. I thought about skipping town without a word. Your life would be easier without me in it, that's for sure. And, hell, I never wanted to be a father in the first place. I never even considered it for myself. Even if someday I fell in love with a man who wanted kids, that's such a distant possibility and so far down the road it's not worth thinking about."

Now that his hard, angry visage was gone, Carson looked young. Technically, he and Jenna were the same age, but studying Carson, she felt old. Tired. So much so that she nearly told both men to leave. She wanted to be alone again. Not that being alone was easy, but it was predictable. Predictability sounded really damn good at the moment. The bottle of whiskey drew her attention. If ever there was a night she needed a drink, this was it.

"You'd regret that," Matt said in a tone of restrained emotion.

Jenna tore her focus from the whiskey to look at him.

He sat with his back against the side of the truck bed, his elbows propped on his knees and his hands clasped together. He wasn't talking to her, but to Carson. "It'd eat you up. Maybe not right now, but someday." His eyes were dark and intense, his jaw tight. "I have a medical condition that makes it so I can't have kids of my own. You might not understand how lucky you are, but I'd give anything to be in your position right now. Anything."

"What are you talking about? You're already a great dad to Tommy. You're what he needs, not me."

Matt gave a slow shake of his head. "He needs you, too. He needs to know his biological father is a stand-up guy and cares about him. I know it must be scary as hell to take this step, but my dad always told me that nobody ever said doing the right thing was easy." He paused and pressed his lips together hard, his eyes unfocused, as if some dark thought was passing through his mind. "That's . . . uh . . . I'm not sure I truly understood that adage until tonight." He cleared his throat. "I told you I'm going to help you through this transition and I meant every word. As far as me being Tommy's dad—" He rolled his eyes to Jenna and pinned her with an inscrutable look. "Jenna and I are going to have to talk about that."

She wrenched her face away to stare into the darkness. Goddamn, did they have to? Jenna didn't think she had it in her to explain herself or be berated any more tonight.

Carson toed the bottom of her shoe. "You might find it interesting to know that Matt told me before we came back outside that he'd shoot to kill if I ever pulled a gun on you again or scared you in any way." He offered Jenna a contrite, tight-lipped grin. "I'm so sorry I did that. I had no idea why you'd made the choices you had. I was so pissed at you and this town that I wasn't in my right mind. All the shit I went through here, all the rage I felt, it came rushing back to me and I did a lousy job controlling it."

Jenna's heart squeezed at the revelation that Matt had threatened Carson on her behalf. Lord, she wished she didn't love him. She wished she didn't want him in her life so badly that a huge hole had opened up inside her at the thought of being without him.

Carson thought Matt was going to be around for her and Tommy in a forever kind of way. How could she tell him that Matt didn't want her? That she was too damaged to be worthy of his love? She gave another look at the whiskey bottle, then stood and leapt over the side of the truck.

Chapter Twenty-Two

Both men tracked Jenna's movement. She paced the gravel next to the truck, keeping her attention on Carson. "You should know that I never stopped thinking about what you went through, the beating, the cover-up by your parents. I'm haunted by what happened to you to this day, differently than it haunts you, I know, but it changed my life all the same. It's time that we faced the truth that the reasons I never let on about you being Tommy's father haven't changed.

"This stupid, small-minded town isn't safe for Tommy and me. It never was and it never will be, especially now that you've come out publicly. That's why Tommy and I are moving to Santa Fe this week. We'd already planned to and I've got it all set up, so you don't need to worry."

Fire shone in Carson's eyes. "I hadn't thought that far ahead yet, but you're right about this place. Shit. What do we do now?" He pushed his fingers into his hair, the wheels clearly turning in his mind.

"We don't do anything. Hate like that is too insidious to weed out. Bucky, Lance, and Kyle aren't the only violent bigots in Quay County," Jenna said.

"I can't not do something. If I take care of those three assholes at the rodeo like I'd originally planned, then maybe

I'll send a message to the others like them that you and Tommy aren't to be messed with. In five days, my leave is over and I've got to report for duty in San Diego. I won't be here to protect you and Tommy after that. I've got to do everything I can."

Jenna hadn't thought about how being on active duty might affect Carson's choices. She pressed her palm to her forehead as a whole new strain of questions flashed through her mind. When was his next deployment? Was he planning to be a career soldier? Even if he wanted to be a part of Tommy's life, father and son may not ever live in the same state. If he wanted visitation rights, did that mean Tommy would have to fly to wherever Carson was stationed? That was, if Carson wanted to be a part of Tommy's life.

Matt stood. "Hey, listen, violence isn't a solid plan. You're on the sheriff's department's radar now. They'll be expecting you to try something, and if you get arrested, that doesn't help Jenna and Tommy, and it would take away all your choices for your future."

Carson threw his hands in the air. "What good am I if I can't go after the bullies that would threaten my . . . my . . ."

"Your son?" Matt supplied. "He's our son, too, and you being arrested wouldn't be what's best for any of us."

Jenna gaped at him. *He's our son, too?*

But Matt wasn't done. "You said you went into the Marines to get strong so you could come back and hurt the people who hurt you, but the truth is, now that you have the strength and skill to do harm, you have to be man enough not to. If you want to get those guys who hurt you, I can help you with that. I'm a lawyer. We'll get those bastards where it really hurts—in court."

Carson's fire was doused. He dropped onto the side of the truck bed, hunching into the arms he'd propped on his knees. "I hope you're right. I hate feeling this helpless."

"I know what you mean, but you're making the right call. You and I, we'll talk, okay? I know the Quay County district attorney well, and so does Vaughn. You'll be here for five days, which is enough time for you to meet with her and the sheriff's department so they can start building a case against Bucky, Lance, and Kyle. You want me to call Vaughn in the morning and make arrangements for you to meet with him and the D.A. for an interview?"

Carson took another hit from the whiskey bottle. "Thank you. That would be good. Will you be there, too?"

Matt squeezed his shoulder. "If that's what you want, then absolutely."

Carson nodded. With a sigh that drew his shoulders up and made him look more at peace than he had been since arriving at her house that night, he turned his focus to Jenna. "You said you were moving to Santa Fe? What's up with that?"

"Yes, we are. And we won't be back except to visit my sisters. I'll make sure you have my contact information. After you've had time to think, we can talk about how you want to handle things with Tommy."

"Where are you going to live—with Matt?"

Why did everybody assume she planned to move in with a man? Didn't anybody have the modern sensibility to think she might be competent enough to live on her own? "I found an apartment. I've got a job lined up with the state as a software programmer. Good starting salary, great benefits, retirement plan—the works. Tommy's already signed up for kindergarten there and everything."

She could tell the news threw him off-kilter again. "You'll be programming computers? How did you manage to get a job like that?"

"I've been going to college." A flash of panic still seized her when she said the words, but she sounded strong and confident. A definite improvement.

"She graduates next month from UNM as a computer engineer," Matt added. Though his eyes and expression remained dark and guarded, his tone carried a note of pride in it, as it always did when he talked about her schooling.

Huffing, Carson grinned at her like he was impressed. "You never needed any of us, Jenna. You were always above the fray, better than the rest of us. You really have your shit together."

She tried not to laugh outright at the assessment. "Not exactly."

Rubbing her arms, she walked to the picket fence and studied her little cottage. It'd been the foreman's house back in the farm's heyday. After he had been let go, it'd sat empty until Tommy was two, when her mom's health began to spiral downward and she no longer tolerated Tommy's little-boy energy or his occasional "terrible twos" tantrums. Jenna and Rachel had decided it was time to spruce up the cottage and move her and Tommy out of the big house.

It'd been a great choice. Jenna liked the solitude. It was so much easier to study in secret out from under her parents' and Rachel's watchful eyes. She'd miss her home when she moved to Santa Fe. She'd miss wide open spaces and horses and seeing Rachel every day. Moving was the right decision on many levels, and she had no regrets or second thoughts, but that didn't mean she wasn't allowed to get sentimental about what she was leaving behind.

A hand on her shoulder made her jump.

"Jenna . . . ," Matt said.

She inhaled, countering the raw, ready-to-shatter feeling pervading her by drawing herself up tall, straight-spined and proud. "I get it now, what you were saying about how messed up I am," she said in a quiet voice for his ears only. "Tommy deserves better than a pathological liar for a mother. I'm going to get myself some professional help in

Santa Fe. You don't have to stick around for all that. You said you wouldn't leave, but I won't hold you to it. Like I told Carson, you're free to walk away and never look back. No one will think less of you for it. Tommy and I are going to be fine."

It took a lot of swallowing and teeth grinding not to shed any tears, but she managed it. She looked him in the eye and poured every last ounce of her fraying strength into her expression.

Balling his hands in his pockets, he turned his face up to the sky and released a tremulous exhale. When he dropped his chin again and looked at her, his eyes were crowded with moisture. With a blink, a tear rolled over his cheek. He smashed his lips together and cleared his throat. "I have a lot to apologize for. And I'm going to. But first, I need to make it absolutely clear that I will not be walking away from you—from us—again. Not tonight, and not for the rest of my life."

He swiped at the tear, but three more followed. "What I'm trying to say is that it's up to you to keep me from turning into one of those creepy stalker guys because I'm not going anywhere."

She tried to smile at his lame attempt at levity, but her heart was too heavy to bear it.

"Guys?" Carson called to them. "I'm going to get out of here, give you two some space. I have a lot to think about. Jenna, are you still going to be in town tomorrow?"

"Yes."

He stowed the whiskey bottle under the backseat again. "I'll come back in the morning. Maybe we can talk about . . ." He scratched his neck, chortling. "Actually, I have no idea what we'll talk about. Where we go from here, I guess."

"You're going to choose to be in Tommy's life, right?" Matt asked. "You're not bailing, are you?"

Even though Carson's expression turned apologetic and

distressed, Jenna was glad Matt had asked because the same question had been weighing on her mind. "I don't know, man. I really don't. Are you going to be here tomorrow, too?"

"Definitely."

Carson opened the driver's-side door. "We'll talk then. About Tommy and my case against Bucky, Lance, and Kyle."

"I'm looking forward to that," Matt said. "I'll let you know when the D.A. is available for a meeting."

They watched him leave in heavy silence.

"Carson's not a bad man," Matt said, staring at the darkness where they'd last seen the taillights of Carson's truck. "Misguided and angry, but I think he's going to step up."

Jenna surprised herself by hoping he did because Matt was right; that would be best for Tommy. "Whether he does or not, Tommy and I are going to be fine." The only dicey part was figuring out how to get through her last month of school while juggling her mommy duties in a new town and new apartment without her support network close by. After that, life would get easier—at least, she had to hope it would.

"Of course you two will be fine. I'm going to see to it that you are."

Probably because it'd been a long, draining day, Jenna's throat tightened at his words and tears threatened in her eyes all over again. "I meant what I said, Matt. You don't have any obligations where Tommy and I are concerned. I lied to you more than once, about big things, and I don't expect you to overlook that. I'm so sorry. It was never my intention to hurt you like I did."

He set his hands on her shoulders and turned her to face him. "I meant what I said, too. I'm not leaving. This isn't about obligations or how much I love Tommy, this is about honoring and loving the most magnificent person I've ever met for the rest of her life."

"Matt, please . . ."

"I can't live without you, Jenna. More importantly, I don't want to. I know I let you down, but I want to be there when you graduate. I want to be there when you come home after your first day of your new job. I want to make love to you under the stars and draw you dirty stick-figure drawings and dance with you every chance I get. I want to tuck Tommy in every night and sing him the cowboy song and take him camping. And I want to help Carson figure out how to be a dad to Tommy, too."

Jenna closed her eyes. They were such pretty words, but she felt so raw, so vulnerable. How could she trust what he said was true?

Matt rubbed her arms. "I've dedicated my life to helping people, yet I'm doing a terrible job helping myself. I was so wrapped up in your choice to keep Tommy's paternity from Carson, so jealous of the gift he'd been given, that I didn't see the gift you'd already given me. The gift of your love, of opening your heart and family to me. You invited me into Tommy's life, into your life, and I couldn't see the blessing that was right in front of my face.

"When we first got together, I asked you to think hard about whether or not you could live with my flaws. You accepted me. You decided to love me anyway. And I didn't hold up my end of the bargain. You're not a pathological liar. You don't have any more wrong with you than any other man or woman in this world does, including me. It was reprehensible that I lashed out at you like that. I was so afraid of getting hurt that I hurt the most important person in my life."

His words filled her with a fresh surge of hope. Maybe there was a chance for them after all. She did need to correct him about one point first, though. She opened her eyes and placed a hand over his heart. "For the record, I didn't decide to love you anyway, despite your genetic condition. I decided that I loved you period. There was no compromising or settling involved. I fell in love with you and that's all there is to it."

His eyes welled with tears anew. "I can't tell you what it means to me to know you think about it like that. To know you love me, there are no words."

She smoothed her hand over his shirt. "You would really co-father Tommy with Carson?"

On a huff, he smiled, his brows raised, and shook his head. "It wasn't what I ever dreamed for myself, but I'm on board with it one hundred percent. Men co-father kids all the time—dads sharing duties with stepdads, gay dads— there are all kinds of blended families out there. I honestly hope Carson does step up because it would be best for Tommy—and him. But if Carson doesn't, Tommy will still have me. He'll never want for love."

She liked the way he was thinking. She liked it a lot. Kids could use all the parents, aunts, uncles, and grandparents they could get. "No, he won't." The raw wound of vulnerability still nagged at her, though. Despite Matt's words, despite the love they had for each other, it didn't change the fact that in her moment of greatest need, he'd walked away.

"You're thinking something dark. What is it?"

She looked into his eyes, tempted to withhold the truth. But she thought better of it. If they were to have any chance of a future together, she had to be completely honest from here on out. "When I needed you most, your instinct was to think the worst of me. How do I know you won't do that again if I give you my heart?" Her face crumpled and she could no longer hold back her tears. She wrenched her face to the side, looking out over the darkened hills, fighting for composure.

She felt a tug on her hands and turned back to look. Matt

had dropped to his knees before her. His eyes and cheeks were as wet as hers. "Jenna Sorentino, I love you and I swear to you that I will never walk out on you again, no matter what. I need another chance at us. I need you to save me. Please. Save me from a lifetime of regret over what I ruined with my petty, misguided pride. I don't want to live without you, Jenna. You give me breath, you give me hope, you give me strength. Save me from the hell that a life without you would be."

She touched his face, love blooming inside her, crowding out her heartache. The man whom she'd once thought was only interested in people he could save wanted her to save him. What a turn-about. "What if we saved each other?"

"I like that idea." He stood and slid fingers along her cheeks, cradling her face as he lowered his lips to hers for a kiss that told her how very deeply he loved her. Giving a little purr in the back of her throat to let him know how welcome his touch was, she opened her lips for him, opened her arms, opened her heart.

When the kiss ended, he stroked her hair. "There's only one thing left to do tonight." He fished his phone from his pocket. "Jenna, may I have this dance?"

Wiping the last of the tears from her eyes, she beamed at him. "Only if it's a waltz."

Skimming through his music library, he smiled so big that her favorite dimple appeared. "Of course. That's my favorite."

"Mine, too."

He set his phone on a rock and kissed her again. "I knew that already."

As the phone played opening notes of the same song they'd waltzed to at the Sarsaparilla Saloon, he took her hand, met her in closed hold, and stepped her back into the grass.

Epilogue

"He's not going to show. I know it."

"Yes, he is," Rachel shot back. "He said he would, so he will."

Amy shouldered her way between Rachel and Jenna. "He's not here yet. Maybe Jenna has a point. How much longer should we wait for him? What if we can't find seats?"

Rachel scowled. "There you go planting ideas in her head, making her even more worried. Don't you have enough sense to keep your mouth shut, or has pregnancy robbed you of that precious skill?"

Amy shifted her weight with a sassy swish to her hips. "That would be a precious skill you know nothing about. You're such a smart-ass, I bet you could sit on a carton of ice cream and tell what flavor it is."

Jenna groaned and covered her face with her hands. "You two are killing me. I'm freaking out here. This day is too important to me for you two to ruin it with your bickering."

"I've got just the thing we need," Amy said. She turned and looked at the group of their family and friends standing off to the side. Kellan, Jake, and Vaughn were deep in discussion with Mr. Dixon, Tina, and Sloane. "Kellan? Did you bring that—" She brought her cupped hand up to her mouth like she was drinking from it.

"Huh? Oh!" He felt around in the inner pocket of his flannel shirt and produced a stainless-steel flask, which he handed off to Amy with a smile.

Amy pushed it into Jenna's hands. "Here. This'll help you relax."

Jenna made the mistake of sniffing the opening. Alcohol tingled up her nose and brought on a sneezing fit. "What is that?"

Amy grinned. "Just a splash of New Mexico's finest tequila."

"Gimme that," Rachel said, lifting the flask from Jenna's hands. She took a long pull from it and scrunched her face up. "Yep. That'll do. But I still don't understand why you can't pack whiskey."

Amy frowned with mock-offense. "Jenna likes tequila."

"Actually, I don't."

Rachel rolled her eyes. "You're about to graduate college. Of course you like tequila. All college kids do. I think it's in the student handbook." She handed the flask back to Jenna. "Drink up."

Jenna took a swig. It wasn't so bad and maybe it would help her stop worrying about her special day being perfect. "You know, this stuff is all right."

Amy beamed. "I told you. And don't worry, Rach, we'll switch the flask to whiskey in time for your wedding next weekend."

Rachel took another hit of tequila, grimacing afterward. "I'm not going to need it because we're not hosting a circus party like you and Kellan did."

"You might be surprised by how nervous getting married will make you."

"Marrying Vaughn is the best, easiest decision I've ever

made. I'm pretty damn sure nerves aren't going to be an issue." She handed the flask back to Jenna, who was starting to feel that nice, warm, relaxed tequila effect. "Speaking of tying the knot, how soon before we're allowed to pester you and Matt about getting married?"

Jenna scanned the parking lot looking for Matt, but didn't see him yet. "Maybe he already asked me."

Amy gasped. Rachel snorted in disbelief.

Jenna allowed a coy smile to break out on her face. She almost couldn't wait to share the news with her sisters, but she and Matt had decided to keep their engagement a secret for a little while, something just for the two of them to enjoy in private before they shouted it from the rooftops. "Maybe we decided to keep it to ourselves until after Rachel's wedding so we don't steal your spotlight."

"Well, you're in luck because I hate the spotlight." Rachel made a sweeping gesture with her hand. "Steal away."

"We will soon. I promise. What I can tell you is that we aren't going to wait too long because we plan to apply to be adoptive parents as soon as possible since the process takes so long."

"A brother or sister for Tommy and a new cousin for Kellan's and my baby? That's going to be wonderful. What about you and Vaughn, Rachel? Any plans for kids?"

Rachel shook her head. "Eventually. Right now we're just in love with being in love, if you know what I mean."

"Do I ever," Jenna said.

Coming up behind Vaughn, Kellan, and Jake were Carrie and her new man, a strapping jock type who was a whole head taller than her. Carrie waved to Jenna, then introduced the guy to the circle of family and friends.

Jenna trotted up next to her and gave her a hug.

"Careful not to muss up your hat or robe," Carrie said.

"These duds look great on you. I'm so proud of you, sweetie."

"I couldn't have done this without your support. You know that, right?"

They hugged again. "I love having you as my honorary sister," Carrie said. "And next year, you can sit in the audience and cheer me on when I graduate."

"Sisters are the best. Honorary and otherwise. I can't wait to cheer you on. Graduating will be one item you can finally check off your bucket list."

"That isn't the only thing," Carrie said, pointing to the back of her new man. "Huge," she whispered, holding her hands apart to a length estimate Jenna was pretty sure wasn't humanly possible.

Jenna flashed her a thumbs-up. Good for her. Dispelling urban legends and getting her rocks off with a cute guy all at the same time. Not bad for a summer's work.

"Where are the boys?" Carrie asked.

"Matt dropped us off at the entrance. He and Tommy are finding parking."

"Good luck with that. This place is packed."

"They should be here soon."

"How's Carson's case going? Last you told me, the D.A. had filed charges against the men who beat him up."

Jenna nodded. In the weeks since Carson had first sat down with the Quay County district attorney and Vaughn to tell his story, Catcher Creek was getting a tough lesson in the kind of hatred that had infected the town and had too long been ignored. A deep divide had risen to the surface between Carson's supporters and those who couldn't bring themselves to believe that the town's golden-boy rodeo champs were anything less than angelic. Between the fall-out from Carson's case and the widespread revelation that he was Tommy's daddy, Jenna couldn't have been more grateful she'd gotten Tommy out of town when she did.

"The D.A. got the FBI involved because of the hate-crime aspect of Carson's case. Bucky, Lance, and Kyle were charged last week with conspiracy, attempted murder, and violation of federal hate crime laws."

"Specifically, the Matthew Shepard and James Byrd Jr. Hate Crimes Prevention Act," Vaughn added, moseying their way. It was uncanny, how fine-tuned Vaughn's hearing was. If he and Rachel ever did get around to having kids, he was going to make one heck of a father. "That makes what Bucky, Lance, and Kyle did a federal hate crime. When the courts are done with them, those bastards aren't going anywhere but the exercise yard of a prison for a long, long time."

"At least they pleaded guilty so Carson is spared from enduring a trial."

Carrie's eyes got huge. "They pleaded guilty?"

"Only after Carson's parents stepped forward as witnesses. His mother had taken photographs of Carson after the beating because she thought that someday she might need them for some reason. And it turned out there'd been a security video from out front of the family's feed store that captured the three men following Carson around the side of the store, baseball bats in their hands." She hadn't seen the video and didn't want to. It was horrifying enough to imagine. "All this time, she'd been holding on to the evidence, failing to find the courage to step forward and tell the police what happened to her son until now."

"Still, that doesn't seem very courageous of her to only step forward after charges had already been filed. Carson's the brave one."

"Agreed." She gave the parking lot another scan, searching for familiar faces as her stomach twisted into knots.

And then she spotted them. Matt was power-walking, dodging parked cars with Tommy on his shoulders. "There's my boys."

Once they were safely out of the parking lot, Matt swung Tommy down and bridged the rest of the distance to Jenna. He tugged on her tassel. "You look great, Miss College Graduate."

"Thank you." She gave him a quick kiss, then gave one to Tommy.

"Is that tequila on your breath?" Matt asked. "I thought you didn't drink."

"Well, Amy had Kellan bring a flask. It's practically tradition now for these types of things. I'm kind of glad she did. I'm getting worried that Carson won't show."

"He'll be here. I guarantee it. He applied for special leave and came all the way out from San Diego to cheer you on."

"And meet with the FBI prosecutors again."

Matt slid an arm around her waist. "That too. But not until he's all done cheering for one of his oldest friends."

She looked at her watch. "I've got to line up soon, but you have a little time to stall before you have to find your seats so you can look for him."

"He'll be here," Matt repeated, kissing her cheek. "Keep the faith."

"That's what I told her," Rachel said. "It was little Nancy Naysayer here who got her worried all over again." She hooked a thumb in Amy's direction.

Amy socked Rachel in the shoulder. "I did not. Don't forget who brought the tequila." She gave Jenna a once-over, then reached for her head. "Let me straighten your hat. It's almost showtime." She fiddled with Jenna's hair, moving bobby pins around. "You know what's neat? I graduated from a chef academy, but you're the first Sorentino to earn a college degree." She choked up on the last word. If it'd been anyone but Amy, Jenna would've attributed the high emotions to pregnancy hormones, but Amy was just being Amy.

What shocked Jenna most was that Rachel's eyes were wet, too. "We're really proud of you, sis."

Jenna rubbed Amy's arm. "Thank you. I'm sorry I didn't know how to tell you guys about my schooling sooner."

"Water under the bridge," Rachel said, sniffing. "I've said it before, but it's worth saying again. Do you have any idea how much I love being your sister?"

Jenna threw her arms around Rachel and Amy and pulled them into a hug. "I bet it's as much as I love being both of yours."

"Carson!" Tommy squealed. Jenna pivoted in time to see her little guy running toward Carson's open arms.

"I made it," Carson said, panting. To the group, he added, "I almost didn't because I got stuck behind a double parker. I was freaking out, but I found a way around. Thank goodness."

When Tommy reached him, Carson swung him off the ground and gave him a tickle on the ribs. "Hey, little man. I missed you. Your daddy sends me pictures of you all the time so I can see how big you're getting."

He and Jenna had made a lot of strides toward figuring out their plans for co-parenting. Tommy knew in his own way that Carson was his father, but Carson wasn't comfortable referring to himself as a daddy and Jenna and Matt had no desire to push him too hard too fast, not with the emotional toll of his criminal case weighing on him. For the time being, Tommy was happy, as were Carson, Matt, and Jenna, and that was all that mattered.

Matt took Jenna's hand and leaned in close. "Told you he'd be here."

Sometimes, Jenna couldn't believe how lucky she was. She had a new career on the horizon, a lifetime of love with Matt, a healthy son, two sisters and brothers-in-law she cherished and who cherished her, and a fresh start ahead of her in Santa Fe. There was only one thing left for her to do.

She clapped her hands to get everyone's attention. "Okay, y'all. I'm outta here. Next time you see me, I'll be a college graduate." Then she walked into the fray of the staging area to the claps and cheers of everyone she held dear in this world, her biggest fans—her family.

**Don't miss these other Catcher Creek romances
by Melissa Cutler!**

The Trouble With Cowboys

It was their parents' ranch, through the good days and the bad. But if they want to hang on to their land, their pride, and their family, the three Sorentino sisters will have to reinvent it from the ground up—and one of them just may reinvent herself in the process . . .

Cowboys have never been good for Amy Sorentino. First her hard-riding father bankrupted the family farm. Then her all-hat-no-cattle boyfriend sold her out on national television, ending her promising career as a chef. Now she and her squabbling sisters have partnered up in a final attempt to save their land by starting an inn and local restaurant. So it figures that with everything on the line, Amy's key supplier is just the kind of Stetson-tipping, heartbreaking bad boy she's sworn to avoid. But Kellan Reed has a few secrets of his own—and cowboy or not, Amy can't resist this kind of wild ride . . .

Cowboy Justice

Transforming their parents' run-down ranch in Catcher Creek, New Mexico, into a tourist destination is the toughest challenge the three Sorentino sisters ever faced. But now one of them has another fight on her hands—to keep from falling for the sexy town sheriff—again . . .

Rachel Sorentino has spent her whole life protecting her siblings from trouble—only to run headlong into it herself. Her first regret about shooting at the vandals targeting her family ranch is that her aim wasn't better. Her second is that when bullets started flying, it was Sheriff Vaughn Cooper's number she dialed. Vaughn is the mistake she keeps on making, a cowboy lawman who cuts through Rachel's surface bravado to the vulnerability no one else sees. And no matter how inconvenient their attraction—for his career, her tangled case, and his already battered heart—there's no denying what feels so irresistibly right . . .

Thrilling Fiction from

GEORGINA GENTRY

My Heroes Have Always Been Cowboys	978-0-8217-7959-0	$6.99US/$8.99CAN
Rio: The Texans	978-1-4201-0851-4	$6.99US/$8.99CAN
Diablo: The Texans	978-1-4201-0850-7	$6.99US/$8.99CAN
To Seduce a Texan	978-0-8217-7992-7	$6.99US/$8.49CAN
To Wed a Texan	978-0-8217-7991-0	$6.99US/$8.49CAN

Available Wherever Books Are Sold!

Visit our website at www.kensingtonbooks.com